Grace Paley was born in New York in 19 2 ish parents who arrived from Russia at the turn of the ce.... ..ey settled in the poor quarter of Lower East Side Manhattan, her mother working in sweatshops, her father struggling to become a doctor. She grew up amidst the vivid life of immigrant New York, a creature of two cultures, her father teaching her Yiddish and Russian, the people around her – those improbable people you meet every day in the street – providing the raw material for her future work.

She had little formal education – she was too busy writing poetry and reading voraciously to finish school – and began to write fiction in the fifties. Her first volume of short stories was *The Little Disturbances of Man* (1959). Throughout the sixties her stories appeared in *Esquire*, *The Atlantic* and *New American Review*; in 1974 a second volume, *Enormous Changes at the Last Minute* was published and in 1985, *Later the Same Day* (both of these are also published by Virago). *Begin Again*, a collection of her poetry, was published in 1993.

She has never published a novel: 'Art is too long,' she has said, 'and life is too short. There's a lot more to do in life than just writing.' Grace Paley has a son and a daughter and has taught literature at Columbia College, Syracuse University and Sarah Lawrence College in New York, but her most important distraction from writing is politics. She is a pacifist and has devoted enormous energy to anti-war movements, in particular to her long and active commitment to end the war in Vietnam.

Grace Paley lives in Vermont.

GRACE PALEY

THE
COLLECTED
STORIES

A *Virago* book

Published by Virago Press 1998

First published in the United States by Farrar, Straus and Giroux 1994

A CIP catalogue record for this book is available from the British Library

ISBN 1 86049 423 4

Typeset by M Rules in Melior
Printed and bound in Great Britain by Clays Ltd, St Ives plc

Virago
A Division of
Little, Brown and Company (UK)
Brettenham House
Lancaster Place
London WC2E 7EN

*It seems right to dedicate this collection to my
friend Sybil Claiborne, my colleague in the Writing
and Mother Trade. I visited her fifth-floor
apartment on Barrow Street one day in 1957.
There before my very eyes were her two husbands
disappointed by the eggs. After that we talked and
talked for nearly forty years. Then she died.
Three days before that, she said slowly, with the
delicacy of an unsatisfied person with only a dozen
words left, Grace, the real question is –
how are we to live our lives?*

Contents

ENORMOUS CHANGES AT THE LAST MINUTE

LATER THE SAME DAY

Two Ears, Three Lucks

In 1954 or '55 I decided to write a story. I had written a few nice paragraphs with some first-class sentences in them, but I hadn't known how to let women and men into the language, nor could I find the story in those pieces of prose. I'd been writing poems since childhood. It was poetry that I read with the greatest pleasure.

But in 1954 or '55 I needed to speak in some inventive way about our female and male lives in those years. Some knowledge was creating a real physical pressure, probably in the middle of my chest – maybe just to the right of the heart. I was beginning to suffer the storyteller's pain: Listen! I *have* to tell you something! I simply hadn't known how to do it in poetry. Other writers have understood easily, but I seem to have been singing along on the gift of one ear, the ear in charge of literature.

Then the first of two small lucks happened. I became sick enough for the children to remain in Greenwich House After School until suppertime for several weeks, but not so sick that I couldn't sit at our living-room table to write or type all day. I began the story 'Goodbye and Good Luck' and to my surprise carried it through to the end. So much prose. Then 'The Contest.' A couple of months later I finished 'A Woman, Young and Old.' Thinking about it some years later I understood I'd found my other ear. Writing the stories had allowed it – suddenly – to do its job, to remember the street language and the home language with its Russian and Yiddish accents, a language my early characters knew well, the only language I spoke. Two ears, one for literature, one for home, are useful for writers.

When I sent these three stories out into the world of periodicals, they did not do well.

I had been reading the current fiction, fifties fiction, a masculine fiction, whether traditional, avant-garde, or – later – Beat. As a former boy myself (in the sense that many little girls reading *Tom Sawyer* know they've found their true boy selves) I had been sold pretty early on the idea that I might not be writing the important serious stuff. As a grown-up woman, I had no choice. Everyday life, kitchen life, children life had been handed to me, my portion, the beginning of big luck, though I didn't know it.

One dark day in our dark basement apartment, a father slumped in our fat chair, waiting to retrieve his two kids, my children's friends. Just before leaving with them, he looked at me. He said that his former wife, the mother of his children, my friend Tibby, had asked him to read my stories. I probably said, Oh, you don't have to bother. But he did have to. A couple of weeks later he came for the children again. This time he sat down at our kitchen table (in the same room as our living-room table). He asked if I could write seven more stories like the three he'd read. He said he'd publish the book. Doubleday would publish them. He was Ken McCormick, an editor who could say that and it would happen. Of course, selling short stories was not a particularly hopeful business. He suggested that I write a novel next. (I tried for a couple of years. I failed.)

Well, that was luck, wasn't it? I don't say this to minimize the stories. I worked conscientiously to write them as truthfully and as beautifully as I could; but so do others, yet they are not usually visited with contracts.

I have called that meeting and that publication my little lucks. Not because they weren't overwhelming. They certainly changed my life. They are little only for their personal size and private pleasure.

As for the big luck: that has to do with political movements, history that happens to you while you're doing the dishes, wars that men plan for their sons, our sons.

I was a woman writing at the early moment when small drops of worried resentment and noble rage were secretly, slowly building into the second wave of the women's movement. I didn't know my small-drop presence or usefulness in this accumulation. Others like Ruth Herschberger, who wrote Adam's Rib in 1948, and Tillie Olsen, who was writing her stories through the forties and fifties, had more consciousness than I and suffered more. This great wave would crest half a generation later, leaving men sputtering and anxious, but somewhat improved for the crashing bath.

Every woman writing in these years has had to swim in that feminist wave. No matter what she thinks of it, even if she bravely swims against it, she has been supported by it – the buoyancy, the noise, the saltiness.

Since writing *The Little Disturbances of Man*, I have often left home. I have received great gifts from my political work as a pacifist and feminist, traveled on political tasks to Vietnam during that war, to Sweden, Russia, Central America, and seen China and Chile and reported on these meetings. Therefore, some of the people who work for me in *Enormous Changes* and *Later the Same Day* have had to share those journeys with me. Some, of course, are still quite young, having been born in the seventies or eighties.

But many of them are still the companions of my big luck. Starting from the neighborhoods of my childhood and my children's childhood, in demonstrations in children's parks or the grownups' Pentagon, in lively neighborhood walks against the Gulf War, in harsh confrontations with ourselves and others, we have remained interested and active in literature and the world and are now growing old together.

G.P.

THE LITTLE
DISTURBANCES
OF MAN
(1959)

Goodbye and Good Luck

I was popular in certain circles, says Aunt Rose. I wasn't no thinner then, only more stationary in the flesh. In time to come, Lillie, don't be surprised – change is a fact of God. From this no one is excused. Only a person like your mama stands on one foot, she don't notice how big her behind is getting and sings in the canary's ear for thirty years. Who's listening? Papa's in the shop. You and Seymour, thinking about yourself. So she waits in a spotless kitchen for a kind word and thinks – poor Rosie . . .

Poor Rosie! If there was more life in my little sister, she would know my heart is a regular college of feelings and there is such information between my corset and me that her whole married life is a kindergarten.

Nowadays you could find me any time in a hotel, uptown or downtown. Who needs an apartment to live like a maid with a dustrag in the hand, sneezing? I'm in very good with the bus-boys, it's more interesting than home, all kinds of people, everybody with a reason . . .

And my reason, Lillie, is a long time ago I said to the forelady, 'Missus, if I can't sit by the window, I can't sit.' 'If you can't sit, girlie,' she says politely, 'go stand on the street corner.' And that's how I got unemployed in novelty wear.

For my next job I answered an ad which said: 'Refined young

lady, medium salary, cultural organization.' I went by trolley to the address, the Russian Art Theater of Second Avenue, where they played only the best Yiddish plays. They needed a ticket seller, someone like me, who likes the public but is very sharp on crooks. The man who interviewed me was the manager, a certain type.

Immediately he said: 'Rosie Lieber, you surely got a build on you!'

'It takes all kinds, Mr. Krimberg.'

'Don't misunderstand me, little girl,' he said. 'I appreciate, I appreciate. A young lady lacking fore and aft, her blood is so busy warming the toes and the fingertips, it don't have time to circulate where it's most required.'

Everybody likes kindness. I said to him: 'Only don't be fresh, Mr. Krimberg, and we'll make a good bargain.'

We did: Nine dollars a week, a glass of tea every night, a free ticket once a week for Mama, and I could go watch rehearsals any time I want.

My first nine dollars was in the grocer's hands ready to move on already, when Krimberg said to me, 'Rosie, here's a great gentleman, a member of this remarkable theater, wants to meet you, impressed no doubt by your big brown eyes.'

And who was it, Lillie? Listen to me, before my very eyes was Volodya Vlashkin, called by the people of those days the Valentino of Second Avenue. I took one look, and I said to myself: Where did a Jewish boy grow up so big? 'Just outside Kiev,' he told me.

How? 'My mama nursed me till I was six. I was the only boy in the village to have such health.'

'My goodness, Vlashkin, six years old! She must have had shredded wheat there, not breasts, poor woman.'

'My mother was beautiful,' he said. 'She had eyes like stars.'

He had such a way of expressing himself, it brought tears.

To Krimberg, Vlashkin said after this introduction: 'Who is responsible for hiding this wonderful young person in a cage?'

'That is where the ticket seller sells.'

'So, David, go in there and sell tickets for a half hour. I have something in mind in regards to the future of this girl and this company. Go, David, be a good boy. And you, Miss Lieber, please, I suggest Feinberg's for a glass of tea. The rehearsals are long. I enjoy a quiet interlude with a friendly person.'

So he took me there, Feinberg's, then around the corner, a place so full of Hungarians, it was deafening. In the back room was a table of honor for him. On the tablecloth embroidered by the lady of the house was *Here Vlashkin Eats*. We finished one glass of tea in quietness, out of thirst, when I finally made up my mind what to say.

'Mr. Vlashkin, I saw you a couple weeks ago, even before I started working here, in *The Sea Gull*. Believe me, if I was that girl, I wouldn't look even for a minute on the young bourgeois fellow. He could fall out of the play altogether. How Chekhov could put him in the same play as you, I can't understand.'

'You liked me?' he asked, taking my hand and kindly patting it. 'Well, well, young people still like me . . . so, and you like the theater too? Good. And you, Rose, you know you have such a nice hand, so warm to the touch, such a fine skin, tell me, why do you wear a scarf around your neck? You only hide your young, young throat. These are not olden times, my child, to live in shame.'

'Who's ashamed?' I said, taking off the kerchief, but my hand right away went to the kerchief's place, because the truth is, it really was olden times, and I was still of a nature to melt with shame.

'Have some more tea, my dear.'

'No, thank you, I am a samovar already.'

'Dorfmann!' he hollered like a king. 'Bring this child a seltzer with fresh ice!'

In weeks to follow I had the privilege to know him better and better as a person – also the opportunity to see him in his profession. The time was autumn; the theater full of coming and going. Rehearsing without end. After *The Sea Gull* flopped, *The Salesman from Istanbul* played, a great success.

Here the ladies went crazy. On the opening night, in the middle of the first scene, one missus – a widow or her husband worked too long hours – began to clap and sing out, 'Oi, oi, Vlashkin.' Soon there was such a tumult, the actors had to stop acting. Vlashkin stepped forward. Only not Vlashkin to the eyes . . . a younger man with pitch-black hair, lively on restless feet, his mouth clever. A half a century later at the end of the play he came out again, a gray philosopher, a student of life from only reading books, his hands as smooth as silk . . . I cried to think who I was – nothing – and such a man could look at me with interest.

Then I got a small raise, due to he kindly put in a good word for me, and also for fifty cents a night I was given the pleasure together with cousins, in-laws, and plain stage-struck kids to be part of a crowd scene and to see like he saw every single night the hundreds of pale faces waiting for his feelings to make them laugh or bend down their heads in sorrow.

The sad day came, I kissed my mama goodbye. Vlashkin helped me to get a reasonable room near the theater to be more free. Also my outstanding friend would have a place to recline away from the noise of the dressing rooms. She cried and she cried. 'This is a different way of living, Mama,' I said. 'Besides, I am driven by love.'

'You! You, a nothing, a rotten hole in a piece of cheese, are you telling me what is life?' she screamed.

Very insulted, I went away from her. But I am good-natured – you know fat people are like that – kind, and I thought to myself, poor Mama . . . it is true she got more of an idea of life than me. She married who she didn't like, a sick man, his spirit already swallowed up by God. He never washed. He had an unhappy smell. His teeth fell out, his hair disappeared, he got smaller, shriveled up little by little, till goodbye and good luck he was gone and only came to Mama's mind when she went to the mail-box under the stairs to get the electric bill. In memory of him and out of respect for mankind, I decided to live for love.

Don't laugh, you ignorant girl.

Do you think it was easy for me? I had to give Mama a little something. Ruthie was saving up together with your papa for linens, a couple knives and forks. In the morning I had to do piecework if I wanted to keep by myself. So I made flowers. Before lunch time every day a whole garden grew on my table.

This was my independence, Lillie dear, blooming, but it didn't have no roots and its face was paper.

Meanwhile Krimberg went after me too. No doubt observing the success of Vlashkin, he thought, Aha, open sesame . . . Others in the company similar. After me in those years were the following: Krimberg I mentioned. Carl Zimmer, played innocent young fellows with a wig. Charlie Peel, a Christian who fell in the soup by accident, a creator of beautiful sets. 'Color is his middle name,' says Vlashkin, always to the point.

I put this in to show you your fat old aunt was not crazy out of loneliness. In those noisy years I had friends among interesting people who admired me for reasons of youth and that I was a first-class listener.

The actresses – Raisele, Marya, Esther Leopold – were only interested in tomorrow. After them was the rich men, producers, the whole garment center; their past is a pincushion, future the eye of a needle.

Finally the day came, I no longer could keep my tact in my mouth. I said: 'Vlashkin, I hear by carrier pigeon you have a wife, children, the whole combination.'

'True, I don't tell stories. I make no pretense.'

'That isn't the question. What is this lady like? It hurts me to ask, but tell me, Vlashkin . . . a man's life is something I don't clearly see.'

'Little girl, I have told you a hundred times, this small room is the convent of my troubled spirit. Here I come to your innocent shelter to refresh myself in the midst of an agonized life.'

'Ach, Vlashkin, serious, serious, who is this lady?'

'Rosie, she is a fine woman of the middle classes, a good mother to my children, three in number, girls all, a good cook, in her youth handsome, now no longer young. You see, could I be more frank? I entrust you, dear, with my soul.'

It was some few months later at the New Year's ball of the Russian Artists Club, I met Mrs. Vlashkin, a woman with black hair in a low bun, straight and too proud. She sat at a small table speaking in a deep voice to whoever stopped a moment to converse. Her Yiddish was perfect, each word cut like a special jewel. I looked at her. She noticed me like she noticed everybody, cold like Christmas morning. Then she got tired. Vlashkin called a taxi and I never saw her again. Poor woman, she did not know I was on the same stage with her. The poison I was to her role, she did not know.

Later on that night in front of my door I said to Vlashkin, 'No more. This isn't for me. I am sick from it all. I am no home breaker.'

'Girlie,' he said, 'don't be foolish.'

'No, no, goodbye, good luck,' I said. 'I am sincere.'

So I went and stayed with Mama for a week's vacation and cleaned up all the closets and scrubbed the walls till the paint came off. She was very grateful, all the same her hard life made her say, 'Now we see the end. If you live like a bum, you are finally a lunatic.'

After this few days I came back to my life. When we met, me and Vlashkin, we said only hello and goodbye, and then for a few sad years, with the head we nodded as if to say, 'Yes, yes, I know who you are.'

Meanwhile in the field was a whole new strategy. Your mama and your grandmama brought around – boys. Your own father had a brother, you never even seen him. Ruben. A serious fellow, his idealism was his hat and his coat. 'Rosie, I offer you a big new free happy unusual life.' How? 'With me, we will raise up the sands of Palestine to make a nation. That is the land of tomorrow for us Jews.' 'Ha-ha, Ruben, I'll go tomorrow then.' 'Rosie!' says Ruben. 'We need strong women like you, mothers and farmers.' 'You don't fool me, Ruben, what you need is dray horses. But for that you need more money.' 'I don't like your attitude, Rose.' 'In that case, go and multiply. Goodbye.'

Another fellow: Yonkel Gurstein, a regular sport, dressed to kill, with such an excitable nature. In those days – it looks to me like yesterday – the youngest girls wore undergarments like Battle Creek, Michigan. To him it was a matter of seconds. Where did he practice, a Jewish boy? Nowadays I suppose it is easier, Lillie? My goodness, I ain't asking you nothing – touchy, touchy . . .

Well, by now you must know yourself, honey, whatever you do, life don't stop. It only sits a minute and dreams a dream.

While I was saying to all these silly youngsters 'no, no, no,' Vlashkin went to Europe and toured a few seasons . . . Moscow, Prague, London, even Berlin – already a pessimistic place. When he came back he wrote a book you could get from the library even today, *The Jewish Actor Abroad*. If someday you're interested enough in my lonesome years, you could read it. You could absorb a flavor of the man from the book. No, no, I am not mentioned. After all, who am I?

When the book came out I stopped him in the street to say congratulations. But I am not a liar, so I pointed out, too, the egotism of many parts – even the critics said something along such lines.

'Talk is cheap,' Vlashkin answered me. 'But who are the critics? Tell me, do they create? Not to mention,' he continues, 'there is a line in Shakespeare in one of the plays from the great history of England. It says, 'Self-loving is not so vile a sin, my liege, as self-neglecting.' This idea also appears in modern times in the moralistic followers of Freud . . . Rosie, are you listening? You asked a question. By the way, you look very well. How come no wedding ring?'

I walked away from this conversation in tears. But this talking in the street opened the happy road up for more discussions. In regard to many things . . . For instance, the management – very narrow-minded – wouldn't give him any more certain young men's parts. Fools. What youngest man knew enough about life to be as young as him?

'Rosie, Rosie,' he said to me one day, 'I see by the clock on your rosy, rosy face you must be thirty.'

'The hands are slow, Vlashkin. On a week before Thursday I was thirty-four.'

'Is that so? Rosie, I worry about you. It has been on my mind to talk to you. You are losing your time. Do you understand it? A woman should not lose her time.'

'Oi, Vlashkin, if you are my friend, what is time?'

For this he had no answer, only looked at me surprised. We went instead, full of interest but not with our former speed, up to my new place on Ninety-fourth Street. The same pictures on the wall, all of Vlashkin, only now everything painted red and black, which was stylish, and new upholstery.

A few years ago there was a book by another member of that fine company, an actress, the one that learned English very good and went uptown – Marya Kavkaz, in which she says certain things regarding Vlashkin. Such as, he was her lover for eleven years, she's not ashamed to write this down. Without respect for him, his wife and children, or even others who also may have feelings in the matter.

Now, Lillie, don't be surprised. This is called a fact of life. An actor's soul must be like a diamond. The more faces it got the more shining is his name. Honey, you will no doubt love and marry one man and have a couple kids and be happy forever till you die tired. More than that, a person like us don't have to know. But a great artist like Volodya Vlashkin . . . in order to make a job on the stage, he's got to practice. I understand it now, to him life is like a rehearsal.

Myself, when I saw him in *The Father-in-Law* – an older man in love with a darling young girl, his son's wife, played by Raisele Maisel – I cried. What he said to this girl, how he whispered such sweetness, how all his hot feelings were on his face . . . Lillie, all this experience he had with me. The very words were the same. You can imagine how proud I was.

So the story creeps to an end.

I noticed it first on my mother's face, the rotten handwriting of time, scribbled up and down her cheeks, across her forehead back and forth – a child could read – it said old, old, old. But it troubled my heart most to see these realities scratched on Vlashkin's wonderful expression.

First the company fell apart. The theater ended. Esther Leopold died from being very aged. Krimberg had a heart attack. Marya went to Broadway. Also Raisele changed her name to Roslyn and was a big comical hit in the movies. Vlashkin himself, no place to go, retired. It said in the paper, 'An actor without peer, he will write his memoirs and spend his last years in the bosom of his family among his thriving grandchildren, the apple of his wife's doting eye.'

This is journalism.

We made for him a great dinner of honor. At this dinner I said to him, for the last time, I thought, 'Goodbye, dear friend, topic of my life, now we part.' And to myself I said further: Finished. This is your lonesome bed. A lady what they call fat and fifty. You made it personally. From this lonesome bed you will finally fall to a bed not so lonesome, only crowded with a million bones.

And now comes? Lillie, guess.

Last week, washing my underwear in the basin, I get a buzz on the phone. 'Excuse me, is this the Rose Lieber formerly connected with the Russian Art Theater?'

'It is.'

'Well, well, how do you do, Rose? This is Vlashkin.'

'Vlashkin! Volodya Vlashkin?'

'In fact. How are you, Rose?'

'Living, Vlashkin, thank you.'

'You are all right? Really, Rose? Your health is good? You are working?'

'My health, considering the weight it must carry, is first-class. I am back for some years now where I started, in novelty wear.'

'Very interesting.'

'Listen, Vlashkin, tell me the truth, what's on your mind?'

'My mind? Rosie, I am looking up an old friend, an old warm-hearted companion of more joyful days. My circumstances, by the way, are changed. I am retired, as you know. Also I am a free man.'

'What? What do you mean?'

'Mrs. Vlashkin is divorcing me.'

'What come over her? Did you start drinking or something from melancholy?'

'She is divorcing me for adultery.'

'But, Vlashkin, you should excuse me, don't be insulted, but you got maybe seventeen, eighteen years on me, and even me, all this nonsense – this daydreams and nightmares – is mostly for the pleasure of conversation alone.'

'I pointed all this out to her. My dear, I said, my time is past, my blood is as dry as my bones. The truth is, Rose, she isn't accustomed to have a man around all day, reading out loud from the papers the interesting events of our time, waiting for breakfast, waiting for lunch. So all day she gets madder and madder. By nighttime a furious old lady gives me my supper. She has information from the last fifty years to pepper my soup. Surely there was a Judas in that theater, saying every day, 'Vlashkin, Vlashkin, Vlashkin . . .' and while my heart was circulating with his smiles he was on the wire passing the dope to my wife.'

'Such a foolish end, Volodya, to such a lively story. What is your plans?'

'First, could I ask you for dinner and the theater – uptown, of course? After this . . . we are old friends. I have money to burn. What your heart desires. Others are like grass, the north wind of time has cut out their heart. Of you, Rosie, I re-create only kindness. What a woman should be to a man, you were to me. Do you think, Rosie, a couple of old pals like us could have a few good times among the material things of this world?'

My answer, Lillie, in a minute was altogether. 'Yes, yes, come up,' I said. 'Ask the room by the switchboard, let us talk.'

So he came that night and every night in the week, we talked of his long life. Even at the end of time, a fascinating man. And like men are, too, till time's end, trying to get away in one piece.

'Listen, Rosie,' he explains the other day. 'I was married to my wife, do you realize, nearly half a century. What good was it? Look at the bitterness. The more I think of it, the more I think we would be fools to marry.'

'Volodya Vlashkin,' I told him straight, 'when I was young I warmed your cold back many a night, no questions asked. You admit it, I didn't make no demands. I was softhearted. I didn't want to be called Rosie Lieber, a breaker up of homes. But now, Vlashkin, you are a free man. How could you ask me to go with you on trains to stay in strange hotels, among Americans, not your wife? Be ashamed.'

So now, darling Lillie, tell this story to your mama from your young mouth. She don't listen to a word from me. She only screams, 'I'll faint, I'll faint.' Tell her after all I'll have a husband, which, as everybody knows, a woman should have at least one before the end of the story.

My goodness, I am already late. Give me a kiss. After all, I watched you grow from a plain seed. So give me a couple wishes on my wedding day. A long and happy life. Many years of love. Hug Mama, tell her from Aunt Rose, goodbye and good luck.

A Woman, Young and Old

My mother was born not too very long ago of my grandma, who named lots of others, girls and boys, all starting fresh. It wasn't love so much, my grandma said, but she never could call a spade a spade. She was imagination-minded, read stories all day, and sighed all night, till my grandpa, to get near her at all, had to use that particular medium.

That was the basic trouble. My mother was sad to be so surrounded by brothers and sisters, none of them more good-natured than she. It's all part of the violence in the atmosphere is a theory – wars, deception, broken homes, all the irremediableness of modern life. To meet her problem my mother screams.

She swears she wouldn't scream if she had a man of her own, but all the aunts and uncles, solitary or wed, are noisy. My grandpa is not only noisy, he beats people up, that is to say – members of the family. He whacked my mother every day of her life. If anyone ever touched me, I'd reduce them to fall-out.

Grandma saves all her change for us. My uncle Johnson is in the nuthouse. The others are here and now, but Aunty Liz is seventeen and my mother talks to her as though she were totally grown up. Only the other day she told her she was just dying for a man, a real one, and was sick of raising two girls in a world just bristling with goddamn phallic symbols. Lizzy said yes, she knew how it was, time frittered by, and what you needed was a strong kind hand at the hem of your skirt. That's what the acoustics of this barn have to take.

My father, I have been told several hundred times, was a really stunning Latin. Full of *savoir-faire*, *joie de vivre*, and so forth. They were deeply and irrevocably in love till Joanna and I revoked everything for them. Mother doesn't want me to feel rejected, but she doesn't want to feel rejected herself, so she says *I* was too noisy and cried every single night. And then Joanna was the final blight and wanted titty all day *and* all night. '. . . a wife,' he said, 'is a beloved mistress until the children come and then . . .' He would just leave it hanging in French, but whenever I'd hear *les enfants*, I'd throw toys at him, guessing his intended slight. He said *les filles* instead, but I caught that petty evasion in no time. We pummeled him with noise and toys, but our affection was his serious burden is Mother's idea, and one day he did not come home for supper.

Mother waited up reading *Le Monde*, but he did not come home at midnight to make love. He missed breakfast and lunch the next day. In fact, where is he now? Killed in the Resistance, says Mother. A postcard two weeks later told her and still tells us all, for that matter, whenever it's passed around: 'I have been lonely for France for five years. Now for the rest of my life I must be lonely for you.'

'You've been conned, Mother,' I said one day while we were preparing dinner.

'Conned?' she muttered. 'You speak a different language than me. You don't know a thing yet, you weren't even born. You know perfectly well, misfortune aside, I'd take another Frenchman – Oh, Josephine,' she continued, her voice reaching strictly for the edge of the sound barrier, 'oh, Josephine, to these loathsomes in this miserable country I'm a joke, a real ha-ha. But over there they'd know me. They would just feel me boiling out to meet them. Lousy grammar and all, in French, I swear I could write Shakespeare.'

I turned away in despair. I felt like crying.

'Don't laugh,' she said, 'someday I'll disappear Air France and surprise you all with a nice curly Frenchman just like your daddy. Oh, how you would have loved your father. A growing-up girl with a man like that in the vicinity constantly. You'd thank me.'

'I thank you anyway, Mother dear,' I replied, 'but keep your taste in your own hatch. When I'm as old as Aunt Lizzy I might like American soldiers. Or a Marine, I think. I already like some soldiers, especially Corporal Brownstar.'

'Is *that* your idea of a man?' asked Mother, rowdy with contempt.

Then she reconsidered Corporal Brownstar. 'Well, maybe you're right. Those powerful-looking boots . . . Very masculine.'

'Oh?'

'I know, I know. I'm artistic and I sometimes hold two views at once. I realize that Lizzy's going around with him and it does something. Look at Lizzy and you see the girl your father saw. Just like me. Wonderful carriage. Marvelous muscle tone. She could have any man she wanted.'

'She's already had some she wanted.'

At that very moment my grandma, the nick-of-time banker, came in, proud to have saved $4.65 for us. 'Whew, I'm so warm,' she sighed. 'Well, here it is. Now a nice dinner, Marvine, I beg of you, a little effort. Josie, run and get an avocado, and Marvine, please don't be small about the butter. And Josie dear, it's awful warm out and your mama won't mind. You're nearly a young lady. Would you like a sip of icy beer?'

Wasn't that respectful? To return the compliment I drank half a glass, though I hate that fizz. We broiled and steamed and sliced and chopped, and it was a wonderful dinner. I did the cooking and Mother did the sauces. We sicked her on with mouth-watering memories of another more gourmet time and, purely flattered, she made one sauce too many and we had it for dessert on saltines, with iced *café au lait*. While I cleared the dishes, Joanna, everybody's piece of fluff, sat on Grandma's lap telling her each single credible detail of her eight hours at summer day camp.

'Women,' said Grandma in appreciation, 'have been the pleasure and consolation of my entire life. From the beginning I cherished all the little girls with their clean faces and their listening ears . . .'

'Men are different than women,' said Joanna, and it's the only thing she says in this entire story.

'That's true,' said Grandma, 'it's the men that've always troubled me. Men and boys . . . I suppose I don't understand them. But think of it consecutively, all in a row, Johnson, Revere, and Drummond . . . after all, where did they start from but me? But all of them, all all all, each single one of them is gone, far away in heart and body.'

'Ah, Grandma,' I said, hoping to console, 'they were all so grouchy, anyway. I don't miss them a bit.'

Grandma gave me a miserable look. 'Everyone's sons are like that,' she explained. 'First grouchy, then gone.'

After that she sat in grieving sorrow. Joanna curled herself round the hassock at her feet, hugged it, and slept. Mother got her last week's copy of *Le Monde* out of the piano bench and calmed herself with a story about a farmer in Provence who had raped his niece and killed his mother and lived happily for thirty-eight years into respected old age before the nosy prefect caught up with him. She translated it into our derivative mother tongue while I did the dishes.

Nighttime came and communication was revived at last by our doorbell, which is full of initiative. It was Lizzy and she did bring Corporal Brownstar. We sent Joanna out for beer and soft drinks and the dancing started right away. He cooperatively danced with everyone. I slipped away to my room for a moment and painted a lot of lipstick neatly on my big mouth and hooked a walleyed brassiere around my ribs to make him understand that I was older than Joanna.

He said to me, 'You're peaches and cream, you're gonna be quite a girl someday, Alice in Wonderland.'

'I am a girl already, Corporal.'

'Uh *huh*,' he said, squeezing my left bottom.

Lizzy passed the punch and handed out Ritz crackers and danced with Mother and Joanna whenever the corporal danced with me. She was delighted to see him so popular, and it just passed her happy head that he was the only man there. At the peak of the evening he said: 'You may all call me Browny.'

We sang air force songs then until 2 a.m., and Grandma said the songs hadn't changed much since her war. 'The soldiers are younger though,' she said. 'Son, you look like your mother is still worried about you.'

'No reason to worry about me, I got a lot of irons in the fire. I get advanced all the time, as a matter of fact. Stern to stern,' he said, winking at Lizzy, 'I'm O.K. . . . By the way,' he continued, 'could you folks put me up? I wouldn't mind sleeping on the floor.'

'The floor?' expostulated Mother. 'Are you out of your mind? A soldier of the Republic. My God! We have a cot. You know . . . an army cot. Set it up and sleep the sleep of the just, Corporal.'

'Oh, goodness' – Grandma yawned – 'talking about bed – Marvine, your dad must be home by now. I'd better be getting back.'

Browny decided in a courteous way to take Lizzy and Grandma home. By the time he returned, Mother and Joanna had wrapped their lonesome arms around each other and gone to sleep.

I sneakily watched him from behind the drapes scrubbing himself down without consideration for his skin. Then, shining and naked, he crawled between the sheets in totality.

I unshod myself and tiptoed into the kitchen. I poured him a cold beer. I came straight to him and sat down by his side. 'Here's a nice beer, Browny. I thought you might be hot after such a long walk.'

'Why, thanks, Alice Palace Pudding and Pie, I happen to be pretty damn hot. You're a real pal.'

He heaved himself up and got that beer into his gut in one gulp. I looked at him down to his belly button. He put the empty glass on the floor and grinned at me. He burped into my face for a joke and then I had to speak the truth. 'Oh, Browny,' I said, 'I just love you so.' I threw my arms around his middle and leaned my face into the golden hairs of his chest.

'Hey, pudding, take it easy. I like you too. You're a doll.'

Then I kissed him right on the mouth.

'Josephine, who the hell taught you that?'

'I taught myself. I practiced on my wrist. See?'

'Josephine!' he said again. 'Josephine, you're a liar. You're one hell of a liar!'

After that his affection increased, and he hugged me too and kissed me right on the mouth.

'Well,' I kidded, 'who taught you that? Lizzy?'

'Shut up,' he said, and the more he loved me the less he allowed of conversation.

I lay down beside him, and I was really surprised the way a man is transformed by his feelings. He loved me all over myself, and to show I understood his meaning I whispered: 'Browny, what do you want? Browny, do you want to do it?'

Well! He jumped out of bed then and flapped the sheet around his shoulders and groaned, 'Oh, Christ . . . Oh,' he said, 'I could be arrested. I could be picked up by M.P.'s and spend the rest of my life in jail.' He looked at me. 'For godsakes button your shirt. Your mother'll wake up in a minute.'

'Browny, what's the matter?'

'You're a child and you're too damn smart for your own good. Don't you understand? This could ruin my whole life.'

'But, Browny . . .'

'The trouble I could get into! I could be busted. You're a baby. It's a joke. A person could marry a baby like you, but it's criminal to lay a hand on your shoulder. That's funny, ha-ha-ha.'

'Oh, Browny, I would love to be married to you.'

He sat down at the edge of the cot and drew me to his lap. 'Gee, what a funny kid you are. You really like me so much?'

'I love you. I'd be a first-class wife, Browny – do you realize I take care of this whole house? When Mother isn't working, she spends her whole time mulling over Daddy. I'm the one who does Joanna's hair every day. I iron her dresses. I could even have a baby for you, Browny, I know just how to –'

'No! Oh no. Don't let anyone ever talk you into that. Not till you're eighteen. You ought to stay tidy as a doll and not strain your skin at least till you're eighteen.'

'Browny, don't you get lonesome in that camp? I mean if Lizzy isn't around and I'm not around . . . Don't you think I have a nice figure?'

'Oh, I guess . . .' He laughed, and put his hand warmly under my shirt. 'It's pretty damn nice, considering it ain't even quite done.'

I couldn't hold my desire down, and I kissed him again right into his talking mouth and smack against his teeth. 'Oh, Browny, I would take care of you.'

'O.K., O.K.,' he said, pushing me kindly away. 'O.K., now listen, go to sleep before we really cook up a stew. Go to sleep. You're a sweet kid. Sleep it off. You ain't even begun to see how wide the world is. It's a surprise even to a man like me.'

'But my mind is settled.'

'Go to sleep, go sleep,' he said, still holding my hand and patting it. 'You look almost like Lizzy now.'

'Oh, but I'm different. I know exactly what I want.'

'Go to sleep, little girl,' he said for the last time. I took his hand and kissed each brown fingertip and then ran into my room and took all my clothes off and, as bare as my lonesome soul, I slept.

The next day was Saturday and I was glad. Mother is a waitress all weekend at the Paris Coffee House, where she has been learning French from the waiters ever since Daddy disappeared. She's lucky because she really loves her work; she's crazy about the customers, the coffee, the decor, and is only miserable when she gets home.

I gave her breakfast on the front porch at about 10 a.m. and Joanna walked her to the bus. 'Cook the corporal some of those frozen sausages,' she called out in her middle range.

I hoped he'd wake up so we could start some more love, but instead Lizzy stepped over our sagging threshold. 'Came over to fix Browny some breakfast,' she said efficiently.

'Oh?' I looked her childlike in the eye. 'I think *I* ought to do it, Aunty Liz, because he and I are probably getting married. Don't you think I ought to in that case?'

'What? Say that slowly, Josephine.'

'You heard me, Aunty Liz.'

She flopped in a dirndl heap on the stairs. '*I* don't even feel old enough to get married and *I've* been seventeen since Christmas time. Did he really ask you?'

'We've been talking about it,' I said, and that was true. 'I'm in love with him, Lizzy.' Tears prevented my vision.

'Oh, love . . . I've been in love twelve times since I was your age.'

'Not me, I've settled on Browny. I'm going to get a job and send him to college after his draft is over . . . He's very smart.'

'Oh, smart . . . everybody's smart.'

'No, they are not.'

When she left I kissed Browny on both eyes, like the Sleeping Beauty, and he stretched and woke up in a conflagration of hunger.

'Breakfast, breakfast, breakfast,' he bellowed.

I fed him and he said, 'Wow, the guys would really laugh, me thiefin' the cradle this way.'

'Don't feel like that. I make a good impression on people, Browny. There've been lots of men more grown than you who've made a fuss over me.'

'Ha-ha,' he remarked.

I made him quit that kind of laughing and started him on some kisses, and we had a cheerful morning.

'Browny,' I said at lunch, 'I'm going to tell Mother we're getting married.'

'Don't she have enough troubles of her own?'

'No, no,' I said. 'She's all for love. She's crazy about it.'

'Well, think about it a minute, baby face. After all, I might get shipped out to some troubled area and be knocked over by a crazy native. You read about something like that every day. Anyway, wouldn't it be fun to have a real secret engagement for a while? How about it?'

'Not me,' I said, remembering everything I'd ever heard from Liz about the opportunism of men, how they will sometimes dedicate with seeming goodwill thirty days and nights, sleeping and waking, of truth and deceit to the achievement of a moment's pleasure. 'Secret engagement! Some might agree to a plan like that, but not me.'

Then I knew he liked me, because he walked around the table and played with the curls of my home permanent a minute and whispered, 'The guys would really laugh, but I get a big bang out of you.'

Then I wasn't sure he liked me, because he looked at his watch and asked it: 'Where the hell is Lizzy?'

I had to do the shopping and put off some local merchants in a muddle of innocence, which is my main Saturday chore. I ran all the way. It didn't take very long, but as I rattled up the stairs and into the hall, I heard the thumping tail of a conversation. Browny was saying, 'It's your fault, Liz.'

'I couldn't care less,' she said. 'I suppose you get something out of playing around with a child.'

'Oh no, you don't get it at all . . .'

'I can't say I want it.'

'Goddamnit,' said Browny, 'you don't listen to a person. I think you stink.'

'Really?' Turning to go, she smashed the screen door in my face and jammed my instep with the heel of her lavender pump.

'Tell your mother we will,' Browny yelled when he saw me. 'She stinks, that Liz, goddamnit. Tell your mother tonight.'

I did my best during that passing afternoon to make Browny more friendly. I sat on his lap and he drank beer and tickled me. I laughed, and pretty soon I understood the game and how it had to have variety and ran shrieking from him till he could catch me in a comfortable place, the living-room sofa or my own bedroom.

'You're O.K.,' he said. 'You are. I'm crazy about you, Josephine. You're a lot of fun.'

So that night at 9:15 when Mother came home I made her some iced tea and cornered her in the kitchen and locked the door. 'I want to tell you something about me and Corporal Brownstar. Don't say a word, Mother. We're going to be married.'

'What?' she said. 'Married?' she screeched. 'Are you crazy? You can't even get a job without working papers yet. You can't even get working papers. You're a baby. Are you kidding me? You're my little fish. You're not fourteen yet.'

'Well, I decided we could wait until next month when I will be fourteen. Then, I decided, we can get married.'

'You can't, my God! Nobody gets married at fourteen, nobody, nobody. I don't know a soul.'

'Oh, Mother, people do, you always see them in the paper. The worst that could happen is it would get in the paper.'

'But I didn't realize you had much to do with him. Isn't he Lizzy's? That's not nice – to take him away from her. That's a rotten sneaky trick. You're a sneak. Women should stick together. Didn't you learn anything yet?'

'Well, she doesn't want to get married and I do. And it's essential to Browny to get married. He's a very clean-living boy, and when his furlough's over he doesn't want to go back to those camp followers and other people's wives. You have to appreciate that in him, Mother – it's a quality.'

'You're a baby,' she droned. 'You're my slippery little fish.'

Browny rattled the kitchen doorknob ten minutes too early.

'Oh, come in,' I said, disgusted.

'How's stuff? Everything settled? What do you say, Marvine?'

'I say shove it, Corporal! What's wrong with Lizzy? You and she were really beautiful together. You looked like twin stars in the summer sky. Now I realize I don't like your looks much. Who's your mother and father? I never even heard much about them. For all I know, you got an uncle in Alcatraz. And your teeth are in terrible shape. I thought the army takes care of things like that. You just don't look so hot to me.'

'No reason to be personal, Marvine.'

'But she's a baby. What if she becomes pregnant and bubbles up her entire constitution? This isn't India. Did you ever read what happened to the insides of those Indian child brides?'

'Oh, he's very gentle, Mother.'

'What?' she said, construing the worst.

That conference persisted for about two hours. We drank a couple of pitcherfuls of raspberry Kool-Aid we'd been saving for Joanna's twelfth birthday party the next day. No one had a dime, and we couldn't find Grandma.

Later on, decently before midnight, Lizzy showed up. She had a lieutenant (j.g.) with her and she introduced him around as Sid. She didn't introduce him to Browny, because she has stated time and time again that officers and enlisted men ought not to mix socially. As soon as the lieutenant took Mother's hand in greeting, I could see he was astonished. He began to perspire visibly in long welts down his back and in the gabardine armpits of his summer uniform. Mother was in one of those sullen, indolent moods which really put a fire under some men. She was just beady to think of my stubborn decision and how my life contained the roots of excitement.

'France is where I belong,' she murmured to him. 'Paris, Marseilles, places like that, where men like women and don't chase little girls.'

'I have a lot of sympathy with the Gallic temperament and I do like a real woman,' he said hopefully.

'Sympathy is not enough.' Her voice rose to the requirements of her natural disposition. 'Empathy is what I need. The empathy of a true friend is what I have lived without for years.'

'Oh yes, I feel all that, empathy too.' He fell deeply into his heart, from which he could scarcely be heard . . . 'I like a woman who's had some contact with life, cradled little ones, felt the pangs of birth, known the death of loved ones . . .'

'. . . and of love,' she added sadly. 'That's unusual in a young good-looking man.'

'Yet that's my particular preference.'

Lizzy, Browny, and I borrowed a dollar from him while he sat in idyllic stupor and we wandered out for some ice cream. We took Joanna because we were sorry to have drunk up her whole party. When we returned with a bottle of black-raspberry soda, no one was in sight. 'I'm beginning to feel like a procurer,' said Lizzy.

That's how come Mother finally said yes. Her moral turpitude took such a lively turn that she gave us money for a Wassermann. She called Dr. Gilmar and told him to be gentle with the needles. 'It's my own little girl, Doctor. Little Josie that you pulled right out of me yourself. She's so headstrong. Oh, Doctor, remember me and Charles? She's a rough little customer, just like me.'

Due to the results of this test, which is a law, and despite Browny's disbelief, we could not get married. Grandma, always philosophical with the advantage of years, said that young men sowing wild oats were often nipped in the bud, so to speak, and. that modern science would soon unite us. Ha-ha-ha, I laugh in recollection.

Mother never even noticed. It passed her by completely, because of large events in her own life. When Browny left for camp drowned in penicillin and damp with chagrin, she gave him a giant jar of Loft's Sour Balls and a can of walnut rum tobacco.

Then she went ahead with her own life. Without any of the disenchantment Browny and I had suffered, the lieutenant and Mother got married. We were content, all of us, though it's common knowledge that she has never been divorced from Daddy. The name next to hers on the marriage license is Sidney LaValle, Jr., Lieut. (j.g.), U.S.N. An earlier, curlier generation of LaValles came to Michigan from Quebec, and Sid has a couple of usable idioms in Mother's favorite tongue.

I have received one card from Browny. It shows an aerial view of Joplin, Mo. It says: 'Hi, kid, chin up, love, Browny. P.S. Health improved.'

Living as I do on a turnpike of discouragement, I am glad to hear the incessant happy noises in the next room. I enjoyed hugging with Browny's body, though I don't believe I was more to him than a hope for civilian success. Joanna has moved in with me. Though she grinds her teeth well into daylight, I am grateful for her company. Since I have been engaged, she looks up to me. She is a real cuddly girl.

The Pale Pink Roast

Pale green greeted him, grubby buds for nut trees. Packed with lunch, Peter strode into the park. He kicked aside the disappointed acorns and endowed a grand admiring grin to two young girls.

Anna saw him straddling the daffodils, a rosy man in about the third flush of youth. He got into Judy's eye too. Acquisitive and quick, she screamed, 'There's Daddy!'

Well, that's who he was, mouth open, addled by visions. He was unsettled by a collusion of charm, a conspiracy of curly hairdos and shiny faces. A year ago, in plain view, Anna had begun to decline into withering years, just as he swelled to the maximum of manhood, spitting pipe smoke, patched with tweed, an advertisement of a lover who startled men and detained the ladies.

Now Judy leaped over the back of a bench and lunged into his arms. 'Oh, Peter dear,' she whispered, 'I didn't even know you were going to meet us.'

'God, you're getting big, kiddo. Where's your teeth?' he asked. He hugged her tightly, a fifty-pound sack of his very own. 'Say, Judy, I'm glad you still have a pussycat's sniffy nose and a pussycat's soft white fur.'

'I do not,' she giggled.

'Oh yes,' he said. He dropped her to her springy hind legs but held on to one smooth front paw. 'But you'd better keep your claws in or I'll drop you right into the Hudson River.'

'Aw, Peter,' said Judy, 'quit it.'

Peter changed the subject and turned to Anna. 'You don't look half bad, you know.'

'Thank you,' she replied politely, 'neither do you.'

'Look at me, I'm a real outdoorski these days.'

She allowed thirty seconds of silence, into which he turned, singing like a summer bird, 'We danced around the Maypole, the Maypole, the Maypole . . .

'Well, when'd you get in?' he asked.

'About a week ago.'

'You never called.'

'Yes, I did, Peter. I called you at least twenty-seven times. You're never home. Petey must be in love somewhere, I said to myself.'

'What is this thing,' he sang in tune, 'called love?'

'Peter, I want you to do me a favor,' she started again. 'Peter, could you take Judy for the weekend? We've just moved to this new place and I have a lot of work to do. I just don't want her in my hair. Peter?'

'Ah, that's why you called.'

'Oh, for godsakes,' Anna said. 'I really called to ask you to become my lover. That's the real reason.'

'O.K., O.K. Don't be bitter, Anna.' He stretched forth a bene-dicting arm. 'Come in peace, go in peace. Of course I'll take her. I like her. She's my kid.'

'Bitter?' she asked.

Peter sighed. He turned the palms of his hands up as though to guess at rain. Anna knew him, theme and choreography. The sunshiny spring afternoon seeped through his fingers. He looked up at the witnessing heavens to keep what he could. He dropped his arms and let the rest go.

'O.K.,' he said. 'Let's go. I'd like to see your place. I'm full of ideas. You should see my living room, Anna. I might even go into interior decorating if things don't pick up. Come on. I'll get the ladder out of the basement. I could move a couple of trunks. I'm crazy about heavy work. You get out of life what you put into it. Right? Let's ditch the kid. I'm not your enemy.'

'Who is?' she asked.

'Off my back, Anna. I mean it. I'll get someone to keep an eye on Judy. Just shut up.' He searched for a familiar face among the Sunday strollers. 'Hey, you,' he finally called to an old pal on whom two chicks were leaning. 'Hey, you glass-eyed louse, c'mere.'

'Not just any of your idiot friends,' whispered Anna, enraged.

All three soft-shoed it over to Peter. They passed out happy hellos, also a bag of dried apricots. Peter spoke to one of the girls. He patted her little-boy haircut. 'Well, well, baby, you have certainly changed. You must have had a very good winter.'

'Oh yes, thanks,' she admitted.

'Say, be my friend, doll, will you? There's Judy over there. Remember? She was nuts about you when she was little. How about it? Keep an eye on her about an hour or two?'

'Sure, Petey, I'd love to. I'm not busy today. Judy! She was cute. I was nuts about her.'

'Anna,' said Peter, 'this is Louie; she was a real friend that year you worked. She helped me out with Judy. She was great, a lifesaver.'

'You're Anna,' Louie said hospitably. 'Oh, I think Judy's cute. We were nuts about each other. You have one smart kid. She's *really* smart.'

'Thank you,' said Anna.

Judy had gone off to talk to the ice-cream man. She returned licking a double-lime Popsicle. 'You have to give him ten cents,' she said. 'He didn't even remember me to give me trust.'

Suddenly she saw Louie. 'Oooh!' she shrieked. 'It's Louie. Louie, Louie, Louie!' They pinched each other's cheeks, rubbed noses like the Eskimoses, and fluttered lashes like kissing angels do. Louie looked around proudly. 'Gee whiz, the kid didn't forget me. How do you like that?'

Peter fished in his pockets for some change. Louie said, 'Don't be ridiculous. It's on me.' 'O.K., girls,' Peter said. 'You two go on. Live it up. Eat supper out. Enjoy yourselves. Keep in touch.'

'I guess they do know each other,' said Anna, absolutely dispirited, waving goodbye.

'There!' said Peter. 'If you want to do things, do things.'

He took her arm. His other elbow cut their way through a gathering clutter of men and boys. 'Going, going, gone,' he said. 'So long, fellows.'

Within five minutes Anna unlocked the door of her new apartment, her snappy city leasehold, with a brand-new key.

In the wide foyer, on the parquet path narrowed by rows of cardboard boxes, Peter stood stock-still and whistled a dozen bars of Beethoven's Fifth Symphony. 'Mama,' he moaned in joy, 'let me live!'

A vista of rooms and doors to rooms, double glass doors, single hard-oak doors, narrow closet doors, a homeful of rooms wired with hallways stretched before. 'Oh, Anna, it's a far cry . . . Who's paying for it?'

'Not you; don't worry.'

'That's not the point, Mary and Joseph!' He waved his arms at a chandelier. 'Now, Anna, I like to see my friends set up this way. You think I'm kidding.'

'*I'm* kidding,' said Anna.

'Come on, what's really cooking? You look so great, you look like a chick on the sincere make. Playing it cool and living it warm, you know . . .'

'Quit dreaming, Petey,' she said irritably. But he had stripped his back to his undershirt and had started to move records into record cabinets. He stopped to say, 'How about me putting up the Venetian blinds?' Then she softened and offered one kindness: 'Peter, you're the one who really looks wonderful. You look just – well – healthy.'

'I take care of myself, Anna. That's why. Vegetables, high proteins. I'm not the night owl I was. Grapefruits, sunlight, oh sunlight, that's my dear love now.'

'You always did take care of yourself, Peter.'

'No, Anna, this is different.' He stopped and settled on a box of curtains. 'I mean it's not egocentric and selfish, the way I used to be. Now it has a real philosophical basis. Don't mix me up with biology. Look at me, what do you see?'

Anna had read that cannibals, tasting man, saw him thereafter as the great pig, the pale pink roast.

'Peter, Peter, pumpkin eater,' Anna said.

'Ah no, that's not what I mean. You know what you see? A structure of flesh. You know when it hit me? About two years ago, around the time we were breaking up, you and me. I took my grandpa to the bathroom one time when I was over there visiting – you remember him, Anna, that old jerk, the one that was so mad, he didn't want to die . . . I was leaning on the door; he was sitting on the pot concentrating on his guts. Just to make conversation – I thought it'd help him relax – I said, 'Pop? Pop, if you had it all to do over again, what would you do different? Any real hot tips?'

'He came up with an answer right away. 'Peter,' he said, 'I'd go to a gym every goddamn day of my life; the hell with the job, the hell with the women. Peter, I'd build my body up till God Hisself wouldn't know how to tear it apart. Look at me Peter,' he said. 'I been a mean sonofabitch the last fifteen years. Why? I'll tell you why. This structure, this . . . this thing' – he pinched himself across his stomach and his knees – 'this me' – he cracked himself sidewise across his jaw – 'this is got to be maintained. The reason is, Peter: *It is the dwelling place of the soul.* In the end, long life is the reward, strength, and beauty.' '

'Oh, Peter!' said Anna. 'Are you working?'

'Man,' said Peter, 'you got the same itsy-bitsy motivations. Of course I'm working. How the hell do you think I live? Did you get your eight-fifty a week out in Scroungeville or not?'

'Eight-fifty is right.'

'O.K., O.K. Then listen. I have a vitamin compound that costs me twelve-eighty a hundred. Fifty dollars a year for basic maintenance and repair.'

'Did the old guy die?'

'Mother! Yes! Of course he died.'

'I'm sorry. He wasn't so bad. He liked Judy.'

'Bad or good, Anna, he got his time in, he lived long enough to teach the next generation. By the way, I don't think you've put on an ounce.'

'Thanks.'

'And the kid looks great. You do take good care of her. You were always a good mother. I'll bet you broil her stuff and all.'

'Sometimes,' she said.

'Let her live in the air,' said Peter. 'I bet you do. Let her love her body.'

'Let her,' said Anna sadly.

'To work, to work, where strike committees shirk,' sang Peter. '*Is* the ladder in the cellar?'

'No, no, in that kitchen closet. The real tall closet.'

Then Peter put up the Venetian blinds, followed by curtains. He distributed books among the available bookcases. He glued the second drawer of Judy's bureau. Although all the furniture had not been installed, there were shelves for Judy's toys. He had no trouble with them at all. He whistled while he worked.

Then he swept the debris into a corner of the kitchen. He put a pot of coffee on the stove. 'Coffee?' he called. 'In a minute,' Anna said. He stabilized the swinging kitchen door and came upon Anna, winding a clock in the living room whose wide windows on the world he had personally draped. 'Busy, busy,' he said.

Like a good and happy man increasing his virtue, he kissed her. She did not move away from him. She remained in the embrace of his right arm, her face nuzzling his shoulder, her eyes closed. He tipped her chin to look and measure opportunity. She could not open her eyes. Honorably he searched, but on her face he met no quarrel.

She was faint and leaden, a sure sign in Anna, if he remembered correctly, of passion. 'Shall we dance?' he asked softly, a family joke. With great care, a patient lover, he undid the sixteen tiny buttons of her pretty dress and in Judy's room on Judy's bed he took her at once without a word. Afterward, having established tenancy, he rewarded her with kisses. But he dressed quickly because he was obligated by the stories of his life to remind her of transience.

'Petey,' Anna said, having drawn sheets and blankets to her chin. 'Go on into the kitchen. I think the coffee's all boiled out.'

He started a new pot. Then he returned to help her with the innumerable little cloth buttons. 'Say, Anna, this dress is wild. It must've cost a dime.'

'A quarter,' she said.

'You know, we could have some pretty good times together every now and then if you weren't so damn resentful.'

'Did you have a real good time, Petey?'

'Oh, the best,' he said, kissing her lightly. 'You know, I like the way your hair is now,' he said.

'I have it done once a week.'

'Hey, say it pays, baby. It does wonders. What's up, what's up? That's what I want to know. Where'd the classy TV come from? And that fabulous desk . . . Say, somebody's an operator.'

'My husband is,' said Anna.

Petey sat absolutely still, but frowned, marking his clear forehead with vertical lines of pain. Consuming the black fact, gritting his teeth to retain it, he said, 'My God, Anna! That was a terrible thing to do.'

'I thought it was so great.'

'Oh, Anna, that's not the point. You should have said something first. Where is he? Where is this stupid sonofabitch while his wife is getting laid?'

'He's in Rochester. That's where I met him. He's a lovely person. He's moving his business. It takes time. Peter, please. He'll be here in a couple of days.'

'You're great, Anna. Man, you're great. You wiggle your ass. You make a donkey out of me and him both. You could've said no. No – excuse me, Petey – no. I'm not that hard up. Why'd you do it? Revenge? Meanness? Why?'

He buttoned his jacket and moved among the cardboard boxes and the new chairs, looking for a newspaper or a package. He hadn't brought a thing. He stopped before the hallway mirror to brush his hair. 'That's it!' he said, and walked slowly to the door.

'Where are you going, Peter?' Anna called across the foyer, a place for noisy children and forgotten umbrellas. 'Wait a minute, Peter. Honest to God, listen to me, I did it for love.'

He stopped to look at her. He looked at her coldly.

Anna was crying. 'I really mean it, Peter, I did it for love.'

'Love?' he asked. 'Really?' He smiled. He was embarrassed but happy. 'Well!' he said. With the fingers of both hands he tossed her a kiss.

'Oh, Anna, then good night,' he said. 'You're a good kid. Honest, I wish you the best, the best of everything, the very best.'

In no time at all his cheerful face appeared at the door of the spring dusk. In the street among peaceable strangers he did a handstand. Then easy and impervious, in full control, he cartwheeled eastward into the source of night.

The Loudest Voice

There is a certain place where dumbwaiters boom, doors slam, dishes crash; every window is a mother's mouth bidding the street shut up, go skate somewhere else, come home. My voice is the loudest.

There, my own mother is still as full of breathing as me and the grocer stands up to speak to her. 'Mrs. Abramowitz,' he says, 'people should not be afraid of their children.'

'Ah, Mr. Bialik,' my mother replies, 'if you say to her or her father "Ssh," they say, "In the grave it will be quiet."'

'From Coney Island to the cemetery,' says my papa. 'It's the same subway; it's the same fare.'

I am right next to the pickle barrel. My pinky is making tiny whirlpools in the brine. I stop a moment to announce: 'Campbell's Tomato Soup. Campbell's Vegetable Beef Soup. Campbell's S-c-otch Broth . . .'

'Be quiet,' the grocer says, 'the labels are coming off.'

'Please, Shirley, be a little quiet,' my mother begs me.

In that place the whole street groans: Be quiet! Be quiet! but steals from the happy chorus of my inside self not a tittle or a jot.

There, too, but just around the corner, is a red brick building that has been old for many years. Every morning the children stand before it in double lines which must be straight. They are not insulted. They are waiting anyway.

I am usually among them. I am, in fact, the first, since I begin with 'A.'

One cold morning the monitor tapped me on the shoulder. 'Go to Room 409, Shirley Abramowitz,' he said. I did as I was told. I went in a hurry up a down staircase to Room 409, which contained sixth-graders. I had to wait at the desk without wiggling until Mr. Hilton, their teacher, had time to speak.

After five minutes he said, 'Shirley?'

'What?' I whispered.

He said, 'My! My! Shirley Abramowitz! They told me you had a particularly loud, clear voice and read with lots of expression. Could that be true?'

'Oh yes,' I whispered.

'In that case, don't be silly; I might very well be your teacher someday. Speak up, speak up.'

'Yes,' I shouted.

'More like it,' he said. 'Now, Shirley, can you put a ribbon in your hair or a bobby pin? It's too messy.'

'Yes!' I bawled.

'Now, now, calm down.' He turned to the class. 'Children, not a sound. Open at page 39. Read till 52. When you finish, start again.' He looked me over once more. 'Now, Shirley, you know, I suppose, that Christmas is coming. We are preparing a beautiful play. Most of the parts have been given out. But I still need a child with a strong voice, lots of stamina. Do you know what stamina is? You do? Smart kid. You know, I heard you read 'The Lord is my shepherd' in Assembly yesterday. I was very impressed. Wonderful delivery. Mrs. Jordan, your teacher, speaks highly of you. Now listen to me, Shirley Abramowitz, if you want to take the part and be in the play, repeat after me, "I swear to work harder than I ever did before."'

I looked to heaven and said at once, 'Oh, I swear.' I kissed my pinky and looked at God.

'That is an actor's life, my dear,' he explained. 'Like a soldier's, never tardy or disobedient to his general, the director. Everything,' he said, 'absolutely everything will depend on you.'

That afternoon, all over the building, children scraped and scrubbed the turkeys and the sheaves of corn off the schoolroom windows. Goodbye Thanksgiving. The next morning a monitor brought red paper and green paper from the office. We made new shapes and hung them on the walls and glued them to the doors.

The teachers became happier and happier. Their heads were ringing like the bells of childhood. My best friend, Evie, was prone to evil, but she did not get a single demerit for whispering. We learned 'Holy Night' without an error. 'How wonderful!' said Miss Glacé, the student teacher. 'To think that some of you don't even speak the language!' We learned 'Deck the Halls' and 'Hark! The Herald Angels' . . . They weren't ashamed and we weren't embarrassed.

Oh, but when my mother heard about it all, she said to my father: 'Misha, you don't know what's going on there. Cramer is the head of the Tickets Committee.'

'Who?' asked my father. 'Cramer? Oh yes, an active woman.'

'Active? Active has to have a reason. Listen,' she said sadly, 'I'm surprised to see my neighbors making tra-la-la for Christmas.'

My father couldn't think of what to say to that. Then he decided: 'You're in America! Clara, you wanted to come here. In Palestine the Arabs would be eating you alive. Europe you had pogroms. Argentina is full of Indians. Here you got Christmas . . . Some joke, ha?'

'Very funny, Misha. What is becoming of you? If we came to a new country a long time ago to run away from tyrants, and instead we fall into a creeping pogrom, that our children learn a lot of lies, so what's the joke? Ach, Misha, your idealism is going away.'

'So is your sense of humor.'

'That I never had, but idealism you had a lot of.'

'I'm the same Misha Abramovitch, I didn't change an iota. Ask anyone.'

'Only ask me,' says my mama, may she rest in peace. 'I got the answer.'

Meanwhile the neighbors had to think of what to say too.

Marty's father said: 'You know, he has a very important part, my boy.'

'Mine also,' said Mr. Sauerfeld.

'Not my boy!' said Mrs. Klieg. 'I said to him no. The answer is no. When I say no! I mean no!'

The rabbi's wife said, 'It's disgusting!' But no one listened to her. Under the narrow sky of God's great wisdom she wore a strawberry-blond wig.

Every day was noisy and full of experience. I was Right-hand Man. Mr. Hilton said: 'How could I get along without you, Shirley?'

He said: 'Your mother and father ought to get down on their knees every night and thank God for giving them a child like you.'

He also said: 'You're absolutely a pleasure to work with, my dear, dear child.'

Sometimes he said: 'For godsakes, what did I do with the script? Shirley! Shirley! Find it.'

Then I answered quietly: 'Here it is, Mr. Hilton.'

Once in a while, when he was very tired, he would cry out: 'Shirley, I'm just tired of screaming at those kids. Will you tell Ira Pushkov not to come in till Lester points to that star the second time?'

Then I roared: 'Ira Pushkov, what's the matter with you? Dope! Mr. Hilton told you five times already, don't come in till Lester points to that star the second time.'

'Ach, Clara,' my father asked, 'what does she do there till six o'clock she can't even put the plates on the table?'

'Christmas,' said my mother coldly.

'Ho! Ho!' my father said. 'Christmas. What's the harm? After all, history teaches everyone. We learn from reading this is a holiday from pagan times also, candles, lights, even Hanukkah. So we learn it's not altogether Christian. So if they think it's a private holiday, they're only ignorant, not patriotic. What belongs to history belongs to all men. You want to go back to the Middle Ages?

Is it better to shave your head with a second-hand razor? Does it hurt Shirley to learn to speak up? It does not. So maybe someday she won't live between the kitchen and the shop. She's not a fool.'

I thank you, Papa, for your kindness. It is true about me to this day. I am foolish but I am not a fool.

That night my father kissed me and said with great interest in my career, 'Shirley, tomorrow's your big day. Congrats.'

'Save it,' my mother said. Then she shut all the windows in order to prevent tonsillitis.

In the morning it snowed. On the street corner a tree had been decorated for us by a kind city administration. In order to miss its chilly shadow our neighbors walked three blocks east to buy a loaf of bread. The butcher pulled down black window shades to keep the colored lights from shining on his chickens. Oh, not me. On the way to school, with both my hands I tossed it a kiss of tolerance. Poor thing, it was a stranger in Egypt.

I walked straight into the auditorium past the staring children. 'Go ahead, Shirley!' said the monitors. Four boys, big for their age, had already started work as propmen and stagehands.

Mr. Hilton was very nervous. He was not even happy. Whatever he started to say ended in a sideward look of sadness. He sat slumped in the middle of the first row and asked me to help Miss Glacé. I did this, although she thought my voice too resonant and said, 'Show-off!'

Parents began to arrive long before we were ready. They wanted to make a good impression. From among the yards of drapes I peeked out at the audience. I saw my embarrassed mother.

Ira, Lester, and Meyer were pasted to their beards by Miss Glacé. She almost forgot to thread the star on its wire, but I reminded her. I coughed a few times to clear my throat. Miss Glacé looked around and saw that everyone was in costume and on line waiting to play his part. She whispered, 'All right . . .' Then:

Jackie Sauerfeld, the prettiest boy in first grade, parted the curtains with his skinny elbow and in a high voice sang out:

Parents dear
We are here
To make a Christmas play in time.
It we give
In narrative
And illustrate with pantomime.

He disappeared.

My voice burst immediately from the wings to the great shock of Ira, Lester, and Meyer, who were waiting for it but were surprised all the same.

'I remember, I remember, the house where I was born . . .'

Miss Glacé yanked the curtain open and there it was, the house – an old hayloft, where Celia Kornbluh lay in the straw with Cindy Lou, her favorite doll. Ira, Lester, and Meyer moved slowly from the wings toward her, sometimes pointing to a moving star and sometimes ahead to Cindy Lou.

It was a long story and it was a sad story. I carefully pronounced all the words about my lonesome childhood, while little Eddie Braunstein wandered upstage and down with his shepherd's stick, looking for sheep. I brought up lonesomeness again, and not being understood at all except by some women everybody hated. Eddie was too small for that and Marty Groff took his place, wearing his father's prayer shawl. I announced twelve friends, and half the boys in the fourth grade gathered round Marty, who stood on an orange crate while my voice harangued. Sorrowful and loud, I declaimed about love and God and Man, but because of the terrible deceit of Abie Stock we came suddenly to a famous moment. Marty, whose remembering tongue I was, waited at the foot of the cross. He stared desperately at the audience. I groaned, 'My God, my God, why hast thou forsaken me?' The soldiers who were sheiks grabbed poor Marty to pin him up to die, but he wrenched free, turned again to the audience, and spread his arms aloft to show despair and the end. I murmured at the top of my voice, 'The rest is silence, but as everyone in this room, in this city – in this world – now knows, I shall have life eternal.'

That night Mrs. Kornbluh visited our kitchen for a glass of tea.

'How's the virgin?' asked my father with a look of concern.

'For a man with a daughter, you got a fresh mouth, Abramovitch.'

'Here,' said my father kindly, 'have some lemon, it'll sweeten your disposition.'

They debated a little in Yiddish, then fell in a puddle of Russian and Polish. What I understood next was my father, who said, 'Still and all, it was certainly a beautiful affair, you have to admit, introducing us to the beliefs of a different culture.'

'Well, yes,' said Mrs. Kornbluh. 'The only thing . . . you know Charlie Turner – that cute boy in Celia's class – a couple others? They got very small parts or no part at all. In very bad taste, it seemed to me. After all, it's their religion.'

'Ach,' explained my mother, 'what could Mr. Hilton do? They got very small voices; after all, why should they holler? The English language they know from the beginning by heart. They're blond like angels. You think it's so important they should get in the play? Christmas . . . the whole piece of goods . . . they own it.'

I listened and listened until I couldn't listen anymore. Too sleepy, I climbed out of bed and kneeled. I made a little church of my hands and said, 'Hear, O Israel . . .' Then I called out in Yiddish, 'Please, good night, good night. Ssh.' My father said, 'Ssh yourself,' and slammed the kitchen door.

I was happy. I fell asleep at once. I had prayed for everybody: my talking family, cousins far away, passersby, and all the lonesome Christians. I expected to be heard. My voice was certainly the loudest.

The Contest

Up early or late, it never matters, the day gets away from me. Summer or winter, the shade of trees or their hard shadow, I never get into my Rice Krispies till noon.

I am ambitious, but it's a long-range thing with me. I have my confidential sights on a star, but there's half a lifetime to get to it. Meanwhile I keep my eyes open and am well dressed.

I told the examining psychiatrist for the army: Yes, I like girls. And I do. Not my sister – a pimp's dream. But girls, slim and tender or really stacked, dark brown at their centers, smeared by time. Not my mother, who should've stayed in Freud. I *have* got a sense of humor.

My last girl was Jewish, which is often a warm kind of girl, concerned about food intake and employability. They don't like you to work too hard, I understand, until you're hooked and then, you bastard, sweat!

A medium girl, size twelve, a clay pot with handles – she could be grasped. I met her in the rain outside some cultural activity at Cooper Union or Washington Irving High School. She had no umbrella and I did, so I walked her home to my house. There she remained for several hours, a yawning cavity, half asleep. The rain rained on the ailanthus tree outside my window, the wind rattled the shutters of my old-fashioned window, and I took my time making coffee and carving an ounce of pound cake. I don't believe in force and I would have waited, but her loneliness was very great.

We had quite a nice time for a few weeks. She brought rolls and bagels from wherever the stuff can still be requisitioned. On Sundays she'd come out of Brooklyn with a chicken to roast. She thought I was too skinny. I am, but girls like it. If you're fat, they can see immediately that you'll never need their unique talent for warmth.

Spring came. She said: 'Where are we going?' In just those words! Now I have met this attitude before. Apparently, for most women good food and fun for all are too much of a good thing.

The sun absorbed July and she said it again. 'Freddy, if we're not going anywhere, I'm not going along anymore.' We were beach-driven those windy Sundays: her mother must have told her what to say. She said it with such imprisoned conviction.

One Friday night in September I came home from an unlucky party. All the faces had been strange. There were no extra girls, and after some muted conversation with the glorious properties of other men, I felt terrible and went home.

In an armchair, looking at an *Art News* full of Dutchmen who had lived eighty years in forty, was Dorothy. And by her side an overnight case. I could hardly see her face when she stood to greet me, but she made tea first and steamed some of my ardor into the damp night.

'Listen, Freddy,' she said. 'I told my mother I was visiting Leona in Washington for two days and I fixed it with Leona. Everyone'll cover me' – pouring tea and producing seeded tarts from some secret Flatbush Avenue bakery – all this to change the course of a man's appetite and enable conversation to go forward.

'No, listen, Freddy, you don't take yourself seriously, and that's the reason you can't take anything else – a job, or a – a relationship – seriously . . . Freddy, you don't listen. You'll laugh, but you're very barbaric. You live at your nerve ends. If you're near a radio, you listen to music; if you're near an open icebox, you stuff yourself; if a girl is within ten feet of you, you have her stripped and on the spit.'

'Now, Dotty, don't be so graphic,' I said. 'Every man is his own rotisserie.'

What a nice girl! Say something vulgar and she'd suddenly be all over me, blushing bitterly, glad that the East River separated her from her mother. Poor girl, she was avid.

And she was giving. By Sunday night I had ended half a dozen conversations and nipped their moral judgments at the homiletic root. By Sunday night I had said I love you Dotty, twice. By Monday morning I realized the extent of my commitment and I don't mind saying it prevented my going to a job I had swung on Friday.

My impression of women is that they mean well but are driven to an obsessive end by greedy tradition. When Dot found out that I'd decided against that job (what job? a job, that's all) she took action. She returned my copy of *Nineteen Eighty-four* and said in a note that I could keep the six wineglasses her mother had lent me.

Well, I did miss her; you don't meet such wide-open kindness every day. She was no fool either. I'd say peasant wisdom is what she had. Not too much education. Her hair was long and dark. I had always seen it in neat little coiffures or reparably disarrayed, until that weekend.

It was staggering.

I missed her. And then I didn't have too much luck after that. Very little money to spend, and girls are primordial with intuition. There was one nice little married girl whose husband was puttering around in another postal zone, but her heart wasn't in it. I got some windy copy to do through my brother-in-law, a clean-cut croupier who is always crackling bank notes at family parties. Things picked up.

Out of my gasbag profits one weekend I was propelled into the Craggy-moor, a high-pressure resort, a star-studded haven with eleven hundred acres of golf course. When I returned, exhausted but modest, there she was, right in my parlor-floor front. With a

few gasping, kind words and a modern gimmick, she hoped to
breathe eternity into a mortal matter, love.

'Ah, Dotty,' I said, holding out my accepting arms. 'I'm always
glad to see you.'

Of course she explained. 'I didn't come for that really, Freddy.
I came to talk to you. We have a terrific chance to make some real
money, if you'll only be serious a half hour. You're so clever, and
you ought to direct yourself to something. God, you could live in
the country. I mean, even if you kept living alone, you could
have a decent place on a decent street instead of this dump.'

I kissed the tip of her nose. 'If you want to be very serious, Dot,
let's get out and walk. Come on, get your coat on and tell me all
about how to make money.'

She did. We walked out to the park and scattered autumn
leaves for an hour. 'Now don't laugh, Freddy,' she told me.
'There's a Yiddish paper called *Morgenlicht*. It's running a contest: Jews in the News. Every day they put in a picture and two
descriptions. You have to say who the three people are, add one
more fact about them, and then send it in by midnight that night.
It runs three months at least.'

'A hundred Jews in the news?' I said. 'What a tolerant country!
So, Dot, what do you get for this useful information?'

'First prize, five thousand dollars and a trip to Israel. Also on
return two days each in the three largest European capitals in the
Free West.'

'Very nice,' I said. 'What's the idea, though? To uncover the
ones that've been passing?'

'Freddy, why do you look at everything inside out? They're
just proud of themselves, and they want to make Jews everywhere proud of their contribution to this country. Aren't you
proud?'

'Woe to the crown of pride!'

'I don't care what you think. The point is, we know somebody
who knows somebody on the paper – he writes a special article
once a week – we don't know him really, but our family name is
familiar to him. So we have a very good chance if we really do it.

Look how smart you are, Freddy. I can't do it myself, Freddy, you have to help me. It's a thing I made up my mind to do anyway. If Dotty Wasserman really makes up her mind, it's practically done.'

I hadn't noticed this obstinacy in her character before. I had none in my own. Every weekday night after work she leaned thoughtfully on my desk, wearing for warmth a Harris-tweed jacket that ruined the nap of my arm. Somewhere out of doors a strand of copper in constant agitation carried information from her mother's Brooklyn phone to her ear.

Peering over her shoulder, I would sometimes discover a three-quarter view of a newsworthy Jew or a full view of a half Jew. The fraction did not interfere with the rules. They were glad to extract him and be proud.

The longer we worked the prouder Dotty became. Her face flushed, she'd raise her head from the hieroglyphics and read her own translation: 'A gray-headed gentleman very much respected; an intimate of Cabinet members; a true friend to a couple of Presidents; often seen in the park, sitting on a bench.'

'Bernard Baruch!' I snapped.

And then a hard one: 'Has contributed to the easiness of inter-state commerce; his creation is worth millions and was completed last year. Still he has time for Deborah, Susan, Judith, and Nancy, his four daughters.'

For this I smoked and guzzled a hot eggnog Dot had whipped up to give me strength and girth. I stared at the stove, the ceiling, my irritable shutters – then I said calmly: 'Chaim Pazzi – he's a bridge architect.' I never forget a name, no matter what typeface it appears in.

'Imagine it, Freddy. I didn't even know there was a Jew who had such accomplishment in that field.'

Actually, it sometimes took as much as an hour to attach a real name to a list of exaggerated attributes. When it took that long I couldn't help muttering, 'Well, we've uncovered another one. Put him on the list for Van 2.'

Dotty'd say sadly, 'I have to believe you're joking.'

Well, why do you think she liked me? All you little psycho-analyzed people, now say it at once, in a chorus: 'Because she is a masochist and you are a sadist.'

No. I was very good to her. And to all the love she gave me, I responded. And I kept all our appointments and called her on Fridays to remind her about Saturday, and when I had money I brought her flowers and once earrings and once a black brassiere I saw advertised in the paper with some cleverly stitched windows for ventilation. I still have it. She never dared take it home.

But I will not be eaten by any woman.

My poor old mother died with a sizable chunk of me stuck in her gullet. I was in the army at the time, but I understand her last words were: 'Introduce Freddy to Eleanor Farbstein.' Consider the nerve of that woman. Including me in a codicil. She left my sister to that ad man and culinary expert with a crew cut. She left my father to the commiseration of aunts, while me, her prize possession and the best piece of meat in the freezer of her heart, she left to Ellen Farbstein.

As a matter of fact, Dotty said it herself. 'I never went with a fellow who paid as much attention as you, Freddy. You're always there. I know if I'm lonesome or depressed all I have to do is call you and you'll meet me downtown and drop whatever you're doing. Don't think I don't appreciate it.'

The established truth is, I wasn't doing much. My brother-in-law could have kept me in clover, but he pretended I was a specialist in certain ornate copy infrequently called for by his concern. Therefore I was able to give my wit, energy, and attention to Jews in the News – *Morgenlicht*, the Morning Paper That Comes Out the Night Before.

And so we reached the end. Dot really believed we'd win. I was almost persuaded. Drinking hot chocolate and screwdrivers, we fantasized six weeks away.

We won.

I received a 9 a.m. phone call one mid-week morning. 'Rise and shine, Frederick P. Sims. We did it. You see, whatever you really try to do, you can do.'

She quit work at noon and met me for lunch at an outdoor café in the Village, full of smiles and corrupt with pride. We ate very well and I had to hear the following information – part of it I'd suspected.

It was all in her name. Of course her mother had to get some. She had helped with the translation because Dotty had very little Yiddish actually (not to mention her worry about the security of her old age); and it was necessary, they had decided in midnight conference, to send some money to their old aunt Lise, who had gotten out of Europe only ninety minutes before it was sealed forever and was now in Toronto among strangers, having lost most of her mind.

The trip abroad to Israel and three other European capitals was for two (2). They had to be married. If our papers could not include one that proved our conjunction by law, she would sail alone. Before I could make my accumulating statement, she shrieked oh! her mother was waiting in front of Lord and Taylor's. And she was off.

I smoked my miserable encrusted pipe and considered my position.

Meanwhile in another part of the city, wheels were moving, presses humming, and the next day the facts were composed from right to left across the masthead of *Morgenlicht*:

! SNIW NAMRESSAW YTTOD
SREWSNA EHT LLA SWONK LRIG NYLKOORB

Neatly boxed below, a picture of Dot and me eating lunch recalled a bright flash that had illuminated the rice pudding the day before, as I sat drenched in the fizzle of my modest hopes.

I sent Dotty a postcard. It said: 'No can do.'

The final arrangements were complicated due to the reluctance of the Israeli government to permit egress to dollar bills which were making the grandest tour of all. Once inside that province of cosmopolitans, the dollar was expected to resign its hedonistic role as an American toy and begin the presbyterian life of a tool.

Within two weeks letters came from abroad bearing this information and containing photographs of Dotty smiling at a kibbutz, leaning sympathetically on a wailing wall, unctuous in an orange grove.

I decided to take a permanent job for a couple of months in an agency, attaching the following copy to photographs of upright men!

THIS IS BILL FEARY. HE IS THE MAN WHO WILL TAKE YOUR ORDER FOR — TONS OF RED LABEL FERTILIZER. HE KNOWS THE MIDWEST. HE KNOWS YOUR NEEDS. CALL HIM BILL AND CALL HIM NOW.

I was neat and brown-eyed, innocent and alert, offended by the chicanery of my fellows, powered by decency, going straight up.

The lean-shanked girls had been brought to New York by tractor and they were going straight up too, through the purgatory of man's avarice to Whore's Heaven, the Palace of Possessions.

While I labored at my dreams, Dotty spent some money to see the leaning tower of Pisa and ride in a gondola. She decided to stay in London at least two weeks because she felt at home there. And so all this profit was at last being left in the hands of foreigners who would invest it to their own advantage.

One misty day the boom of foghorns rolling round Manhattan Island reminded me of a cablegram I had determined to ignore. ARRIVING QUEEN ELIZABETH WEDNESDAY 4 P.M. I ignored it successfully all day and was casual with a couple of cool blondes. And went home and was lonely. I was lonely all evening. I tried writing a letter to an athletic girl I'd met in a ski lodge a few weeks before . . . I thought of calling some friends, but the pure unmentionable fact is that women isolate you. There was no one to call.

I went out for an evening paper. Read it. Listened to the radio. Went out for a morning paper. Had a beer. Read the paper and waited for the calculation of morning.

I never went to work the next day or the day after. No word came from Dot. She must have been crawling with guilt. Poor girl . . .

I finally wrote her a letter. It was very strong.

My dear Dorothy:

When I consider our relationship and recall its seasons, the summer sun that shone on it and the winter snows it plowed through, I can still find no reason for your unconscionable behavior. I realize that you were motivated by the hideous examples of your mother and all the mothers before her. You were, in a word, a prostitute. The love and friendship I gave were apparently not enough. What did you want? You gave me the swamp waters of your affection to drown in, and because I refused you planned this desperate revenge.

In all earnestness, I helped you, combing my memory for those of our faith who have touched the press-happy nerves of this nation.

What did you want?

Marriage?

Ah, that's it! A happy daddy-and-mommy home. The home-happy day you could put your hair up in curlers, swab cream in the corner of your eyes . . . I'm not sure all this is for Fred.

I am twenty-nine years old and not getting any younger. All around me boy graduates have attached their bow legs to the Ladder of Success. Dotty Wasserman, Dotty Wasserman, what can I say to you? If you think I have been harsh, face the fact that you haven't dared face me.

We had some wonderful times together. We could have them again. This is a great opportunity to start on a more human basis. You cannot impose your narrow view of life on me. Make up your mind, Dotty Wasserman.

　　　　　　　　　　Sincerely with recollected affection,

　　　　　　　　　　　　　　　　　F.

P.S. This is your *last* chance.

Two weeks later I received a one-hundred-dollar bill.

A week after that at my door I found a carefully packed leather portfolio, hand-sewn in Italy, and a projector with a box of slides showing interesting views of Europe and North Africa. And after that, nothing at all.

An Interest in Life

My husband gave me a broom one Christmas. This wasn't right. No one can tell me it was meant kindly.

'I don't want you not to have anything for Christmas while I'm away in the army,' he said. 'Virginia, please look at it. It comes with this fancy dustpan. It hangs off a stick. Look at it, will you? Are you blind or cross-eyed?'

'Thanks, chum,' I said. I had always wanted a dustpan hooked up that way. It was a good one. My husband doesn't shop in bargain basements or January sales.

Still and all, in spite of the quality, it was a mean present to give a woman you planned on never seeing again, a person you had children with and got onto all the time, drunk or sober, even when everybody had to get up early in the morning.

I asked him if he could wait and join the army in a half hour, as I had to get the groceries. I don't like to leave kids alone in a three-room apartment full of gas and electricity. Fire may break out from a nasty remark. Or the oldest decides to get even with the youngest.

'Just this once,' he said. 'But you better figure out how to get along without me.'

'You're a handicapped person mentally,' I said. 'You should've been institutionalized years ago.' I slammed the door. I didn't want to see him pack his underwear and ironed shirts.

I never got farther than the front stoop, though, because there was Mrs. Raftery, wringing her hands, tears in her eyes as though she had a monopoly on all the good news.

'Mrs. Raftery!' I said, putting my arm around her. 'Don't cry.' She leaned on me because I am such a horsey build. 'Don't cry, Mrs. Raftery, please!' I said.

'That's like you, Virginia. Always looking at the ugly side of things. 'Take in the wash. It's rainin'!' That's you. You're the first one knows it when the dumbwaiter breaks.'

'Oh, come on now, that's not so. It just isn't so,' I said. 'I'm the exact opposite.'

'Did you see Mrs. Cullen yet?' she asked, paying no attention. 'Where?'

'Virginia!' she said, shocked. 'She's passed away. The whole house knows it. They've got her in white like a bride and you never saw a beautiful creature like that. She must be eighty. Her husband's proud.'

'She was never more than an acquaintance; she didn't have any children,' I said.

'Well, I don't care about that. Now, Virginia, you do what I say now, you go downstairs and you say like this – listen to me – say, 'I hear, Mr. Cullen, your wife's passed away. I'm sorry.' Then ask him how he is. Then you ought to go around the corner and see her. She's in Witson & Wayde. Then you ought to go over to the church when they carry her over.'

'It's not my church,' I said.

'That's no reason, Virginia. You go up like this,' she said, parting from me to do a prancy dance. 'Up the big front steps, into the church you go. It's beautiful in there. You can't help kneeling only for a minute. Then round to the right. Then up the other stairway. Then you come to a great oak door that's arched above you, then,' she said, seizing a deep, deep breath, for all the good it would do her, 'and then turn the knob slo-owly and open the door and see for yourself: Our Blessed Mother is in charge. Beautiful. Beautiful. Beautiful.'

I sighed in and I groaned out, so as to melt a certain pain around my heart. A steel ring like arthritis, at my age.

'You are a groaner,' Mrs. Raftery said, gawking into my mouth.

'I am not,' I said. I got a whiff of her, a terrible cheap wine lush.

My husband threw a penny at the door from the inside to take my notice from Mrs. Raftery. He rattled the glass door to make sure I looked at him. He had a fat duffel bag on each shoulder. Where did he acquire so much worldly possession? What was in them? My grandma's goose feathers from across the ocean? Or all the diaper-service diapers? To this day the truth is shrouded in mystery.

'What the hell are you doing, Virginia?' he said, dumping them at my feet. 'Standing out here on your hind legs telling everybody your business? The army gives you a certain time, for godsakes, they're not kidding.' Then he said, 'I beg your pardon,' to Mrs. Raftery. He took hold of me with his two arms as though in love and pressed his body hard against mine so that I could feel him for the last time and suffer my loss. Then he kissed me in a mean way to nearly split my lip. Then he winked and said, 'That's all for now,' and skipped off into the future, duffel bags full of rags.

He left me in an embarrassing situation, nearly fainting, in front of that old widow, who can't even remember the half of it. 'He's a crock,' said Mrs. Raftery. 'Is he leaving for good or just temporarily, Virginia?'

'Oh, he's probably deserting me,' I said, and sat down on the stoop, pulling my big knees up to my chin.

'If that's the case, tell the Welfare right away,' she said. 'He's a bum, leaving you just before Christmas. Tell the cops,' she said. 'They'll provide the toys for the little kids gladly. And don't forget to let the grocer in on it. He won't be so hard on you expecting payment.'

She saw that sadness was stretched worldwide across my face. Mrs. Raftery isn't the worst person. She said, 'Look around for comfort, dear.' With a nervous finger she pointed to the truckers eating lunch on their haunches across the street, leaning on the loading platforms. She waved her hand to include in all the men marching up and down in search of a decent luncheonette. She didn't leave out the six longshoremen loafing under the fish-market marquee. 'If their lungs and stomachs ain't crushed by overwork, they disappear somewhere in the world. Don't be disappointed, Virginia. I don't know a man living'd last you a lifetime.'

Ten days later Girard asked, 'Where's Daddy?'

'Ask me no questions, I'll tell you no lies.' I didn't want the children to know the facts. Present or past, a child should have a father.

'Where *is* Daddy?' Girard asked the week after that.

'He joined the army,' I said.

'He made my bunk bed,' said Philip.

'The truth shall make ye free,' I said.

Then I sat down with pencil and pad to get in control of my resources. The facts, when I added and subtracted them, were that my husband had left me with fourteen dollars, and the rent unpaid, in an emergency state. He'd claimed he was sorry to do this, but my opinion is, out of sight, out of mind. 'The city won't let you starve,' he'd said. 'After all, you're half the population. You're keeping up the good work. Without you the race would die out. Who'd pay the taxes? Who'd keep the streets clean? There wouldn't be no army. A man like me wouldn't have no place to go.'

I sent Girard right down to Mrs. Raftery with a request about the whereabouts of Welfare. She responded R.S.V.P. with an extra comment in left-handed script: 'Poor Girard . . . he's never the boy my John was!'

Who asked her?

I called on Welfare right after the new year. In no time I discovered that they're rigged up to deal with liars, and if you're truthful it's disappointing to them. They may even refuse to handle your case if you're too truthful.

They asked sensible questions at first. They asked where my husband had enlisted. I didn't know. They put some letter writers and agents after him. 'He's not in the United States Army,' they said. 'Try the Brazilian Army,' I suggested.

They have no sense of kidding around. They're not the least bit lighthearted and they tried. 'Oh no,' they said. 'That was incorrect. He is not in the Brazilian Army.'

'No?' I said. 'How strange! He must be in the Mexican Navy.'

By law, they had to hound his brothers. They wrote to his brother who has a first-class card in the Teamsters and owns an apartment house in California. They asked his two brothers in Jersey to help me. They have large families. Rightfully they laughed. Then they wrote to Thomas, the oldest, the smart one (the one they all worked so hard for years to keep him in college until his brains could pay off). He was the one who sent ten dollars immediately, saying, 'What a bastard! I'll send something time to time, Ginny, but whatever you do, don't tell the authorities.' Of course I never did. Soon they began to guess they were better people than me, that I was in trouble because I deserved it, and then they liked me better.

But they never fixed my refrigerator. Every time I called I said patiently, 'The milk is sour . . .' I said, 'Corn beef went bad.' Sitting in that beer-stinking phone booth in Felan's for the sixth time (sixty cents) with the baby on my lap and Barbie tapping at the glass door with an American flag, I cried into the secretary's hardhearted ear, 'I bought real butter for the holiday, and it's rancid . . .' They said, 'You'll have to get a better bid on the repair job.'

While I waited indoors for a man to bid, Girard took to swinging back and forth on top of the bathroom door, just to soothe himself, giving me the laugh, dreamy, nibbling calcimine off the ceiling. On first sight Mrs. Raftery said, 'Whack the monkey, he'd be better off on arsenic.'

But Girard is my son and I'm the judge. It means a terrible thing for the future, though I don't know what to call it.

It was from constantly thinking of my foreknowledge on this and other subjects, it was from observing when I put my lipstick on daily, how my face was just curling up to die, that John Raftery came from Jersey to rescue me.

On Thursdays, anyway, John Raftery took the tubes in to visit his mother. The whole house knew it. She was cheerful even before breakfast. She sang out loud in a girlish brogue that only came to tongue for grand occasions. Hanging out the wash, she blushed to recall what a remarkable boy her John had been. 'Ask the sisters around the corner,' she said to the open kitchen windows. 'They'll never forget John.'

That particular night after supper Mrs. Raftery said to her son, 'John, how come you don't say hello to your old friend Virginia? She's had hard luck and she's gloomy.'

'Is that so, Mother?' he said, and immediately climbed two flights to knock at my door.

'Oh, John,' I said at the sight of him, hat in hand in a white shirt and blue-striped tie, spick-and-span, a Sunday-school man. 'Hello!'

'Welcome, John!' I said. 'Sit down. Come right in. How are you? You look awfully good. You do. Tell me, how've you been all this time, John?'

'How've I been?' he asked thoughtfully. To answer within reason, he described his life with Margaret, marriage, work, and children up to the present day.

I had nothing good to report. Now that he had put the subject around before my very eyes, every burnt-up day of my life smoked in shame, and I couldn't even get a clear view of the good half hours.

'Of course,' he said, 'you do have lovely children. Noticeable-looking, Virginia. Good looks is always something to be thankful for.'

'Thankful?' I said. 'I don't have to thank anything but my own foolishness for four children when I'm twenty-six years old, deserted, and poverty-struck, regardless of looks. A man can't help it, but I could have behaved better.'

'Don't be so cruel on yourself, Ginny,' he said. 'Children come from God.'

'You're still great on holy subjects, aren't you? You know damn well where children come from.'

He did know. His red face reddened further. John Raftery has had that color coming out on him boy and man from keeping his rages so inward.

Still he made more sense in his conversation after that, and I poured fresh tea to tell him how my husband used to like me because I was a passionate person. That was until he took a look around and saw how in the long run this life only meant more of the same thing. He tried to turn away from me once he came to this understanding, and make me hate him. His face changed. He gave up his brand of cigarettes, which we had in common. He threw out the two pairs of socks I knitted by hand. 'If there's anything I hate in this world, it's navy blue,' he said. Oh, I could have dyed them. I would have done anything for him, if he were only not too sorry to ask me.

'You were a nice kid in those days,' said John, referring to certain Saturday nights. 'A wild, nice kid.'

'Aaah,' I said, disgusted. Whatever I was then was on the way to where I am now. 'I was fresh. If I had a kid like me, I'd slap her cross-eyed.'

The very next Thursday John gave me a beautiful radio with a record player. 'Enjoy yourself,' he said. That really made Welfare speechless. We didn't own any records, but the investigator saw my burden was lightened and he scribbled a dozen pages about it in his notebook.

On the third Thursday he brought a walking doll (twenty-four inches) for Linda and Barbie with a card inscribed, 'A baby doll for a couple of dolls.' He had also had a couple of drinks at his mother's, and this made him want to dance. 'La-la-la,' he sang, a ramrod swaying in my kitchen chair. 'La-la-la, let yourself go . . .'

'You gotta give a little,' he sang, 'live a little . . .' He said, 'Virginia, may I have this dance?'

'Sssh, we finally got them asleep. Please, turn the radio down. Quiet. Deathly silence, John Raftery.'

'Let me do your dishes, Virginia.'

'Don't be silly, you're a guest in my house,' I said. 'I still regard you as a guest.'

'I want to do something for you, Virginia.'

'Tell me I'm the most gorgeous thing,' I said, dipping my arm to the funny bone in dish soup.

He didn't answer. 'I'm having a lot of trouble at work' was all he said. Then I heard him push the chair back. He came up behind me, put his arms around my waistline, and kissed my cheek. He whirled me around and took my hands. He said, 'An old friend is better than rubies.' He looked me in the eye. He held my attention by trying to be honest. And he kissed me a short sweet kiss on my mouth.

'Please sit down, Virginia,' he said. He kneeled before me and put his head in my lap. I was stirred by so much activity. Then he looked up at me and, as though proposing marriage for life, he offered – because he was drunk – to place his immortal soul in peril to comfort me.

First I said, 'Thank you.' Then I said, 'No.'

I was sorry for him, but he's devout, a leader of the Fathers' Club at his church, active in all the lay groups for charities, orphans, etc. I knew that if he stayed late to love with me, he would not do it lightly but would in the end pay terrible penance and ruin his long life. The responsibility would be on me.

So I said no.

And Barbie is such a light sleeper. All she has to do, I thought, is wake up and wander in and see her mother and her new friend John with his pants around his knees, wrestling on the kitchen table. A vision like that could affect a kid for life.

I said no.

Everyone in this building is so goddamn nosy. That evening I had to say no.

But John came to visit, anyway, on the fourth Thursday. This time he brought the discarded dresses of Margaret's daughters, organdy party dresses and glazed cotton for every day. He gently admired Barbara and Linda, his blue eyes rolling to back up a couple of dozen oohs and ahs.

Even Philip, who thinks God gave him just a certain number of hellos and he better save them for the final judgment, Philip leaned on John and said, 'Why don't you bring your boy to play with me? I don't have nobody who to play with.' (Philip's a liar. There must be at least seventy-one children in this house, pale pink to medium brown, English-talking and gibbering in Spanish, rough-and-tough boys, the Lone Ranger's bloody pals, or the exact picture of Supermouse. If a boy wanted a friend, he could pick the very one out of his neighbors.)

Also, Girard is a cold fish. He was in a lonesome despair. Sometimes he looked in the mirror and said, 'How come I have such an ugly face? My nose is funny. Mostly people don't like me.' He was a liar too. Girard has a face like his father's. His eyes are the color of those little blue plums in August. He looks like an advertisement in a magazine. He could be a child model and make a lot of money. He is my first child, and if he thinks he is ugly, I think I am ugly.

John said, 'I can't stand to see a boy mope like that . . . What do the Sisters say in school?'

'He doesn't pay attention is all they say. You can't get much out of them.'

'My middle boy was like that,' said John. 'Couldn't take an interest. Aaah, I wish I didn't have all that headache on the job. I'd grab Girard by the collar and make him take notice of the world. I wish I could ask him out to Jersey to play in all that space.'

'Why not?' I said.

'Why, Virginia, I'm surprised you don't know why not. You know I can't take your children out to meet my children.'

I felt a lot of strong arthritis in my ribs.

'My mother's the funny one, Virginia.' He felt he had to continue with the subject matter. 'I don't know. I guess she likes the idea of bugging Margaret. She says, 'You goin' up, John?' 'Yes, Mother,' I say. 'Behave yourself, John,' she says. 'That husband might come home and hacksaw you into hell. You're a Catholic man, John,' she says. But I figured it out. She likes to know I'm in the building. I swear, Virginia, she wishes me the best of luck.'

'I do too, John,' I said. We drank a last glass of beer to make sure of a peaceful sleep. 'Good night, Virginia,' he said, looping his muffler neatly under his chin. 'Don't worry. I'll be thinking of what to do about Girard.'

I got into the big bed that I share with the girls in the little room. For once I had no trouble falling asleep. I only had to worry about Linda and Barbara and Philip. It was a great relief to me that John had taken over the thinking about Girard.

John was sincere. That's true. He paid a lot of attention to Girard, smoking out all his sneaky sorrows. He registered him into a wild pack of Cub Scouts that went up to the Bronx once a week to let off steam. He gave him a Junior Erector Set. And sometimes when his family wasn't listening he prayed at great length for him.

One Sunday, Sister Veronica said in her sweet voice from another life, 'He's not worse. He might even be a little better. How are *you*, Virginia?' putting her hand on mine. Everybody around here acts like they know everything.

'Just fine,' I said.

'We ought to start on Philip,' John said, 'if it's true Girard's improving. '

'You should've been a social worker, John.'

'A lot of people have noticed that about me,' said John.

'Your mother was always acting so crazy about you, how come she didn't knock herself out a little to see you in college? Like we did for Thomas?'

'Now, Virginia, be fair. She's a poor old woman. My father was a weak earner. She had to have my wages, and I'll tell you, Virginia, I'm not sorry. Look at Thomas. He's still in school. Drop him in this jungle and he'd be devoured. He hasn't had a touch of real life. And here I am with a good chunk of a family, a home of my own, a name in the building trades. One thing I have to tell you, the poor old woman is sorry. I said one day (oh, in passing – years ago) that I might marry you. She stuck a knife in herself. It's a fact. Not more than an eighth of an inch. You never saw such a gory Sunday. One thing – you would have been a better daughter-in-law to her than Margaret.'

'Marry me?' I said.

'Well, yes . . . Aaah – I always liked you, then . . . Why do you think I'd sit in the shade of this kitchen every Thursday night? For godsakes, the only warm thing around here is this teacup. Yes sir, I did want to marry you, Virginia.'

'No kidding, John? Really?' It was nice to know. Better late than never, to learn you were desired in youth.

I didn't tell John, but the truth is, I would never have married him. Once I met my husband with his winking looks, he was my only interest. Wild as I had been with John and others, I turned all my wildness over to him and then there was no question in my mind.

Still, face facts, if my husband didn't budge on in life, it was my fault. On me, as they say, be it. I greeted the morn with a song. I had a hello for everyone but the landlord. Ask the people on the block, come or go – even the Spanish ones, with their sad dark faces – they have to smile when they see me.

But for his own comfort, he should have done better lifewise and moneywise. I was happy, but I am now in possession of knowledge that this is wrong. Happiness isn't so bad for a woman. She gets fatter, she gets older, she could lie down, nuzzling a regiment of men and little kids, she could just die of the pleasure. But men are different, they have to own money, or they have to be famous, or everybody on the block has to look up to them from the cellar stairs.

A woman counts her children and acts snotty, like she invented life, but men must do well in the world. I know that men are not fooled by being happy.

'A funny guy,' said John, guessing where my thoughts had gone. 'What stopped him up? He was nobody's fool. He had a funny thing about him, Virginia, if you don't mind my saying so. He wasn't much distance up, but he was all set and ready to be looking down on us all.'

'He was very smart, John. You don't realize that. His hobby was crossword puzzles, and I said to him real often, as did others around here, that he ought to go out on the "$64 Question." Why not? But he laughed. You know what he said? He said, "That proves how dumb you are if you think I'm smart.'''

'A funny guy,' said John. 'Get it all off your chest,' he said. 'Talk it out, Virginia; it's the only way to kill the pain.'

By and large, I was happy to oblige. Still I could not carry through about certain cruel remarks. It was like trying to move back into the dry mouth of a nightmare to remember that the last day I was happy was the middle of a week in March, when I told my husband I was going to have Linda. Barbara was five months old to the hour. The boys were three and four. I had to tell him. It was the last day with anything happy about it.

Later on he said, 'Oh, you make me so sick, you're so goddamn big and fat, you look like a goddamn brownstone, the way you're squared off in front.'

'Well, where are you going tonight?' I asked.

'How should I know?' he said. 'Your big ass takes up the whole goddamn bed,' he said. 'There's no room for me.' He bought a sleeping bag and slept on the floor.

I couldn't believe it. I would start every morning fresh. I couldn't believe that he would turn against me so, while I was still young and even his friends still liked me.

But he did, he turned absolutely against me and became no friend of mine. 'All you ever think about is making babies. This place stinks like the men's room in the BMT. It's a fucking *pissoir*.' He was strong on truth all through the year. 'That kid eats more than the five of us put together,' he said. 'Stop stuffing your face, you fat dumbbell,' he said to Philip.

Then he worked on the neighbors. 'Get that nosy old bag out of here,' he said. 'If she comes on once more with "my son in the building trades" I'll squash her for the cat.'

Then he turned on Spielvogel, the checker, his oldest friend, who only visited on holidays and never spoke to me (shy, the way some bachelors are). 'That sonofabitch, don't hand me that friendship crap, all he's after is your ass. That's what I need – a little shitmaker of his using up the air in this flat.'

And then there was no one else to dispose of. We were left alone fair and square, facing each other.

'Now, Virginia,' he said, 'I come to the end of my rope. I see a black wall ahead of me. What the hell am I supposed to do? I only got one life. Should I lie down and die? I don't know what to do anymore. I'll give it to you straight, Virginia, if I stick around, you can't help it, you'll hate me . . .'

'I hate you right now,' I said. 'So do whatever you like.'

'This place drives me nuts,' he mumbled. 'I don't know what to do around here. I want to get you a present. Something.'

'I told you, do whatever you like. Buy me a rat trap for rats.'

That's when he went down to the House Appliance Store, and he brought back a new broom and a classy dustpan.

'A new broom sweeps clean,' he said. 'I got to get out of here,' he said. 'I'm going nuts.' Then he began to stuff the duffel bags, and I went to the grocery store but was stopped by Mrs. Raftery, who had to tell me what she considered so beautiful – death – then he kissed and went to join some army somewhere.

I didn't tell John any of this, because I think it makes a woman look too bad to tell on how another man has treated her. He begins to see her through the other man's eyes, a sitting duck, a skinful of flaws. After all, I had come to depend on John. All my husband's friends were strangers now, though I had always said to them, 'Feel welcome.'

And the family men in the building looked too cunning, as though they had all personally deserted me. If they met me on the stairs, they carried the heaviest groceries up and helped bring Linda's stroller down, but they never asked me a question worth answering at all.

Besides that, Girard and Philip taught the girls the days of the week: Monday, Tuesday, Wednesday, Johnday, Friday. They waited for him once a week, under the hallway lamp, half asleep like bugs in the sun, sitting in their little chairs with their names on in gold, a birth present from my mother-in-law. At fifteen after eight he punctually came, to read a story, pass out some kisses, and tuck them into bed.

But one night, after a long Johnday of them squealing my eardrum split, after a rainy afternoon with brother constantly raising up his hand against brother, with the girls near ready to go to court over the proper ownership of Melinda Lee, the twenty-four-inch walking doll, the doorbell rang three times. Not any of those times did John's face greet me.

I was too ashamed to call down to Mrs. Raftery, and she was too mean to knock on my door and explain.

He didn't come the following Thursday either. Girard said sadly, 'He must've run away, John.'

I had to give him up after two weeks' absence and no word. I didn't know how to tell the children: something about right and wrong, goodness and meanness, men and women. I had it all at my fingertips, ready to hand over. But I didn't think I ought to take mistakes and truth away from them. Who knows? They might make a truer friend in this world somewhere than I have ever made. So I just put them to bed and sat in the kitchen and cried.

In the middle of my third beer, searching in my mind for the next step, I found the decision to go on *Strike It Rich*. I scrounged some paper and pencil from the toy box and I listed all my troubles, which must be done in order to qualify. The list when complete could have brought tears to the eye of God if He had a minute. At the sight of it my bitterness began to improve. All that is really necessary for survival of the fittest, it seems, is an interest in life, good, bad, or peculiar.

As always happens in these cases where you have begun to help yourself with plans, news comes from an opposite direction. The doorbell rang, two short and two long – meaning John.

My first thought was to wake the children and make them happy. 'No! No!' he said. 'Please don't put yourself to that trouble. Virginia, I'm dog-tired,' he said. 'Dog-tired. My job is a damn headache. It's too much. It's all day and it scuttles my mind at night, and in the end who does the credit go to?

'Virginia,' he said, 'I don't know if I can come anymore. I've been wanting to tell you. I just don't know. What's it all about? Could you answer me if I asked you? I can't figure this whole thing out at all.'

I started the tea steeping because his fingers when I touched them were cold. I didn't speak. I tried looking at it from his man point of view, and I thought he had to take a bus, the tubes, and a subway to see me; and then the subway, the tubes, and a bus to go back home at 1 a.m. It wouldn't be any trouble at all for him to part with us forever. I thought about my life, and I gave strongest consideration to my children. If given the choice, I decided to choose not to live without him.

'What's that?' he asked, pointing to my careful list of troubles. 'Writing a letter?'

'Oh no,' I said, 'it's for *Strike It Rich*. I hope to go on the program.'

'Virginia, for goodness' sakes,' he said, giving it a glance, 'you don't have a ghost. They'd laugh you out of the studio. Those people really suffer.'

'Are you sure, John?' I asked.

'No question in my mind at all,' said John. 'Have you ever seen that program? I mean, in addition to all of this – the little disturbances of man' – he waved a scornful hand at my list – 'they *suffer*. They live in the forefront of tornadoes, their lives are washed off by floods – catastrophes of God. Oh, Virginia.'

'Are you sure, John?'

'For goodness' sake . . .'

Sadly I put my list away. Still, if things got worse, I could always make use of it.

Once that was settled, I acted on an earlier decision. I pushed his cup of scalding tea aside. I wedged myself onto his lap between his hard belt buckle and the table. I put my arms around his neck and said, 'How come you're so cold, John?' He has a kind face and he knew how to look astonished. He said, 'Why, Virginia, I'm getting warmer.' We laughed.

John became a lover to me that night.

Mrs. Raftery is sometimes silly and sick from her private source of cheap wine. She expects John often. 'Honor your mother, what's the matter with you, John?' she complains. 'Honor. Honor.'

'Virginia dear,' she says. 'You never would've taken John away to Jersey like Margaret. I wish he'd've married you.'

'You didn't like me much in those days.'

'That's a lie,' she says. I know she's a hypocrite, but no more than the rest of the world.

What is remarkable to me is that it doesn't seem to conscience John as I thought it might. It is still hard to believe that a man who sends out the Ten Commandments every year for a Christmas card can be so easy buttoning and unbuttoning.

Of course we must be very careful not to wake the children or disturb the neighbors, who will enjoy another person's excitement just so far, and then the pleasure enrages them. We must be very careful for ourselves too, for when my husband comes back, realizing the babies are in school and everything easier, he won't forgive me if I've started it all up again — noisy signs of life that are so much trouble to a man.

We haven't seen him in two and a half years. Although people have suggested it, I do not want the police or Intelligence or a private eye or anyone to go after him to bring him back. I know that if he expected to stay away forever he would have written and said so. As it is, I just don't know what evening, any time, he may appear. Sometimes, stumbling over a blockbuster of a dream at midnight, I wake up to vision his soft arrival.

He comes in the door with his old key. He gives me a strict look and says, 'Well, you look older, Virginia.' 'So do you,' I say, although he hasn't changed a bit.

He settles in the kitchen because the children are asleep all over the rest of the house. I unknot his tie and offer him a cold sandwich. He raps my backside, paying attention to the bounce. I walk around him as though he were a Maypole, kissing as I go.

I didn't like the army much,' he says. 'Next time I think I might go join the Merchant Marine.'

'What army?' I say.

'It's pretty much the same everywhere,' he says.

'I wouldn't be a bit surprised,' I say.

'I lost my cuff link, goddamnit,' he says, and drops to the floor to look for it. I go down too on my knees, but I know he never had a cuff link in his life. Still I would do a lot for him.

'Got you off your feet that time,' he says, laughing. 'Oh yes, I did.' And before I can even make myself half comfortable on that polka-dotted linoleum, he got onto me right where we were, and the truth is, we were so happy, we forgot the precautions.

An Irrevocable Diameter

One day in August, in a quiet little suburb hot with cars and zoned for parks, I, Charles C. Charley, met a girl named Cindy. There were lots of Cindys strolling in the woods that afternoon, but mine was a real citizen with yellow hair that never curled (it hung). When I came across her, she had left the woods to lie around her father's attic. She rested on an army cot, her head on no pillow, smoking a cigarette that stood straight up, a dreamy funnel. Ashes fell gently to her chest, which was relatively new, covered by Dacron and Egyptian cotton, and waiting to be popular.

I had just installed an air conditioner, 20 percent off and late in the season. That's how I make a living. I bring ease to noxious kitchens and fuming bedrooms. People who have tried to live by cross ventilation alone have thanked me.

On the first floor the system was in working order, absolutely perfect and guaranteed. Upstairs, under a low unfinished ceiling, that Cindy lay in the deadest center of an August day. Her forehead was damp, mouth slightly open between drags, a furious and sweaty face, hardly made up except around the eyes, but certainly cared for, cheeks scrubbed and eyebrows brushed, a lifetime's deposit of vitamins, the shiny daughter of cash in the bank.

'Aren't you hot?' I inquired.

'Boiling,' she said.

'Why stay up here?' I asked like a good joe.

'That's my business,' she said.

'Ah, come on, little one,' I said, 'don't be grouchy.'

'What's it to you?' she asked.

I took her cigarette and killed it between forefinger and thumb. Then she looked at me and saw me for what I was, not an ordinary union brother but a perfectly comfortable way to spend five minutes.

'What's your name?' she asked.

'Charles,' I said.

'Is this your business? Are you the boss?'

'I am,' I said.

'Listen, Charles, when you were in high school, did you know exactly what your interests were?'

'Yes,' I said. 'Girls.'

She turned over on her side so we could really talk this out head-on. I stooped to meet her. She smiled. 'Charles, I'm almost finished with school and I can't even decide what to take in college. I don't really want to be anything. I don't know what to do,' she said. 'What do you think I should do?'

I gave her a serious answer, a handful of wisdom. 'In the first place, don't let them shove. Who do they think they're kidding? Most people wouldn't know if they had a million years what they wanted to be. They just sort of become.'

She raised a golden brow. 'Do you think so, Charles? Are you sure? Listen, how old are *you*?'

'Thirty-two,' I said as quick as nighttime in the tropics. 'Thirty-two,' I repeated to reassure myself, since I was subtracting three years wasted in the army as well as the first two years of my life, which I can't remember a damn thing about anyway.

'You seem older.'

'Isn't thirty-two old enough? Is it too old?'

'Oh no, Charles, I don't like kids. I mean they're mostly boring. They don't have a remark to make on anything worth listening to.

They think they're the greatest. They don't even dance very well.'

She fell back, her arms swinging on either side of the cot. She stared at the ceiling. 'If you want to know something,' she said, 'they don't even know how to kiss.'

Then lightly on the very tip of her nose, I, Charles C. Charley, kissed her once and, if it may be sworn, in jest.

To this she replied, 'Are you married, by any chance?'

'No,' I said, 'are you?'

'Oh, Charles,' she said, 'how could I be married? I haven't even graduated yet.'

'You must be a junior,' I said, licking my lips.

'Oh, Charles,' she said, 'that's what I mean. If you were a kid like Mike or Sully or someone, you'd go crazy. Whenever they kiss me, you'd think their whole life was going to change. Honestly, Charles, they lose their breath, they sneeze – just when you're getting in the mood. They stop in the middle to tell you a dirty joke.'

'Imagine that!' I said. 'How about trying someone over sixteen?'

'Don't fish,' she said in a peaceful, happy way. 'Anyway, talk very low. In fact, whisper. If my father comes home and hears me even mention kissing, he'll kill us both.'

I laughed. My little factories of admiration had started to hum and I missed her meaning.

What I observed was the way everything about this Cindy was new and unused. Her parts, visible or wrapped, were tooled for display. All the exaggerated bones of childhood and old age were bedded down in a cozy consistency of girl;

I offered her another cigarette. I stood up and, ducking the rafters, walked back and forth alongside the cot. She held her fresh cigarette aloft and crossed her eyes at it. Ashes fell, little fine feathers. I leaned forward until I was close enough for comfort. I blew them all away.

I thought of praying for divine guidance in line with the great spiritual renaissance of our time. But I am all thumbs in that kind of deciduous conversation. I asked myself, did I, as God's creature under the stars, have the right to evade an event, a factual occurrence, to parry an experience or even a small peradventure?

I relit her cigarette. Then I said, with no pacing at all, like a person who lacks aptitude, 'What do you think, Cindy, listen, will you have trouble with your family about dating me? I'd like to spend a nice long evening with you. I haven't talked to someone your age in a long time. Or we could go swimming, dancing, I don't know. I don't want you to have any trouble, though. Would it help if *I* asked your mother? Do you think she'd let you?'

'That'll be the day,' she said. 'No one tells *me* who to go out with. No one. I've got a new bathing suit, Charles. I'd love to go.'

'I bet you look like a potato sack in it.'

'Oh, Charley, quit kidding.'

'O.K.,' I said. 'But don't call me Charley. Charley is my last name. Charles is my first. There's a "C" in the middle. Charles C. Charley is who I am.'

'O.K.,' she said. 'My name is Cindy.'

'I know that,' I said.

Then I said goodbye and left her nearly drowned in perspiration, still prone, smoking another cigarette, and staring dreamily at a beam from which hung an old doll's house with four upstairs bedrooms.

Outside I made lighthearted obeisance to the entire household, from rumpus room to expanding attic. I hopped onto my three-wheeled scooter and went forward on spectacular errands of mercy across the sycamore-studded seat of this fat county.

At 4 a.m. of the following Saturday morning I delivered Cindy to her eight-room house with two and a half bathrooms. Mrs. Graham was waiting. She didn't look at me at all. She began to cry. She sniffed and stopped crying. 'Cindy, it's so late. Daddy went to the police. We were frightened about you. He went to see the lieutenant.' Then she waited, forlorn. Before her very eyes the friend she had been raising for years, the rejuvenating confidante, had deserted her. I was sorry. I thought Cindy ought to get her a cold drink. I wanted to say, 'Don't worry, Mrs. Graham. I didn't knock the kid up.'

But Cindy burned. 'I am just sick of this crap!' she yelled. 'I am heartily and utterly sick of being pushed around. Every time I come home a little late, you call the police. This is the third time, the third time. I am sick of you and Daddy. I hate this place. I hate living here. I told you last year. I hate it here. I'm sick of this place and the phony trains and no buses and I can't drive. I hate the kids around here. They're all dopes. You follow me around. I hate the two of you. I wish I was in China.' She stamped her feet three times, then ran up to her room.

In this way she avoided her father, who came growling past me where I still stood in the doorway. I was comforting Mrs. Graham. 'You know adolescence is a very difficult period . . .' But he interrupted. He looked over his shoulder, saw it was really me, and turned like a man to say it to my face. 'You sonofabitch, where the hell were you?'

'Nothing to worry about, Mr. Graham. We just took a boat ride.'

'You'd better call the police and tell them Cindy's home, Alvin,' said Mrs. Graham.

'Where to?' he said. 'Greenwich Village?'

'No, no,' I said reasonably. 'I took Cindy out to Pottsburg – it's one of those amusement parks there on the other side of the harbor. It's a two-hour ride. There's dancing on the boat. We missed a boat and had to wait two more hours, and then we missed the train.'

'This boat goes straight to Pottsburg?'

'Oh yes,' I said.

'Alvin,' said Mrs. Graham, 'please call the police. They'll be all over town.'

'O.K., O.K.,' he said. 'Where's Cynthy Anne?'

'Asleep probably,' Mrs. Graham said. 'Please, Alvin.'

'O.K., O.K.,' he said. 'You go up too, Ellie. Go on, don't argue. Go on up and go to sleep. I want to talk to Mr. What's-His-Name for a couple of minutes. Go on now, Ellie, before I get sore.

'Now, you!' he said, turning to me. 'Let's go into my den.' He pointed to it with a meaty shoulder. I went before him.

I could not really see him through the 4 a.m. haze, but I got the outlines. He was a big guy with a few years on me, a little more money, status, and enough community standing to freeze him where he stood. All he could do was bellow like a bull in his own parlor, crinolines cracking all around him.

'You know, sonny,' he said, leaning forward in a friendly way, 'if you don't keep away from my kid – in fact, if I ever see you with her again – I'm gonna bring this knee right up' – pointing to it – 'and let you have it.'

'What did *I* do?'

'You didn't do anything and you're not going to. Stay away . . . Listen,' he said intimately, man to man. 'What good is she? She's only a kid. She isn't even sure which end is up.'

I looked to see if he really believed that. From the relaxed condition of his face and the sincere look in his eyes, I had to say to myself, yes, that's what he believes.

'Mr. Graham,' I said, 'I called for Cindy at her own door. Your wife met me. I did not come sneaking around.'

'Don't give me any crap,' he said.

'Well, all right, Mr. Graham,' I said. 'I'm the last guy to create a situation. What do you want me to do?'

'I don't want you near this place.'

I pretended to give it some thought. But my course was clear. I had to sleep two hours before morning at least. 'I'll tell you what, Mr. Graham. I'm the last guy to create a situation. I just won't see Cindy anymore. But there's something we ought to do – from her point of view. The hell with me . . .'

'The hell with you is right,' he said. 'What?'

'I think a little note's in order, a little letter explaining about all this. I don't want her to think I hate her. You got to watch out with kids that age. They're sensitive. I'd like to write to her.'

'O.K.,' he said. 'That's a good idea, Charley. You do that little thing, and as far as I'm concerned we can call it square. I know how it is in the outfield, boy. Cold. I don't blame you for trying. But this kid's got a family to watch out for her. And I'll tell you another thing. I'm the kind of father, I'm not ashamed to beat the shit out of her if I have to, and the *Ladies' Home Journal* can cry in their soda pop, for all I care. O.K.?' he asked, standing up to conclude. 'Everything O.K.?

'I'm dying on my dogs,' he said in a kindlier tone. Then in a last snarl at the passing stranger he said, 'But you better not try this neighborhood again.'

'Well, so long,' I said, hopefully passing out of his life. 'Don't take any woolen condoms.' But when he cantered out to look for me, I was gone.

Two days later I was sitting peacefully in my little office, which is shaded by a dying sycamore. I had three signed-for, cash-on-delivery jobs ahead of me, and if I weren't a relaxed guy I would have been out cramming my just rewards. I was reading a little book called *Medieval People*, which I enjoyed because I am interested in man as a person. It's a hobby. (I should have been a psychologist. I have an ear.) I was eating a hero sandwich. Above my head was a sign in gold which declared AERI AIR CONDITIONERS. Up the Aeri Mountain, Down the Rushing Glen, Aeri Goes Wherever, Man Builds Homes for Men.

The telephone gave its half-turned-off buzz. It was Cindy, to whom I offered a joyous hello, but she was crying. She said three times, 'Oh, I'm sorry. Oh, I'm sorry. Oh, I'm sorry.'

'I am too, honey.' I thought of how to console her. 'But you know there's some justice to it. Your daddy's really planning a lovely future for you.'

'No, Charles, that's not it. You don't know what happened. Charles, it's terrible. It's all my fault; he's going to put you in jail. But he got me so mad . . . It's my fault, Charles. He's crazy, he really means it.'

On the pale reflection in the colorless window glass, I blanched. 'O.K.,' I said. 'Don't cry any more. Tell me the truth.'

'Oh, Charles . . .' she said. Then she described the events of the previous evening. Here they are. I have taken them right out of Cindy's mouth.

'Cindy,' Mr. Graham said, 'I don't want you to go around with a man like that – old enough to be your father almost.'

'Oh, for godsakes, Daddy, he's very nice. He's a wonderful dancer.'

'I don't like it, Cindy. Not at all. I don't even like your dancing with him. There are a lot of things you don't know about people and things, Cindy. I don't like you dancing with him. I don't approve of a man of that age even putting his arm around a teenager like you. You know I want the best for you, Cindy Anne. I want you to have a full and successful life. Keeping up your friendship with him, even if it's as innocent and pleasant as you claim, would be a real hindrance. I want you to go away to school and have a wonderful time with fellows your own age, dancing with them, and, you know, you might fall in love or something . . . I'm not so stupid and blind. You know, I was young once too.'

'Oh, Daddy, there's still plenty of life in you, for goodness' sakes.'

'I hope so, Cindy. But what I want to tell you, honey, is that I've asked this man Charles to please stay away from you and write you a nice letter and he agreed, because, after all, you are a very pretty girl and people can often be tempted to do things they don't want to do, no matter how nice they are.'

'You asked him to stay away?'

'Yes.'

'And he agreed?'

'Yes, he did.'

'Did he say he might be tempted?'

'Well . . .'

'Did he say he *might* be tempted?'

'Well, actually, he said he . . .'

'He just agreed? He didn't even get angry? He didn't even *want* to see me again?'

'He'll write you, honey.'

'He'll write me? Did he say he'll write me? That's all? Who does he think I am? An idiot? A dope? A little nitwit from West Main Street? Where does he get off? That fat slob . . . What does he think I am? Didn't he even *want* to see me again? He's gonna write me?'

'Cindy!'

'That's all? That's what he wanted me for? He's gonna write me a letter? Daddy . . . Daddy . . .'

'Cindy! What happened last night?'

'Why do you go stick your nose in my business? Doesn't anything ever happen to you? I was just getting along fine for five minutes. Why do you always sit around the house with your nose in my business?'

'Cindy, were you fooling around with that man?'

'Why can't you leave me alone for five minutes? Doesn't anyone else want you around anymore someplace? What do you want from me?'

'Cindy.' He gripped her wrist. 'Cindy! Answer me this minute. Were you?'

'Stop yelling. I'm not deaf.'

'Cindy, were you fooling around with that man? Answer!'

'Leave me alone,' she cried. 'Just leave me alone.'

'You answer me this minute,' he shouted.

'I'll answer you, all right,' she said. 'I was not fooling around. I was not fooling. You asked me. I was not fooling. I went upstairs where the lifeboat is and I lay down right underneath it and I did it with Charles.'

'What did you do?' gasped her father.

'And I ruined my blue dress,' she screamed. 'And you're so dumb you didn't even know it.'

'Your blue dress?' he asked, scarcely breathing to hear the answer. 'Cindy Anne, why?'

'Because I wanted to. I wanted to.'

'What?' he asked dimly.

'I wanted to, Daddy,' she said.

'Oh my God!' he said. 'My God, my God, what did I do?'

Half an hour later Mrs. Graham returned loaded with goodies from the KrissKross Shopping Center. Cindy was crying in the kitchen, and in the TV room Mr. Graham sat in his red leatherette, eyes closed; his pale lips whispered, 'It's statutory rape . . . It's transporting a minor . . .'

Cindy, my little pal, came lolling down the courtroom aisle with a big red smile, friend to the entire court. She wiggled a little in order to convey the notion that she was really a juvenile whore and I was not accountable. Nobody believed her. She was obviously only the singed daughter of a Campfire Girl.

Besides – philosophically and with a heavy hand – I had decided my fate was written. O.K., O.K., O.K., I said to the world and, staring inward, I overcame my incarceration anxiety. If a period of self-revelation under spartan circumstances was indicated, I was willing to accept the fact that this mysterious move of His might be meant to perform wonders. (Nehru, I understand, composed most of his books in jail.) Do not assume any particular religiosity in me. I have no indoctrinated notion about what He is like: size, shape, or high I.Q.

Adjustments aside, I was embarrassed by the sudden appearance of my mother, who had been hounded from home by the local papers. She sat as close to me as the courtroom design would allow and muttered when apropos, 'She's a tramp,' or 'You're an idiot.' Once we were allowed to speak to each other: she said, 'What a wild Indian you turned into, Charles.'

Was she kidding? Was she proud? Why did she even care? Me, Charles C. Charley, puffed and scared, I am not the baby who lay suffocating under her left tit. I am not the boy who waited for her every night at the factory gate. I am not even anymore the draftee who sent her portable pieces of an Italian church.

'What kind of a boy was your son?' my stupid lawyer asked. She peered at him, her fat face the soundboard of silence. 'I said, Mrs. Charley, what kind of a boy was your son?'

After a few disengaged moments she replied, 'I don't know

much about any of my boys; they're a surprise to me.' Then her lips met and her hands clasped each other and she hadn't another comment on that subject.

My legal adviser, a real nobody from nothing, was trying to invent an environment of familial madness from which I could not have hoped to recover. 'That is certainly an odd name, in combination with his last name, Charles C. Charley, Mrs. Charley. How did this naming come about?'

'What is your name, sir?' asked my mother politely.

With a boyish grin he replied, 'Edward Johnson, ma'am.'

'Ha! Ha! Ha!' said my mother.

When it was my turn, he asked, 'And weren't you in love with young Miss Graham, that flirtatious young woman, when you lost your head? Weren't you?'

'Generally speaking,' I replied, 'there's love in physical union. It's referred to in Western literature as an act of love.'

'That's true,' he said, not cerebrating noticeably. 'And you loved Miss Graham, didn't you?' Here he pointed to her where she sat. Her hair had been washed that early morning. She wore a golden Chinese slip of a dress with little slits, probably to flash her tan calves through. Her sweet round rump nestled in the hard pew of the law.

'I suppose I did,' I said.

At last the attorney for the prosecuting victim had a chance. at me. He had known Cindy since she was an even younger child than she was a child at present, he said, using just those words. He was close to tears. Not a hair was rooted in his head. This is description, not adventitious comment, which I can't afford, since I am unpleasantly hirsute.

Even now, time having awarded some dimension, I don't understand his line of questioning nor the line of questioning of my own brainless lawyer. I had pleaded guilty. I was not opposed to punishment, since our happy performance, it turned out, had a criminal aspect. Still they talked. I realize they had their training to consider – all those years at school. Men like these must milk the moment or sleep forever.

'Well,' he began, blinking a tear, 'Charles C. Charley, you have told us that you loved that little girl at that moment but did not love her before or after and have not since?'

'I have no reason to lie,' I said. 'I am in the hand of God.'

'Who?' the judge shouted.

Then they all mumbled together in an effort to figure out what could be done with the contemptible use of pious nomenclature. They could not say, of course, that we are not in the hand of God when, for all they knew, we are.

Mr. Graham's gleaming attorney returned to me. 'Mr. Charley, did you love Cindy Graham at that moment?'

'I did,' I said.

'But you do not love her now?' he asked.

'I haven't thought about it,' I said.

'Would you marry her?' he demanded, twisting his head toward the jury. He felt sly.

'She's just a child,' I said. 'How could I marry her? Marriage requires all sorts of responsibility. She isn't ready for anything like that. And besides, the age difference . . . it's too great. Be realistic,' I adjured his muddled head.

'You would *not* marry her?' he asked, his voice rising to a clinch.

'No, sir.'

'Good enough to force sex on but not good enough to cherish for life?'

'Well,' I said calmly, refusing to respond to his hysteria, and without mentioning names, 'actually it's six of one and half a dozen of the other.'

'And so you, a mature man, an adult, you took it upon yourself, knowing something about the pitfalls before a young girl, this child, still growing, Cynthia Anne Graham, you took it upon yourself to decide she was ready to have her virginity ravaged to satisfy your own selfish rotten lust.'

After that little bit of banter I clammed up. Because Cindy was going to live among them forever, I was so silent that even now I am breathless with self-respect.

These castaways on life's sodden beach were under the impression that I was the first. I was not. I am not an inventive or creative person, I take a cue from the universe, I have never been the first anywhere. Actually, in this case, I was no more than fifth or sixth. I don't say this to be disparaging of Cindy. A person has to start somewhere. Why was Mr. Graham so baffled by truth? Gourmets everywhere begin with voracious appetites before they can come to the finesse of taste. I had seen it happen before; in five or six years, a beautiful and particular woman, she might marry some contributing citizen and resign her light habits to him. None of my adversaries was more than ten years my senior, but their memories were short (as mine would be if I weren't sure at all times to keep in touch with youth).

In the middle of my thinking, while the court waited patiently for a true answer, Cindy burst into wild tears, screaming, 'Leave him alone, you leave him alone. It's not his fault if I'm wild. I'll tell the whole world how wild I am if you don't shut up. I made him do it, I made him do it . . .'

From my narrow-eyed view the court seemed to constrict into a shuddering sailor's knot. Cindy's mother and father unraveled her, and two civil-service employees hustled her out. The opposing lawyers buzzed together and then with the judge. A pair of newspapermen staggered from one convulsive group to another. My mother took advantage of the disorganization to say, 'Charles, they're bugheaded.'

The paid principals nodded their heads. The judge asked for order, then a recess. My attorney and two cops led me into a brown-paneled room where a board-meeting mahogany table was surrounded by board-meeting chairs. 'You didn't give one sensible answer,' my attorney complained. 'Now listen to me. Just sit down here and keep your mouth shut, for godsakes. I'm going to talk to the Grahams.'

Except for some bored surveillance, I was alone for one hour and a half. In that time I reviewed Cindy and all her accessories, also the meaning of truth. I was just tangent to the Great Circle of Life, of which I am one irrevocable diameter, when my mother appeared. She had had time to go shopping for some wheat germ and carrots and apples full of unsprayed bacteria. The state of her health requires these innocent staples. Mr. and Mrs. Graham followed, and my little grimy Cindy. Mrs. Graham kept tissuing some of the black eye stuff off her smeared cheeks. Mr. Graham, sensible when answering or questioning and never devious, said, 'All right, Charles, all right. We've decided to withdraw charges. You and Cindy will get married.'

'What?' I said.

'You heard me the first time . . . I'm against it. I think a punk like you is better off in jail. For my money, you could rot in jail. I've seen worse guys but not much worse. You took advantage of a damn silly kid. You and Cindy get married next week. Meanwhile you'll be at our house, Charley. Cindy's missed enough school. This is a very important year for her. I'll tell you one thing. You better play it straight, Charley, or I'll split your skull with a kitchen knife.'

'Say . . .' I said.

My mother piped up. 'Charles,' she said, 'son, think about it a minute. What'll happen to me if you go to jail? She's very pretty. You're not getting younger. What'll happen to me? Son . . .' she said.

She turned to Mrs. Graham. 'It's hard to be old and dependent this way. I hope you have plenty of insurance.'

Mrs. Graham patted her shoulder.

My mother regarded this as invitation to enlarge. 'When you really think about it, it's all a fuss about nothing. I always. say, let them enjoy themselves when they're young. You know,' she said, her eyes hazy in the crowded past, 'at least it gives you something to look back on.'

Mrs. Graham removed her hand and blushed in fear.

'Don't you want to marry me?' asked Cindy, tears starting again.

'Honey . . .' I said.

'Then it's settled,' Mr. Graham said. 'I'll find a good house in the neighborhood. No children for a while, Charley, she's got to finish school. As for you,' he said, getting down to brass tacks, 'the truth is, you have a fair business. I want my accountant to go over the books. If they're what I expect, you'll be cooking with gas in six months. You'll be the biggest conditioning outlet in the county. You're a goddamn slob, you haven't begun to realize your potential in a community like ours.'

'I wish I could smoke,' I said.

'No smoking here,' my lawyer said, having brought my entire life to a successful conclusion.

In this way I assuaged the people in charge, and I live with Cindy in events which are current.

Through the agency of my father-in-law I have acquired a first-class food-freezer and refrigerator franchise. If you can imagine anything so reprehensible, it was obtained right out from under the nose of a man who has been in the business for thirty years, a man who dreamt of that franchise as his reward for unceasing labor in the kitchens of America. If someone would hand me the first stone, I would not be ashamed to throw it. But at whom?

Living with Cindy has many pleasures. One acquires important knowledge in the dwelling place of another generation. First things first, she always has a kind word for the future. It is my opinion that she will be a marvelous woman in six or seven years. I wish her luck; by then we will be strangers.

Two Short Sad Stories from a Long and Happy Life

1
The Used-Boy Raisers

There were two husbands disappointed by eggs.

I don't like them that way either, I said. Make your own eggs. They sighed in unison. One man was livid; one was pallid.

There isn't a drink around here, is there? asked Livid.

Never find one here, said Pallid. Don't look; driest damn house. Pallid pushed the eggs away, pain and disgust his escutcheon.

Livid said, Now really, isn't there a drink? Beer? he hoped.

Nothing, said Pallid, who'd been through the pantries, closets, and refrigerators looking for a white shirt.

You're damn right, I said. I buttoned the high button of my powder-blue duster. I reached under the kitchen table for a brown paper bag full of an embroidery which asked God to Bless Our Home.

I was completing this motto for the protection of my sons, who were also Livids. It is true that some months earlier, from a far place – the British plains in Africa – he had written hospitably to Pallid: I do think they're fine boys, you understand. I love them too, but Faith is their mother and now Faith is your wife. I'm so much away. If you want to think of them as yours, old man, go ahead.

Why, thank you, Pallid had replied, airmail, overwhelmed. Then he implored the boys, when not in use, to play in their own room. He made all efforts to be kind.

Now as we talked of time past and upon us, I pierced the ranch house that nestles in the shade of a cloud and a Norway maple, just under the golden script.

Ha-ha, said Livid, dripping coffee on his pajama pants, you'll never guess whom I met up with, Faith.

Who? I asked.

Saw your old boyfriend Clifford at the Green Coq. He looks well. One thing must be said – he addressed Pallid – she takes good care of her men.

True, said Pallid.

How is he? I asked coolly. What's he doing? I haven't seen him in two years.

Oh, you'll never guess. He's marrying. A darling girl. She was with him. Little tootsies, little round bottom, little tummy – she must be twenty-two, but she looks seventeen. One long yellow braid down her back. A darling girl. Stubby nose, fat little under-lip. Her eyes put on in pencil. Shoulders down like a dancer . . . slender neck. Oh, darling, darling.

You certainly observed her, said Pallid.

I have a functioning retina, said Livid. Then he went on. Better watch out, Faith. You'd be surprised, the dear little chicks are hatching out all over the place. All the sunny schoolgirls rolling their big black eyes. I hope you're really settled this time. To me, whatever is under the dam is in another county; however, in my life you remain an important person historically, he said. And that's why I feel justified in warning you. I must warn you. Watch out, sweetheart! he said, leaning forward to whisper harshly and give me a terrible bellyache.

What's all this about? asked Pallid innocently. In the first place, she's settled . . . and then she's still an attractive woman. Look at her.

Oh yes, said Livid, looking. An attractive woman. Magnificent, sometimes.

We were silent for several seconds in honor of that generous remark.

Then Livid said, Yes, magnificent, but I just wanted to warn you, Faith.

He pushed his eggs aside finally and remembered Clifford. A mystery wrapped in an enigma . . . I wonder why he wants to marry.

I don't know, it just ties a man down, I said.

And yet, said Pallid seriously, what would I be without marriage? In luminous recollection – a gay dog, he replied.

At this moment, the boys entered: Richard the horse thief and Tonto the crack shot.

Daddy! they shouted. They touched Livid, tickled him, unbuttoned his pajama top, whistled at the several gray hairs coloring his chest. They tweaked his ear and rubbed his beard the wrong way.

Well, well, he cautioned. How are you boys, have you been well? You look fine. Sturdy. How are your grades? he inquired. He dreamed that they were just up from Eton for the holidays.

I don't go to school, said Tonto. I go to the park.

I'd like to hear the child read, said Livid.

Me. I can read, Daddy, said Richard. I have a book with a hundred pages.

Well, well, said Livid. Get it.

I kindled a fresh pot of coffee. I scrubbed cups and harassed Pallid into opening a sticky jar of damson-plum jam. Very shortly, what could be read had been, and Livid, knotting the tie strings of his pants vigorously, approached me at the stove. Faith, he admonished, that boy can't read a tinker's damn. Seven years old.

Eight years old, I said.

Yes, said Pallid, who had just remembered the soap cabinet and was rummaging in it for a pint. If they were my sons in actuality as they are in everyday life, I would send them to one of the good parochial schools in the neighborhood where reading is taught. Reading. St. Bartholomew's, St. Bernard's, St. Joseph's.

Livid became deep purple and gasped. Over my dead body.

Merde, he said in deference to the children. I've said, yes, you may think of the boys as your own, but if I ever hear they've come within an inch of that church, I'll run you through, you bastard. I was fourteen years old when in my own good sense I walked out of that grotto of deception, head up. You sonofabitch, I don't give a damn how *au courant* it is these days, how gracious to be seen under a dome on Sunday . . . Shit! Hypocrisy. Corruption. Cave dwellers. Idiots. Morons.

Recalling childhood and home, poor Livid writhed in his seat. Pallid listened, head to one side, his brows gathering the onsets of grief.

You know, he said slowly, we iconoclasts . . . we freethinkers . . . we latter-day Masons . . . we idealists . . . we dreamers . . . we are never far from our nervous old mother, the Church. She is never far from us.

Wherever we are, we can hear, no matter how faint, her hourly bells, tolling the countryside, reverberating in the cities, bringing to our civilized minds the passionate deed of Mary. Every hour on the hour we are startled with remembrance of what was done for us. FOR US.

Livid muttered in great pain, Those bastards, oh oh oh, those contemptible, goddamnable bastards. Do we have to do the nineteenth century all over again? All right, he bellowed, facing us all, I'm ready. That Newman! He turned to me for approval.

You know, I said, this subject has never especially interested me. It's your little dish of lava.

Pallid spoke softly, staring past the arched purple windows of his soul. I myself, although I lost God a long time ago, have never lost faith.

What the hell are you talking about, you moron? roared Livid.

I have never lost my love for the wisdom of the Church of the World. When I go to sleep at night, I inadvertently pray. I also do so when I rise. It is not to God, it is to that unifying memory out of childhood. The first words I ever wrote were: What are the sacraments? Faith, can you ever forget your old grandfather intoning Kaddish? It will sound in your ears forever.

Are you kidding? I was furious to be drawn into their conflict. Kaddish? What do I know about Kaddish. Who's dead? You know my opinions perfectly well. I believe in the Diaspora, not only as a fact but a tenet. I'm against Israel on technical grounds. I'm very disappointed that they decided to become a nation in my life-time. I believe in the Diaspora. After all, they *are* the chosen people. Don't laugh. They really are. But once they're huddled in one little corner of a desert, they're like anyone else: Frenchies, Italians, temporal nationalities. Jews have one hope only – to remain a remnant in the basement of world affairs – no, I mean something else – a splinter in the toe of civilizations, a victim to aggravate the conscience.

Livid and Pallid were astonished at my outburst, since I rarely express my opinion on any serious matter but only live out my destiny, which is to be, until my expiration date, laughingly the servant of man.

I continued. I hear they don't even look like Jews anymore. A bunch of dirt farmers with no time to read.

They're your own people, Pallid accused, dilating in the nos-tril, clenching his jaw. And they're under the severest attack. This is not the time to revile them.

I had resumed my embroidery. I sighed. My needle was now deep in the clouds, which were pearl gray and late afternoon. I am only trying to say that they aren't meant for geographies but for history. They are not supposed to take up space but to con-tinue in time.

They looked at me with such grief that I decided to consider all sides of the matter. I said, Christ probably had all that trou-ble – now that you mention it – because he knew he was going to gain the whole world but he forgot Jerusalem.

When you married us, said Pallid, and accused me, didn't you forget Jerusalem?

I never forget a thing, I said. Anyway, guess what. I just read somewhere that England is bankrupt. The country is wadded with installment paper.

Livid's hand trembled as he offered Pallid a light. Nonsense, he said. That's not true. Nonsense. The great British Island is the tight little fist of the punching arm of the Commonwealth.

What's true is true, I said, smiling.

Well, I said, since no one stirred, do you think you'll ever get to work today? Either of you?

Oh my dear, I haven't even seen you and the boys in over a year. It's quite pleasant and cozy here this morning, said Livid.

Yes, isn't it? said Pallid, the surprised host. Besides, it's Saturday.

How do you find the boys? I asked Livid, the progenitor.

American, American, rowdy, uncontrolled. But you look well, Faith. Plumper, but womanly and well.

Very well, said Pallid, pleased.

But the boys, Faith. Shouldn't they be started on something? Just lining up little plastic cowboys. It's silly, really.

They're so young, apologized Pallid, the used-boy raiser.

You'd both better go to work, I suggested, knotting the pearl-gray late-afternoon thread. Please put the dishes in the sink first. Please. I'm sorry about the eggs.

Livid yawned, stretched, peeked at the clock, sighed. Saturday or no, alas, my time is not my own. I've got an appointment downtown in about forty-five minutes, he said.

I do too, said Pallid. I'll join you on the subway.

I'm taking a cab, said Livid.

I'll split it with you, said Pallid.

They left for the bathroom, where they shared things nicely – shaving equipment, washstand, shower, and so forth.

I made the beds and put the aluminum cot away. Livid would find a hotel room by nightfall. I did the dishes and organized the greedy day: dinosaurs in the morning, park in the afternoon, peanut butter in between, and at the end of it all, to reward us for a week of beans endured, a noble rib roast with little onions, dumplings, and pink applesauce.

Faith, I'm going now, Livid called from the hall. I put my shopping list aside and went to collect the boys, who were wandering among the rooms looking for Robin Hood. Go say goodbye to your father, I whispered.

Which one? they asked.

The real father, I said. Richard ran to Livid. They shook hands manfully. Pallid embraced Tonto and was kissed eleven times for his affection.

Goodbye now, Faith, said Livid. Call me if you want anything at all. Anything at all, my dear. Warmly with sweet propriety he kissed my cheek. Ascendant, Pallid kissed me with considerable business behind the ear.

Goodbye, I said to them.

I must admit that they were at last clean and neat, rather attractive, shiny men in their thirties, with the grand affairs of the day ahead of them. Dark night, the search for pleasure and oblivion were well ahead. Goodbye, I said, have a nice day. Goodbye, they said once more, and set off in pride on paths which are not my concern.

2
A Subject of Childhood

At home one Saturday and every Saturday, Richard drew eight-by-eleven portraits of stick men waving their arms. Tonto held a plastic horse in his hand and named it Tonto because its eyes were painted blue as his had been. I revised the hem of last year's dress in order to be up to the minute, chic, and *au courant* in the midst of spring. Strangers would murmur, 'Look at her, isn't she wonderful? Who's her couturier?'

Clifford scrubbed under the shower, singing a Russian folk song. He rose in a treble of cold water to high C, followed by the scourging of the flesh. At last after four hots and three colds, he was strong and happy and he entered the living room, a steaming emanation. His face was round and rosy. He was noticeably hairless on the head. What prevented rain and shower water from running foolishly down his face? Heavy dark downsloping brows. Beneath these his eyes were round and dark, amazed. This Clifford, my close friend, was guileless. He would not hurt a fly and he was a vegetarian.

As always, he was glad to see us. He had wrapped a large sunbathing towel around his damp body. 'Behold the man!' he shouted, and let the towel fall. He stood for a moment, gleaming and pleasant. Richard and Tonto glanced at him. 'Cover yourself, for godsakes, Clifford,' I said.

'Take it easy, Faith,' he called to the ear of reason, 'the world is changing.' Actually propriety did not embarrass him. It did not serve him. He peeked from behind the rubber plant where his pants, under and over, were heaped. When he reappeared, snapped and buttoned, he said, 'Wake up, wake up. What's everyone slouching around for? ' He poked Richard in the tummy. 'A little muscle tone there, boy. Wake up.'

Richard said, 'I want to draw, Clifford.'

'You can draw any time. I'm not always here. Draw tomorrow, Rich. Come on – fight me, boy. Fight. Come on . . . let's go, get me. You better get started, Richy, 'cause I'm gonna really punch you one. Here I come, ready or not!'

'Here *I* come,' said Tonto, dropping his horse, and he whacked Clifford hard across the kidneys.

'Who did that?' asked Clifford. 'What boy did that?'

'Me, me,' said Tonto, jumping up and down. 'Did I hurt you bad?'

'Killed me, yes sir, yes you did, and now I'm going to get you.' He whirled. 'I'm going to tickle you, that's what.' He raised Tonto high above his head, a disposable item, then pitched him into the air-foam belly of the couch.

Richard tiptoed with the teddy bear to a gentle rise, the sofa cushion, from which he crowned Clifford three times.

'Oh, I'm getting killed,' cried Clifford. 'They're all after me. They're very rough.' Richard kicked him in the shin. 'That's it,' said Clifford. 'Get it out! Get it all out! Boys! Out! Out!'

Tonto spit right into his eye. He wiped his cheek. He feinted and dodged the teddy bear that was coming down again on his bowed head. Tonto leaped onto his back and got hold of his ears. 'Ouch,' said Clifford.

Richard found a tube of rubber cement in the bookcase and squirted it at Clifford's hairy chest.

'I'm wild,' said Richard. 'I am, I'm wild.'

'So am I,' said Tonto. 'I'm the wildest boy in the whole park.' He tugged at Clifford's ears. 'I'll ride you away. I'm an elephant boy.'

'He's a lazy camel,' screamed Richard. 'Bubbles, I want you to work.'

'Pretend I'm the djinn,' said Tonto in a high wail. 'Giddap, Clifford.'

'Me, me, me,' said Richard, sinking to the floor. 'It's me. I'm a poison snake,' he said, slithering to Clifford's foot. 'I'm a poison snake,' he said, resting his chin on Clifford's instep. 'I'm a terrible poison snake,' he swore. Then he raised his head like the adder he is, and after a prolonged hiss, with all his new front teeth, he bit poor Clifford above the bone, in his Achilles' heel, which is his weak left ankle.

'Oh no, oh no . . .' Clifford moaned, then folded neatly at all joints.

'Mommy, Mommy, Mommy,' cried Richard, for Clifford fell, twelve stone, on him.

'Oh, it's me,' screamed Tonto, an elephant boy thrown by his horse, headlong into a trap of table legs.

And he was the one I reached first. I hugged him to my lap. 'Mommy,' he sobbed, 'my head hurts me. I wish I could get inside you.' Richard lay, a crushed snake in the middle of the floor, without breath, without tears, angry.

Well, what of Clifford? He had hoisted his sorrowful self into an armchair and lay there lisping on a bloody tongue which he himself had bitten, 'Faith, Faith, the accumulator, the accumulator!'

Bruised and tear-stricken, the children agreed to go to bed. They forgot to say it was too early to nap. They forget to ask for their bears. They lay side by side and clutched each other's thumb. Here was the love that myth or legend has imposed on brothers.

I re-entered the living room, where Clifford sat, a cone like an astrologer's hat on his skin-punctured place. Just exactly there, universal energies converged. The stationary sun, the breathless air in which the planets swing were empowered now to make him well, to act, in their remarkable art, like aspirin.

'We've got to have a serious talk,' he said. 'I really can't take those kids. I mean, Faith, you know yourself I've tried and tried. But you've done something to them, corrupted their instincts in some way or other. Here we were; having an absolutely marvelous time, rolling around making all kinds of free noise, and look what happened – like every other time, someone got hurt. I mean I'm really hurt. We should have all been relaxed. Easy. It should have been all easy. Our bodies should have been so easy. No one should've been hurt, Faith.'

'Do you mean it's my fault you all got hurt?'

'No doubt about it, Faith, you've done a rotten job.'

'Rotten job?' I said.

'Lousy,' he said.

I gave him one more chance. 'Lousy?' I asked.

'Oh my God! Stinking!' he said.

Therefore, the following – a compendium of motivations and griefs, life to date:

Truthfully, Mondays through Fridays – because of success at work – my ego is hot; I am a star; whoever can be warmed by me, I may oblige. The flat scale stones of abuse that fly into that speedy atmosphere are utterly consumed. Untouched, I glow my little thermodynamic way.

On Saturday mornings in my own home, however, I face the sociological law called the Obtrusion of Incontrovertibles. For I have raised these kids, with one hand typing behind my back to earn a living. I have raised them all alone without a father to identify themselves with in the bathroom like all the other little boys in the playground. Laugh. I was forced by inclement management into a yellow-dog contract with Bohemia, such as it survives. I have stuck by it despite the encroachments of kind relatives who offer ski pants, piano lessons, tickets to the rodeo. Meanwhile I have serviced Richard and Tonto, taught them to keep clean and hold an open heart on the subjects of childhood. We have in fact risen mightily from toilets in the hall and scavenging in great cardboard boxes at the Salvation Army for underwear and socks. It has been my perversity to do this alone, except for the one year their father was living in Chicago with Claudia Lowenstill and she was horrified that he only sent bicycles on the fifth birthday. A whole year of gas and electricity, rent and phone payments followed. One day she caught him in the swiveling light of truth, a grand figure who took a strong stand on a barrel of soapsuds and went down clean. He is now on the gold coast of another continent, enchanted by the survival of clandestine civilizations. Courts of kitchen drama cannot touch him.

All the same, I gave Clifford one more opportunity to renege and be my friend. I said, 'Stinking? I raised them lousy?'

This time he didn't bother to answer because he had become busy gathering his clothes from different parts of the room.

Air was filtering out of my two collapsing lungs. Water rose, bubbling to enter, and I would have died of instantaneous pneumonia – something I never have heard of – if my hand had not got hold of a glass ashtray and, entirely apart from my personal decision, flung it.

Clifford was on his hands and knees looking for the socks he'd left under the armchair on Friday. His back was to me; his head convenient to the trajectory. And he would have passed away a blithering idiot had I not been blind with tears and only torn off what is anyway a vestigial earlobe.

Still, Clifford is a gentle person, a consortment of sweet dispositions. The sight of all the blood paralyzed him. He hulked, shuddering; he waited on his knees to be signaled once more by Death, the Sheriff from the Styx.

'You don't say things like that to a woman,' I whispered. 'You damn stupid jackass. You just don't say anything like that to a woman. Wash yourself, moron, you're bleeding to death.'

I left him alone to tie a tourniquet around his windpipe or doctor himself according to present-day plans for administering first aid in the Great Globular and Coming War.

I tiptoed into the bedroom to look at the children. They were asleep. I covered them and kissed Tonto, my baby, and 'Richard, what a big boy you are,' I said. I kissed him too. I sat on the floor, rubbing my cheek on Richard's rubbly fleece blanket until their sweet breathing in deep sleep quieted me.

A couple of hours later Richard and Tonto woke up picking their noses, sneezing, grumpy, then glad. They admired the ticktack-toes of Band-Aid I had created to honor their wounds. Richard ate soup and Tonto ate ham. They didn't inquire about Clifford, since he had a key which had always opened the door in or out.

That key lay at rest in the earth of my rubber plant. I felt discontinued. There was no one I wanted to offer it to.

'Still hungry, boys?' I asked. 'No, sir,' said Tonto. 'I'm full up to here,' leveling at the eyes.

'I'll tell you what.' I came through with a stunning notion. 'Go on down and play.'

'Don't shove, miss,' said Richard.

I looked out the front window. Four flights below, armed to the teeth, Lester Stukopf waited for the enemy. Carelessly I gave Richard this classified information. 'Is he all alone?' asked Richard.

'He is,' I said.

'O.K., O.K.' Richard gazed sadly at me. 'Only, Faith, remember, I'm going down because I feel like it. Not because you told me.'

'Well, naturally,' I said.

'Not me,' said Tonto.

'Oh, don't be silly, you go too, Tonto. It's so nice and sunny. Take your new guns that Daddy sent you. Go on, Tonto.'

'No, sir, I hate Richard and I hate Lester. I hate those guns. They're baby guns. He thinks I'm a baby. You better send him a picture.'

'Oh, Tonto —'

'He thinks I suck my thumb. He thinks I wet my bed. That's why he sends me baby guns.'

'No, no, honey. You're no baby. Everybody knows you're a big boy.'

'He is not,' said Richard. 'And he does so suck his thumb and he does so wet his bed.'

'Richard,' I said, 'Richard, if you don't have anything good to say, shut your rotten mouth. That doesn't help Tonto, to keep reminding him.'

'Goodbye,' said Richard, refusing to discuss, but very high and first-born. Sometimes he is nasty, but he is never lazy. He returned in forty-five seconds from the first floor to shout, 'As long as he doesn't wet my bed, what do I care?'

Tonto did not hear him. He was brushing his teeth, which he sometimes does vigorously seven times a day, hoping they will loosen. I think they are loosening.

I served myself hot coffee in the living room. I organized comfort in the armchair, poured the coffee black into a white mug that said MAMA, tapped cigarette ash into a ceramic hand-hollowed by Richard. I looked into the square bright window of daylight to ask myself the sapping question: What is man that woman lies down to adore him?

At the very question mark Tonto came softly, sneaky in socks, to say, 'I have to holler something to Richard, Mother.'

'Don't lean out that window, Tonto. Please, it makes me nervous.'

'I have to tell him something.'

'No.'

'Oh yes,' he said. 'It's awful important, Faith. I really *have* to.'

How could I permit it? If he should fall, everyone would think I had neglected them, drinking beer in the kitchen or putting eye cream on at the vanity table behind closed doors. Besides, I would be bereaved forever. My grandmother mourned all her days for some kid who'd died of earache at the age of five. All the other children, in their own municipal-pension and federal welfare years, gathered to complain at her deathside when she was ninety-one and heard her murmur, 'Oh, oh, Anita, breathe a little, try to breathe, my little baby.'

With tears in my eyes I said, 'O.K., Tonto, I'll hold on to you. You can tell Richard anything you have to.'

He leaned out onto the air. I held fast to one thick little knee. 'Richie,' he howled. 'Richie, hey, Richie!' Richard looked up, probably shielding his eyes, searching for the voice. 'Richie, hey, listen, I'm playing with your new birthday-present army fort and all them men.'

Then he banged the window shut as though he knew nothing about the nature of glass and tore into the bathroom to brush his teeth once more in triumphant ritual. Singing through toothpaste and gargle, 'I bet he's mad,' and in lower key, 'He deserves it, he stinks.'

'So do you,' I shouted furiously. While I sighed for my grand-mother's loss, he had raised up his big mouth against his brother. 'You really stink!'

'Now listen to me. I want you to get out of here. Go on down and play. I need ten minutes all alone. Anthony, I might kill you if you stay up here.'

He reappeared, smelling like peppermint sticks at Christmas. He stood on one foot, looked up into my high eyes, and said, 'O.K., Faith. Kill me.'

I had to sit immediately then, so he could believe I was his size and stop picking on me.

'Please,' I said gently, 'go out with your brother. I have to think, Tonto.'

'I don't wanna. I don't have to go anyplace I don't wanna,' he said. 'I want to stay right here with you.'

'Oh, please, Tonto, I have to clean the house. You won't be able to do a thing or start a good game or anything.'

'I don't care,' he said. 'I want to stay here with you. I want to stay right next to you.'

'O.K., Tonto. O.K. I'll tell you what, go to your room for a couple of minutes, honey, go ahead.'

'No,' he said, climbing onto my lap. 'I want to be a baby and stay right next to you every minute.'

'Oh, Tonto,' I said, 'please, Tonto.' I tried to pry him loose, but he put his arm around my neck and curled up right there in my lap, thumb in mouth, to be my baby.

'Oh, Tonto,' I said, despairing of one solitary minute. 'Why can't you go play with Richard? You'll have fun.'

'No,' he said, 'I don't care if Richard goes away, or Clifford. They can go do whatever they wanna do. I don't even care. I'm never gonna go away. I'm gonna stay right next to you forever, Faith.'

'Oh, Tonto,' I said. He took his thumb out of his mouth and placed his open hand, its fingers stretching wide, across my breast. 'I love you, Mama,' he said.

'Love,' I said. 'Oh love, Anthony, I know.'

I held him so and rocked him. I cradled him. I closed my eyes and leaned on his dark head. But the sun in its course emerged from among the water towers of downtown office buildings and suddenly shone white and bright on me. Then through the short fat fingers of my son, interred forever, like a black-and-white-barred king in Alcatraz, my heart lit up in stripes.

In Time Which Made a Monkey of Us All

No doubt that is Eddie Teitelbaum on the topmost step of 1434, a dark-jawed, bossy youth in need of repair. He is dredging a cavity with a Fudgsicle stick. He is twitching the cotton in his ear. He is sniffing and snarling and swallowing spit because of rotten drainage. But he does not give a damn. Physicalities aside, he is only knee-deep so far in man's inhumanity; he is reconciled to his father's hair-shirted Jacob, Itzik Halbfunt; he is resigned to his place in this brick-lined Utrillo which runs east and west, flat in the sun, a couple of thousand stoop steps. On each step there is probably someone he knows. For the present, no names.

Now look at the little kids that came in those days to buzz at his feet. That is what they did, they gathered in this canyon pass, rumbling at the knee of his glowering personality. Some days he heeded them a long and wiggily line which they followed up and down the street, around the corner, and back to 1434.

On dark days he made elephants, dogs, rabbits, and long-tailed mice for them out of pipe cleaners. 'You can also make a neat ass cleaner this way,' he told them for a laugh, which turned their mothers entirely against him. Well, he was a poor sloppy bastard then, worked Saturdays, Sundays, summers, and holidays, no union contract in his father's pet shop. But pennywise as regards the kids, he was bubble-gum foolish, for bubble gum strengthens the jaw. He never worried about teeth but approved of dentures and, for that matter, all prostheses.

In the end, man will probably peel his skin (said Eddie) to favor durable plastics, at which time, kaput the race problem. A man will be any color he chooses or translucent too, if the shape and hue of intestines can be made fashionable. Eddie had lots of advance information which did not turn a hair of his head, for he talked of the ineluctable future; but all his buddies, square or queer, clever and sentimental, pricked their ears in tears.

He also warned them of the spies who peeked from windows or plopped like stones on the street, which was the kids' by all unentailed rights. Mrs. Goredinsky, head spy the consistency of fresh putty, sat on an orange crate every morning, her eye on the door of 1434. Also Mrs. Green, Republican poll watcher in November – the rest of the year she waited in her off-the-street doorway, her hand trembling, her head turning one way, then the other.

'Tennis, anyone?' asked Carl Clop, the super's son.

'Let her live,' said Eddie, marking time.

Then one day old Clop, the super, rose from the cellar, scrambling the kids before him with the clatter of bottle tops. He took a stance five steps below Eddie, leaned on his broom, and prepared to make conversation.

'What's the matter, son?' he asked. 'Where's your pals?'

'Under the kitchen table,' said Eddie. 'They got juiced on apricot nectar.'

'Go on, Eddie; you got an in. Who's the bum leaves Kleenex in the halls?'

'I don't know. Goredinsky has a cold for months.'

'Aah, her, what you got against her, a old pot of cabbage soup? You always make a remark on her.'

Out of a dark window in second-floor front a tiny voice sang to the tune of 'My Country, 'Tis of Thee':

Mrs. Goredinsky was a spy
Caught by the FBI.
Tomorrow she will die –
  Won't that be good?

'Get a load of that, Clop,' said Eddie. 'Nobody has any privacy around here, you notice? Listen to me, Clop, in the country in superbia, every sonofabitch has a garage to tinker in. On account of that, great ideas, brilliant inventions come from out of town. Why the hell shouldn't we produce as fine minds as anybody else?'

Now Eddie was just helping Clop out, talkwise, maintaining relations with authority, so to speak. He would have ended the conversation right then and there, since at that moment he was in the mental act of inventing a cockroach segregator, a device which would kill only that cockroach which emigrated out of its pitchy crack into the corn flakes of people. If properly conceived and delicately contrived, all the other cockroaches would be left alone to gum up the laths and multiply and finally inherit the entire congressional district. Why not?

'Not so dumb,' said Mr. Clop. 'Privacy.' Then he let Eddie have a bewhiskered, dead-eye, sideways leer. 'What you need privacy for, you? To stick it into girls?'

No reply.

Clop retrieved the conversation. 'So that's how it goes, that's how they get ahead of us, the farmers. What do you know? How come someone don't figure it out, to educate you kids up a little, especially in summer? The city's the one pays the most taxes. Anyway, what the hell you do on the stoop all day? How come Carl hangs out in front of Michailovitch, morning noon night, every time I look up? Come on, get the hell off the stoop here, you Teitelbaum,' he yelled. 'Stupids. Stick the Kleenex in your pocket.' He gave Eddie a splintery whisk with the broom. He turned away, frowning, thinking. 'Go 'way, bums,' he mumbled at two loitering infants, maybe four years old.

Nevertheless, Clop was a man of grave instinct, a serious man.

Three days later he offered Eddie the key to the bicycle and carriage room of 1436, the corner and strategic building.

'For thinking up inventions,' said Clop. 'What are we, animals?' He went on to tell that he was proud to be associated
with scientific research. So many boys were out bumming, on
the tramp, tramp, tramp. Carl, his own son, looked bad, played
poker day and night under the stairs with Shmul, the rabbi's
son, a Yankee in a skullcap.* Therefore, Clop begged Eddie to
persuade Carl to do a little something in his line of thinking and
follow-through. He really liked science very much, Mr. Clop
said, but needed a little encouragement, since he had no
mother.

'O.K., O.K.' Eddie was willing. 'He can help me figure out a
rocket to the moon.'

'The moon?' Mr. Clop asked. He peeked out the cellar window
at a piece of noonday sky.

Right before Eddie's mirage-making eyes for his immediate
use was a sink, electricity, gas outlets, and assorted plumbing
pipes. What else is basic to any laboratory? Do you think that the
Institute for Advanced Study started out any stronger than that,
or all the little padlocked cyclotron houses? The beginning of
everything is damp and small, but wide-armed oaks – according
to myth, legend, and the folktales of the people – from solitary
acorns grow.

Eddie's first chore was the perfection of the cockroach segregator. At cost plus 6 percent, he trailed some low-voltage wire all
around local kitchen baseboards, which immediately returned
to its gummy environment under the linoleum the cockroach
which could take a hint. It electrocuted the stubborn fools not
meant by Darwin anyway to survive.

There was nothing particularly original in this work. Eddie
would be the first to concede that he had been thinking about the

* *Yankee in a Skullcap: My Day & Night in the East Bronx*, Shmul Klein,
Mitzvah Press.

country and cows all summer, as well as barbed wire, and had simply applied recollected knowledge to the peculiar conditions of his environment.

'What a hell of a summer this is turning into,' said Carl, plucking a bug off the lab's wire. 'I mean, we ought to have some fun too, Eddie. How about it? I mean, if we were a club, we would be more well rounded.'

'Everyone wants fun,' said Eddie.

'I don't mean real fun,' said Carl. 'We could be a science club. But just you and me – No, I'm sick of that crap. Get some more guys in. Make it an organization, Eddie.'

'Why not?' said Eddie, anxious to get to work.

'Great. I've been thinking of some names. How's . . . Advanseers . . . Get it?'

'Stinks.'

'I thought of a funny one . . . like on those little cards. How about The Thimkers?'

'Very funny.'

Carl didn't press it. 'All right. But we have to get some more members.'

'Two,' said Eddie, thinking a short laugh.

'Well, O.K. But, Eddie, what about girls? I mean, after all, women have the vote a long time. They're doctors and . . . What about Madame Curie? There's others.'

'Please, Carl, lay off. We got about thirteen miles of wire left. I got to figure out something.'

Carl couldn't stop. He liked girls all around him, he said. They made him a sunny, cheerful guy. He could think of wonderful witticisms when they were present. Especially Rita Niskov and Stella Rosenzweig.

He would like to go on, describing, as an example, the Spitz twins, how they were so top-heavy but with hips like boys. Hadn't Eddie seen them afloat at the Seymour Street Pool, water-winged by their airtight tits?

Also darling little Stella Rosenzweig, like a Vassar girl despite being only in third-term high. When you danced with her, you could feel something like pinpricks, because although she was little she was extremely pointed.

Eddie was absolutely flipped by a groundswell of lust just before lunch. To save himself, he coldly said, 'No, no. No girls. Saturday nights they can come over for a little dancing, a little petting. Fix up the place. No girls in the middle of the week.'

He promised, however, to maintain an open line between Carl and the Spitz twins by recruiting for immediate membership their brother Arnold. That was a lucky, quiet choice. Arnold needed a corner in which to paint. He stated that daylight would eventually disappear and with it the myths about north light. He founded in that dark cellar a school of painters called the Light Breakers, who still work together in a loft on East Twenty-ninth Street under two 25-watt bulbs.

On Carl's recommendation Shmul Klein was ingathered, a great fourth hand, but Eddie said no card tables. Shmul had the face of an unentrammeled guy. Did he make book after school? No, no, he said, rumors multiplied: the truth was single.

He was a journalist of life, as Eddie was a journeyman in knowledge. When questioned about his future, he would guess that he was destined to trip over grants, carrying a fearsome load of scholarships on his way to a soft job in advertising, using a fraction of his potential.

Well, there were others, of course, who glinted around, seeking membership under the impression that a neighborhood cathouse was being established. Eddie laughed and pointed to a market glutted by individual initiative, not to mention the way the bottom has fallen out of the virgin as moral counterweight.

It took time out of Eddie to be a club. Whole afternoons and weekends were lost for public reasons. The boys asked him to hold open meetings so that the club's actual disposition would be appreciated by the parents of girls. Eddie talked then on 'The Dispersal of the Galaxies and the Conservation of Matter.' Carl applauded twice, in an anarchy of enthusiasm. Mr. Clop listened, was impressed, asked what he could do for them, and then tied their wattage into Mrs. Goredinsky's meter.

Eddie offered political lectures, too, as these are times which, if man were human, could titillate his soul. From the four-by-six room which Eddie shared with Itzik Halbfunt, his father's monkey, he saw configurations of disaster revise the sky before anyone even smelled smoke.

'Who was the enemy?' he asked, to needle a little historicity into his clubmates. 'Was it the People of the Sea? Troy? Rome? The Saracens? The Huns? The Russians? The colonies in Africa, the stinking proletariat? The hot owners of capital?'

Typically he did not answer. He let them weave these broad questions on poor pinheaded looms while he slipped into Michailovitch's for a celery tonic.

He shared his profits from the cockroach segregator with the others. This way they took an interest and were courteous enough to heed his philosophic approach, as did the clients to whom he pointed out a human duty to interfere with nature as little as possible except for food-getting (survival), a seminal tragedy which obtains in the wild forests as well.

Reading, thinking on matters beyond the scope of the physical and chemical sciences carried his work from the idealistic cockroach segregator to a telephone dial system for people on relief within a ten-block radius – and finally to the well-known War Attenuator, which activated all his novitiate lab assistants but featured his own lonely patience.

'Eddie, Eddie, you take too much time,' said his father. 'What about us?'

'You,' said Eddie.

How could he forget his responsibilities at the Teitelbaum Zoo, a pet shop where three or four mutts, scabby with sawdust, slept in the window? A hundred gallons of goldfish were glassed inside, four canaries singing tu-wit-tu-wu – all waited for him to dump the seeds, the hash, the mash into their dinner buckets. Poor Itzik Halbfunt, the monkey from Paris, France, waited too, nibbling his beret. Itzik looked like Mr. Teitelbaum's uncle who had died of Jewishness in the epidemics of '40, '41. For this reason he would never be sold. 'Too bad,' is an outsider's comment, as a certain local Italian would have paid maybe $45 for that monkey.

In sorrow Mr. Teitelbaum had turned away forever from his neighbor, man, and for life, then, he squinted like a cat and hopped like a bird and drooped like a dog. Like a parrot, all he could say and repeat when Eddie made his evening break was, 'Eddie, don't leave the door open, me and the birds will fly away.'

'If you got wings, Papa, fly,' said Eddie. And that was Eddie's life for years and years, from childhood on: he shoveled dog shit and birdseed, watching the goldfish float and feed and die in a big glass of water far away from China.

One Monday morning in July, bright and hot and early, Eddie called the boys together for assignments in reconnaissance and mapping. Carl knew the basement extremely well, but Eddie wanted a special listing of doors and windows, their conditions established. There were three buildings involved in this series, 1432, 1434, 1436. He requested that they keep a diary in order to arrive at viable statistics on how many ladies used the laundry facilities at what hours, how hot the hot water generally was at certain specific times.

'Because we are going to work with gases now. Gas expands, compresses, diffuses, and may be liquefied. If there is any danger involved at any point, I will handle it and be responsible. Just don't act like damn fools. I promise you,' he added bitterly, 'a lot of fun.'

He asked them to develop a little competence with tools. Carl as the son of Clop, plumber, electrician, and repairman, was a happy, aggressive teacher. In the noisy washing-machine hours of morning, under Carl's supervision, they drilled barely visible holes in the basement walls and pipe-fitted long-wear rubber tubes. The first series of tests required a network of delicate ducts.

'I am the vena cava and the aorta,' Eddie paraphrased. 'Whatever goes from me must return to me. You be the engineers. Figure out the best way to nourish all outlying areas.'

By 'nourish,' Shmul pointed out, he really meant 'suffocate.'

On the twenty-ninth of July they were ready. At 8:13 a.m. the first small-scale, small-area test took place. At 8:12 a.m., just before the moment of pff,* all the business of the cellars was being transacted – garbage transferred from small cans into large ones; early wide-awake grandmas, rocky with insomnia, dumped wash into the big tubs; boys in swimming trunks rolled baby carriages out into the cool morning. A coal truck arrived, shifted, backed up across the sidewalk, stopped, shoved its black ramp into one sooty cellar window, and commenced to roar.

Mr. Clop's radio was loud. As he worked, rolling the cans, hoisting them with Carl's help up the wooden cellar steps, arguing with the coalmen about the right of way, he listened to the news. He wanted to know if the sun would roll out, flashy as ever; if there was a chance for rain, as his brother grew tomatoes in Jersey.

At 8:13 a.m. the alarm clock in the laboratory gave the ringing word. Eddie touched a button in the substructure of an ordinary glass coffeepot, from whose spout two tubes proceeded into the wall. A soft hiss followed: the coffeepot steamed and clouded and cleared.

Forty seconds later Mr. Clop howled, 'Jesus, who farted?' although the smell was not quite like that at all, Eddie the concoctor knew. It was at least *meant* to be greener, skunkier, closer to the deterrents built into animals and flowers, but stronger. He was informed immediately of a certain success by the bellows of the coal delivery men, the high cries of the old ladies.

Satisfied, Eddie touched another button, this at the base of Mrs. Spitz's reconstructed vacuum cleaner. The reverse process used no more than two minutes. The glass clouded, the spout was stoppered, the genie returned.

Eddie knew it would take the boys a little longer to get free of their observation posts and the people who were observing them. During that speck of time his heart sank as hearts may do after a

---

* *The moment of Pff: An Urban Boyhood*, Shmul Klein, Mitzvah Press.

great act of love. He suffered a migraine from acceding desolation. When Carl brought excited news, he listened sadly, for what is life? he thought.

'God, great!' cried Carl. 'History-making! Crazee! Eddie, Eddie, a mystery! No one knows how what where . . .'

'Yet,' Eddie said. 'You better quiet down, Carl.'

'But listen, Eddie, nobody can figure it out,' said Carl. 'How long did it last? It ended before that fat dope, Goredinsky, got out of our toilet. She was hollering and pulling up her bloomers and pulling down her dress. I watched from the door. It laid me sidewise. She's not even supposed to use that toilet. It's ours.'

'Yeh,' said Eddie.

'Wait a minute, wait a minute, listen. My father kept saying, "Jesus dear, did I forget to open an exhaust someplace? Jesus dear, what did I do? Did I wreck up the flues? Tell me, tell me, give me a hint!"'

'Your father's a very nice old guy,' Eddie said coldly.

'Oh, I know that,' said Carl.

'Wonderful head,' said Arnold, who had just entered.

'Look at my father,' Eddie said, taking the dim and agitated view. 'Look at him, he sits in that store, he doesn't shave, maybe twice a week. Sometimes he doesn't move an hour or two. His nose drips, so the birds know he's living. That lousy sonofabitch, he used to be a whole expert on world history, he supports a stinking zoo and that filthy monkey that can't even piss straight' . . . Bitterness for his cramped style and secondhand pants took his breath away. So he laughed and let them have the facts. 'You know, my old man was so hard up just before he got married and he got such terrific respect for women (he respects women, let me tell you) that you know what he did? He snuck into the Bronx Zoo and he rammed it up a chimpanzee there. You're surprised, aren't you! Listen to me, they shipped that baby away to France. If my father'd've owned up, we'd've been rich. It makes me sore to think about. He'd've been the greatest buggerer in recorded history. He'd be wanted in pigsties and stud farms. They'd telegraph him a note from Irkutsk to get in on those crazy cross-pollination experiments. What he could do to winter wheat! That cocksucker tells everyone he went over to Paris to see if his cousins were alive. He went over to get my big brother Itzik. To bring him home. To aggravate my mother and me.'

'Aw . . .' said Carl.

'So that's it,' said Shmul, a late reporter, playing alongside Eddie. 'That's how you got so smart. Constant competition with an oddball sibling . . . Aha . . .'

'Please,' said Arnold, his sketch pad wobbly on his knee. 'Please, Eddie, raise your arms like that again, like you just did when you were mad. It gives me an idea.'

'Jerks,' said Eddie, and spat on the spotless laboratory floor. 'A bunch of jerks.'

Still and all, the nineteenth-century idea that progress is immanent is absolutely correct. For his sadness dwindled and early August was a time of hard work and glorious conviviality. The mystery of the powerful non-toxic gas from an unknowable source remained. The boys kept their secret. Outsiders wondered. They knew. They swilled Coke like a regiment which has captured all the enemy pinball machines without registering a single tilt.

Saturday nights at the lab were happy, ringing with 45 r.p.m.s, surrounded by wonderful women. All kinds of whistling adventures were recorded by Shmul . . . He had it all written down: how one night Mr. Clop wandered in looking for fuses and found Arnold doing life sketches of Rita Niskov. She held a retort over one breast in order to make technical complications for Arnold, who was ambitious. 'Keep it up, keep it up, son,' mumbled Clop, to whom it was all a misunderstanding.

And another night Blanchie Spitz took off everything but her drawers and her brassière and because of a teaspoon of rum in a quart and a half of Coke decided to do setting-up exercises to the tune of the 'Nutcracker Suite.' 'Ah, Blanchie,' said Carl, nearly nauseous with love, 'do me a belly dance, baby.' 'I don't know what a belly dance is, Carl,' she said, and to the count of eight went into a deep knee bend. Arnold lassoed her with Rita's skirt, which he happened to have in his hand. He dragged Blanchie off to a corner, where he slapped her, dressed her, asked her what her fee was and did it include relatives, and before she could answer he slapped her again, then took her home, Rita's skirt flung over one shoulder. This kind of event will turn an entire neighborhood against the most intense chronology of good works. Rita's skirt, hung by a buttonhole, fluttered for two days from the iron cellar railing and was unclaimed. Girls, Shmul editorialized in his little book, live a stone-age life in a blown-glass cave.

Eddie had to receive most of this chattery matter from Shmul. The truth is that Eddie did not take frequent part in the festivities, as Saturday was his father's movie night. Mr. Teitelbaum would have closed the shop, but the manager of the Loew's refused to sell Itzik a ticket. 'Show me,' said Mr. Teitelbaum, 'where it says no monkeys.' 'Please,' said the manager, 'this is my busy night.' Itzik had never been alone, for although he was a brilliant monkey, in the world of men he is dumb. 'Ach,' said Mr. Teitelbaum, 'you know what it's like to have a monkey for a pet? It's like raising up a moron. You get very attached, no matter what, and very tied down.'

'Still and all, things are picking up around here,' said Carl.

About a week after the unpleasant incident with the girls (which eventually drove the entire Niskov family about six blocks uptown where they were unknown), Eddie asked for an off-schedule meeting. School was due to begin in three weeks, and he was determined to complete the series which would prove his War Attenuator marketable among the nations.

'Don't exaggerate,' said Shmul. 'What we have here is a big smell.'

'Non-toxic,' Eddie pointed out. 'No matter how concentrated, non-toxic. Don't forget that, Klein, because that's the beauty of it. An instrument of war that will not kill. Imagine that.'

'O.K.,' he said. 'I concede. So?'

'Shmul, you got an eye. What did the people do during the last test? Did they choke? Did their eyes run? What happened?'

'I already told you, Eddie. Nothing happened. They only ran. They ran like hell. They held their noses and they tore out the door and a couple of kids crawled up the coal ramp. Everybody gave a yelp and then ran.'

'What about your father, Carl?'

'Oh, for Christ's sake, if I told you once, I told you twenty times, he got out fast. Then he stood on the steps, holding his nose and figuring who to pass the buck to.'

'Well, that's what I mean, boys. It's the lesson of the cockroach segregator. The peaceful guy who listens to the warning of his senses will survive generations of defeat. Who needs the inheritance of the louse with all that miserable virulence in his nucleic acid? Who? I haven't worked out the political strategy altogether, but our job here, anyway, is just to figure out the technology.'

'O.K., now the rubber tubes have to be extended up to the first and second floor of 1432, 1434, 1436 – the three attached buildings. Do not drill into Michailovitch on the corner, as this could seep into the ice-cream containers and fudge and stuff, and I haven't tested out all comestibles. If you work today and tomorrow, we should be done by Thursday. On Friday the test goes forward; by noon we ought to have all reports and know what we have. Any questions? Carl, get the tools, you're in charge. I have to fix this goddamn percolator and see what the motor's like. We'll meet on Friday morning. Same time – 7:30 a.m.'

Then Eddie hurried back to the shop to clean the bird cages which he had forgotten about for days because of the excitement in his mind. Itzik offered him a banana. He accepted. Itzik peeled it for him, then got a banana for himself. He threw the peels into the trash can, for which Eddie kissed him on his foolish face. He jumped to Eddie's shoulder to tease the birds. Eddie did not like him to do this, for those birds will give you psittacosis (said Eddie) if you aggravate them too much. This is an untested hypothesis, but it makes sense; as you know, people who loathe you will sneeze in your face when their mucous membranes are most swollen or when their throat is host to all kinds of cocci.

'Don't, Itzikel,' he said gently, and put the monkey down. Then

Itzik hung from Eddie's shoulder by one long arm, eating the banana behind his back. 'That's how I like to see you,' said Mr. Teitelbaum when he looked into the shop. 'Once in a while anyway.'

Eddie was near the end of a long summer's labor. He could bear being peaceful and happy.

On Friday morning Carl, Arnold, and Shmul waited outside. They had plenty of bubble gum and lollipops in which Eddie had personally invested. They were responsible for maintaining equilibrium among the little children who might panic. They also had notebooks, and in these reports each boy was expected to cover only one building.

Inside, Eddie played a staccato note on the button under the percolator. After that it was very simple. People poured from the three buildings. Tenants on the upper floors, which were not involved, poked their heads out the windows because of the commotion. The controls were so fine that they had gotten only the barest whiff and had assumed it to be the normal smell of morning rising from the cracked back of the fish market three blocks east.

Eddie had agreed not to leave the laboratory until reports came in from the other boys. He was perplexed when half an hour had passed and they did not appear. There wasn't even a book to read. So he busied himself disconnecting his home-constructed appliances, funneling the residue powder into a paper envelope which he kept in his back pocket. Suddenly he worried about everyone. What could happen to Itsy Bitsy Michailovitch, who sat outside his father's store spinning a yo-yo and singing a no-song to himself all day? He was in fact a goddamn helpless idiot. What about Mrs. Spitz, who would surely stop to put her corset on and would faint away and maybe crack her skull on a piece of rococo mahogany? What about heart failure in people over forty? What about the little Susskind kids? They were so wild, so baffled out of sense, they might jump into the dumbwaiter shaft.

He was scrubbing the sink, trying to uproot his miserable notions, when the door opened. Two policemen came in and put their hands on him. Eddie looked up and saw his father. Their eyes met and because of irrevocable pain, held. That was the moment (said Shmul, later on after that and other facts) that Eddie fell headfirst into the black heart of a deep depression. This despair required all his personal attention for years.

No one could make proper contact with him again, to tell him the news. Did he know that he had caused the death of all his father's stock? Even the three turtles, damn it, every last minnow, even the worms that were the fishes' Sunday dinner had wriggled their last. The birds were dead at the bottom of their clean cages.

Itzik Halbfunt lay in a coma from which he would not recover. He lay in Eddie's bed on Eddie's new mattress, between Eddie's sheets. 'Let him die at home,' said Mr. Teitelbaum, 'not with a bunch of poodles at Speyer's.'

He caressed his scrawny shoulder that was itchy and furry and cried, 'Halbfunt, Halbfunt, you were my little friend.'

No matter how lovingly a person or a doctor rapped at the door to Eddie's mind, Eddie refused to say 'Come in.' Carl Clop called loudly, taking a long distance, local stop, suburban train several times to tell Eddie that it was really he who had thought it would be wonderful to see old Teitelbaum run screaming with hysterical Itzik. For the pleasure this sight would give, Carl had connected the rubber tubes to a small vent between the basement of 1436 and the rear of the pet shop. He had waited at the corner and, sure enough, they had come at last, Mr. Teitelbaum running and Itzik gasping for breath. Clop's bad luck, said Clop to have a son who wasn't serious.

Eddie was remanded to the custody of Dr. Scott Tully, director of A Home for Boys, in something less than three weeks. The police impounded Shmul's notebooks but learned only literary things about faces and the sex habits of adolescent boys. Also found was an outline of a paper Eddie had planned for the anti-vivisectionist press, describing his adventures as a self-prepared subject for the gas tolerance experiments. It was entitled NO GUINEA PIG FRONTS FOR ME. As any outsider can judge, this is an insane idea.

Eddie was cared for at A Home for Boys by a white-frocked attendant, cross-eyed and muscle-bound, with strong canines oppressing his lower lip, a nose neatly broken and sloppily jointed. This was Jim Sunn and he was kind to Eddie. 'Because he's no trouble to me, Mr. Teitelbaum, he's a good boy. If he opens his eyes wide, I know he wants to go to the bathroom. He ain't crazy, Mr. Teitelbaum, he just got nothing to say right now, is all. I seen a lot of cases, don't you worry.'

Mr. Teitelbaum didn't have too much to say himself, and this made him feel united with Eddie. He came every Sunday and sat with him in silence on a bench in the garden behind A Home; in bad weather they met in the parlor, a jolly rectangle scattered with small hooked rugs. They sat for one hour opposite one another in comfortable chairs, peaceful people, then Eddie opened his eyes wide and Jim Sunn said, 'O.K. Let's go, buddy. Shut-eye don't hurt the kings of the jungle. Bears hibernate.' Mr. Teitelbaum stood on his tiptoes and enfolded Eddie in his arms. 'Sonny, don't worry so much,' he said, then went home.

This situation prevailed for two years. One cold winter day Mr. Teitelbaum had the flu and couldn't visit. 'Where the hell's my father?' Eddie growled.

That was the opener. After that Eddie said other things. Before the week had ended, Eddie said, 'I'm sick of peppers, Jim. They give me gas.'

A week later he said, 'What's the news? Long Island sink yet?'

Dr. Tully had never anticipated Eddie's return. ('Once they go up this road, they're gone,' he had confided to the newspapermen.) He invited a consultant from a competing but friendly establishment. He was at last able to give Eddie a Rorschach, which restored his confidence in his original pessimism.

'Let him have more responsibility,' the consultant suggested, which they did at once, allowing him because of his background to visit the A Home for Boys' Zoo. He was permitted to fondle a rabbit and tease two box turtles. There was a fawn, caged and sick. Also a swinging monkey, but Eddie didn't bat an eyelash.

That night he vomited. 'What's with the peppers, Jimmy? Can't that dope cook? Only with peppers?'

Dr. Tully explained that Eddie was now a helper. As soon as there was a vacancy, he would be given sole responsibility for one animal. 'Thank God,' Mr. Teitelbaum said. 'A dumb animal is a good friend.'

At last a boy was cured, sent home to his mother; a vacancy existed. Dr. Tully considered this a fortunate vacancy, for the cured boy had been in charge of the most popular snake in the zoo. The popularity of the snake had made the boy very popular. The popularity of the boy had increased his self-confidence; he had become vice-president of the Boys' Assembly; he had acquired friends and sycophants, he had become happy, cured, and had been returned to society.

On the very first day Eddie proved his mettle. He cleaned the cage with his right hand, holding the snake way out with his left. He had many admirers immediately.

'When you go home, could I have the job?' asked a very pleasant small boy who was only mildly retarded, but some father was willing to lay out a fortune because he was ashamed. 'I'm not going anywhere, sonny,' said Eddie. 'I like it here.'

On certain afternoons, shortly after milk and cookies, Eddie had to bring a little white mouse to his snake. He slipped the mouse into the cage, and that is why this snake was so popular: the snake did not eat the mouse immediately. At four o'clock the boys began to gather. They watched the mouse cowering in the corner. They watched the lazy snake wait for his hungry feelings to tickle him all along his curly interior. Every now and then he hiked his spine and raised his head, and the boys breathed hard. Sometime between four-thirty and six o'clock he would begin to slither aimlessly around the cage. The boys laid small bets on the time, winning and losing chunks of chocolate cake or a handful of raisins. Suddenly, but without fuss (and one had to be really watching), the snake stretched his long body, opened his big mouth, and gulped the little live mouse, who always went down squeaking.

Eddie could not disapprove, because this was truly the nature of the snake. But he pulled his cap down over his eyes and turned away.

Jimmy Sunn told him at supper one night, 'Guess what I heard. I heard you're acquiring back your identity. Not bad.'

'My identity?' asked Eddie.

A week later Eddie handed in a letter of resignation. He sent a copy to his father. The letter said: 'Thank you, Dr. Tully. I know who I am. I am no mouse killer. I am Eddie Teitelbaum, the Father of the Stink Bomb, and I am known for my Dedication to Cause and my Fearlessness in the Face of Effect. Do not bother me anymore. I have nothing to say. Sincerely.'

Dr. Tully wrote a report in which he pointed with pride to his consistent pessimism in the case of Eddie Teitelbaum. This was considered remarkable, in the face of so much hope, and it was remembered by his peers.

While Eddie was making the decision to go out of his mind as soon as possible, other decisions were being made elsewhere. Mr. Teitelbaum, for instance, decided to die of grief and old age – which frequently overlap – and that was the final decision for all Teitelbaums. Shmul sat down to think and was disowned by his father.

Arnold ran away to East Twenty-ninth Street, where he built up a lovely bordello of naked oils at considerable effort and expense .

But Carl, the son of Clop, had tasted with Eddie's tongue. He went to school and stayed for years in order to become an atomic physicist for the navy. Nowadays on the 8:07 Carl sails out into the hophead currents of our time, fights the undertow with little beep-beep signals. He has retained his cheerful disposition and for this service to the world has just received a wife who was washed out of the Rockettes for being too beautiful.

The War Attenuator has been bottled weak under pressure. It is sometimes called Teitelbaum's Mixture, and its ingredients have been translated into Spanish on the label. It is one of the greatest bug killers of all time. Unfortunately it is sometimes hard on philodendrons and old family rubber plants.

Mrs. Goredinsky still prefers to have her kitchen protected by the Segregator. An old-fashioned lady, she drops in bulk to her knees to scrub the floor. She cannot help seeing the cockroach caught and broiled in his own juice by the busy A.C. She flicks the cockroach off the wall. She smiles and praises Eddie.

The Floating Truth

The day I knocked, all the slats were flat. 'Where are you, Lionel?'
I shouted. 'In the do-funny?'

'For goodness' sake, be quiet,' he said, unlatching the back
door. 'I'm the other side of the coin.'

I nicked him with my forefinger. 'You don't ring right, Charley.
You're counterfeit.'

'Come on in and settle,' he said. 'Keep your hat on. The coat
rack's out of order.'

I had visited before. The seats were washable plaid plastic –
easy to care for – and underfoot was the usual door-to-door fuzz.
In graceful disarray philodendrons rose and fell from the back
window ledge.

'How in the world can you see to drive, Marlon?'

'Well, baby, I don't drive it much,' he said. 'It isn't safe.'

He offered me an apple from the glove compartment.

'Nature's toothbrush,' I said dreamily. 'How've you been,
Eddie?'

He sighed. 'Things never looked better.'

He hopped out the front door and crawled in the rear. He was
not a seat climber. 'Truthfully, I would have phoned you no later
than tonight,' he said. He snapped the blinds horizontal, and
from the east the morning glared at our pale faces. He took a

paper and pencil out of a small mahogany file cabinet built along the rear of the front seat. 'Let's get down to brass tacks,' he said. 'What do you want to do?'

'What does anyone want to do?'

'Let me ask the questions,' he said. 'What do you want to do?'

'Oh . . . something worthwhile,' I said. 'Well, make a contribution . . . you know what I mean . . . help out somehow . . . do good.'

'Please!' he said bitterly. 'Don't waste my time. Every sonofabitch wants to do good.'

'Why, that's nice,' I said. 'What a wonderful social trend. In these terrible times it's marvelous news.'

'It's marvelous news . . .' he squeaked in a high girl-voice. 'Don't be an idiot. All of time is terrible. You should have lived in a little farming village during the Hundred Years' War. Anyway, do you realize you're paying me by the hour? Let's get started. What can you *do*?'

I was surprised to hear that I was paying him by the hour. Still, for all I know, despite their appearance, these times may not be terrible at all.

'I can type. I went to business school for three months and I can type.'

'Don't worry,' he said. 'I've gotten jobs for virgins. I could place a pediatrician in the Geriatric Clinic.'

'If you're so great, Bubbles, how come you don't even have a home?'

'I've only just found myself,' he said, turning inward. On the outside he was a mirror image of a face with a dead center. His eyes were blue. The pupils were dark and immovable. He never saw anything out of the corner of his eye but swiveled his whole head to stare at it. His hair was blond, darkening in a terrible rush before the gray could become general. All his sex characteristics were secondary, which did not prevent him from asking me after our first day's work, 'Give me a bunny hug, baby?' I didn't mind at all and did, goosing him gently. It seemed to me he'd like that a lot. I am not considered wild, but I am kind.

I scraped a ham sandwich out of my dungarees and offered him half. '*Gasoline* is what I need,' he said peevishly. 'I was going to call for a man who invited me to La Vie for a business deal.'

Just then the phone rang. He lunged over the front seat for it. 'What good luck, Edsel,' he chortled. 'You got me just as I was pulling up to a meter. Hold it a moment while I disengage.' He made grunting noises as though great effort were involved because of tonnage, then resumed his conversation. 'Yes? About tonight? I'm not sure I can make it . . . I've got to be out all day . . .'

I waved a one-dollar bill across the windshield mirror. 'Ah . . . make it quarter to ten, so I have time to eat . . . No, that's not necessary . . . No . . . Well, if you insist, at least allow me to call for you. I'll stop by at eight-thirty . . . Great . . . It'll be marvelous to talk with you again. *Arrivederci*.'

'Here,' I said, 'is a dollar. Petrol.'

'I appreciate it,' he said.

The Edsel he met at eight-thirty, honking his horn before a canopied doorman, was Jonathan Stubblefield, but don't try to reach him because he's unlisted. His eyes were pale as the moon. They drove here and yon, hip-flasked, unwatered and unsodaed, uniced and defrosted, looped in one another's consonants. Lack of communication made them appear to be lovers.

'Do you have a friend?' asked Jonathan Stubblefield. 'Yes, a girl,' said my pal, his nose always to the grindstone. Jonathan Stubblefield misunderstood. 'Hotcha!' he replied. 'I have a friend myself, but the goddamn family – What do you think of the family?' he asked, trying to make sense of his entire life.

'The Family of Man? Oh, I believe in it. But look here, Edsel . . . this girl I'm talking about is not a sexual partner. She's a business associate. Lively, alert, young, charming, clever, enthusiastic. How can you use her?'

'Oh boy,' said Jonathan Stubblefield, stupefied. 'Upside down, cross-country, her choice. Any way she says.'

'You still misunderstand me. It's her business affairs I'm in charge of.'

'Oh,' said Jonathan Stubblefield. 'Oh,' he said, 'in that case send me a résumé,' and passed out.

'But you didn't tell him anything about me,' I complained the following afternoon.

'Why should I? He didn't tell me anything about himself. Do you think his real name is Stubblefield? What's the matter with you? Don't put yourself on a platter. What are you – a roast duck, everything removable with a lousy piece of flatware? Be secret. Turn over on your side. Let them guess if you're stuffed. That's how I got where I am.'

The organization of his ideas was all wrong; I was drawn to the memory of myself – a mere stripling of a girl – the day I learned that the shortest distance between two points is a great circle.

'Anyway, you ought to think in shorter sentences,' he suggested, although I hadn't said a word. Old Richard-the-Liver-Headed, he saw right through to the heart of the matter, my syntax.

'Well, now, just go somewhere for a couple of days. Home, maybe. How about home? Go to the movies. I don't give a damn where you go. I'll have the résumé ready. I've pinpointed Edsel. He's avid to have an employee.'

'I'll do what you say.' I had to get started somehow. I had been out of school six weeks and was beginning to feel nearly unemployable.

I ducked out of the car. A cop came to the door and squinted authoritatively. 'Listen, Squatface, I told you Tuesday, get this hearse to a mummery.' He was one of those college cops, in it for the pension. Security is an essential. How else face the future?

'Ran out of gas,' my chum whispered as soft as soup.

'Here's a dollar,' I replied. 'More petrol.'

It rained for three days. On the fourth morning, I received a telegram. PHONE OUT OF ORDER. MEET ME USUAL PLACE. SEE EDSEL. LIKE FLYNN, YOU'RE IN.

At noon I found them admiring new white tires. (These are the good times.) I was all dressed up and they were all dressed up. Jonathan Stubblefield observed me. His eyes *were* pale as the moon. He winked and a tear rolled down his smooth cheek. 'I have an occluded lachrymal duct,' he explained.

'Let's go to the Vilamar Cafeteria, where we can talk.' He added with pride, 'It's on me.'

We proceeded at once, single file, Stubblefield leading. In the cafeteria we seated ourselves deferentially around a rotating altar of condiments and began in communal reverence.

'You seem so young,' said Jonathan Stubblefield. 'I can't really believe that time has passed. Take a good look at me. A man of thirty-one. Inside my head, a photostatic account of Pearl Harbor. I can still see it so clear . . . the snow just stippling the rocks –'

'Snow?'

'Snow. The absolute quiet and then that wild hum and then the noise. And then the whole world plunged into disaster.'

'Oh my!'

'You were too young. But I remember – Geneva, Yalta, the San Francisco conference, much-scoffed-at Acheson; those days were the hope of the world. I remember it like yesterday.'

'You do?'

'What sort of memories can you young people of today have? You have a reputation for clothes and dope. You have no sense of history; you have no tragic sense. What is Alsace-Lorraine? Can you tell me, my dear? What problem does it face, even today? You don't know. Not innocent, but ignorant.'

'You're right,' I said.

'Of course,' he said. 'You can't deny it. The truth finds its own level and floats.'

'Coffee?' asked Roderick the middleman.

'Not me,' said Edsel. 'Baked apple for me. And salmon salad. Jell-O maybe. I'm on a diet.' He patted his tummy. 'Now tell me about yourself. I want to know you better.'

I tossed my ponytail, agleam with natural oils, and said: 'What can I say?'

'You can tell me about yourself. Who you are, where you come from, what your interests are, your hobbies. Who's your favorite boyfriend, for instance?'

I told him who I was, where I came from, what my interests and my hobbies were. 'But I'm still waiting for Mr. Right to come out of the West.'

'You and I have a lot in common,' he said sadly. 'I'm still waiting for Mr. Right too. I'm paraphrasing, of course. I mean Miss Right.

'You know, you dress beautifully. You look like a rose. Yes, a rose is what is indicated.' He touched gently that part of the décolletage furthest from my chin.

He looked at his watch, which had a barometer tucked in somewhere along its circumference. 'Pressure rising; I've got to run. Tell our friend "excuse me" for me. Tell him you're hired, pending résumé. I've got to have that résumé. I don't do business without documentation.'

He stood up and transported his gaze slowly from the lady's rest room to the steam counter, the short order table, the grand coffee urns, and finally to the great doors which rested where their rubber stoppers had established them.

'I am lord of all I survey,' he murmured. He smiled beneficently on my shining face, then turned on his heels, like the sound of the old order changing, and disappeared into the Götterdämmerung of the revolving doors.

'Oh, Everett, what an interesting man!' I said. We split the salmon salad, but Jell-O reminds me of junket.

'Well, what do you think of him? Not bad. He's the wave of the future. A man who can use leisure. Here's the résumé.' He was very businesslike and continued, as he buttered a hard seeded roll, to give me orders for my own good. 'Type it. Do a nice job . . . only it has to look home-typed; the only one of its kind. Maybe you ought to make a mistake. If he thinks you've plastered the city with them, you're finished . . . Look it over. It's a day's work, and I'm kind of proud of it.'

I riffled and read. 'Say, it's three pages, legal size. Do you know it's three pages?'

'Aha!' he said in pride.

'Oh, please, it's ridiculous. What'll I do if he calls any of these people?'

'No, no, no. He *wants* to hire you. He's crazy about you; he wants to be your friend. When he sees all these words, he'll be happy and feel free. He may not even read them.'

I looked it over again. These are only a few of the jobs with which he had papered my past. The first, in advertising:

The Green House: In eight exciting months I brought The Green House's name before the public in seven ways – all inexpensive: two-color posters were distributed. No copy used. A green house on an eggshell-white background. Two-color matchbooks – no copy. Two-color personal cards for all personnel. The Green House itself was finally painted green. Here and there throughout the city where people least expected it (park benches, lampposts, etc.), the question asked in green paint: What Is Green? In infinitesimal green print below and to the right the reply: The Green House is green.

'What in hell is The Green House?'

'I don't know.' He giggled.

Here's another; this, under the heading of Public Relations:

The Philadelphia: An association of professionals working in the law and allied fields hired me to bring law and its possibilities to women everywhere. I traveled throughout the country for five months by bus, station wagon, train, and also by air under the name of Gladys Hand. Within nine months there were 11 percent more users of legal services. The average fee had jumped $7.20 over the previous year. Crowded court calendars required statute revisions in seven states. The Philadelphia ascribed these improvements to my work in their behalf.

And more:

The Kitchen Institute: Through the medium of The Kitchen Institute Press's 'The Kettle Calls,' we inaugurated a high-pressure plan to return women to the kitchen. 'The kitchen you are leaving may be your home' was one of many slogans used. By radio and television, as well as by ads taken in men's publications and on men's pages in newspapers (sports, finance, etc.), men were told to ask their wives as they came in the door each night: 'What's cooking?' In this way the prestige of women in kitchens everywhere was enhanced and the need and desire for kitchens accelerated.

At the very end, as though it were of no importance whatsoever, he had typed 'More Facts' and then listed: Single, twenty-three, Grad. Green Valley College for Women. Additional Courses, Sorbonne, in Short Story Writing and Public Speaking. Social Chairman of GO in high school.

'Oh, for God's sake,' I said. 'That last is pretty silly.'

'It may be silly to you, but if he reads it at all he'll certainly read the last line and he'll like that. 'A girl who was lightheaded enough to be social chairman in high school may still be spinning,' is the way I see it.'

'But listen,' I told him two days later. 'I'm not twenty-three.'

'You will be, you will be,' he assured me.

That afternoon I was helping him water the philodendrons. I was a little excited about being on the threshold of my future, and some water dripped down the back seat and filled the crevices of the upholstery.

'My God, you infuriate me sometimes,' he said, tearing the watering can from my hand. 'Can't you watch what you're doing?' Poor Dick, he was a covey of twittering angers. 'You're so damn stupid!' he screamed. He poured the dregs into an open ashtray and sprinkled the windows. 'Get something, get something,' he cried. I ran down to the store and bought an old Sunday *Times* to help clean up the mess. I realized that, against great odds, he was only trying to make a home. When I returned he was on the phone: 'Can't have you down here. Place is incredible! Let me pick you up. I want to close the deal. It's been pending too long . . . I said 10 percent . . . 10 percent is what I want. That's not excessive.'

'What deal?' I asked.

'Big deal,' he replied sotto voce. 'O.K.'

The phone rang again. 'Edsel!' He beamed. 'Long time no see.

Long time no hear also . . . Of course,' he said. 'Haha. 'Can she do shorthand?' Baby, he wants to know if you can do shorthand! Ha-ha, Edsel, she's a speed demon!'

'I can't,' I whispered.

He twisted his trunk to reach me and then kicked me on the shin.

He hung up. 'O.K.,' he said. 'Go on over. He's all yours. Good luck. You'll get my bill in the morning mail.'

Well, that is how I got my first job. I entered the business world, my senses alert. I quietly watched and voraciously listened. Every 9 a.m. in the five-day week I opened the heavy oak door on which a sign in Old Regal said STUBBLEFIELD. I kept my pencils sharpened. I read the morning papers in the morning and the evening papers in the afternoon, in case some question about current events should arise.

It was true, he had been avid to have an employee and seemed happy. Often his mother called to ask him to please come to lunch or cocktails. Occasionally his father called but left no name. At decent intervals I was instructed to say he was out of town on business. He entrusted me with the key, and when he was away for two or three days, I was in full charge.

I had planned to remain with the job for at least a year, to learn office procedure and persistence.

But one Monday at about 10 a.m. the door opened and a camel-hair blonde, all textured in cashmere, appeared. 'I've just been hired by Mr. Stubblefield,' she said, 'via Western Union.' She flapped a manila half sheet under my nose. 'I met him in Bronxville last graduation day.' She looked around. There were mauve walls and army-colored file cabinets. 'I just love a two-girl office,' she said, expecting to be my friend. 'What's he like? Does he give severance pay?'

She was followed by a desk and a Long Island boy from the Bell Telephone Company. I didn't say anything to anyone but filed my *Time* and unfolded my New York *Herald Tribune*. I resharpened my pencil and proceeded to underline whatever required underlining.

'A lot of paperwork?' asked Serena, a cool revision of my former self. I had nothing to say.

Jonathan Stubblefield poked his snout out of the inner office. 'Get to know each other, girls. You're exactly the same age.'

That information unsettled me.

'You don't know how old I am,' I said. 'Anyway, what do you need her for? I'm doing a job. I'm doing as good a job as you require. This is a deliberate slap in my face. It is.'

'We're in the middle of an expanding economy, for goodness' sake!' said Jonathan Stubblefield. 'Don't be sentimental. Besides, I thought we could do with some college people.'

'But there isn't enough work to go around,' I said bravely. 'There's nothing to do.'

'It's my company, isn't it?' he said belligerently. 'If I want to, I can hire forty people to do nothing. NOTHING.'

I looked at Jonathan Stubblefield, a man in tears – but only because of his lachrymal ducts – a man nevertheless with truth on his side.

'There's room for everybody,' he said. But he would not reconsider. He probably never really liked me in the first place.

As I had never used the phone for private conversations, I had to wait until five to call my vocational counselor from a phone booth.

'Come on down, baby,' he said, giving me his latitude and longitude. 'I don't know what you want to talk about. You owe me fifteen dollars already.'

Because of crosstown traffic, it was nearly dark by the time I reached him. I had purchased a rare roast beef sandwich with coleslaw and gift-wrapped it with two green rubber bands. But he laughed in my face. 'I only eat out these days; I hate puttering around with drinks and dishes.' We gave the sandwich to a passing child, who immediately ripped off the aluminum foil and dumped the food into the gutter. She folded the foil neatly and slipped it into her pocket.

Surly Sam turned on the car heater and dimmed the lights. 'Oh my,' I said, 'it's lovely here now. What are those – crocuses?'

'Yes,' he said, 'crocuses. I take some pride in raising them in the fall.'

'Lovely! ' I repeated.

'Well,' he said, 'what's on your mind? How's the job?'

'What job? You call that a job?'

'You're a character!' he said, laying it all at my door. 'What'd you expect to do – give polio shots?'

'What's so wrong with that? That's not the most terrible thing in the world.'

He entangled all my hopes in one popeyed look. 'And where would you go from there? Let me tell you something. I sent you to Edsel . . . I worked three days on that résumé for him, because I believe that Edsel is going places and anyone on board will be going with him. Believe me, what you're now doing constitutes some of the finest experience available to a young person who wants to set sail for tomorrow.

'Ah yes,' he continued philosophically, swiveling slightly to see how absorbent I looked, 'ah yes – you could do more. Now if you were really sincere, you could take your shoes off and stand on a street corner with a sign saying: HE DIED FOR ME.' He paused. I didn't comment, because I was waiting for that particular hint that would tell me where I was going, in case it was there. 'Or else,' he suggested, brightening, 'leave the habitations of men – like me.'

My heart sank in terror.

He felt he had gone far enough, and we leaned back in the rosy decor, smoking across one artless silence after another. Finally he grimaced out of his usual face, raised an eyebrow, and swiveled. 'Ah, what's the use, baby?'

'How true,' I said. I owed him something, and in due time I paid him something. Beyond that it was the Sabbath. 'It's morning, Morton,' I said. 'Good night!'

He walked me to the rump of the car.

'I'm not mad,' I said. We shook hands and I went my way.

I was directed to the future, but it is hard for me to part with experience. Before I reached the subway entrance, I turned for a last look. He stood in front of the car, glancing up and down the street. There wasn't a soul in his sight. Not even me.

Then he peed. He did not pee like a boy who expects to span a continent, but like a man – in a puddle.

'Good night!' I called, hoping to startle him. He never heard me but stared at the dusty trash he had driven out of the gutters through oblique tunnels that led to the sea. He tightened his belt and hunched his shoulders against the weather. Having left the habitations of men, you can understand he had a special problem. When he was conveniently located he stopped in the city park. At other times he had to use dark one-way streets to help maintain the water levels of this airsick earth.

I gathered fifteen cents from several pockets and started down the subway steps when I heard him shout. In all modesty, I think he was calling me . . . 'Hey, beautiful!' he asseverated. 'You're pretty damn diurnal yourself.'

ENORMOUS CHANGES AT THE TIME
(1974)

Wants

I saw my ex-husband in the street. I was sitting on the steps of the new library.

Hello, my life, I said. We had once been married for twenty-seven years, so I felt justified.

He said, What? What life? No life of mine.

I said, O.K. I don't argue when there's real disagreement. I got up and went into the library to see how much I owed them.

The librarian said $32 even and you've owed it for eighteen years. I didn't deny anything. Because I don't understand how time passes. I have had those books. I have often thought of them. The library is only two blocks away.

My ex-husband followed me to the Books Returned desk. He interrupted the librarian, who had more to tell. In many ways, he said, as I look back, I attribute the dissolution of our marriage to the fact that you never invited the Bertrams to dinner.

That's possible, I said. But really, if you remember: first, my father was sick that Friday, then the children were born, then I had those Tuesday-night meetings, then the war began. Then we didn't seem to know them anymore. But you're right. I should have had them to dinner.

I gave the librarian a check for $32. Immediately she trusted me, put my past behind her, wiped the record clean, which is just what most other municipal and/or state bureaucracies will not do.

I checked out the two Edith Wharton books I had just returned because I'd read them so long ago and they are more apropos now than ever. They were *The House of Mirth* and *The Children*, which is about how life in the United States in New York changed in twenty-seven years fifty years ago.

A nice thing I do remember is breakfast, my ex-husband said. I was surprised. All we ever had was coffee. Then I remembered there was a hole in the back of the kitchen closet which opened into the apartment next door. There, they always ate sugar-cured smoked bacon. It gave us a very grand feeling about breakfast, but we never got stuffed and sluggish.

That was when we were poor, I said.

When were we ever rich? he asked.

Oh, as time went on, as our responsibilities increased, we didn't go in need. You took adequate financial care, I reminded him. The children went to camp four weeks a year and in decent ponchos with sleeping bags and boots, just like everyone else. They looked very nice. Our place was warm in winter, and we had nice red pillows and things.

I wanted a sailboat, he said. But you didn't want anything.

Don't be bitter, I said. It's never too late.

No, he said with a great deal of bitterness. I may get a sailboat. As a matter of fact I have money down on an eighteen-foot two-rigger. I'm doing well this year and can look forward to better. But as for you, it's too late. You'll always want nothing.

He had had a habit throughout the twenty-seven years of making a narrow remark which, like a plumber's snake, could work its way through the ear down the throat, halfway to my heart. He would then disappear, leaving me choking with equipment. What I mean is, I sat down on the library steps and he went away.

I looked through *The House of Mirth*, but lost interest. I felt extremely accused. Now, it's true, I'm short of requests and absolute requirements. But I do want *something*.

I want, for instance, to be a different person. I want to be the woman who brings these two books back in two weeks. I want to be the effective citizen who changes the school system and addresses the Board of Estimate on the troubles of this dear urban center.

I *had* promised my children to end the war before they grew up.

I wanted to have been married forever to one person, my ex-husband or my present one. Either has enough character for a whole life, which as it turns out is really not such a long time. You couldn't exhaust either man's qualities or get under the rock of his reasons in one short life.

Just this morning I looked out the window to watch the street for a while and saw that the little sycamores the city had dreamily planted a couple of years before the kids were born had come that day to the prime of their lives.

Well! I decided to bring those two books back to the library. Which proves that when a person or an event comes along to jolt or appraise me I *can* take some appropriate action, although I am better known for my hospitable remarks.

Debts

A lady called me up today. She said she was in possession of her family archives. She had heard I was a writer. She wondered if I would help her write about her grandfather, a famous innovator and dreamer of the Yiddish theater. I said I had already used every single thing I knew about the Yiddish theater to write one story, and I didn't have time to learn any more, then write about it. There is a long time in me between knowing and telling. She offered a share of the profits, but that is something too inorganic. It would never rush her grandfather's life into any literature I could make.

The next day, my friend Lucia and I had coffee and we talked about this woman. Lucia explained to me that it was probably hard to have family archives or even only stories about outstanding grandparents or uncles when one was sixty or seventy and there was no writer in the family and the children were in the middle of their own lives. She said it was a pity to lose all this inheritance just because of one's own mortality. I said yes, I did understand. We drank more coffee. Then I went home.

I thought about our conversation. Actually, I owed nothing to the lady who'd called. It was possible that I did owe something to my own family and the families of my friends. That is, to tell their stories as simply as possible, in order, you might say, to save a few lives.

Because it was her idea, the first story is Lucia's. I tell it so that some people will remember Lucia's grandmother, also her mother, who in this story is eight or nine.

The grandmother's name was Maria. The mother's name was Anna. They lived on Mott Street in Manhattan in the early 1900s. Maria was married to a man named Michael. He had worked hard, but bad luck and awful memories had driven him to the Hospital for the Insane on Welfare Island.

Every morning Anna took the long trip by trolley and train and trolley again to bring him his hot dinner. He could not eat the meals at the hospital. When Anna rode out of the stone streets of Manhattan over the bridge to the countryside of Welfare Island, she was always surprised. She played for a long time on the green banks of the river. She picked wildflowers in the fields, and then she went up to the men's ward.

One afternoon, she arrived as usual. Michael felt very weak and asked her to lean on his back and support him while he sat at the edge of the bed eating dinner. She did so, and that is how come, when he fell back and died, it was in her thin little arms that he lay. He was very heavy. She held him so, just for a minute or two, then let him fall to the bed. She told an orderly and went home. She didn't cry because she didn't like him. She spoke first to a neighbor, and then together they told her mother.

Now this is the main part of the story:

The man Michael was not her father. Her father had died when she was little. Maria, with the other small children, had tried to live through the hard times in the best way. She moved in with different, nearly related families in the neighborhood and worked hard helping out in their houses. She worked well, and it happened that she was also known for the fine bread she baked. She would live in a good friend's house for a while baking magnificent bread. But soon, the husband of the house would say, 'Maria bakes wonderful bread. Why can't you learn to bake bread like that?' He would probably then seem to admire her in other ways. Wisely, the wife would ask Maria to please find another home.

One day at the spring street festival, she met a man named Michael, a relative of friends. They couldn't marry because Michael had a wife in Italy. In order to live with him, Maria explained the following truths to her reasonable head:

1. This man Michael was tall with a peculiar scar on his shoulder. Her husband had been unusually tall and had had a scar on his shoulder.
2. This man was redheaded. Her dead husband had been redheaded.
3. This man was a tailor. Her husband had been a tailor.
4. His name was Michael. Her husband had been called Michael.

In this way, persuading her own understanding, Maria was able to not live alone at an important time in her life, to have a father for the good of her children's character, a man in her bed for comfort, a husband to serve. Still and all, though he died in her arms, Anna, the child, didn't like him at all. It was a pity, because he had always called her 'my little one'. Every day she had visited him, she had found him in the hallway waiting, or at the edge of his white bed, and she had called out, 'Hey, Zio, here's your dinner. Mama sent it. I have to go now.'

Distance

You would certainly be glad to meet me. I was the lady who appreciated youth. Yes, all that happy time, I was not like some. It did not go by me like a flitting dream. Tuesdays and Wednesdays was as gay as Saturday nights.

Have I suffered since? No sir, we've had as good times as this country gives: cars, renting in Jersey summers, TV the minute it first came out, everything grand for the kitchen. I have no complaints worth troubling the manager about.

Still, it is like a long hopeless homesickness my missing those young days. To me, they're like my own place that I have gone away from forever, and I have lived all the time since among great pleasures but in a foreign town. Well, O.K. Farewell, certain years.

But that's why I have an understanding of that girl Ginny downstairs and her kids. They're runty, underdeveloped. No sun, no beef. Noodles, beans, cabbage. Well, my mother off the boat knew better than that.

Once upon a time, as they say, her house was the spit of mine. You could hear it up and down the air shaft, the singing from her kitchen, banjo playing in the parlor, she would admit it first, there was a tambourine in the bedroom. Her husband wasn't American. He had black hair – like Gypsies do.

And everything then was spotless, the kitchen was all inlay like broken-up bathroom tiles, pale lavender. Formica on all surfaces, everything bright. The shine of the pots and pans was turned to stun the eyes of company . . . you could see it, the mischievousness of that family home.

Of course, on account of misery now, she's always dirty. Crying crying crying. She would not let tap water touch her.

Five ladies on the block, old friends, nosy, me not included, got up a meeting and wrote a petition to Child Welfare. I already knew it was useless, as the requirement is more than dirt, drunkenness, and a little once-in-a-while whoring. That is probably something why the children in our city are in such a state. I've noticed it for years, though it's not my business. Mothers and fathers get up when they wish, half being snuggled in relief, go to bed in the afternoon with their rumpy bumpy sweethearts pumping away before 3 p.m. (So help me.) Child Welfare does not show its concern. No matter who writes them. People of influence, known in the district, even the district leader, my cousin Leonie, who put her all into electing the mayor, she doesn't get a reply if she sends in a note. So why should I, as I'm nothing but a Primary Day poll watcher?

Anyhow there are different kinds coming into this neighborhood, and I do not mean the colored people alone. I mean people like you and me, religious, clean, many of these have gone rotten. I go along with live and let live, but what of the children?

Ginny's husband ran off with a Puerto Rican girl who shaved between the legs. This is common knowledge and well known or I'd never say it. When Ginny heard that he was going around with this girl, she did it too, hoping to entice him back, but he got nauseated by her and that tipped the scales.

Men fall for terrible weirdos in a dumb way more and more as they get older; my old man, fond of me as he constantly was, often did. I never give it the courtesy of my attention. My advice to mothers and wives: Do not imitate the dimwit's girlfriends. You will be damnfool-looking, what with your age and all. Have you heard the saying 'Old dough won't rise in a new oven'?

Well, you know it, I know it, even the punks and the queers that have wiggled their way into this building are in on the inside dope. John, my son, is a constant attendant now at that Ginny's poor grubby flat. Tired, who can blame him, of his Margaret's shiny face all pitted and potted by Jersey smog. My grandchildren, of which I have close to six, are pale, as the sun can't have a chance through the oil in Jersey. Even the leaves of the trees there won't turn a greenish green.

John! Look me in the eye once in a while! What a good little twig you were always, we did try to get you out with the boys and you did go when we asked you. After school when he was eight or so, we got him into a bunch of Cub Scouts, a very raw bunch with a jawful of curse words. All of them tough and wild, but at attention when the master came among them. Right turn! You would've thought the United States Marines was in charge they was that accurate in marching, and my husband on Tuesday nights taught them what he recalled from being a sergeant. Hup! two, three, four! I guess is what he knew. But John, good as his posture was, when he come home I give him a hug and a kiss and 'What'd you do today at Scouts, son? Have a parade, darling?'

'Oh no, Mother,' says he. 'Mrs. McClennon was collecting money the whole time for the district-wide picnic, so I just got the crayons and I drew this here picture of Our Blessed Mother,' he says.

That's my John. And if you come with a Polaroid Land camera, you couldn't snap much clearer.

People have asked and it's none of their business: Why didn't the two of you (meaning Jack and me – both working) send the one boy you had left to college?

Well now to be honest, he would have had only grief in college. Truth: he was not bright. His father was not bright, and he inherited his father's brains. Our Michael was clever. But Michael is dead. We had it all talked over, his father and me, the conclusion we come to: a trade. My husband Jack was well established in the union from its early struggle, he was strong and loyal. John just floated in on the ease of recommendation and being related. We were wise. It's proved.

For now (this very minute) he's a successful man with a wonderful name in the building trade, and he has a small side business in cement plaques, his own beautiful home, and every kid of his dressed like the priest's nephew.

But don't think I'm the only one that seen Ginny and John when they were the pearls of this pitchy pigsty block. Oh, there were many, and they are still around holding the picture in the muck under their skulls, like crabs. And I am never surprised when they speak of it, when they try to make something of it, that nice-looking time, as though I was in charge of its passing.

'Ha,' Jack said about twenty times that year, 'she's a wild little bird. Our Johnny's dying . . . Watch her.'

O.K. Wild enough, I guess. But no wilder than me when *I* was seventeen, as I never told him, that whole year, long ago, mashing the grass of Central Park with Anthony Aldo. Why I'd put my wildness up against any wildness of present day, though I didn't want Jack to know. For he was a simple man . . . Put in the hours of a wop, thank God pulled the overtime of a decent American. I didn't like to worry worry worry him. He was kindness itself, as they say.

He come home 6 p.m. I come home 6:15 p.m. from where I was afternoon cashier. Put supper up. Seven o'clock, we ate it up and washed the dishes; 7:45 p.m. sharp, if there was no company present and the boy out visiting, he liked his pussy. Quick and very neat. By 8:15 he had showered every bit of it away. I give him his little whiskey. He tried that blabbermouth *Journal-American* for news of the world. It was too much. Good night, Mr. Raftery, my pal.

Leaving me, thank goodness, the cream of the TV and a cup of sweet wine till midnight. Though I liked the attentions as a man he daily give me as a woman, it hardly seemed to tire me as it exhausted him. I could stay with the *Late Show* not fluttering an eyelid till the very end of the last commercial. My wildness as a girl is my own life's business, no one else's.

Now: As a token for friendship under God, John'd given Ginny his high-school GO pin, though he was already a working man. He couldn't of given her his union card (that never got customary), though he did take her to a famous dinner in honor of Klaus Schnauer: thirty-five years at Camillo, the only heinie they ever let into that American local; he was a disgusting fat-bottomed Nazi so help me, he could've turned you into a pink Commie, his ass, excuse me, was that fat. Well, as usual for that young-hearted gang, Saturday night went on and on, it give a terrible jolt to Sunday morning, and John staggered in to breakfast, not shaved or anything. (A man, husband, son, or lodger should be shaved at breakfast.) 'Mother,' he said, 'I am going to ask Virginia to marry me.'

'I told you so,' said my husband and dropped the funnies on his bacon.

'You are?' I said.

'I am, and if God is good, she'll have me.'

'No blasphemy intended,' I said, 'but He'll have to be off in the old country fishing if she says yes.'

'Mother!' said John. He is a nice boy, loyal to friends and good.

'She'll go out with anyone at all,' I said.

'Oh, Mother!' said John, meaning they weren't engaged, and she could do what she wanted.

'Go out is nothing,' I said. 'I seen her only last Friday night with Pete, his arm around her, going into Phelan's.'

'Pete's like that, Mother,' meaning it was no fault of hers.

'Then what of last Saturday night, you had to go to the show yourself as if there wasn't no one else in the Borough of Manhattan to take to a movie, and when you was gone I seen her buy two Cokes at Carlo's and head straight to the third floor to John Kameron's . . .'

'So? So?'

'. . . and come out at 11 p.m. and *his* arm was around her.'

'So?'

'. . . and his hand was well under her sweater.'

'That's not so, Mother.'

'It *is* so, and tell me, young man, how you'll feel married to a girl that every wild boy on the block has been leaning his thumbs on her titties like she was a Carvel dairy counter, tell me that? '

'Dolly!' says Jack. 'You went too far.'

John just looked at me as red and dumb as a baby's knees.

'I haven't gone far enough into the facts, and I'm not ready to come out yet, and you listen to me, Johnny Raftery, you're somebody's jackass, I'll tell you, you look out that front window and I bet you if you got yourself your dad's spyglass you would see some track of your little lady. I think there are evenings she don't get out of the back of that trailer truck parked over there. and it's no trouble at all for Pete or Kameron's half-witted kid to get his way of her. Listen Johnny, there isn't a grown-up woman who was sitting on the stoop last Sunday when it was so damn windy that doesn't know that Ginny don't wear underpants.

'Oh, Dolly,' says my husband, and plops his head into his hands.

'I'm going, Mother, that's libel, I'll have her sue you for libel,' dopey John starts to holler out of his tomato-red face. 'I'm going and I'll ask her and I love her and I don't care what you say. Truth or lies, I don't care.'

'And if you go, Johnny,' I said, calm as a dead fish, my eyes rolling up to pray and be heeded, 'this is what I must do,' and I took a kitchen knife, a bit blunt, and plunged it at least an eighth of an inch in the fat of my heart. I guess that the heart of a middle-aged lady is jammed in deeper than an eighth of an inch, for I am here to tell the tale. But some blood did come soon, to my son's staring; it touched my nightie and spread out on my bathrobe, and it was as red on my apron as a picture in an Italian church. John fell down on his knees and hid his head in my lap . He cried, 'Mother, Mother, you've hurt yourself. ' My husband didn't say a word to me. He kept his madness in his teeth, but he told me later, Face it: the feelings in his heart was cracked.

I met Ginny the next morning in Carlo's store. She didn't look at me. Then she did. Then she said, 'It's a nice day, Mrs. Raftery.'

'Mm,' I said. (It was.) 'How can you tell the kind of day it is?' (I don't know what I meant by that.)

'What's wrong, Mrs. Raftery?' she said.

'Hah! wrong?' I asked.

'Well, you know, I mean, you act mad at me, you don't seem to like me this morning.' She made a little laugh.

'I do. I like you a great deal,' I said, outwitting her. 'It's you, you know, you don't like Johnny. You don't.'

'What?' she said, her head popping up to catch sight of that reply.

'Don't don't don't,' I said. 'Don't don't!' I hollered, giving Ginny's arm a tug. 'Let's get out of here. Ginny, you don't like John. You'd let him court you, squeeze you, and he's very good, he wouldn't press you further.'

'You ought to mind your business,' says Ginny very soft, me being the elder (but with tears).

'My son is my business.'

'No,' she says, 'he's his own.'

'My son is my business. I have one son left, and he's my business.'

'No,' she says. 'He's his own.'

MY SON IS MY BUSINESS. BY LOVE AND DUTY.

'Oh no,' she says. Soft because I am the older one, but very strong. (I've noticed it. All of a sudden they look at you, and then it comes to them, young people, they are bound to outlast you, so they temper up their icy steel and stare into about an inch away from you a lot. Have you noticed it?)

At home, I said, 'Jack now, the boy needs guidance. Do you want him to spend the rest of his life in bed with an orphan on welfare? '

'Oh,' said Jack. 'She's an orphan, is she? It's just her mother that's dead. What has one thing to do with another? You're a pushy damn woman, Dolly. I don't know what use you are . . .'

What came next often happens in a family, causing sorrow at the time. Looking back, it's a speck compared to life.

For: Following this conversation, Jack didn't deal with me at all, and he broke his many years' after-supper habits and took long walks. That's what killed him, I think, for he was a habitual person.

And: Alongside him on one of these walks was seen a skinny crosstown lady, known to many people over by Tompkins Square – wears a giant Ukrainian cross in and out of the tub, to keep from going down the drain, I guess.

'In that case, the hell with you,' is what I said. 'I don't care. Get yourself a cold-water flat on Avenue D.'

'Why not? I'll go. O.K.,' said Jack. I think he figured a couple of weeks' vacation with his little cuntski and her color television would cool his requirements.

'Stay off the block,' I said, 'you slippery relic. I'll send your shirts by the diaper-service man.'

'Mother,' said poor John, when he noticed his dad's absence, 'what's happening to you? The way you talk. To Dad. It's the wine, Mother. I know it.'

'You're a bloated beer guzzler!' I said quietly. (People that drink beer are envious against the ones in favor of wine. Though my dad was a mick in cotton socks, in his house, we had a choice.)

'No, Mother, I mean you're not clear sometimes.'

'Crazy, you mean, son. Huh? Split personality?'

'Something's wrong!' he said. 'Don't you want Dad back?' He was nervous to his fingernails.

'Mind your business, he'll be back, it's happened before, Mr. Two-Weeks-Old.'

'What?' he said, horrified.

'You're blind as a bat, Mr. Just Born. Where was you three Christmases ago?'

'What! But Mother! Didn't you feel terrible? Terrible! How'd you stand for him acting that way? Dad!'

'Now quit it, John, you're a damnfool kid. Sure I don't want to look at his dumb face being pleased. That'd kill.'

'Mother, it's not right.'

'Phoo, go to work and mind your business, sonny boy.'

'It is my business,' he said, 'and don't call me sonny.'

About two months later, John came home with Margaret, both of them blistered from Lake Hopatcong-at ninety-four degrees. I will be fair. She was not yet ruined by Jersey air, and she was not too terrible-looking, at least to the eye of a cleanminded boy.

'This is Margaret,' he says. 'She's from Monmouth, Jersey.'

'Just come over on the *Queen Mary*, dear?' I asked for the joke in it.

'I have to get her home for supper. Her father's strict.'

'Sure,' I said, 'have a Coke first.'

'Oh, thank you so much,' says Margaret. 'Thank you, thank you, thank you, Mrs. Raftery.'

'Has she blood in her?' hollered Jack after his shower. He had come home by then, skinny and dissatisfied. Is there satisfaction anywhere in getting old?

John didn't inquire an O.K. of his dad or me, nor answer to nobody Yes or No. He was that age that couldn't live without a wife. He had to use this Margaret.

It was his time to go forward like we all did once. And he has. Number One: She is kept plugged up with babies. Number Two: As people nowadays need a house, he has bought one and tangled it around in Latin bushes. Nobody but the principal at Holy Redeemer High knows what the little tags on the twigs say. Every evening after hard work you can find him with a hose scrubbing down his lawn. His oldest kid is now fourteen and useless. The littlest one is four, and she reminds me of me with the flashiest eyes and a little tongue sharpened to a scrappy point.

'How come you never named one for *me*, Margaret?' I asked her straight in her face.

'Oh,' she said, 'there's only the two girls, Teresa, for my mother, and Cathleen, for my best sister. The very next'll be for you.'

'What? Next! Are you trying to kill my son?' I asked her. 'Why he has to be working nights as it is. You don't look well, you know. You ought to see a smart Jewish doctor and get your tubes tied up.'

'Oh,' she said, 'never!'

I have to tease a little to grapple any sort of a reply out of her. But mostly it doesn't work. It is something like I am a crazy construction worker in conversation with fresh cement. Can there be more in the world like her? Don't answer. Time will pass in spite of her slow wits.

In fact it has, for here we are in the present, which is happening now, and I am a famous widow babysitter for whoever thinks I am unbalanced but within reason. I am a grand storybook reader to the little ones. I read like an actress, Joan Crawford or Maureen O'Sullivan, my voice is deeper than it was. So I do make a little extra for needs, though my Johnny sees to the luxuries I must have. I won't move away to strangers. This is my family street, and I don't need to.

And of course as friendship never ends, Johnny comes twice a week foɪ his entertainment to Ginny. Ginny and I do not talk a word, though we often pass. She knows I am right as well as victorious. She's had it unusually lovely (most people don't) – a chance to be some years with a young fellow like Blackie that gave her great rattling shivers, top to bottom, though it was all cut off before youth ended. And as for my Johnny, he now absolutely has her as originally planned and desired, and she depends on him in all things. She requires him. Her children lean on him. They climb up his knees to his shoulder. They cry out the window for him, *John*, *John*, if his dumb Margaret keeps him home.

It's a pity to have become so right and Jack's off stalking the innocent angels.

I wait on the stoop steps to see John on summer nights, as he hasn't enough time to visit me and Ginny both, and I need the sight of him, though I don't know why. I like the street anyway, and the hot night when the ice-cream truck brings all the dirty kids and the big nifty boys with their hunting-around eyes. I put a touch of burgundy on my strawberry ice-cream cone as my father said we could on Sunday, which drives these sozzle-headed ladies up the brown brick wall, so help me Mary.

Now, some serious questions, so far unasked:

What the devil is it all about, the noisiness and the speediness, when it's no distance at all? How come John had to 'put all them courtesy calls into Margaret on his lifelong trip to Ginny? Also, Jack, what was his real nature? Was he for or against? And that Anthony, what *did* he have in mind as I knuckled under again and again (and I know I was the starter)? He did not get me pregnant as in books it happens at once. How come the French priest said to me, crying tears and against his order, 'Oh no, Dolly, if you are *enceinte* [meaning pregnant], he will certainly marry you, poor child, now smile, poor child, for that is the Church's promise to infants born.' To which, how come, tough and cheery as I used to be, all I could say before going off to live and die was: 'No, Father, he doesn't love me.'

Faith in the Afternoon

As for you, fellow independent thinker of the Western Bloc, if you have anything sensible to say, don't wait. Shout it out loud right this minute. In twenty years, give or take a spring, your grandchildren will be lying in sandboxes all over the world, their ears to the ground, listening for signals from long ago. In fact, kneeling now on the great plains in a snootful of gray dust, what do you hear? Pigs oinking, potatoes peeling, Indians running, winter coming?

Faith's head is under the pillow nearly any weekday midnight, asweat with dreams, and she is seasick with ocean sounds, the squealing wind stuck in its rearing tail by high tide.

That is because her grandfather, scoring the salty sea, skated for miles along the Baltic's icy beaches, with a frozen herring in his pocket. And she, all ears, was born in Coney Island.

Who are her antecedents? Mama and Papa of course. Her environment? A brother and a sister with their own sorrow to lead by the nose out of this life. All together they would make a goddamn quadruped bilingual hermaphrodite. Even so, proving their excellence, they bear her no rancor and are always anxious to see her, to see the boys, to take the poor fatherless boys to a picnic with their boys, for a walk, to an ocean, glad to say, we saw Mama

in the Children of Judea, she sends love . . . They never say
snidely, as the siblings of others might, It wouldn't hurt you to
run over, Faith, it's only a subway ride . . .

Hope and Faith and even Charles – who comes glowering
around once a year to see if Faith's capacity for survival has not
been overwhelmed by her susceptibility to abuse – begged their
parents to reconsider the decision to put money down and move
into the Children of Judea. 'Mother,' said Hope, taking off her
eyeglasses, for she did not like even that little window of glass to
come between their mother and herself. 'Now, Mother, how will
you make out with all those *yentas*? Some of them don't even
speak English.' 'I have spoken altogether too much English in my
life,' said Mrs. Darwin. 'If I really liked English that much, I
would move to England.' 'Why don't you go to Israel?' asked
Charles. 'That would at least make sense to people.' 'And leave
you?' she asked, tears in her eyes at the thought of them all alone,
wrecking their lives on the shoals of every day, without her tear-
ful gaze attending.

When Faith thinks of her mother and father in any year, young
or impersonally aged, she notices that they are squatting on the
shore, staring with light eyes at the white waves. Then Faith feels
herself so damply in the swim of things that she considers crawling Channels and Hellesponts and even taking a master's degree
in education in order to exult at last in a profession and get out of
the horseshit trades of this lofty land.

Certain facts may become useful. The Darwins moved to
Coney Island for the air. There was not enough air in Yorkville,
where the grandmother had been planted among German Nazis
and Irish bums by Faith's grandfather, who soon departed alone
in blue pajamas, for death.

Her grandmother pretended she was German in just the same
way that Faith pretends she is an American. Faith's mother flew
in the fat face of all that and, once safely among her own kind in
Coney Island, learned real Yiddish, helped Faith's father, who
was not so good at foreign languages, and as soon as all the verbs
and necessary nouns had been collected under the roof of her

mouth, she took an oath to expostulate in Yiddish and grieve only in Yiddish, and she has kept that oath to this day.

Faith has only visited her parents once since she began to understand that because of Ricardo she would have to be unhappy for a while. Faith really is an American and she was raised up like everyone else to the true assumption of happiness.

No doubt about it, squinting in any direction she is absolutely miserable. She is ashamed of this before her parents. 'You should get help,' says Hope. 'Psychiatry was invented for people like you, Faithful,' says Charles. 'My little blondie, life is short. I'll lay out a certain amount of cash,' says her father. 'When will you be a person,' says her mother.

Their minds are on matters. Severed Jerusalem; the Second World War still occupies their arguments; peaceful uses of atomic energy (is it necessary altogether?); new little waves of anti-Semitism lap the quiet beaches of their accomplishment.

They are naturally disgusted with Faith and her ridiculous position right in the middle of prosperous times. They are ashamed of her willful unhappiness.

All right! Shame then! Shame on them all!

That Ricardo, Faith's first husband, was a sophisticated man. He was proud and happy because men liked him. He was really, he said, a man's man. Like any true man's man, he ran after women too. He was often seen running, in fact, after certain young women on West Eighth Street or leaping little fences in Bedford Mews to catch up with some dear little pussycat.

He called them pet names, which generally referred to certain flaws in their appearance. He called Faith Baldy, although she is not and never will be bald. She is fine-haired and fair, and regards it as part of the lightness of her general construction that when she gathers her hair into an ordinary topknot, the stuff escapes around the contour of her face, making her wisp-haired and easy to blush. He is now living with a shapely girl with white round arms and he calls her Fatty.

When in New York, Faith's first husband lives within floating distance of the Green Coq, a prospering bar where he is well known and greeted loudly as he enters, shoving his current woman gallantly before. He introduces her around – hey, this is Fatty or Baldy. Once there was Bugsy, dragged up from the gutter where she loved to roll immies with Russell the bartender. Then Ricardo, to save her from becoming an old tea bag (his joke), hoisted her on the pulpy rods of his paperbacked culture high above her class, and she still administers her troubles from there, poor girl, her knees gallivanting in air.

Bugsy lives forever behind the Horney curtain of Faith's mind, a terrible end, for she used to be an ordinarily reprehensible derelict, but by the time Ricardo had helped her through two abortions and one lousy winter, she became an alcoholic and a whore for money. She soon gave up spreading for the usual rewards, which are an evening's companionship and a weekend of late breakfasts.

Bugsy was before Faith. Ricardo agreed to be Faith's husband for a couple of years anyway, because Faith in happy overindulgence had become pregnant. Almost at once, she suffered a natural miscarriage, but it was too late. They had been securely married by the state for six weeks when that happened, and so, like the gentleman he may very well be, he resigned himself to her love – a medium-sized, beefy-shouldered man, Indian-black hair, straight and coarse to the fingers, lavender eyes – Faith is perfectly willing to say it herself, to any good listener: she loved Ricardo. She began indeed to love herself, to love the properties which, for a couple of years anyway, extracted such heart-warming activity from him.

Well, Faith argues whenever someone says, 'Oh really, Faithy, what do you mean – love?' She must have loved Ricardo. She had two boys with him. She had them to honor him and his way of loving when sober. He believed and often shouted out loud in the Green Coq, that Newcastle into which he reeled every night, blind with coal, that she'd had those kids to make him a bloody nine-to-fiver.

Nothing, said Faith in those simple days, was further from her mind. For her public part, she had made reasoned statements in the playground, and in the A&P while queued up for the cashier, that odd jobs were a splendid way of making out if you had together agreed on a substandard way of life. For, she explained to the ladies in whom she had confided her entire life, how can a man know his children if he is always out working? How true, that is the trouble with children today, replied the ladies, wishing to be her friend, they never see their daddies.

'Mama,' Faith said, the last time she visited the Children of Judea, 'Ricardo and I aren't going to be together so much anymore.'

'Faithy!' said her mother. 'You have a terrible temper. No, no, listen to me. It happens to many people in their lives. He'll be back in a couple of days. After all, the children . . . just say you're sorry. It isn't even a hill of beans. Nonsense. I thought he was much improved when he was here a couple of months ago. Don't give it a thought. Clean up the house, put in a steak. Tell the children be a little quiet, send them next door for the television. He'll be home before you know it. Don't pay attention. Do up your hair something special. Papa would be more than glad to give you a little cash. We're not poverty-stricken, you know. You only have to tell us you want help. Don't worry. He'll walk in the door tomorrow. When you get home, he'll be turning on the hi-fi.'

'Oh, Mama, Mama, he's tone deaf.'

'Ai, Faithy, you have to do your life a little better than this.'

They sat silently together, their eyes cast down by shame. The doorknob rattled. 'My God, Hegel-Shtein,' whispered Mrs. Darwin. 'Ssh, Faith, don't tell Hegel-Shtein. She thinks everything is her business. Don't even leave a hint.'

Mrs. Hegel-Shtein, president of the Grandmothers' Wool Socks Association, rolled in on oiled wheelchair wheels. She brought a lapful of multicolored wool in skeins. She was an old lady. Mrs. Darwin was really not an old lady. Mrs. Hegel-Shtein had organized this Active Association because children today wear cotton socks all winter. The grandmothers who lose heat at their extremities at a terrible clip are naturally more sensitive to these facts than the present avocated generation of mothers.

'Shalom, darling,' said Mrs. Darwin to Mrs. Hegel-Shtein. 'How's tricks?' she asked bravely.

'Aah,' said Mrs. Hegel-Shtein. 'Mrs. Essie Shifer resigned on account of her wrists.'

'Really? Well, let her come sit with us. Company is healthy.'

'Please, please, what's the therapy value if she only sits? Phooey!' said Mrs. Hegel-Shtein. 'Excuse me, don't tell me that's Faith. Faith? Imagine that. Hope I know, but this is really Faith. So it turns out you really have a little time to see your mother . . . What luck for her you won't be busy forever.'

'Oh, Gittel, I beg you, be quiet,' Faith's mortified mother said. 'I must beg you. Faith comes when she can. She's a mother. She has two little small boys. She works. Did you forget, Gittel, what it was like in those days when they're little babies? Who comes first? The children . . . the little children, they come first.'

'Sure, sure, first, I know all about first. Didn't Archie come first? I had a big honor. I got a Christmas card from Florida from Mr. and Mrs. First. Listen to me, foolish people. I went by them to stay in the summer place, in the woods, near rivers. Only it got no ventilation, the whole place smells from termites and the dog. Please, I beg him, please, Mr. First, I'm a old woman, be sorry for me, I need extra air, leave your door open, I beg, I beg. No, not a word. Bang, every night eleven o'clock, the door gets shut like a rock. For a ten-minute business they close themselves up a whole night long.

'I'm better off in a old ladies' home, I told them. Nobody there is ashamed of a little cross ventilation.'

Mrs. Darwin blushed. Faith said, 'Don't be such a clock watcher, Mrs. Hegel-Shtein.'

Mrs. Hegel-Shtein, who always seemed to know Faith better than Faith knew Mrs. Hegel-Shtein, said, 'All right, all right. You're here, Faithy, don't be lazy. Help out. Here. Hold it, this wool on your hands, your mama will make a ball.' Faith didn't mind. She held the wool out on her arms. Mrs. Darwin twisted and turned it round and round. Mrs. Hegel-Shtein directed in a loud voice, wheeling back and forth and pointing out serious mistakes. 'Celia, Celia,' she cried, 'it should be rounder, you're making a square. Faithy, be more steadier. Move a little. You got infantile paralysis?'

'More wool, more wool,' said Mrs. Darwin, dropping one completed ball into a shopping bag. They were busy as bees in a ladies' murmur about life and lives. They worked. They took vital facts from one another and looked as dedicated as a kibbutz.

The door to Mr. and Mrs. Darwin's room had remained open. Old bearded men walked by, thumbs linked behind their backs, all alike, the leftover army of the Lord. They had stuffed the morning papers under their mattresses, and because of the sorrowful current events they hurried up to the Temple of Judea on the sixth floor, from which they could more easily communicate with God. Ladies leaned on sticks stiffly, their articulations jammed with calcium. They knocked on the open door and said, 'Oi, busy . . .' or 'Mrs. Hegel-Shtein, don't you ever stop?' No one said much to Faith's mother, the vice-president of the Grandmothers' Wool Socks Association.

Hope had warned her: 'Mother, you are only sixty-five years old. You look fifty-five.' 'Youth is in the heart, Hopey. I feel older than Grandma. It's the way I'm constituted. Anyway Papa is practically seventy, he deserves a rest. We have some advantage that we're young enough to make a good adjustment. By the time we're old and miserable, it'll be like at home here.' 'Mother, you'll certainly be an object of suspicion, an interloper, you'll have enemies everywhere.' Hope had been sent to camp lots of years as a kid; she knew a thing or two about group living.

Opposite Faith, her mother swaddled the fat turquoise balls in more and more turquoise wool. Faith swayed gently back and forth along with her outstretched wool-wound arms. It hurt her most filial feelings that, in this acute society, Mrs. Hegel-Shtein should be sought after, admired, indulged . . .

'Well, Ma, what do you hear from the neighborhood?' Faith

asked. She thought they could pass some cheery moments before the hovering shadow of Ricardo shoved a fat thumb in her eye.

'Ah, nothing much,' Mrs. Darwin said.

'Nothing much?' asked Mrs. Hegel-Shtein. 'I heard you correctly said nothing much? You got a letter today from Slovinsky family, your heart stuck in your teeth, Celia, you want to hide this from little innocent Faith. Little baby Faithy. Ssh. Don't tell little children? Hah?'

'Gittel, I must beg you. I have reasons. I must beg you, don't mix in. Oh, I must beg you, Gittel, not to push anymore, I want to say nothing much on this subject.'

'Idiots!' Mrs. Hegel-Shtein whispered low and harsh.

'Did you really hear from the Slovinskys, Mama, really? Oh, you know I'm always interested in Tessie. Oh, you remember what a lot of fun Tess and I used to have when we were kids. I liked her. I never didn't like her.' For some reason Faith addressed Mrs. Hegel-Shtein: 'She was a very beautiful girl.'

'Oh, yeh, beautiful. Young. Beautiful. Very old story. Naturally. Gittel, you stopped winding? Why? The meeting is tonight. Tell Faithy all about Slovinsky, her pal. Faithy got coddled from life already too much.'

'Gittel, I said shut up!' said Mrs. Darwin. 'Shut up!'

(Then to all concerned a short dear remembrance arrived. A policeman, thumping after him along the boardwalk, had arrested Mr. Darwin one Saturday afternoon. He had been distributing leaflets for the Sholem Aleichem School and disagreeing reasonably with his second cousin, who had a different opinion about the past and the future. The leaflet cried out in Yiddish: 'Parents! A little child's voice calls to you, "Papa, Mama, what does it mean to be a Jew in the world today?"' Mrs. Darwin watched them from the boardwalk bench, where she sat getting sun with a shopping bag full of leaflets. The policeman shouted furiously at Mr. and Mrs. Darwin and the old cousin, for they were in an illegal place. Then Faith's mother said to him in the Mayflower voice of a disappearing image of life, 'Shut up, you Cossack!' 'You see,' said Mr. Darwin, 'to a Jew the word "shut up" is a terrible expression, a dirty word, like a sin, because in the beginning, if I remember correctly, was the word! It's a great assault. Get it?')

'Celia, if you don't tell this story now, I roll right out and I don't roll in very soon. Life is life. Everybody today is coddlers.'

'Mama, I want to hear anything you know about Tess, anyway. Please tell me,' Faith asked. 'If you don't tell me, I'll call up Hope. I bet you told her.'

'All stubborn people,' said Mrs. Darwin. 'All right. Tess Slovinsky. You know about the first tragedy, Faith? The first tragedy was she had a child born a monster. A real monster. Nobody saw it. They put it in a home. All right. Then the second child. They went right away ahead immediately and they tried and they had a second child. This one was born full of allergies. It had rashes from orange juice. It choked from milk. Its eyes swoll up from going to the country. All right. Then her husband, Arnold Lever, a very pleasant boy, got a cancer. They chopped off a finger. It got worse. They chopped off a hand. It didn't help. Faithy, that was the end of a lovely boy. That's the letter I got this morning just before you came.'

Mrs. Darwin stopped. Then she looked up at Mrs. Hegel-Shtein and Faith. 'He was an only son,' she said. Mrs. Hegel-Shtein gasped. 'You said an only son!' On deep tracks, the tears rolled down her old cheeks. But she had smiled so peculiarly for seventy-seven years that they suddenly swerved wildly toward her ears and hung like glass from each lobe.

Faith watched her cry and was indifferent. Then she thought a terrible thought. She thought that if Ricardo had lost a leg or so, that would certainly have kept him home. This cheered her a little, but not for long.

'Oh, Mama, Mama, Tessie never guessed what was going to happen to her. We used to play house and she never guessed.'

'Who guesses?' screamed Mrs. Hegel-Shtein. 'Archie is laying down this minute in Florida. Sun is shining on him. He's guessing?'

Mrs. Hegel-Shtein fluttered Faith's heart. She rattled her ribs.

She squashed her sorrow as though it were actually the least toxic of all the world's great poisons.

However, the first one to live with the facts was Mrs. Hegel-Shtein. Eyes dry, she said, 'What about Brauns? The old Braun, the uncle, an idiot, a regular Irgunist, is here.'

'June Braun?' Faith asked. 'My friend June Braun? From Brighton Beach Avenue? That one?'

'Of course, only, that isn't so bad,' Mrs. Darwin said, getting into the spirit of things. 'Junie's husband, an engineer in airplanes. Very serious boy. Papa doesn't like him to this day. He was in the movement. They bought a house in Huntington Harbor with a boat, a garage, a garage for the boat. She looked stunning. She had three boys. Brilliant. The husband played golf with the vice-president, a goy. The future was golden. She was active in everything. One morning they woke up. It's midnight. Someone uncovers a little this, a little that. (I mentioned he was in the movement?) In forty-eight hours, he's blacklisted. Good night Huntington Harbor. Today the whole bunch live with the Brauns in four rooms. I'm sorry for the old people.'

'That's awful, Mama,' Faith said. 'The whole country's in a bad way.'

'Still, Faith, times change. This is an unusual country. You'll travel around the world five times over, you wouldn't see a country like this often. She's up, she's down. It's unusual.'

'Well, what else, Mama?' Faith asked. June Braun didn't sorrow her at all. What did June Braun know about pain? If you go in the dark sea over your head, you have to expect drowning cheerfully. Faith believed that June Braun and her husband whatever-his-name-could-be had gone too deeply into the air pocket of America whence all handouts come, and she accepted their suffocation in good spirit.

'What else, Mama? I know, what about Anita Franklin? What about her? God, was she smart in school! The whole senior class was crazy about her. Very chesty. Remember her, she got her period when she was about nine and three-quarters? Or something like that. You knew her mother very well. You were always in cahoots about something. You and Mrs. Franklin. Mama!'

'You sure you really want to hear, Faithy, you won't be so funny afterward?' She liked telling these stories now, but she was not anxious to tell this one. Still she had warned Faith. 'All right. Well, Anita Franklin. Anita Franklin also didn't guess. You remember she was married way ahead of you and Ricardo to a handsome boy from Harvard. Oh, Gittel, you can imagine what hopes her mother and her father had for her happiness. Arthur Mazzano, you know, Sephardic. They lived in Boston and they knew such smart people. Professors, doctors, the finest people. History-book writers, thinking American people. Oh, Faithy darling. I was invited to the house several times, Christmas, Easter. I met their babies. Little blondies like you were, Faith. He got maybe two Ph.D.s, you know, in different subjects. If someone wanted to ask a question, on what subject, they asked Arthur. At eight months their baby walked. I saw it myself. He wrote articles for Jewish magazines you never heard of, Gittel. Then one day, Anita finds out from the horse's mouth itself, he is fooling around with freshmen. Teenagers. In no time it's in the papers, everybody in court, talking talking talking, some say yes, some no, he was only flirting, you know the way a man flirts with youngsters. But it turns out one of the foolish kids is pregnant.'

'Spanish people,' said Mrs. Hegel-Shtein thoughtfully. 'The men don't like their wives so much. They only get married if it's a good idea.'

Faith bowed her head in sorrow for Anita Franklin, whose blood when she was nine and three-quarters burst from her to strike life and hope into the busy heads of all the girls in the fifth and sixth grades. Anita Franklin, she said to herself, do you think you'll make it all alone? How do you sleep at night, Anita Franklin, the sexiest girl in New Utrecht High? How is it these days, now you are never getting laid anymore by clever Arthur Mazzano, the brilliant Sephardic Scholar and Lecturer? Now it is time that leans across you and not handsome, fair Arthur's mouth on yours, or his intelligent Boy Scouty conflagrating fingers.

At this very moment, the thumb of Ricardo's hovering shadow

jabbed her in her left eye, revealing for all the world the shallowness of her water table. Rice could have been planted at that instant on the terraces of her flesh and sprouted in strength and beauty in the floods that overwhelmed her from that moment on through all the afternoon. For herself and Anita Franklin, Faith bowed her head and wept.

'Going already, Faith?' her father asked. He had poked his darling birdy head with poppy pale eyes into the sun-spotted room. He is not especially good-looking. He is ugly. Faith has often thanked the Germ God and the Gene Goddess and the Great Lords of All Nucleic Acid that none of them looks like him, not even Charles, to whom it would not matter, for Charles has the height for any kind of face. They all look a little bit Teutonish, like their grandmother, who thinks she's German, just kind of light and even-featured, with Charles inclining to considerable jaw. People expect decision from Charles because of that jaw, and he has learned to give it to them – the wit of diagnosis, then inescapable treatment, followed by immediate health. In fact, his important colleagues often refer their wives' lower abdominal distress to Charles. Before he is dead he will be famous. Mr. Darwin hopes he will be famous soon, for in that family people do not live long.

Well, this popeyed, pale-beaked father of Faith's peered through the room into the glassy attack of the afternoon sun, couldn't focus on tears, or bitten lips for that matter, but saw Faith rise to look for her jacket in the closet.

'If you really have to go, I'll walk you, Faithy. Sweetheart, I haven't seen you in a long time,' he said. He withdrew to wait in the hallway, well out of the circle of Mrs. Hegel-Shtein's grappling magnetism.

Faith kissed her mother, who whispered into her damp ear, 'Be something, don't be a dishrag. You have two babies to raise.' She kissed Mrs. Hegel-Shtein, because they had been brought up that way, not to hurt anyone's feelings, particularly if they loathed them, and they were much older.

Faith and her father walked through the light-green halls in silence to the life-giving lobby, where rosy, well-dressed families continued to arrive in order to sit for twenty minutes alongside their used-up elders. Some terrible political arguments about Jews in Russia now were taking place near the information desk. Faith paid no attention but moved toward the door, breathing deeply. She tried to keep her father behind her until she could meet the commitments of her face. 'Don't rush, sweetheart,' he said. 'Don't rush, I'm not like these old cockers here, but I am no chicken definitely.'

Gallantly he took her arm. 'What's the good word?' he asked. 'Well, no news isn't bad news, I hope?'

'So long, Chuck!' he called as they passed the iron gate over which, in stunning steel cursive, a welder had inscribed *The Children of Judea*. 'Chuckle, chuckle,' said her father, grasping her elbow more firmly, 'what a name for a grown-up man!'

She turned to give him a big smile. He deserved an enormous smile, but she had only a big one available.

'Listen, Faithl, I wrote a poem, I want you to hear. Listen. I wrote it in Yiddish, I'll translate it in my head:

Childhood passes
Youth passes
Also the prime of life passes.
Old age passes.
Why do you believe, my daughters,
That old age is different?

'What do you say, Faithy? You know a whole bunch of artists and writers.'

'What do I say? Papa.' She stopped stock-still. 'You're marvelous. That's like a Japanese Psalm of David.'

'You think it's good?'

'I love it, Pa. It's marvelous.'

'Well . . . you know, I might give up all this political stuff, if you really like it. I'm at a loss these days. It's a transition. Don't

laugh at me, Faithy. You'll have to survive just such events someday yourself. Learn from life. Mine. I was going to organize the
help. You know, the guards, the elevator boys – colored fellows,
mostly. You notice, they're coming up in the world. Regardless of
hopes, I never expected it in my lifetime. The war, I suppose, did
it. Faith, what do you think? The war made Jews Americans and
Negroes Jews. Ha ha. What do you think of that for an article?
"The Negro: Outside In at Last."'

'Someone wrote something like that.'

'Is that a fact? It's in the air. I tell you, I'm full of ideas. I don't
have a soul to talk to. I'm used to your mother, only a funny thing
happened to her, Faithy. We were so close. We're still friendly,
don't take me the wrong way, but I mean a funny thing, she likes
to be with the women lately. Loves to be with that insane, perse-
cution, delusions-of-grandeur, paranoical Mrs. Hegel-Shtein. I
can't stand her. She isn't a woman men can stand. Still, she got
married. Your mother says, Be polite, Sid; I am polite. I always
loved the ladies to a flaw, Faithy, but Mrs. Hegel-Shtein knocks at
our room at 9 a.m. and I'm an orphan till lunch. She has magic
powers. Also she oils up her wheelchair all afternoon so she can
sneak around. Did you ever hear of a wheelchair you couldn't
hear coming? My child, believe me, what your mother sees in her
is a shady mystery. How could I put it? That woman has a whole
bag of spitballs for the world. And also a bitter crippled life.'

They had come to the subway entrance. 'Well, Pa, I guess I
have to go now. I left the kids with a friend.'

He shut his mouth. Then he laughed. 'Aaah, a talky old
man . . .'

'Oh no, Pa, not at all. No. I loved talking to you, but I left the
kids with a friend, Pa.'

'I know how it is when they're little, you're tied down, Faith.
Oh, we couldn't go anywhere for years. I went only to meetings,
that's all. I didn't like to go to a movie without your mother and
enjoy myself. They didn't have babysitters in those days. A wonderful invention, babysitters. With this invention two people
could be lovers forever.

'Oh!' he gasped, 'my darling girl, excuse me . . .' Faith was surprised at his exclamation because the tears had come to her eyes
before she felt their pain.

'Ah, I see now how the land lies. I see you have trouble. You
picked yourself out a hard world to raise a family.'

'I have to go, Pa.'

'Sure.'

She kissed him and started down the stairs.

'Faith,' he called, 'can you come soon?'

'Oh, Pa,' she said, four steps below him, looking up, 'I can't
come until I'm a little happy.'

'Happy!' He leaned over the rail and tried to hold her eyes. But
that is hard to do, for eyes are born dodgers and know a whole
circumference of ways out of a bad spot. 'Don't be selfish, Faithy,
bring the boys, come.'

'They're so noisy, Pa.'

'Bring the boys, sweetheart. I love their little goyish faces.'

'O.K., O.K.,' she said, wanting only to go quickly. 'I will, Pa, I
will.'

Mr. Darwin reached for her fingers through the rail. He held
them tightly and touched them to her wet cheeks. Then he said,
'Aaah . . .' an explosion of nausea, absolute digestive disgust.
And before she could turn away from the old age of his insulted
face and run home down the subway stairs, he had dropped her
sweating hand out of his own and turned away from her.

Gloomy Tune

There is a family nearly everybody knows. The children of this family are named Bobo, Bibi, Doody, Dodo, Neddy, Yoyo, Butch, Put Put, and Beep.

Some are girls and some are boys.

The girls are mean babysitters for mothers. The boys plan to join the army.

The two oldest mean babysitters go out to parties a lot. Sometimes they jerk people off. They really like to.

They are very narrow-minded. They never have an idea. But they like to be right. They never listen to anyone else's ideas.

One after another, Dodo, Neddy, Yoyo, and Put Put got the sisters at the school into a state. The sisters had to give up on them and they got dumped where they belonged for being fresh: right in the public school.

Around four years old, they began to be bad by cursing, and they went on from there.

First they said ass, then bitch, then fuckn bitch. Then when they got a little bigger, motherfuckn bitch, and so on, but I don't like to say.

The sister was strict first, very angry and cold as ice. You can hardly blame her. She wasn't ever a mother, had children, or done anything like that.

She was strict and she was right to be strict. Of course, no strictness at home is the real reason for boldness and freshness.

Then the sister wanted to try kindness too. She spoke very kindly. She took all her own time to sit, especially with Neddy who was so cute, and she helped him in arithmetic.

She was good. She taught Yoyo checkers. But his mind wasn't on it. When kindness was useless, she had to say in each case, As far as our school is concerned, sorry. God help you, you must go. You don't deserve a wonderful education. There's so many waiting behind you just for the chance.

She went to see their mother, who was doing the wash in a terrible hurry before going to work. I don't know what it is, sister, the mother said. They get in with the tough kids moving in the neighborhood, you know the ones I mean.

Oh, oh, said the sister who was tired of always hearing mean gossip, oh, oh, whose children are we, dear missus, every single one of us?

The mother didn't say a word. Because she knew the sister couldn't understand a thing. Now, the sister didn't know what it was like to live next door to all kinds.

Ah listen sister dear, said the mother, could you keep an eye on Put Put? Bobo's gonna be in any minute to watch out for him. I been late four times already on that job. I better go so help me. What the hell's holding that girl up? You don't know what's gone on in the high schools today. Sister, I know your time ain't your own.

Now you better hurry, said sister, getting to perspire in the place. Oh I am sorry about Neddy. And Yoyo. Oh, how I wish we could hold them.

Of course public school being what it is, they didn't improve. Got worse and began to say, Go suck your father's dick. I don't think they really understood what they were saying.

They never stole. They had a teeny knife. They pushed people on the slides and knocked them all over the playground. They wouldn't murder anyone I think.

They cursed a lot and pushed back a lot. Someone usually

pushed them first or cursed them first. They had a right to curse back or push back.

One day, not later than was expected, Chuchi Gomez slipped in an olive-oil puddle left by a lady whose bottle broke. She picked up the bottle pieces, but didn't do a thing about the oil. I wouldn't know what to do about the oil either.

Chuchi said, turning to Yoyo in back of him, Why you push me bastard?

Who pushed you, you dope? said Yoyo.

You dumb bastard, you push me. I feel over here on my shoulder, you push me.

Aah go on, I didn push you, said Yoyo.

I seen you push me. I feeled you push me. Who you think you go around pushin. Bastard.

Who you callin bastard, you big mouth. You call me a bastard?

Yeh, said Chuchi, the way I figure, you a motherfuckn bastard.

You call me a motherfuckn bastard?

Yeh, you. I call you that. You see this here oil. That's what I call you.

Then Yoyo was so mad because he and Chuchi had plans to go to the dock for eels Sunday. Now he couldn't have any more plans with Chuchi.

So he hollered, You better not say my mother's name, you hear me, Chuchi stinking Gomez. Your whole family's a fuckn bitches starting with your father and mother and Eddie and Ramon and Lilli and all the way the whole bunch and your gramma too.

Then he picked up a board with two nails in it and clonked Chuchi on the shoulder.

That isn't such a bloody place, but with the oil and blood and all, if you got a little vinegar, you could of pickled Chuchi.

Then Chuchi yelped and screamed, Don' you murder me. And he ran home to his gramma who was in charge of him.

His gramma lay right down in bed when she saw Chuchi and hollered, I don' wanna see no more in this bad country. Kill me, I beg you, somebody.

No, no, said Chuchi, don't feel so bad Gramma. It' wasn't my fault. He started it. You better take me to the clinic.

His gramma was disgusted that she couldn't even lie down a minute in her age to holler a little. But she had to take Chuchi to the clinic. They gave him a couple of shots for nail poisoning.

Well you see how Yoyo got well known for using a knife. The people from Greenwich House to Hudson Guild know his name. He is bold and hopeless.

In school he gets prayed for every day by all the kids, girls or boys.

Living

Two weeks before Christmas, Ellen called me and said, 'Faith, I'm dying.' That week I was dying too.

After we talked, I felt worse. I left the kids alone and ran down to the corner for a quick sip among living creatures. But Julie's and all the other bars were full of men and women gulping a hot whiskey before hustling off to make love.

People require strengthening before the acts of life.

I drank a little California Mountain Red at home and thought – why not – wherever you turn someone is shouting give me liberty or I give you death. Perfectly sensible, thing-owning, Church-fearing neighbors flop their hands over their ears at the sound of a siren to keep fallout from taking hold of their internal organs. You have to be cockeyed to love, and blind in order to look out the window at your own ice-cold street.

I really was dying. I was bleeding. The doctor said, 'You can't bleed forever. Either you run out of blood or you stop. No one bleeds forever.'

It seemed *I* was going to bleed forever. When Ellen called to say she was dying, I said this clear sentence: 'Please! I'm dying too, Ellen.'

Then she said, 'Oh, oh, Faithy, I didn't know.' She said, 'Faith, what'll we do? About the kids. Who'll take care of them? I'm too scared to think.'

I was frightened too, but I only wanted the kids to stay out of the bathroom. I didn't worry about them. I worried about me. They were noisy. They came home from school too early. They made a racket.

'I may have another couple of months,' Ellen said. 'The doctor said he never saw anyone with so little will to live. I don't want to live, he thinks. But Faithy, I do, I do. It's just I'm scared.'

I could hardly take my mind off this blood. Its hurry to leave me was draining the red out from under my eyelids and the sunburn off my cheeks. It was all rising from my cold toes to find the quickest way out.

'Life isn't that great Ellen,' I said. 'We've had nothing but crummy days and crummy guys and no money and broke all the time and cockroaches and nothing to do on Sunday but take the kids to Central Park and row on that lousy lake. What's so great, Ellen? What's the big loss? Live a couple more years. See the kids and the whole cruddy thing, every cheese hole in the world go up in heat blast firewaves . . .'

'I want to see it all,' Ellen said.

I felt a great gob making its dizzy exit.

'Can't talk,' I said. 'I think I'm fainting.'

Around the holly season, I began to dry up. My sister took the kids for a while so I could stay home quietly making hemoglobin, red corpuscles, etc., with no interruption. I was in such first-class shape by New Year's, I nearly got knocked up again. My little boys came home. They were tall and handsome.

Three weeks after Christmas, Ellen died. At her funeral at that very neat church on the Bowery, her son took a minute out of crying to tell me, 'Don't worry Faith, my mother made sure of everything. She took care of me from her job. The man came and said so.'

'Oh. Shall I adopt you anyway?' I asked, wondering, if he said yes, where the money, the room, another ten minutes of good nights, where they would all come from. He was a little older than my kids. He would soon need a good encyclopedia, a chemistry set. 'Listen Billy, tell me the truth. Shall I adopt you? '

He stopped all his tears. 'Why thanks. Oh no. I have an uncle in Springfield. I'm going to him. I'll have it O.K. It's in the country. I have cousins there.'

'Well,' I said, relieved. 'I just love you Billy. You're the most wonderful boy. Ellen must be so proud of you.'

He stepped away and said, 'She's not anything of anything, Faith.' Then he went to Springfield. I don't think I'll see him again.

But I often long to talk to Ellen, with whom, after all, I have done a million things in these scary, private years. We drove the kids up every damn rock in Central Park. On Easter Sunday, we pasted white doves on blue posters and prayed on Eighth Street for peace. Then we were tired and screamed at the kids. The boys were babies. For a joke we stapled their snowsuits to our skirts and in a rage of slavery every Saturday for weeks we marched across the bridges that connect Manhattan to the world. We shared apartments, jobs, and stuck-up studs. And then, two weeks before last Christmas, we were dying.

Come On, Ye Sons of Art

The way Zandakis comes on smiling! says Jerry Cook, biggest archbishopric in New Jersey in the palm of his hand; shy saints, relics all kinds; painted monks blessed by the dumbest ladies, bawling madonnas.

Everywhere in America, he says, giving Kitty a morning hour, New Jersey and Long Island man is looking at God and about Him, says Jerry Cook, I dream.

Oh, he says further, turning over to stare, as far as money is concerned, I love the masters. Baby. admit it, the masters are scientists. They add and they multiply. After that they water and they weigh. They're artists. They lay low. They are smiling in a hot bath and the whole damn East Coast leather-goods industry grows up out of the crap in their teeth. They are bulldozers. Two Jew experts in any regular recession can mash twenty-five miserable Syrians. One old Greek, he's half asleep, he puts his marble shoulder on fifty Jews. Right away a hundred thousand plastic briefcases get dumped into bargain bins of Woolworth, New York. Don't mention the Japanese.

Why not? asked Kitty.

Never, said Jerry Cook, no matter to whom, I never mention the Japanese.

Who Cook worked for was Gladstein. There were billings up

and down 46, 1, 22 for maybe 285,000 all in secular goods. If you see a cheap wallet in Orange County, Jerry Cook put it there.

But what is Gladstein compared to Zandakis? Zandakis, so help me, he is touched by the pinky of the Holy Spirit and the palm of Eastern Orthodox. You can see Gladstein from here, put-putting behind that greasy genius, giving out 20-by-60 Flushing building lots at swamp-bottom prices to his wife's nephews. Dumbhead Gladstein is not even afraid of Taiwan. He is on the high seas, but he thinks it's Central Park Lake. He holds a dance for the showoff of it all once a month out on deck, which is a twentieth-floor penthouse over Broadway and Seventh Avenue, the black tidewaters. In the war he turned old maid's sweater buttons into golden captain's buttons and internal security exploded in him – to his fingertips – like a dumdum, and now he includes the switchboard girls in his party, the key-punch girls, the Dictaphone girls, the groovy bookkeepers, he even includes Jerry Cook, very democratic.

Only Karl Marx, the fly in the ointment, knows how come Zandakis turned on Gladstein just when his in-laws loved him the most and ground him into drygoods. In a minute 325,000 little zippered real-leather ladies' change purses were rammed into the digestion of starving Mrs. Lonesome, the Jersey Consumer.

Envy of Zandakis and pain about Gladstein made Jerry Cook bitter.

Business! he said. You think I'm in business. You think Gladstein is business – with his Fulton Street molds and his Florentine bookmarks. You think tobacco pouches is business! He bit his nails.

No! But diamonds! Kitty, say it to me, say diamonds. he said.

O.K. Diamonds, she said.

Well, that's better. That's business. I call that business. I should go right to diamonds. Kitty, it's a fact, old bags, you slip them the salami nice, they buy anything. That's what I hear everywhere.

Don't go into diamonds, said Kitty.

Oh yes, he said, giving the pillow a rabbit punch. I know you

Kitty. You're one of that crowd. You're the kind thinks the world is round. Not like my sister, he said. Not Anna Marie. She knows the real shape. She lived, Anna Marie. What did she have, when she was a kid, what'd my father give her, a little factory to begin with, embroidery, junk, but she's shrewd and crooked and she understands. My two brothers are crooked. Crooked, crooked. They have crooked wives. The only one is not crooked, the one who is straight and dumb like you Kitty – Kitty, Kitty – he said, dragging her to him for a minute's kiss – is her husband, Anna Marie's. He was always dumb and straight, but they have got him now, all knotted up, you wouldn't unravel him if you started in August.

Kitty, with your personality, you should be in some business. Only for a year, to buy and sell, it's a gimmick.

But they are thieves. Baby. My brothers. Oh listen they worked for famous builders one time. They're known. Planit Brothers. Millions of dollars. You don't know reality. Kitty, you're not in contact, if you don't realize what a million dollars is. (It is one and six zeroes running after.) That was the Planit Corner Cottages, Every Cottage a Corner Plot. How they did it was short blocks. Every penny they stole from the government. So? What's the government for? The people? Kitty, you're right. And Planit Brothers is people, a very large family.

Four brothers and three sisters, they wouldn't touch birth control with a basement beam. Orthodox. Constructive fucking. Builders, baby.

Meanwhile my brother Skippy mentions $40,000. Come on! What is $40,000. Ask the bank. Go to the bank. They tear up $40,000. They jump up and down on it. They spit on it. They laugh. You want to sink in one stick of a foundation, the cost is maybe $12,000. It disappears into the ground. Into the ground and farewell.

But listen Kitty. Anna Marie is shrewd. She has a head, hollered Jerry Cook, leaping out of bed and rapping his own with his pointing forefinger. Anna Marie, she tells my brothers, while you're working for Planit, take something, for godsakes. Take a little at a time. Don't be greedy. Don't be dumb. The world is an egg, jackasses, suck it. It's pure protein, you won't get fat on your heart. You might get psychosomatic, but you won't get fat.

Jerry Cook sighed. He fell back into bed, exhausted, and talked softly against Kitty's soft breast. Take something, Anna Marie said, sinks, boilers, stoves, washing machines, lay it up, lay it up. Slowly. Where, my brothers ask, should we lay up? Where? they asked. It was my brothers. I wasn't there. I'm not in on it. Kitty, I don't know why, he said sadly. I'm crooked too.

Sure you are, said Kitty.

You guys make me puke, said Anna Marie. I took care of all that already. She had really done that. Taken care of where to stack it away. She had gone and bought a warehouse. In an auction. Where else do you get one?

Tie! Tie bid! the auctioneer hollers. A quarter of a million, screams one sharpie. At the same simultaneous minute, a quarter of a million, screams the other sharpie. Ha! The auctioneer bangs the gavel. Bang! Tie bid!

I never heard of that, said Kitty.

You sheltered yourself, said Jerry Cook. My sister says to him, Marv. You look like a pig half the time. You look like a punk, you don't look like an auctioneer. What do you look like? Name it. Schlep, he says. Laughs. Right-o. Schlep. Listen, Marv, give me this warehouse for 70,000. I'll slip you back 7 and an Olds. Beautiful car, like a horse, she says. I know your wife's a creep, she don't put out. I'll fix you up nice. You don't deserve to look such a bum. Right away he's grateful. Hahahah, breathes hard. He thinks he's getting laid. What? My sister? Anna Marie. Not her. No. She wouldn't do that. Never. Still, that's what he thinks .

My brothers say, Sure, introduce him. A nice brunette, a blonde, redhead, something from Brooklyn. You know? Not Anna Marie. Too smart. I ain't in the roast-beef business, Skippy, she says to my brother Skippy . . .

Because she's not! Anna Marie could be in any business she chose. She learned from my mother and father. They knew. But what did she do when her time came to do? She looked up at the sky. It was empty. Where else could she put her name and fame? Oh Anna Marie. High-risers! she said. Oh, she could choose to be in anything. She could sell tushies in Paris. She could move blondes in Sweden. Crooked, he said, his heart jumping like a fool in his throat. He sat up straight. High-risers!

On the East Side, on the North Side. Democratic. She put one up in Harlem. She named it. She digs spades. Not what you think, Kitty. Digs them. She sees it coming, Anna Marie. She sees who she's dealing with in ten years, twenty years. Life is before her. You have to watch *The New York Times*. The editorial section, who they're for. *Then* do business.

Harriet Tubman Towers, that's what I name you, twenty-seven stories. Looks out over Central Park, Madison Avenue, the Guggenheim Museum. If you happen to live in the back, the Harlem River, bridges, the South Bronx, and a million slaves.

A colonial power I planted here, she says. She missed the boat though, naming it that way. She's putting up another one more west, she already got the name for it, black, like onyx halls, a sphinx fountain, a small Cleopatra's needle in the playground, you know, for the kids to climb on. *Egypt*, she calls it. They like that. She doesn't build, Anna Marie, till she got the name. In the Village, what do you see, for instance: Cézanne, Van Gogh, St. Germain . . . Jerks, transient tenancy, concessions, vacancies in the second year . . . She reads the papers there, *The Villager*, the *Voice*. She sniffs. Anna Marie is shrewd. Quiet, she looks the contractor in the face. *Franz Kline*. And she is oversubscribed the day after they paste the plans up.

You ought to go into business, Kitty. You're not shrewd. But you're loving and you got tolerance. There's a place for that. You wouldn't be a millionaire, but you'd get out of this neighborhood. What have your kids got here, everywhere they go, shvartzes, spics and spades. Not that I got a thing against them, but who needs the advance guard.

Kitty put her finger over his lips. Ssh, she said. I am tolerant and loving.

Come on, Kitty. Did you like the mockies right out of steerage?

They stunk. Those Yids, you could smell them a precinct away. Beards like a garlic farm. What can you do . . . Europe in those days . . . Europe was backwards. Today you could go into a gym with the very same people. People forget today about the backwardness of Europe.

But listen, Kitty, once my sister decided about high-risers . . .

Who? said Kitty. Decided what?

My sister decided. High-risers. That's where her future was. Way up. She called up Skippy. She called up the bank. They each of them got into their own car and they head for the warehouse. Collateral for a life of investments. The warehouse is laying out there in Jersey, in the sun, beautiful, grass all around, a swamp in the back, barbed wire, electrified in case of trouble, a watchman, the windows clean. The bank takes one look, the warehouse is so stuffed, stovepipes are sticking out the window, cable is rolling off the gutters, the bank doesn't have to look twice. It signs right away on the dotted line.

Oh Anna Marie! Out of her head all that came. Jerry, she asks me, what do you use your head for, headaches? Headaches. How come I'm not one of them, Kitty? I asked Skippy for a house once. He said, Sure, I'll give a $35,000 house for maybe 22. Is that good, Kitty? Should he have given it to me straight, Kitty? Oh, if I could lay my hand on some of that jack, if you figure me out a way.

I wish I could help you be more crooked, said Kitty.

He put his hand on Kitty's high belly. Kitty, I would personally put that kid in Harvard if I could figure the right angle.

Well, what happened to Zandakis?

What'd you bring him up for? He's no businessman, he's a murderer and a creep.

Where's Gladstein?

Him too? He doesn't exist. They hung him up by his thumbs in his five-and-ten on 125th Street with mercerized cotton no. 9.

God?

Kitty, you're laughing at me. Don't laugh.

O.K., said Kitty and leaned back into the deep pillows. She thought life on Sunday was worth two weeks of waiting.

Now me, said Jerry. What I am really: I am the Sunday-breakfast chef. I will make thirty pancakes, six per person, eggs, bacon, fresh ham, and a gallon of juice. I will wake up those lazy kids of yours, and I will feed them and feed them until I see some brains wiggling in their dumb heads. I hate a dumb kid. I always think it's me.

Oh, Jerry, said Kitty, what would I do without you?

Well, you wouldn't be knocked up is one thing, he said.

Is that so? said Kitty.

It wasn't cold, but she snuggled down deep under the blanket. It was her friend Faith's grandmother's patchwork quilt that kept her so warm in the warm room. The old windowshades made the morning dusk. She listened to the song of Jerry's brother Skippy's orange radio which was:

'Come, come, ye sons of art . . .'

The bacon curled fearfully on the hot griddle, the waffles popped out of the toaster, and a countertenor called:

Strike the viol
Touch
  oh touch the lute . . .

Well, it was on account of the queen's birthday, the radio commentator said, that such a lot of joy had been transacted in England the busy country, one day when Purcell lived.

Faith in a Tree

Just when I most needed important conversation, a sniff of the man-wide world, that is, at least one brainy companion who could translate my friendly language into his tongue of undying carnal love, I was forced to lounge in our neighborhood park, surrounded by children.

All the children were there. Among the trees, in the arms of statues, toes in the grass, they hopped in and out of dog shit and dug tunnels into mole holes. Wherever the children ran, their mothers stopped to talk.

What a place in democratic time! One God, who was King of the Jews, who unravels the stars to this day with little hydrogen explosions, He can look down from His Holy Headquarters and see us all: heads of girl, ponytails riding the springtime luck, short black bobs, and an occasional eminence of golden wedding rings. He sees south into Brooklyn how Prospect Park lies in its sand-rooted trees among Japanese gardens and police, and beyond us north to dangerous Central Park. Far north, the deer-eyed eland and kudu survive, grazing the open pits of the Bronx Zoo.

But me, the creation of His soft second thought, I am sitting on the twelve-foot-high, strong, long arm of a sycamore, my feet swinging, and I can only see Kitty, a co-worker in the mother trade – a topnotch craftsman. She is below, leaning on my tree, rumpled in a black cotton skirt made of shroud remnants at about fourteen cents a yard. Another colleague, Anne Kraat, is close by on a hard park bench, gloomy, beautiful, waiting for her luck to change.

Although I can't see them. I know that on the other side of the dry pool, the thick snout of the fountain spout, hurrying along the circumference of the parched sun-struck circle (in which, when Henry James could see, he saw lilies floating), Mrs. Hyme Caraway pokes her terrible seedlings, Gowan, Michael, and Christopher, astride an English bike, a French tricycle, and a Danish tractor. Beside her, talking all the time in fear of no response, Mrs. Steamy Lewis, mother of Matthew, Mark, and Lucy, tells of happy happy life in a thatched hotel on a Greek island where total historical recall is indigenous. Lucy limps along at her skirt in muddy cashmere. Mrs. Steamy Lewis really swings within the seconds of her latitude and swears she will have six, but Mr. Steamy Lewis is not expected to live.

I can easily see Mrs. Junius Finn, my up-the-block neighbor and evening stoop companion, a broad barge, like a lady, moving slow – a couple of redheaded cabooses dragged by clothesline at her stern; on her fat upper deck, Wiltwyck,* a pale three-year-old roaring captain with smoky eyes, shoves his wet thumb into the wind. 'Hurry! Hurry'' he howls. Mrs. Finn goes puff puffing toward the opinionated playground, that sandy harbor.

Along the same channel, but near enough now to spatter with spite, tilting delicately like a boy's sailboat, Lynn Ballard floats past my unconcern to drop light anchor, a large mauve handbag, over the green bench slats. She sighs and looks up to see what (if anything) the heavens are telling. In this way, once a week, toes in, head high and in three-quarter turn, arms at her side, graceful

---

* Wiltwyck is named for the school of his brother Junior, where Junior, who was bad and getting worse, is still bad, but is getting better (as man is perfectible).

as a seal's flippers, she rests, quiet and expensive. She never grabs another mother's kid when he falls and cries. Her particular Michael on his little red bike rides round and round the sandbox, while she dreams of private midnight.

'Like a model,' hollers Mrs. Junius Finn over Lynn Ballard's head.

I'm too close to the subject to remark. I sniff, however, and accidentally take sweetness into my lungs. Because it's the month of May.

Kitty and I are nothing like Lynn Ballard. You will see Kitty's darling face, as I tell her, slowly, but me – quick – what am I? Not bad if you're a basement shopper. On my face are a dozen messages, easy to read, strictly for friends, Bargains Galore! I admit it now.

However, the most ordinary life is illuminated by a great event like fame. Once I was famous. From the meaning of that glow, the modest hardhearted me is descended.

Once, all the New York papers that had the machinery to do so carried a rotogravure picture of me in a stewardess's arms. I was, it is now thought, the third commercial air-flight baby passenger in the entire world. This picture is at the Home now, mounted on laundry cardboard. My mother fixed it with glass to assail eternity. The caption says: One of Our Youngest. Little Faith Decided to Visit Gramma. Here She Is, Gently Cuddled in the Arms of Stewardess Jeannie Carter.

Why would anyone send a little baby anywhere alone? What was my mother trying to prove? That I was independent? That she wasn't the sort to hang on? That in the sensible, socialist, Zionist world of the future, she wouldn't cry at my wedding? 'You're an American child. Free. Independent.' Now what does that mean? I have always required a man to be dependent on, even when it appeared that I had one already. I own two small boys whose dependence on me takes up my lumpen time and my bourgeois feelings. I'm not the least bit ashamed to say that I tie their shoes and I have wiped their backsides well beyond the recommendations of my friends, Ellen and George Hellesbraun, who are psychiatric social workers and appalled. I kiss those kids forty times a day. I punch them just like a father should. When I have a date and come home late at night, I wake them with a couple of good hard shakes to complain about the miserable entertainment. When I'm not furiously exhausted from my low-level job and that bedraggled soot-slimy house, I praise God for them. One Sunday morning, my neighbor, Mrs. Raftery, called the cops because it was 3 a.m. and I was vengefully singing a praising song.

Since I have already mentioned singing, I have to tell you: it is not Sunday. For that reason, all the blue-eyed, boy-faced policemen in the park are worried. They can see that lots of our vitamin-enlarged high-school kids are planning to lug their guitar cases around all day long. They're scared that one of them may strum and sing a mountain melody or that several, a gang, will gather to raise their voices in medieval counterpoint.

Question: Does the world know, does the average freedman realize that, except for a few hours on Sunday afternoon, the playing of fretted instruments is banned by municipal decree? Absolutely forbidden is the song of the flute and oboe.

Answer (explanation): This *is* a great ballswinger of a city on the constant cement-mixing remake, battering and shattering, and a high note out of a wild clarinet could be the decibel to break a citizen's eardrum. But what if you were a city-loving planner leaning on your drawing board? Tears would drop to the delicate drafting sheets.

Well, you won't be pulled in for whistling and here come the whistlers – the young Saturday fathers, open-shirted and ambitious. By and large they are trying to get somewhere and have to go to a lot of parties. They are sleepy but pretend to great energy for the sake of their two-year-old sons (little boys need a recollection of Energy as a male resource). They carry miniature footballs though the season's changing. Then the older fathers trot in, just a few minutes slower, their faces scraped to a clean smile, every one of them wearing a fine gray head and eager eyes, his breath caught, his hand held by the baby daughter of a third intelligent marriage.

One of them, passing my tree, stubs his toe on Kitty's sandal. He shades his eyes to look up at me against my sun. That is Alex O. Steele, who was a man organizing tenant strikes on Ocean Parkway when I was a Coney Island Girl Scout against my mother's socialist will. He says, 'Hey, Faith, how's the world? Heard anything from Ricardo?'

I answer him in lecture form:

Alex Steele. Sasha. Yes. I have heard from Ricardo. Ricardo even at the present moment when I am trying to talk with you in a civilized way, Ricardo has rolled his dove-gray brain into a glob of spit in order to fly secretly into my ear right off the poop deck of Foamline's World Tour Cruiseship *Eastern Sunset*. He is stretched out in my head, exhausted before dawn from falling in love with an *Eastern Sunset* lady passenger on the first leg of her many-masted journey round the nighttimes of the world. He is *this minute* saying to me,

'Arcturus Rise, Orion Fall . . .'

'Cock-proud son of a bitch,' I mutter.

'Ugh,' he says, blinking.

'How are the boys?' I make him say.

'Well, he really wants to know how the boys are,' I reply.

'No, I don't,' he says. 'Please don't answer. Just make sure they don't get killed crossing the street. That's your job.'

'What?' says Alex Steele. 'Speak clearly, Faith, you're garbling like you used to.'

'I'm joking. Forget it. But I did hear from him the other day.' Out of the pocket of my stretch denims I drag a mashed letter with the exotic stamp of a new underdeveloped nation. It is a large stamp with two smiling lions on a field of barbed wire. The letter says: 'I am not well. I hope I never see another rain forest. I am sick. Are you working? Have you seen Ed Snead? He owes me $180. Don't badger him about it if he looks broke. Otherwise send me some to Guerra Verde c/o Dotty Wasserman. Am living here with her. She's on a Children's Mission. Wonderful girl. Reminds me of you ten years ago. She acts on her principles. I *need* the money.'

'That is Ricardo. Isn't it, Alex? I mean, there's no signature.'

'Dotty Wasserman! Alex says. 'So that's where she is . . . a funny plain girl. Faith, let's have lunch some time. I work up in the East Fifties. How're your folks? I hear they put themselves into a Home. They're young for that. Listen! I'm the executive director of Incurables, Inc., a fund-raising organization. We do wonderful things Faith. The speed of life-extending developments . . . By the way, what do you think of this little curly Sharon of mine?'

'Oh, Alex, how old is she? She's darling, she's a little golden baby, I love her. She's a peach.'

'Of course! *She's* a peach, you like anyone better'n you like us,' says my son Richard, who is jealous – because he came first and was deprived at two and one-half by his baby brother of my singlehearted love, my friend Ellie Hellesbraun says. Of course, that's a convenient professional lie, a cheap hindsight, as Richard, my older son, is brilliant, and I knew it from the beginning. When he was a baby all alone with me, and Ricardo, his daddy, was off exploring some deep creepy jungle, we often took the ferry to Staten Island. Then we sometimes took the ferry to Hoboken. We walked bridges, just he and I, I said to him, Richie, see the choo-choos on the barges, Richie, see the strong fast tugboat, see the merchant ships with their tall cranes, see the *United States* sail away for a week and a day, see the Hudson River with its white current. Oh, it isn't really the Hudson River, I told him, it's the North River; it isn't really a river, it's an estuary, part of the sea, I told him, though he was only two. I could tell him scientific things like that, because I considered him absolutely brilliant. See how beautiful the ice is on the river, see the stony palisades, I said, I hugged him, my pussycat, I said, see the interesting world.

So he really has no kicks coming, he's just peevish.

'We're really a problem to you, Faith, we keep you not free,' Richard says. 'Anyway, it's true you're crazy about anyone but us.'

It's true I do like the other kids. I am not too cool t⌐
Sharon really is a peach. But you, you stupid kid, Rich⌐
could match me for pride or you for brilliance? Which one
smart third-grade kids in a class of learned Jews, Presbyteri⌐
and bohemians? You are one of the two smartest and the othe⌐
one is Chinese – Arnold Lee, who does make Richard look a little
simple, I admit it. But did you ever hear of a child who, when
asked to write a sentence for the word 'who' (they were up to the
hard *wh*'s), wrote and then magnificently, with Oriental lisp, read
the following: 'Friend, tell me who among the Shanghai merchants does the largest trade?'*

'That's a typical yak yak out of you, Faith,' says Richard.

'Now Richard, listen to me. Arnold's an interesting boy; you
wouldn't meet a kid like him anywhere but here or Hong Kong.
So use some of these advantages I've given you. I could be living
in the country, which I love, but I know how hard that is on children – I stay here in this creepy slum. I dwell in soot and slime
just so you can meet kids like Arnold Lee and live on this wonderful block with all the Irish and Puerto Ricans, although God
knows why there aren't any Negro children for you to play
with . . .'

'Who needs it?' he says, just to tease me. 'All those guys got
knives anyway. But you don't care if I get killed much, do you?'

How can you answer that boy?

'You don't,' says Mrs. Junius Finn, glad to say a few words.
'You don't have to answer them. God didn't give out tongues for
that. You answer too much, Faith Asbury, and it shows. Nobody
fresher than Richard.'

'Mrs. Finn,' I scream in order to be heard, for she's some distance away and doesn't pay attention the way I do, 'what's so
terrible about fresh. EVIL is bad. WICKED is bad. ROBBING, MURDER,
and PUTTING HEROIN IN YOUR BLOOD is bad.

* The teacher, Marilyn Gewirtz, the only real person in this story, a
child admirer, told me this.

'Blah blah,' she says, deaf to passion. 'Blah to you.'

Despite no education, Mrs. Finn always is more in charge of word meanings than I am. She is especially in charge of Good and Bad. My language limitations here are real. My vocabulary is adequate for writing notes and keeping journals but absolutely useless for an active moral life. If I really knew this language, there would surely be in my head, as there is in Webster's or the *Dictionary of American Slang*, that unreducible verb designed to tell a person like me what to do next.

Mrs. Finn knows my problems because I do not keep them to myself. And I am reminded of them particularly at this moment, for I see her roughly the size of life, held up at the playground by Wyllie, who has rolled off the high ruddy deck of her chest to admire all the English bikes filed in the park bike stand. Of course that is what Junior is upstate for: love that forced possession. At first his father laced him on his behind, cutting the exquisite design known to generations of daddies who labored at home before the rise of industrialism and group therapy. Then Mr. Finn remembered his childhood, that it was Adam's Fall not Junior that was responsible. Now the Finns never see a tenspeed Italian racer without family sighs for Junior, who is still not home as there were about 176 bikes he loved.

Something is wrong with the following tenants: Mrs. Finn, Mrs. Raftery, Ginnie, and me. Everyone else in our building is on the way up through the affluent society, putting five to ten years into low rent before moving to Jersey or Bridgeport. But our four family units, as people are now called, are doomed to stand culturally still as this society moves on its caterpillar treads from ordinary affluent to absolute empire. All this in mind, I name names and dates. 'Mrs. Finn, darling, look at my Richard, the time Junior took his Schwinn and how Richard hid in the coal in the basement thinking of a way to commit suicide,' but she coolly answers, 'Faith, you're not a bit fair, for Junior give it right back when he found out it was Richard's.'

O.K.

Kitty says, 'Faith, you'll fall out of the tree, calm yourself.'

She looks up, rolling her eyes to show direction, and I see a handsome man in narrow pants whom we remember from other Saturdays. He has gone to sit beside Lynn Ballard. He speaks softly to her left ear while she maintains her profile. He has never spoken to her Michael. He is a famous actor trying to persuade her to play opposite him in a new production of *She*. That s what Kitty, my kind friend, says.

I am above that kindness. I often see through the appearance of things right to the apparition itself. It's obvious that he's a week-end queer, talking her into the possibilities of a neighborhood threesome. When her nose quivers and she agrees, he will easily get his really true love, the magnificent manager of the super-market, who has been longing for her at the check-out counter. What they will do then, I haven't the vaguest idea. I am the child of puritans and I'm only halfway here.

'Don't even think like that,' says Kitty. No. She can see a contract in his pocket.

There is no one like Kitty Skazka. Unlike other people who have similar flaws that doom, she is tolerant and loving. I wish Kitty could live forever, bearing daughters and sons to open the heart of man. Meanwhile, mortal, pregnant, she has three green-eyed daughters and they aren't that great. Of course, Kitty thinks they are. And they are no worse than the average gifted, sensitive child of a wholehearted mother and half a dozen transient fathers.

Her youngest girl is Antonia, who has no respect for grown-ups. Kitty has always liked her to have no respect; so in this, she is quite satisfactory to Kitty.

At some right moment on this Saturday afternoon, Antonia decided to talk to Tonto, my second son. He lay on his belly in the grass, his bare heels exposed to the eye of flitting angels, and he worked at a game that included certain ants and other bugs as players.

'Tonto,' she asked. 'what are you playing, can I?'

'No, it's my game, no girls,' Tonto said.

'Are you the boss of the world?' Antonia asked politely.

'Yes,' said Tonto.

He thinks, he really believes, he is. To which I must say, Righto! you are the boss of the world, Anthony, you are prince of the day-care center for the deprived children of working mothers, you are the Lord of the West Side loading zone whenever it rains on Sundays. I have seen you, creepy chief of the dark forest of four ginkgo trees. The Boss! If you would only look up, Anthony, and boss me what to do, I would immediately slide down this scabby bark, ripping my new stretch slacks, and do it.

'Give me a nickel, Faith,' he ordered at once.

'Give him a nickel, Kitty,' I said.

'Nickels, nickels, nickels, whatever happened to pennies?' Anna Kraat asked.

'Anna, you're rich. You're against us,' I whispered, but loud enough to be heard by Mrs. Junius Finn, still stopped at the mouth of the playground.

'Don't blame the rich for everything,' she warned. She herself, despite the personal facts of her economic position, is disgusted with the neurotic rise of the working class.

Lynn Ballard bent her proud and shameless head.

Kitty sighed, shifted her yardage, and began to shorten the hem of the enormous skirt which she was wearing. 'Here's a nickel, love,' she said.

'Oh boy! Love!' said Anna Kraat.

Antonia walked in a wide circle around the sycamore tree and put her arm on Kitty, who sewed, the sun just barely over her left shoulder – a perfect light. At that very moment, a representational artist passed. I think it was Edward Roster. He stopped and kneeled, peering at the scene. He squared them off with a filmmaker's viewfinder and said, 'Ah, what a picture!' then left.

'Number one!' I announced to Kitty, which he was, the very first of the squint-eyed speculators who come by to size up the stock. Pretty soon, depending on age and intention, they would move in groups along the paths or separately take notes in the shadows of the statues.

'The trick,' said Anna, downgrading the world, 'is to know the speculators from the investors . . .'

'I will never live like that. Not I,' Kitty said softly.

'Balls!' I shouted, as two men strolled past us, leaning toward one another. They weren't lovers, they were Jack Resnick and Tom Weed, music lovers inclining toward their transistor, which was playing the 'Chromatic Fantasy.' They paid no attention to us because of their relation to this great music. However, Anna heard them say. 'Jack, do you hear what I hear?' Damnit yes, the overromanticizing and the under-Baching, I can't believe it.'

Well, I must say when darkness covers the earth and great darkness the people, I will think of you: two men with smart ears. I don't believe civilization can do a lot more than educate a person's senses. If it's truth and honor you want to refine, I think the Jews have some insight. Make no images, imitate no God. After all, in His field, the graphic arts, He is pre-eminent. Then let that One who made the tan deserts and the blue Van Allen belt and the green mountains of New England be in charge of Beauty, which He obviously understands, and let man, who was full of forgiveness at Jerusalem, and full of survival at Troy, let man be in charge of Good.

'Faith, will you quit with your all-the-time philosophies,' says Richard, my first- and disapproving-born. Into our midst, he'd galloped, riding an all-day rage. Brand-new ball bearings, roller skates, heavy enough for his big feet, hung round his neck.

I decided not to give in to Richard by responding. I digressed and was free: A cross-eyed man with a red beard became president of the Parent-Teachers Association. He appointed a committee of fun-loving ladies who met in the lunchroom and touched up the coffee with little gurgles of brandy.

He had many clever notions about how to deal with the money shortage in the public schools. One of his great plots was to promote the idea of the integrated school in such a way that private-school people would think their kids were missing the real thing. And at 5 a.m., the envious hour, the very pit of the morning of middle age, they would think of all the public-school children deeply involved in the urban tragedy, something their children might never know. He suggested that one month of public-school attendance might become part of the private-school curriculum, as natural and progressive an experience as a visit to the boiler room in first grade. Funds could be split 50-50 or 30-70 or 40-60 with the Board of Education. If the plan failed, still the projected effort would certainly enhance the prestige of the public school.

Actually something did stir. Delegations of private progressive-school parents attacked the Board of Ed. for what became known as the Shut-out, and finally even the parents-and-teachers associations of the classical schools (whose peculiar concern always had been educating the child's head) began to consider the value of exposing children who had read about the horror at Ilium to ordinary street fights, so they could understand the Iliad better. Public School (in Manhattan) would become a minor like typing, required but secondary.

Mr. Terry Koln, full of initiative, energy, and lightheartedness, was re-elected by unanimous vote and sent on to the United Parents and Federated Teachers Organization as special council member, where in a tiny office all his own he grew marijuana on the windowsills, swearing it was deflowered marigolds.

He was the joy of our P.T.A. But it was soon discovered that he had no children, and Kitty and I have to meet him now surreptitiously in bars.

'Oh,' said Richard, his meanness undeflected by this jolly digression:

> 'The ladies of the P.T.A.
> wear baggies in their blouses
> they talk on telephones all day
> and never clean their houses.'

He really wrote that, my Richard. I thought it was awfully good, rhyme and meter and all, and I brought it to his teacher. I took the afternoon off to bring it to her. 'Are you joking, Mrs. Asbury?' she asked.

Looking into her kind teaching eyes, I remembered schools
and what it might be like certain afternoons and I replied, 'May I
have my Richard, please, he has a dental appointment. His teeth
are just like his father's. Rotten.'

'Do take care of them, Mrs. Asbury.'

'God, yes, it's the least,' I said, taking his hand.

'Faith,' said Richard, who had not gone away. 'Why did you
take me to the dentist that afternoon?'

'I thought you wanted to get out of there.'

'Why? Why? Why?' asked Richard, stamping his feet and
shouting. I didn't answer. I closed my eyes to make him disappear.

'Why not?' asked Philip Alazzano, who was standing there
looking up at me when I opened my eyes.

'Where's Richard?' I asked.

'This is Philip,' Kitty called up to me. 'You know Philip, that
I told you about?'

'Yes?'

'Philip,' she said.

'Oh,' I said and left the arm of the sycamore with as delicate a
jump as can be made by a person afraid of falling, twisting an
ankle, and being out of work for a week.

'I don't mind school,' said Richard, shouting from behind the
tree. 'It's better than listening to her whine.'

He really talks like that.

Philip looked puzzled. 'How old are you, sonny?'

'Nine.'

'Do nine-year-olds talk like that? I think I have a boy who's
nine.'

'Yes,' said Kitty. 'Your Johnny's nine, David's eleven, and
Mike's fourteen.'

'Ah,' said Philip, sighing; he looked up into the tree I'd
flopped from – and there was Judy, Anna's kid, using my nice
warm branch. 'God,' said Philip, 'more!'

Silence followed and embarrassment, because we outnum-
bered him, though clearly, we tenderly liked him.

'How is everything, Kitty?' he said, kneeling to tousle her hair. 'How's everything, my old honey girl? Another one?' He tapped Kitty's tummy lightly with an index finger. 'God!' he said, standing up. 'Say, Kitty, I saw Jerry in Newark day before yesterday. Just like that. He was standing in a square scratching his head.'

'Jerry?' Kitty asked in a high loving squeak. 'Oh. I know. Newark all week . . . Why were you there?'

'Me? I had to see someone, a guy named Vincent Hall, a man in my field.'

'What's your field?' I asked.

'Daisies,' he said. 'I happen to be in the field of daisies.' What an answer! How often does one meet, in this black place, a man, woman, or child who can think up a pastoral reply like that?

For that reason I looked at him. He had dark offended eyes deep in shadow, with a narrow rim of whiteness under the eyes, the result, I invented, of lots of late carousing nights, followed by eye-wrinkling examinations of mortalness. All this had marked him lightly with sobriety, the first enhancing manifest of ravage.

Even Richard is stunned by this uncynical openhearted notation of feeling. Forty bare seconds then, while Jack Resnick puts his transistor into the hollow of an English elm, takes a tattered score of The Messiah out of his rucksack, and writes a short Elizabethan melody in among the long chorus holds to go with the last singing sentence of my ode to Philip.

'Nice day,' said Anna.

'Please, Faith,' said Richard. 'Please. You see that guy over there?' He pointed to a fat boy seated among adults on a park bench not far from listening Lynn Ballard. 'He has a skate key and he won't lend it to me. He stinks. It's your fault you lost the skate key, Faith. You know you did. You never put anything away.'

'Ask him again, Richard.'

'You ask him, Faith. You're a grownup.'

'I will not. You want the skate key, you ask him. You have to go after your own things in this life. I'm not going to be around forever.'

Richard gave me a gloomy, lip-curling look. No. It was worse

than that. It was a baleful, foreboding look; a look which as far as
our far-in-the-future relations were concerned could be named
ill-auguring.

'You never do me a favor, do you?' he said.

'*I'll* go with you, Richard.' Philip grabbed his hand. 'We'll talk
to that kid. He probably hasn't got a friend in the world. I'm not
kidding you, boy, it's hard to be a fat kid.' He rapped his belly,
where, I imagine, certain memories were stored.

Then he took Richard's hand and they went off, man and boy,
to tangle.

'Kitty! Richard just hands him his skate, his hand, and just
goes off with him . . . That's not like my Richard.'

'Children sense how good he is,' said Kitty.

'He's good?'

'He's really not *so* good. Oh, he's good. He's considerate. You
know what kind he is, Faith. But if you don't really want him to
be good, he will be. And he's very strong. Physically. Someday I'll
tell you about him. Not now. He has a special meaning to me.'

Actually everyone has a special meaning to Kitty, even me, a
dictionary of particular generalities, even Anna and all our children.

Kitty sewed as she spoke. She looked like a delegate to a
Conference of Youth from the People's Republic of Ubmonsk
from Lower Tartaria. A single dark braid hung down her back.
She wore a round-necked white blouse with capped sleeves
made of softened muslin, woven for aged bridesbeds. I have
always listened carefully to my friend Kitty's recommendations,
for she has made one mistake after another. Her experience is
invaluable.

Kitty's kids have kept an eye on her from their dear tiniest
times. They listened to her reasons, but the two eldest, without
meaning any disrespect, had made different plans for their lives.
Children are all for John Dewey. Lisa and Nina have never
believed that Kitty's life really worked. They slapped Antonia for
scratching the enameled kitchen table. When Kitty caught them,
she said, 'Antonia's a baby. Come on now girls, what's a table?'

'What's a *table*?' said Lisa. 'What a nut! She wants to know what a table is.'

'Well, Faith,' said Richard, '*he* got the key for me.

Richard and Philip were holding hands, which made Richard look like a little boy with a daddy. I could cry when I think that I always treat Richard as though he's about forty-seven.

Philip felt remarkable to have extracted that key. He's quite a kid, Faith, your boy. I wish that my Johnny in Chicago was as great as Richard here. Is Johnny really nine, Kitty?'

'You bet,' she said.

He kept his puzzled face for some anticipated eventuality and folded down to cross-legged comfort, leaning familiarly on Nina's and Lisa's backs. 'How are you two fairy queens?' he asked and tugged at their long hair gently. He peeked over their shoulders. They were reading Classic Comics, *Ivanhoe* and *Robin Hood*.

'I hate to read,' said Antonia.

'Me too,' hollered Tonto.

'Antonia, I wish *you'd* read more,' said Philip. 'Antonia, little beauty. These two little ones. Forest babies. Little sunny brown creatures. I think you would say, Kitty, that they understand their bodies?'

'Oh, yes, I would,' said Kitty, who believed all that.

Although I'm very shy, I tend to persevere, so I said, 'You're pretty sunny and brown yourself. How do you make out? What are you? An actor or a French teacher, or something?'

'French . . .' Kitty smiled. 'He could teach Sanskrit if he wanted to. Or Filipino or Cambodian.'

'Cambodge . . .' Philip said. He said this softly as though the wars in Indochina might be the next subject for discussion.

'French teacher?' asked Anna Kraat, who had been silent, grieved by spring, for one hour and forty minutes. 'Judy,' she yelled into the crossed branches of the sycamore. 'Judy . . . French . . .'

'So?' said Judy. 'What's so great? Je m'appelle Judy Solomon. Ma père s'appelle Pierre Solomon. How's that, folks?'

'Mon père,' said Anna. 'I told you that before.'

'Who cares?' said Judy, who didn't care.

'She's lost two fathers.' said Anna, 'within three years.'

Tonto stood up to scratch his belly and back, which were itchy with wet grass. 'Mostly nobody has fathers. Anna,' he said.

'Is that true, little boy?' asked Philip.

'Oh yes,' Tonto said. 'My father is in the Equator. They never even had fathers,' pointing to Kitty's daughters. 'Judy has two fathers, Peter and Dr. Kraat. Dr. Kraat takes care of you if you're crazy.'

'Maybe I'll be your father.'

Tonto looked at me. I was too rosy. 'Oh no,' he said. 'Not right now. My father's name is Ricardo. He's a famous explorer. Like an explorer, I mean. He went in the Equator to make contacts. I have two books by him.'

'Do you like him?'

'He's all right.'

'Do you miss him?'

'He's very fresh when he's home.'

'That's enough of that!' I said. It's stupid to let a kid talk badly about his father in front of another man. Men really have too much on their minds without that.

'He's quite a boy,' said Philip. 'You and your brother are real boys.' He turned to me. 'What do I do? Well, I make a living. Here. Chicago. Wherever I am. I'm not in financial trouble. I figured it all out ten years ago. But what I really am, really . . .' he said, driven to lying confidence because he thought he ought to try that life anyway. 'What I truly am is a comedian.'

'That's a joke, that's the first joke you've said.'

'But that's what I want to be . . . a comedian.'

'But you're not funny.'

'But I am. You don't know me yet. I want to be one. I've been a teacher and I've worked for the State Department. And now what I want to be's a comedian. People have changed professions before.'

'You can't be a comedian,' said Anna, 'unless you're funny.'

He took a good look at Anna. Anna's character is terrible, but she's beautiful. It took her husbands about two years apiece to see how bad she was, but it takes the average passer, answerer, or asker about thirty seconds to see how beautiful she is. You can't warn men. As for Kitty and me, well, we love her because she's beautiful.

'Anna's all right,' said Richard.

'Be quiet,' said Philip. 'Say, Anna, are you interested in the French tongue, the French people, French history, or French civilization? '

'No,' said Anna.

'Oh,' he said, disappointed.

'I'm not interested in anything,' said Anna.

'Say!' said Philip, getting absolutely red with excitement, blushing from his earlobes down into his shirt, making me think as I watched the blood descend from his brains that I would like to be the one who was holding his balls very gently, to be exactly present so to speak when all the thumping got there.

Since it was clearly Anna, not I, who would be in that affectionate position, I thought I'd better climb the tree again just for the oxygen or I'd surely suffer the same sudden descent of blood. That's the way nature does things, swishing those quarts and quarts to wherever they're needed for power and action.

Luckily, a banging of pots and pans came out of the playground and a short parade appeared – four or five grownups, a few years behind me in the mommy-and-daddy business, pushing little go-carts with babies in them, a couple of three-year-olds hanging on. They were the main bangers and clangers. The grownups carried three posters. The first showed a prime-living, prime-earning, well-dressed man about thirty-five years old next to a small girl. A question was asked: would you burn a child? In the next poster he placed a burning cigarette on the child's arm. The cool answer was given: WHEN NECESSARY. The third poster carried no words, only a napalmed Vietnamese baby, seared, scarred, with twisted hands.

We were very quiet. Kitty put her head down into the dark skirt of her lap. I trembled. I said, Oh! Anna said to Philip,

'They'll only turn people against them,' and turned against them herself at once.

'You people will have to go,' said Douglas, our neighborhood cop. He had actually arrived a few minutes earlier to tell Kitty to beg Jerry not to sell grass at this end of the park. But he was ready. 'You just have to go,' he said. 'No parades in the park.'

Kitty lifted her head and with sweet bossiness said. 'Hey Doug, leave them alone. They're O.K.'

Tonto said, 'I know that girl, she goes to Greenwich House. You're in the fours,' he told her.

Doug said, 'Listen Tonto, there's a war on. You'll be a soldier too someday. I know you're no sissy like some kids around here. You'll fight for your country.'

'Ha ha,' said Mrs. Junius Finn, 'that'll be the day. Oh, say, can you see?'

The paraders made a little meeting just outside our discussion. They had to decide what next. The four grownups held the tongues of the children's bells until that decision could be made. They were a group of that kind of person.

'What they're doing is treason,' said Douglas. He had decided to explain and educate. 'Signs on sticks aren't allowed. In case of riot. It's for their own protection too. They might turn against each other.' He was afraid that no one would find the real perpetrator if that should happen.

'But Officer, I know these people. They're decent citizens of this community,' said Philip, though he didn't live in the borough, city, or state, let alone vote in it.

Doug looked at him thoroughly. 'Mister, I could take you in for interference.' He pulled his cop voice out of his healthy diaphragm.

'Come on . . .' said Kitty.

'You too,' he said fiercely. 'Disperse,' he said, 'disperse, disperse.'

Behind his back, the meeting had been neatly dispersed for about three minutes. He ran after them, but they continued on the park's circumference, their posters on the carriage handles, very solemn, making friends and enemies.

'They look pretty legal to me,' I hollered after Doug's blue back.

Tonto fastened himself to my leg and stuck his thumb in his mouth.

Richard shouted. 'Ha! Ha!' and punched me. He also began to grind his teeth, which would lead, I knew, to great expense.

'Oh, that's funny, Faith.' he said. He cried, he stamped his feet dangerously, in skates. 'I hate you. I hate your stupid friends. Why didn't they just stand up to that stupid cop and say fuck you. They should of just stood up and hit him.' He ripped his skates off, twisting his bad ankle. 'Gimme that chalk box, Lisa, just give it to me.'

In a fury of tears and disgust, he wrote on the near blacktop in pink flamingo chalk – in letters fifteen feet high, so the entire Saturday walking world could see – WOULD YOU BURN A CHILD? and under it, a little taller, the red reply, WHEN NECESSARY.

And I think that is exactly when events turned me around, changing my hairdo, my job uptown, my style of living and telling. Then I met women and men in different lines of work, whose minds were made up and directed out of that sexy playground by my children's heartfelt brains, I thought more and more and every day about the world.

Samuel

Some boys are very tough. They're afraid of nothing. They are the ones who climb a wall and take a bow at the top. Not only are they brave on the roof, but they make a lot of noise in the darkest part of the cellar where even the super hates to go. They also jiggle and hop on the platform between the locked doors of the subway cars.

Four boys are jiggling on the swaying platform. Their names are Alfred, Calvin, Samuel, and Tom. The men and the women in the cars on either side watch them. They don't like them to jiggle or jump but don't want to interfere. Of course some of the men in the cars were once brave boys like these. One of them had ridden the tail of a speeding truck from New York to Rockaway Beach without getting off, without his sore fingers losing hold. Nothing happened to him then or later. He had made a compact with other boys who preferred to watch: Starting at Eighth Avenue and Fifteenth Street, he would get to some specified place, maybe Twenty-third and the river, by hopping the tops of the moving trucks. This was hard to do when one truck turned a corner in the wrong direction and the nearest truck was a couple of feet too high. He made three or four starts before succeeding. He had gotten this idea from a film at school called *The Romance of*

Logging. He had finished high school, married a good friend, was in a responsible job and going to night school.

These two men and others looked at the four boys jumping and jiggling on the platform and thought, It must be fun to ride that way, especially now the weather is nice and we're out of the tunnel and way high over the Bronx. Then they thought, These kids do seem to be acting sort of stupid. They *are* little. Then they thought of some of the brave things they had done when they were boys and jiggling didn't seem so risky.

The ladies in the car became very angry when they looked at the four boys. Most of them brought their brows together and hoped the boys could see their extreme disapproval. One of the ladies wanted to get up and say, Be careful you dumb kids, get off that platform or I'll call a cop. But three of the boys were Negroes and the fourth was something else she couldn't tell for sure. She was afraid they'd be fresh and laugh at her and embarrass her. She wasn't afraid they'd hit her, but she was afraid of embarrassment. Another lady thought, Their mothers never know where they are. It wasn't true in this particular case. Their mothers all knew that they had gone to see the missile exhibit on Fourteenth Street.

Out on the platform, whenever the train accelerated, the boys would raise their hands and point them up to the sky to act like rockets going off then they rat-tat-tatted the shatterproof glass pane like machine guns, although no machine guns had been exhibited.

For some reason known only to the motorman, the train began a sudden slowdown. The lady who was afraid of embarrassment saw the boys jerk forward and backward and grab the swinging guard chains. She had her own boy at home. She stood up with determination and went to the door. She slid it open and said 'You boys will be hurt. You'll be killed. I'm going to call the conductor if you don't just go into the next car and sit down and be quiet.'

Two of the boys said. 'Yes'm.' and acted as though they were about to go. Two of them blinked their eyes a couple of times and pressed their lips together. The train resumed its speed. The door slid shut, parting the lady and the boys. She leaned against the side door because she had to get off at the next stop.

The boys opened their eyes wide at each other and laughed. The lady blushed. The boys looked at her and laughed harder. They began to pound each other's back. Samuel laughed the hardest and pounded Alfred's back until Alfred coughed and the tears came. Alfred held tight to the chain hook. Samuel pounded him even harder when he saw the tears. He said, 'Why you bawling? You a baby, huh?' and laughed. One of the men whose boyhood had been more watchful than brave became angry. He stood up straight and looked at the boys for a couple of seconds. Then he walked in a citizenly way to the end of the car, where he pulled the emergency cord. Almost at once, with a terrible hiss, the pressure of air abandoned the brakes and the wheels were caught and held.

People standing in the most secure places fell forward, then backward. Samuel had let go of his hold on the chain so he could pound Tom as well as Alfred. All the passengers in the cars whipped back and forth, but he pitched only forward and fell head first to be crushed and killed between the cars.

The train had stopped hard, halfway into the station, and the conductor called at once for the trainmen who knew about this kind of death and how to take the body from the wheels and brakes. There was silence except for passengers from other cars who asked, What happened! What happened! The ladies waited around wondering if he might be an only child. The men recalled other afternoons with very bad endings. The little boys stayed close to each other, leaning and touching shoulders and arms and legs.

When the policeman knocked at the door and told her about it, Samuel's mother began to scream. She screamed all day and moaned all night, though the doctors tried to quiet her with pills.

Oh, oh, she hopelessly cried. She did not know how she could ever find another boy like that one. However, she was a young woman and she became pregnant. Then for a few months she was hopeful. The child born to her was a boy. They brought him to be seen and nursed. She smiled. But immediately she saw that this baby wasn't Samuel. She and her husband together have had other children, but never again will a boy exactly like Samuel be known.

The Burdened Man

The man has the burden of the money. It's needed day after day. More and more of it. For ordinary things and for life. That's why holidays are a hard time for him. Another hard time is the weekend, when he's not making money or furthering himself.

Then he's home and he watches the continuation of his son's life and the continuation of his wife's life. They do not seem to know about the money. They are not stupid. but they leave the hall lights on. They consume electricity. The wife cooks and cooks. She has to make meat. She has to make potatoes and bring orange juice to the table. He is not against being healthy, but rolls baked hot in expensive gas are not necessary. His son makes phone calls. Then his wife makes a phone call. These are immediately clicked into the apparatus of AT&T and added against him by IBM. One day they accidentally buy three newspapers. Another day the boy's out in the yard. He's always careless. Naturally he falls and rips his pants. This expense occurs on a Saturday. On Sunday a neighbor knocks at the door, furious because it's her son's pants that were first borrowed then ripped, and they cost $5.95 and are good narrow-wale corduroy.

When he hears this, the man is beside himself. He does not

know where the money is coming from. The truth is, he makes a very good salary and puts away five dollars a week for his son's college. He has done this every week and now has $2,750 in the bank. But he does not know where the money for *all* of life will come from. At the door, without a word, he gives the neighbor six dollars in cash and receives two cents in change. He looks at the two pennies in his hand. He feels penniless and thinks he will faint. In order to be strong, he throws the two pennies at his neighbor, who screams, then runs. He chases her for two blocks. Her husband can't come to her rescue because he's on Sunday duty. Her children are at the movies. When she reaches the corner mailbox, she leans against it. She turns in fear and throws the six dollars at him. He takes the floating bills out of the air. He pitches them straight from the shoulder with all his strength. They drift like leaves to her coat and she cries out, 'Stop! stop!'

The police arrive at once from somewhere and are disgusted to see two grown-up people throwing money at each other and crying. But the neighborhood is full of shade trees and pretty lawns. The police forgive them and watch them go home in the same direction (because they're next-door neighbors).

They are sorry for each other's anger.

She says: 'I don't need the pants. Billy has plenty of pants.' He says: 'What's the money to me? Six dollars? Chicken feed.'

Then they have coffee at her house and explain everything. They each tell one story about when they were young. After this they become friends and visit one another on Sunday afternoons when both their families are on duty or at the movies.

On Friday nights the man climbs the three flights out of the deep subway. He stops at a bakery just before the bus for his remote neighborhood picks him up. He brings a strawberry short-cake home to his wife and son.

All the same, things changed. Summer came and the neighbor took her three children to a little summer house on the Long Island water. When she returned, she was tanned a light tea color with a touch of orange because of the lotion she had used. It seemed to him that her first and subsequent greetings were very cool. He had answered her cordially. 'You look real great,' he said. 'Thank you,' she said, without mentioning his looks, which the vacation sun had also improved.

One Saturday morning he waited in bed for the house to become quiet and empty. His wife and the boy always went to the supermarket by 9 a.m. When they were finally gone with the cart, the shopping bags, and the car, he began to think that he and his neighbor had talked and talked through many Sundays and now it was time to consider different ways to begin to make love to her.

He wondered if the kitchen might not be the best place to start because it was narrow. She was a decent person with three children and would probably say no just to continue her decency a little longer. She would surely try to get away from his first effort. However, she would never get away if he approached at the dishwashing machine.

Another possibility: If the coffee were already on the table, he might be beside her as she prepared to pour. He would take the coffeepot away from her and put it on the trivet. He would then take her hands and look into her eyes. She would know his meaning at once and start all the arrangements in her mind about ensuring privacy for the next Sunday.

Another possibility: In the living room on the couch before the coffee table, he would straightforwardly yet shyly declare, 'I'm having a terrible time. I want to get together with you.' This was the strongest plan because it required no further plan. He would be able to embrace her right after making his statement; he would lift her skirt, and if she wore no girdle, he could enter her at once.

The next day was Sunday. He called and she said in her new cool way, 'Oh sure, come on over.' In about ten minutes he was waiting for coffee at her dinette table. He had clipped the first four flowering zinnias out of his wife's lawn border and was arranging them in the bowl when he became aware of his neighbor's husband creeping stealthily along the wall toward him. He looked foolish and probably drunk. The man said. 'What . . . what . . .' He knew the husband by appearance only and was embarrassed to see him nearly on his knees in his own house.

'You fucking wop . . .' said the husband. 'You ain't been here twenty minutes you finished already, you cheap quickie cuntsucker . . . in and out . . . that's what she likes, the cold bitch . . .'

'No . . . no . . .' said the man. He was saying 'No no,' to the husband's belief that she was cold. 'No no,' he said, although he didn't know for sure, 'she's not.'

'What you waste your time on that fat bag of tits . . .' said her husband. 'Hey!' said the man. He hadn't thought of that part of her much at all. Mostly he had thought of how she would be under her skirt and of her thighs. He realized the husband was drunk or he would not speak of his wife with such words.

The husband then waved a pistol at him in a drunken way the man had often seen in the movies but never in life. He knew it was all right for the husband to have that pistol because he was a cop.

As a cop he was not unknown. He had once killed a farm boy made crazy by crowds in the city. The boy had run all day in terror round and round Central Park. People thought he was a runner because he wore an undershirt, but he had finally entered the park, and with a kitchen knife he had killed one baby and wounded two or three others. 'Too many people,' he screamed when he killed.

Bravely the cop had disarmed him, but the poor boy pulled another long knife out of his pants-leg pocket and the cop had then had to kill him. He was given a medal for this. He often remembered that afternoon and wondered that he had been brave once, but was not brave enough to have been brave twice.

Now he stared at the man and he tried to remember what inhibition had abandoned him, what fear of his victim had given him energy. How had he decided to kill that crazy boy?

Suddenly the woman came out of the kitchen. She saw that her husband was drunk and bloody-eyed. She saw that he held a pistol and waved it before his eyes as though it could clear fogs and smogs. She remembered that he was a person who had killed.

'Don't touch him.' she screamed at her husband. 'You maniac! Boy-killer! Don't touch him,' she shouted and gathered the man against her whole soft body. He hadn't wanted anything like this, his chin caught in the V neck of her wraparound housedress.

'Just get out of her shirt,' said the husband.

'If you kill him, you kill me,' she said, hugging the man so hard he wondered where to turn his nose to get air.

'O.K., why not, why not!' said the husband. 'Why not, you fucking whore, why not?'

Then his finger pressed the trigger and he shot and shot, the man, the woman, the wall, the picture window, the coffeepot. Looking down, screaming, Whore! whore! he shot straight into the floor, right through his shoe, smashing his toes for life.

The midnight edition of the morning paper said:

QUEENS COP COOLS ROMANCE

Precinct Pals Clap Cop in Cooler

Sgt. Armand Kielly put an end today to his wife's alleged romance with neighbor Alfred Ciaro by shooting up his kitchen, Mrs. Kielly, himself, and his career. Arrested by his own pals from the 115th precinct who claim he has been nervous of late, he faces departmental action. When questioned by this reporter, Mrs. Kielly said, 'No no no.'

The burdened man spent three days in the hospital having his shoulder wound attended to. Hospitalization paid for nearly all. He then sold his house and moved to another neighborhood on another bus line, though the subway stop remained the same. Until old age startled him, he was hardly unhappy again.

In fact, for several years, he could really feel each morning that a mixture of warm refreshments was being pumped out of the chambers of his heart to all his cold extremities.

Enormous Changes at the Last Minute

A young man said he wanted to go to bed with Alexandra because she had an interesting mind. He was a cabdriver and she *had* admired the curly back of his head. Still, she was surprised. He said he would pick her up again in about an hour and a half. Because she was fair and a responsible person, she placed between them a barrier of truthful information. She said, I suppose you don't know many middle-aged women.

You don't look so middle-aged to me. I mean, everyone likes what they like. That is, I'm interested in your point of view, your way of life. Anyway, he said, peering into the mirror, your face is nice and your eyebrows are out of sight.

Make it two hours, she said. I'm visiting my father whom I happen to love.

I love mine too, he said. He just doesn't love me. Too too bad.

O.K. That's enough, she said. Because they had already *had* the following factual and introductory conversation.

How old are your kids?

I have none.

Sorry. Then what do you do for a living?

Children. Early teenage. Adoptions, foster homes. Probation, Troubles – well . . .

Where'd you go to school?

City colleges. What about you?

Oh, me. Lots of places. Antioch. Wisconsin. California. I might go back someday. Someplace else though. Maybe Harvard. Why not?

He leaned on his horn to move a sixteen-wheel trailer truck delivering Kleenex to the A&P.

I wish you'd stop that, she said. I hate that kind of driving.

Why? Oh! You're an idealist! He looked through his rearview mirror straight into her eyes. But were you married? Ever?

Once. For years.

Who to?

It's hard to describe. A revolutionist.

Really? Could I know him? What's his name? We say revolutionary nowadays.

Oh?

By the way, my name's Dennis. I probably like you, he said.

You do, do you? Well, why should you? And let me ask you something. What do you mean by nowadays?

By the birdseed of St. Francis, he said, taking a tiny brogue to the tip of his tongue. I meant no harm.

Nowadays! she said. What does that mean? I guess you think you're kind of brand-new. You're not so brand-new. The telephone was brand-new. The airplane was brand-new. You've been seen on earth before.

Wow! he said. He stopped the cab just short of the hospital entrance. He turned to look at her and make decisions. But you're right, he said sweetly. You know the mind *is* an astonishing, long-living, erotic thing.

Is it? she asked. Then she wondered: What is the life expectancy of the mind?

Eighty years, said her father, glad to be useful. Once he had explained electrical storms before you could find the Book of Knowledge. Now in the cave of old age, he continued to amass wonderful information. But he was sick with oldness. His arteries had a hopeless future, and conversation about all that obsolescent tubing often displaced very interesting subjects.

One day he said, Alexandra! Don't show me the sunset again.
I'm not interested anymore. You know that. She had just pointed
to a simple sunset happening outside his hospital window. It
was a red ball – all alone, without its evening streaking clouds –
a red ball falling hopelessly west, just missing the Hudson River,
Jersey City, Chicago, the Great Plains, the Golden Gate – falling,
falling.

Then in Russian he sighed some Pushkin. Not for me, the
spring. *Nye dyla menya* . . . He slept. She read the large-print edition of *The Guns of August*. A half hour later, he opened his eyes
and told her how, in that morning's *Times*, the Phoenicians had
sailed to Brazil in about 500 B.C. A remarkable people. The
Vikings too were remarkable. He spoke well of the Chinese, the
Jews, the Greeks, the Indians – all the old commercial people.
Actually he had never knocked an entire nation. International
generosity had been started in him during the late nineteenth
century by his young mother and father, candleholders inside
the dark tyranny of the tsars. It was childhood training.
Thoughtfully, he passed it on.

In the hospital bed next to him, a sufferer named John feared
the imminent rise of the blacks of South Africa, the desperate
blacks of Chicago, the yellow Chinese, and the Ottoman Turks.
He had more reason than Alexandra's father to dread the future
because his heart was strong. He would probably live to see it all.
He believed the Turks when they came would bring to New York
City diseases like cholera, virulent scarlet fever, and particularly
leprosy.

Leprosy! for godsakes! said Alexandra. John! Upset yourself
with reality for once! She read aloud from the *Times* about the
bombed, burned lepers' colonies in North Vietnam. Her father
said, Please, Alexandra, today, no propaganda. Why do you constantly pick on the United States? He remembered the first time
he'd seen the American flag on wild Ellis Island. Under its protection and working like a horse, he'd read Dickens, gone to

medical school, and shot like a surface-to-air missile right into
the middle class.

Then he said, But they shouldn't put a flag in the middle of
chocolate pudding. It's ridiculous.

It's Memorial Day, said the nurse's aide, removing his tray.

In the early evening Dennis stood at the door of each room of
Alexandra's apartment. He looked this way and that. Underuse in
a time of population stress, he muttered. He entered the kitchen
and sniffed the kitchen air. It doesn't matter, he said aloud. He
took a fingerful of gravy out of the pot on the stove. Beef stew, he
whispered. Then he opened the door to the freezer compartment
and said, Sweet Jesus! because there were eleven batches of the
same, neatly stacked and frozen. They were for Alexandra's
junkies, whose methadone required lots of protein and carbohy-
drates.

I wouldn't have them in my house. It's a wonder you got a cup
and saucer left. Creeps, said Dennis. However, yes indeed, I will
eat this stuff. Why? Does it make me think of home or of something else? he asked. I think, a movie I once saw.

Apple turnovers! You know I have to admit it, our commune
isn't working too well. Probably because it's in Brooklyn and the
food co-op isn't together. But it's cool, they've accepted the criticism.

You have lots of junk in here, he pointed out after dinner. He
had decided to give the place some respectful attention. He
meant armchairs, lamps, desk sets, her grandmother's wedding
portrait, and an umbrella stand with two of her father's canes.

Um, said Alexandra, it's rent-controlled.

You know what I like to do, Alexandra? I like to sit with a girl
and look at a late movie, he said. It's an experience common to
Americans at this hour. It's important to be like others, to dig the
average dude, you have to be him. Be HIM. It's groovier than a lot
of phony gab. You'd be surprised how friendly you get.

I'm not against friendliness, she said, I'm not even against
Americans.

They watched half of *A Day at the Races*. This is very relaxing, he said. It's kind of long though, isn't it? Then he began to undress. He held out his arms. He said, Alexandra I really can't wait anymore. I'm a sunrise person. I like to go to bed early. Can I stay a few days?

He gave reasons: 1. It was a Memorial Day weekend, and the house in Brooklyn was full of tripping visitors. 2. He was disgusted with them anyway because they'd given up the most beautiful batik work for fashionable tie-dying. 3. He and Alexandra could take some good walks in the morning because all the parks to walk in were the lightest green. He had noticed that the tree on the corner though dying of buses was green at the beginning of many twigs. 4. He could talk to her about the kids, help her to understand their hangups, their incredible virtues. He had missed being one of them by about seven useless years.

So many reasons are not essential, Alexandra said. She offered him a brandy. Holy toads! he said furiously. You *know* I'm not into that. Touched by gloom, he began to remove the heavy shoes he wore for mountain walking. He dropped his pants and stamped on them a couple of times to make sure he and they were disengaged.

Alexandra, in the first summer dress of spring, stood still and watched. She breathed deeply because of having been alone for a year or two. She put her two hands over her ribs to hold her heart in place and also out of modesty to quiet its immodest thud. Then they went to bed in the bedroom and made love until that noisy disturbance ended. She couldn't hear one interior sound. Therefore they slept.

In the morning she became interested in reality again, which she had always liked. She wanted to talk about it. She began with a description of John, her father's neighbor in the hospital.

Turks? Far out! Well he's right. And another thing. Leprosy is coming. It's coming to the Forest Hills County Fair, the Rikers Island Jamboree, the Fillmore East, and the Ecolocountry Gardens in Westchester. In August.

Reality? A lesson in reality? Am I a cabdriver? No. I drive a cab but I am not a cabdriver. I'm a song hawk. A songmaker. I'm a poet, in other words. Do you know that every black man walking down the street today is a poet? But only one white honky devil in ten. One in ten.

Nowadays I write for the Lepers all the time. Fuck poetry. The Lepers dig me. I dig them.

The Lepers? Alexandra said.

Cool! You know them? No? Well, you may have known them under their old name. They used to be called The Split Atom. But they became too popular and their thing is anonymity. That's what they're known for. They'll probably change their name after the summer festivals. They might move to the country and call themselves Winter Moss.

Do you really make a living now?

Oh yes. I do. I do. Among technicians like myself I do.

Now: I financially carry one-third of a twelve-person, three-children commune. I only drive a cab to keep on top of the world of illusion, you know, Alexandra, to rap with the bourgeoisies, the fancy whores, the straight ladies visiting their daddies. Oh, excuse me, he said.

Now, Alexandra, imagine this: two bass guitars, a country violin, one piccolo, and drums. The Lepers' theme song! He sat up in bed. The sun shone on his chest. He had begun to think of breakfast, but he sang so that Alexandra could know him better and dig his substantialness.

ooooh
first my finger goes   goes   goes
then my nose
*   then baby   my toes*

if you love me this way   anyway   any day
I'll go your way
*   my Little Neck rose*

Well? he asked. He looked at Alexandra. Was she going to cry?

I thought you were such a reality freak, Alexandra. That's the way it is in the real world. Anyway! He then said a small prose essay to explain and buttress the poem:

The kids! the kids! Though terrible troubles hang over them, such as the absolute end of the known world quickly by detonation or slowly through the easygoing destruction of natural resources, they are still, even now, optimistic, humorous, and brave. In fact, they intend enormous changes at the last minute.

Come on, said Alexandra, hardhearted, an enemy of generalization, there are all kinds. My boys aren't like that.

Yes, they are, he said, angry. You bring them around. I'll prove it. Anyway, I love them. He tried for about twenty minutes, forgetting breakfast, to show Alexandra how to look at things in this powerful last-half-of-the-century way. She tried. She had always had a progressive if sometimes reformist disposition, but at that moment, listening to him talk, she could see straight ahead over the thick hot rod of love to solitary age and lonesome death.

But there's nothing to fear my dear girl, her father said. When you get there you will not want to live a hell of a lot. Nothing to fear at all. You will be used up. You are like a coal burning, smoldering. Then there's nothing left to burn. Finished. Believe me, he said, although he hadn't been there yet himself, at that moment you won't mind. Alexandra's face was a bit rumpled, listening.

Don't look at me like that! he said. He was too sensitive to her appearance. He hated her to begin to look older the way she'd had to in the last twenty years. He said, Now *I* have seen people die. A large number. Not one or two. Many. They are good and ready. Pain. Despair. Unconsciousness, nightmares. Perfectly good comas, wrecked by nightmares. They are ready. You will be too, Sashka. Don't worry so much.

Ho ho ho, said John in the next bed listening through the curtains. Doc, I'm not ready. I feel terrible, I got lousy nightmares. I don't sleep a wink. But I'm not ready. I can't piss without this tube. Lonesomeness! Boy! Did you ever see one of my kids visiting? No! Still I am not ready. NOT READY. He spelled it out, looking at the ceiling or through it, to the roof garden for incurables, and from there to God.

The next morning Dennis said, I would rather die than go to the hospital.

For godsakes why?

Why? Because I hate to be in the hands of strangers. They don't let you take the pills you got that you know work, then if you need one of their pills, even if you buzz, they don't come. The nurse and three interns are making out in the information booth. I've seen it. It's a high counter, she's answering questions, and they're taking turns banging her from behind.

Dennis! You're too dumb. You sound like some superstitious old lady with rape dreams.

That's cool, he said. I *am* an old lady about my health. I mean I like it. I want my teeth to go right on. Right on sister. He began to sing, then stopped. Listen! Your destiny's in their hands. It's up to them. Do you live? Or are you a hippie crawling creep from their point of view? Then die!

Really. Nobody ever decides to let you die. In fact, that's what's wrong. They decide to keep people alive for years after death has set in.

You mean like your father?

Alexandra leaped out of bed stark naked. My father! Why he's got twenty times your zip.

Cool it! he said. Come back. I was just starting to fuck you and you get so freaked.

And another thing. Don't use that word. I hate it. When you're with a woman you have to use the language that's right for her.

What do you want me to say?

I want you to say, I was just starting to make love to you, etc.

Well, that's true, said Dennis, I was. When she returned to him, he only touched the tips of her fingers, though all of her was

present. He kissed each finger and said right after each kiss, I
want to make love to you. He did this sweetly, not sarcastically.

Dennis, Alexandra said in an embarrassment of recognition,
you look like one of my placements, in fact you look like a kid,
Billy Platoon. His real name is Platon but he calls himself Platoon
so he can go to Vietnam and get killed like his stepbrother. He's a
dreamy boy.

Alexandra, you talk a lot, now hush, no politics.

Alexandra continued for a sentence or two. He carries a stick
with a ball full of nails attached, like some medieval weapon, in
case an enemy from Suffolk Street CIA's him. That's what they
call it.

Never heard that before. Besides I'm jealous. And also I'm the
enemy from Suffolk Street.

No, no, said Alexandra. Then she noticed in her mother's bedroom bureau mirror across the room a small piece of her naked
self. She said, Ugh!

There, there! said Dennis lovingly, caressing what he thought
she'd looked at, a couple of rippled inches between her breast
and belly. It's natural, Alexandra. Men don't change as much as
women. Among all the animals, human females are the only ones
to lose estrogen as they get older.

Is that it? she said.

Then there was nothing to talk about for half an hour.

But how come you knew that? she asked. The things you
know, Dennis. What for?

Why — for my art, he said. And despite his youth he rested
from love the way artists often do in order to sing. He sang:

Camp out
    out in the forest daisy
    under the gallows tree
with the
        ace of pentacles
        and me
            daisy flower

> *What of the*
>   *earth's ecology*
> *you're drivin too fast*
> *Daisy you're drivin alone*
> *Hey Daisy cut the ignition*
>   *let the oil*
>   *back in the stone.*

Oh, I like that one. I admire it! Alexandra said. But in fact! *is* ecology a good word for a song? It's technical . . .

Any word is good, it's the big word today anyway, said Dennis. It's what you do with the word. The language and the idea, they work it out together.

Really? Where do you get most of your ideas?

I don't know if I want to eat or sleep, he said. I think I just want to nuzzle your titty. Talk talk talk. Most? Well, I would say the majority are from a magazine, the *Scientific American*.

During breakfast, language remained on his mind. Because of this, he was silent. After the pancakes, he said, Actually Alexandra, I can use any words I want. And I have. I proved it last week in a conversation just like this one. I asked these blue-eyed cats to give me a dictionary. I just flipped the pages and jabbed and the word I hit was *ophidious*. But I did it, because the word does the dreaming for you. The word.

To a tune that was probably 'On Top of Old Smoky' he sang:

> *The ophidious garden*
> *was invented by Freud*
>
>   *where three ladies murdered*
>   *oh three ladies murdered*
>
> *the pricks of the birds*
>
> *the cobra is buried*
> *the rattlesnake writhes*

in the black snaky garden
in the blue snaky garden

in the hairs of my wives.

More coffee, please, he said with pride and modesty.

It's better than most of your songs, Alexandra said. It's a poem, isn't it? It *is* better.

What? What? It is *not* better, it is not, goddamn. It is not . . . It just isn't . . . oh, excuse me for losing my cool like that.

Forget it sonny, Alexandra said respectfully. I only meant I liked it, but I know, I'm too frank from living alone so much I think. Anyway, how come you always think about wives? Wives, mothers?

Because that's me, said peaceful Dennis. Haven't you noticed it yet? That's my bag. I'm a motherfucker.

Oh, she said, I see. But I'm not a mother, Dennis.

Yes, you are, Alexandra. I've figured out a lot about you. I know. I act like the weekend stud sometimes. But I wrote you a song. Just last night in the cab. I think about you. The Lepers'll never dig it. They don't know too much about life. They're still baby bees trying to make it to the next flower, but some oldtimer'll tape it, some sore dude who's been out of it for a couple of years who wants to grow. He'll smell the shit in it.

Oh
I know something about you baby
*   that's sad*
*   don't be mad*
*   baby*

That you will never have children at
*   rest*
*   at that beautiful breast*
*   my love*

But see

> *everywhere you go, children follow you*
> *for more*
> > *many more*
> *are the children of your life*
> *than the children of the married wife.*

That one is out of the Bible, he said.

Pa. Alexandra said, don t you think a woman in this life ought to have at least one child?

No doubt about it, he said. You should have when you were married to Granofsky, the Communist. We disagreed. He had no sense of humor. He's probably boring the Cubans to death this minute. But he was an intelligent person otherwise. I would have brilliant grandchildren. They would not necessarily have the same politics.

Then he looked at her, her age and possibilities. He softened. You don't look so bad. You could still marry, dear girl. Then he softened further, thinking of hopeless statistics he had just read about the ratio of women to men. Actually! So what! It's not important, Alexandra. According to the Torah, only the man is commanded to multiply. You are not commanded. You have a child, you don't have, God doesn't care. You don't have one, you call in the maid. You say to your husband, Sweetie, get my maid with child. O.K. Well, your husband has anyway been fooling around with the maid for a couple of years, but now it's a respectable business. Good. You don't have to go through the whole thing, nine months, complications, maybe a caesarean, no no pronto, a child for the Lord, Hosanna.

Pa, she said, several weeks later, but what if I did have a baby?

Don't be a fool, he said. Then he gave her a terrible long medical look, which included her entire body. He said, Why do you ask this question? He became red in the face, which had never happened. He took hold of his chest with his right hand, the hospital buzzer with the left. First, he said, I want the nurse! Now! Then he ordered Alexandra: Marry!

*

Dennis said, I don't know how I got into this shit. It's not right, but because your habits and culture are different, I will compromise. What I suggest is this, Alexandra. The three children in our commune belong to us all. No one knows who the father is. It's far out. I swear – by the cock of our hard-up gods, I swear it's beautiful. One of them might be mine. But she doesn't have any distinguishing marks. Why don't you come and live with us and we'll all raise that kid up to be a decent human and humane being in this world. We need a slightly older person, we really do, with a historic sense. We lack that.

Thank you, Alexandra replied. No.

Her father said, Explain it to me, please. For what purpose did you act out this nonsense? For love? At your age. Money? Some conniver flattered you. You probably made him supper. Some starving ne'er-do-well probably wanted a few meals and said, Why not? This middle-aged fool is an easy mark. She'll give me pot roast at night, bacon and eggs in the morning.

No Pa, no, Alexandra said. Please, you'll get sicker.

John in the next bed dying with a strong heart wrote a little note to him. Doc, you're crazy. Don't leave enemies. That girl is loyal! She hasn't missed a Tues., Thurs., or Sat. Did you ever see one of my kids visit? Something else. I feel worse and worse. But I'm still *not ready*.

I want to tell you one more thing, her father said. You are going to embitter my last days and ruin my life.

After that, Alexandra hoped every day for her father's death, so that she could have a child without ruining his interesting life at the very end of it when ruin is absolutely retroactive.

Finally, Dennis said, Then let me at least share the pad with you. It'll be to your advantage.

No, Alexandra said. Please, Dennis. I've got to go to work early. I'm sleepy.

I dig. I've been a joke to you. You've used me in a bad way. That's not cool. That smells under heaven.

No, Alexandra said. Please, shut up. Anyway, how do you know you're the father?

Come on, he said, who else would be?

Alexandra smiled, bit her lip to the edge of blood to show pain politely. She was thinking about the continuity of her work, how to be proud and not lose a productive minute. She thought about the members of her caseload one by one.

She said, Dennis, I know exactly what I'm going to do.

In that case, this is it, I'm splitting.

This is what Alexandra did in order to make good use of the events of her life. She invited three pregnant clients who were fifteen and sixteen years old to live with her. She visited each one and explained to them that she was pregnant too, and that her apartment was very large. Although they had disliked her because she'd always worried more about the boys, they moved out of the homes of their bad-tempered parents within a week. At the very first evening meal they began to give Alexandra good advice about men, which she did appreciate years later. She ensured their health and her own and she took notes as well. She established a precedent in social work which would not be followed or even mentioned in state journals for about five years.

Alexandra's father's life was not ruined, nor did he have to die. Shortly before the baby's birth, he fell hard on the bathroom tiles, cracked his skull, dipped the wires of his brain into his heart's blood. Short circuit! He lost twenty, thirty years in the flood, the faces of nephews, in-laws, the names of two Presidents, and a war. His eyes were rounder, he was often awestruck, but he was smart as ever, and able to begin again with fewer scruples to notice and appreciate.

The baby was born and named Dennis for his father. Of course his last name was Granofsky because of Alexandra's husband, Granofsky the Communist.

The Lepers, who had changed their name to the Edible Amanita, taped the following song in his tiny honor. It was called 'Who? I.'

The lyrics are simple. They are:

Who is the father?
Who is the father
Who is the father

 I! I! I! I!

I am the father
I am the father
I am the father.

Dennis himself sang the solo which was I! I! I! I! in a hoarse enraged prophetic voice. He had been brave to acknowledge the lyrics. After a thirty-eight-hour marathon encounter at his commune, he was asked to leave. The next afternoon he moved to a better brownstone about four blocks away where occasional fatherhood was expected.

On the baby's third birthday, Dennis and the Fair Fields of Corn produced a folk-rock album because that was the new sound and exciting. It was called *For Our Son*. Tuned-in listeners could hear how taps played by the piccolo about forty times a verse flitted in and out of the long dark drumrolls, the ordinary banjo chords, and the fiddle tune which was something but not exactly like 'Lullaby and Good Night.'

Will you come to see me Jack
    When I'm old and very shaky?
Yes I will for you're my dad
    And you've lost your last old lady
    Though you traveled very far
To the highlands and the badlands
    And ripped off the family car
Still, old dad, I won't forsake you.

Will you come to see me Jack?
    Though I'm really not alone.
Still I'd like to see my boy

For we're lonesome for our own.
    Yes I will for you're my dad
Though you dumped me and my brothers
    And you sizzled down the road
Loving other fellows' mothers.

Will you come to see me Jack?
    Though I look like time boiled over.
Growing old is not a lark.
    Yes I will for you're my dad
    Though we never saw a nickel
As we struggled up life's ladder
    I will call you and together
We will cuddle up and see
    What the weather's like in Key West
On the old-age home TV.

This song was sung coast to coast and became famous from the dark Maine woods to Texas's shining gulf. It was responsible for a statistical increase in visitors to old-age homes by the apprehensive middle-aged and the astonished young.

Politics

A group of mothers from our neighborhood went downtown to the Board of Estimate hearing and sang a song. They had contributed the facts and the tunes, but the idea for that kind of political action came from the clever head of a media man floating on the ebbtide of our Lower West Side culture because of the housing shortage. He was from the far middle plains and loved our well-known tribal organization. He said it was the coming thing. Oh? how he loved our old moldy pot New York.

He was also clean-cut and attractive. For that reason the first mother stood up straight when the clerk called her name. She smiled, said excuse me, jammed past the knees of her neighbors, and walked proudly down the aisle of the hearing room. Then she sang, according to some sad melody learned in her mother's kitchen, the following lament requesting better playground facilities.

oh oh oh
will someone please put a high fence
up
around the children's playground
they are playing a game and have
only

one more year of childhood. won't the city
come
or their daddies to keep the bums and
the tramps out of the yard they are too
little now to have the old men wagging their
cricked pricks at them or feeling their
knees and saying to them sweetheart
sweetheart sweetheart. can't the cardinal
keep all these creeps out . . .

She bowed her head and stepped back modestly to allow the recitative for which all the women rose, wherever in the hearing room they happened to be. They said a lovely statement in chorus:

The junkies with smiles can be stopped by intelligent
reorganization of government functions.

Then she stepped forward once more, embarrassed before the high municipal podiums, and continued to sing:

. . . please Mr. Mayor
there's a girl without any pants on they're babies
so help me the Commies just walk in the gate
and put shit in the sand . . .

Raising her arms toward the off-white ceiling of our lovely City Hall, she cried out.

stuff them on a freight train to Brooklyn
your honor, put up a fence
we're mothers oh what
will become of the children . . .

No one on the Board of Estimate, including the mayor, was unimpressed. After the reiteration of the fifth singer, all the officials said so, murmuring ah and oh in a kind of startled arpeggio round lasting maybe three minutes. The comptroller, who was a famous financial nag, said, 'Yes yes yes, in this case, yes, a high 16.8 fence can be put up at once, can be expedited, why not . . .' Then and there, he picked up the phone and called Parks, Traffic and Child Welfare. All were agreeable when they heard his strict voice and temperate language. By noon the next day, the fence was up.

Later that night, an hour or so past moonlight, a young Tactical Patrol Force cop snipped a good-sized hole in the fence for two reasons. His first reason was public: The Big Brothers, a baseball team of young priests who absolutely required exercise, always played at night. They needed entrance and egress. His other reason was personal: There were eleven bats locked up in the locker room. These were, to his little group, an esoteric essential. He, in fact, had already gathered them into his arms like stalks of pussywillow and loaded them into a waiting paddy wagon. He had returned for half a dozen catcher's mitts, when a young woman reporter from the *Lower West Side Sun* noticed him in the locker room.

She asked, because she was trained in the disciplines of curiosity followed by intelligent inquiry, what he was doing there. He replied, 'A police force stripped of its power and shorn by vengeful politicians of the respect due it from the citizenry will arm itself as best it can.' He had a copy of Camus's *The Rebel* in his inside pocket which he showed her for identification purposes. He had mild gray eyes, short eyelashes, a smooth and perfect countenance, white gloves of linen, barely smudged, and was able, therefore, while waiting among the basketballs for apprehension by precinct cops, to inject her with two sons, one Irish and one Italian, who sang to her in dialect all her life.

Northeast Playground

When I went to the playground in the afternoon I met eleven unwed mothers on relief. Only four of them were whores, the rest of them were unwed on principle or because some creep had ditched them.

The babies were all under one year old, very funny and lovable.

When the mothers stuck them in the sandbox, they took up the whole little desert, throwing sand and screeching. A kid with a father at home, acknowledging and willing to support, couldn't get a wet toehold.

How come you're all here? I asked.

By accident, said the first.

A couple of us happened to meet, said the second, liked one another, and introduced friends.

We're like a special-interest group, said a third. That was Janice, a political woman, conscious of power structure and power itself.

A fourth came into the playground with eleven Dixie cups, chocolate and vanilla. She passed them around. What a wonderful calm unity in this group! When I was a mother of babies in this same park, we were not so unified and often quarreled, accusing other children of unhealthy aggression or excessive timidity. He's a ruined wreck, we'd say about some streaky squeaker about two years old. No hope. His eyelids droop. Look how he hangs on to his little armored prick!

Of course, said Janice, if you want to see a beauty, there's Claude, Leni's baby. The doll! said Janice, who had a perfectly good baby of her own in a sling across her chest, asleep in the heat of her protection.

Claude *was* beautiful. He was bouncing on Leni's lap. He was dark brown, though she was white.

Beautiful, I said.

Leni is very unusual, said Janice. She's from Brighton Beach, a street whore, despite her age, weight, and religion.

He's not my baby, said Leni. Some dude owed me and couldn't pay. So he gave me the first little bastard he had. A.D.C. Aid to Dependent Children. Honey, I just stay home now like a mama bear and look at TV. I don't turn a trick a week. He takes all my time, my Claude. Don't you, you little pancake? Eat your ice cream, Claudie, the sun's douchin' it away.

The sixth and seventh unwed mothers were twin sisters who had always dressed alike.

The eighth and ninth were whores and junkies and watched each other's babies when working or flying. They were very handsome dykey women, with other four- and five-year-old children in the child-care center, and their baby girls sat in ribbons and white voile in fine high veneer and chrome imported carriages. They never let the kids play in the sand. They were disgusted to see them get dirty or wet and gave them hell when they did. The girls who were unwed on principle – that included Janice and the twins – considered it rigidity, but not hopeless because of the extenuating environment.

The tenth and eleventh appeared depressed. They'd been ditched and it kept them from total enjoyment of the babies, though they clutched the little butterballs to their hearts or flew into the sandbox at the call of a whimper, hollering, What? What? Who? Who? Who took your shovel? Claude? Leni! Claude!

He's a real boy, said Leni.

These two didn't like to be on relief at all. They were embarrassed but not to the point of rudeness to their friends who weren't ashamed. Still, every now and then they'd make ironic remarks. They were young and very pretty, the way almost all young girls tend to be these days, and would probably never be ditched again. I tried to tell them this and they replied, Thanks! One ironic remark they'd make was, My mother says don't feel bad, Allison's a love-child. The mother was accepting and advanced, but poor.

The afternoon I visited, I asked one or two simple questions and made a statement.

I asked, Wouldn't it be better if you mixed in with the other mothers and babies who are really a friendly bunch?

They said, No.

I asked, What do you think this ghettoization will do to your children?

They smiled proudly.

Then I stated: In a way, it was like this when my children were little babies. The ladies who once wore *I Like Ike* buttons sat on the south side of the sandbox, and the rest of us who were revisionist Communist and revisionist Trotskyite and revisionist Zionist registered Democrats sat on the north side.

In response to my statement, NO kidding! most of them said.

Beat it, said Janice.

The Little Girl

Carter stop by the café early. I just done waxing. He said, I believe I'm having company later on. Let me use your place, Charlie, hear?

I told him, Door is open, go ahead. Man coming for the meter (why I took the lock off). I told him Angie my lodger *could* be home but he strung out most the time. He don't even know when someone practicing the horn in the next room. Carter, you got hours and hours. There ain't no wine there, nothing like it. He said he had some other stuff would keep him on top. That was a joke. Thank you, brother, he said. I told him I believe I *have* tried anything, but to this day, I like whiskey. If you have whiskey, you drunk, but if you pump up with drugs, you just crazy. Yeah, hear that man, he said. Then his eyeballs start walking away.

He went right to the park. Park is full of little soft yellow-haired baby chicks. They ain't but babies. They far from home, and you better believe it, they love them big black cats walking around before lunchtime, jutting their apparatus. They think they gonna leap off that to heaven. Maybe so.

Nowadays, the spades around here got it set out for them. When I was young, *I* put that kettle to cook. *I* stirred it and stirred it. And these dudes just sucking off the gravy.

Next thing: Carter rested himself on the bench. He look this way and that. His pants is tight. His head making pictures. Along comes this child. She just straggling along. Got her big canvas pocketbook and she looking around. Carter hollers out. Hey, sit down, he says. By me, here, you pretty thing. She look sideways. Sits. On the edge.

Where you from, baby? he ask her. Hey, relax, you with friends.

Oh, thank you. Oh, the Midwest, she says. Near Chicago. She want to look good. She ain't from maybe eight hundred miles.

You left home for a visit, you little dandylion you, your boyfriend let you just go?

Oh no, she says. Getting talky. I just left and for good. My mother don't let me do a thing. I got to do the breakfast dishes when I get home from school and clean and do my two brothers' room and they don't have to do nothing. And I got to be home in my room by 10 p.m. weekdays and 12 p.m. just when the fun starts Saturday and nothing is going on in that town. Nothing! It's dead, a sleeping hollow. *And the prejudice, whew!* She blushes up a little, she don't want to hurt his feelings. It's terrible and then they caught me out with a little bit of a roach I got off of some fellow from New York who was passing through and I couldn't get out at all then for a week. They was watching me and watching. They're disgusting and they're so ignorant!

My! Carter says. I don't know how you kids today stand it. The world is changing, that's a fact, and the old folks ain't heard the news. He ruffle with her hair and he lay his cheek on her hair a minute. Testing. And he puts the tip of his tongue along the tip of her ear. He's a fine-looking man, you know, a nice color, medium, not too light. Only thing wrong with him is some blood line in his eye.

I don't know when I seen a prettier chick, he says. Just what we call fattening the pussy. Which wouldn't use up no time he could see. She look at him right away, Oh Lord, I been trudging around. I am tired. Yawns.

He says, I got a nice place, you could just relax and rest and decide what to do next. Take a shower. Whatever you like. Anyways you do is O.K. My, you are sweet. You better'n Miss America. How old you say you was?

Eighteen, she jump right in.

He look at her satisfied, but that was a lie and Carter knew it, I believe. That the Number One I hold against him. Because, why her? Them little girls just flock, they do. A grown man got to use his sense.

Next thing: They set out for my apartment, which is six, seven blocks downtown. Stop for a pizza 'Mm this is good, she says (she is so simple). She says, They don't make 'em this way back home.

They proceed. I seen Carter courting before. Canvas pocketbook across his shoulder. They holding hands maybe and handswinging.

Open the front door of 149, but when they through struggling up them four flights, she *got* to be disappointed, you know my place, nothing there. I got my cot. There's a table. There two chairs. Blanket on the bed. And a pillow. And a old greasy pillow slip. I'm too old now to give up my grizzily greasy head, but I sure wish I was a young buck, I would let my Afro flare *out*.

She got to be disappointed.

Wait a minute, he says, goes into the kitchen and brings back ice water, a box of pretzels. Oh, thank you, she says. Just what I wanted. Then he says, Rest yourself, darling, and she lie down. Down, right in her coffin.

You like to smoke? Ain't that peaceful, he says. Oh, it is, she says. It sure is peaceful. People don't know.

Then they finish up. Just adrifting in agreement, and he says, You like to ball? She says, Man! Do I! Then he put up her dress and take down her panties and tickle her here and there, nibbling away. He says, You like that, baby? Man! I sure do, she says. A colored boy done that to me once back home, it sure feels good.

Right then he get off his clothes. Gonna tend to business. Now, the bad thing there is, the way Carter told it, and I know it so, those little girls come around looking for what they used to, hot dog. And what they get is knockwurst. You know we are like that. Matter of fact, Carter did force her. Had to. She starting to holler, Ow, it hurts, you killing me, it hurts. But Carter told me, it was her asked for it. Tried to get away, but he had been stiff as stone since morning when he stop by the store. He wasn't *about* to let her run.

Did you hit her? I said. Now Carter, I ain't gonna tell anyone. But I got to know.

I might of hauled off and let her have it once or twice. Stupid little cunt asked for it, didn't she? She was so little, there wasn't enough meat on her thigh bone to feed a sick dog. She could of wriggled by the scoop in my armpit if I had let her. Our black women ain't a bit like that, I told you Charlie. They cook it up, they eat the mess they made. They proud.

I didn't let that ride too long. Carter's head moves quick, but he don't dust me. I ask him, How come when they passing the plate and you *is* presented with the choice, you say like the prettiest dude, A little of that white stuff, please, man?

I don't! He hollered like I had chopped his neck. And I won't! He grab my shirt front. It was a dirty old work shirt and it tore to bits in his hand. He got solemn. Shit! You right! They are poison! They killing me! That diet gonna send me upstate for nothin but *bone* diet and I got piles as is.

Joking by the side of the grave trench. That's why I used to like him. He wasn't usual. That's why I like to pass time with Carter in the park in the early evening.

Be cool, I said.

Right on, he said.

He told me he just done shooting them little cotton-head darkies into her when Mangie Angie Emporiore lean on the doorway. Girl lying on my bloody cot pulling up a sheet, crying, bleeding out between her legs. Carter had tore her up some. You know, Charlie, he said, I ain't one of your little Jewboy buddies with half of it cut off. Angie peering and peering. Carter stood up out of his working position. He took a quick look at Angie, heisted his pants, and split. He told me, Man, I couldn't stay there, that dumb cunt sniffling and that blood spreading out around her, she didn't get up to protect herself, she was disgusting, and that low white bug, your friend, crawled in from under the kitchen sink. Now on, you don't live with no white junkie, hear me Charlie, they can't use it.

Where you going now Carter? I ask him. To the pigs, he says and jabs his elbow downtown. I hear they looking for me.

That exactly what he done, and he never seen free daylight since.

Not too long that same day they came by for me. They know where I am. At the station they said, You sleep somewhere else tonight and tomorrow night. Your place padlocked. You wouldn't want to see it, Charlie. You in the clear. We know your whereabouts to the minute. Sergeant could see I didn't know nothing. Didn't want to tell me neither. I'll explain it. They had put out a warrant for Angel. Didn't want me speaking to him. Telling him anything.

Hector the beat cop over here can't keep nothing to himself. They are like that. Spanish people. Chatter chatter. What he said: You move, Charlie. You don't want to see that place again. Bed smashed in. That little girl broken up in the bottom of the airshaft on top of the garbage and busted glass. She just tossed out that toilet window wide awake alive. They know that. Death occur on ground contact.

The next day I learned worse. Hector found me outside the store. My buffer swiped. Couldn't work. He said, Every bone between her knee and her rib cage broken, splintered. She been brutally assaulted with a blunt instrument or a fist before death.

Worse than that, on her leg high up, inside, she been bitten like a animal bit her and bit her and tore her little meat she had on her. I said, All right, Hector. Shut up. Don't speak.

They put her picture in the paper every day for five days, and when her mother and daddy came on the fifth day, they said, The name of our child is Juniper. She is fourteen years old. She been a little rebellious but the kids today all like that.

Then court. I had a small job to say, Yes, it was my place. Yes,

I told Carter he could use it. Yes, Angie was my roommate and sometimes he lay around there for days. He owed me two months' rent. That the reason I didn't put him out.

In court Carter said, Yes, I did force her, but he said he didn't do nothing else.

Angie said, I did smack her when I seen what she done, but I never bit her, your honor, I ain't no animal, that black hippie must of.

Nobody said – they couldn't drag out of anyone – they lacking the evidence who it was picked her up like she was nothing, a bag of busted bones, and dumped her out the fifth-floor window.

But wasn't it a shame, them two studs. Why they take it out on her? After so many fluffy little chicks. They could of played her easy. Why Carter seen it many times hisself. She could of stayed the summer. We just like the UN. Every state in the union stop by. She would of got her higher education right on the fifth-floor front. September, her mama and daddy would come for her and they whip her bottom, we know that. We been in this world long enough. We seen lots of the little girls. They go home, then after a while they get to be grown womens, they integrating the swimming pool and picketing the supermarket, they blink their eyes and shut their mouth and grin.

But that was my room and my bed, so I don't forget it. I don't stop thinking, That child . . . That child . . . And it come to me yesterday, I lay down after work: Maybe it wasn't no one. Maybe she pull herself the way she was, crumpled, to that open window. She was tore up, she must of thought she was gutted inside her skin. She must of been in a horror what she got to remember – what her folks would see. Her life look to be disgusting like a squashed fish, so what she did: she made up some power somehow and raise herself up that windowsill and hook herself onto it and then what I see, she just topple herself out. That what I think right now.

That is what happened.

A Conversation with My Father

My father is eighty-six years old and in bed. His heart, that bloody motor, is equally old and will not do certain jobs anymore. It still floods his head with brainy light. But it won't let his legs carry the weight of his body around the house. Despite my metaphors, this muscle failure is not due to his old heart, he says, but to a potassium shortage. Sitting on one pillow, leaning on three, he offers last-minute advice and makes a request.

'I would like you to write a simple story just once more,' he says, 'the kind Maupassant wrote, or Chekhov, the kind you used to write. Just recognizable people and then write down what happened to them next.'

I say, 'Yes, why not? That's possible.' I want to please him, though I don't remember writing that way. I *would* like to try to tell such a story, if he means the kind that begins: 'There was a woman . . .' followed by plot, the absolute line between two points which I've always despised. Not for literary reasons, but because it takes all hope away. Everyone, real or invented, deserves the open destiny of life.

Finally I thought of a story that had been happening for a couple of years right across the street. I wrote it down, then read it aloud. 'Pa,' I said, 'how about this? Do you mean something like this?'

> Once in my time there was a woman and she had a son. They lived nicely, in a small apartment in Manhattan. This boy at about fifteen became a junkie, which is not unusual in our neighborhood. In order to maintain her close friendship with him, she became a junkie too. She said it was part of the youth culture, with which she felt very much at home. After a while, for a number of reasons, the boy gave it all up and left the city and his mother in disgust. Hopeless and alone, she grieved. We all visit her.

'O.K., Pa, that's it,' I said, 'an unadorned and miserable tale.'

'But that's not what I mean,' my father said. 'You misunderstood me on purpose. You know there's a lot more to it. You know that. You left everything out. Turgenev wouldn't do that. Chekhov wouldn't do that. There are in fact Russian writers you never heard of, you don't have an inkling of, as good as anyone, who can write a plain ordinary story, who would not leave out what you have left out. I object not to facts but to people sitting in trees talking senselessly, voices from who knows where . . .'

'Forget that one, Pa, what have I left out now? In this one?'

'Her looks, for instance.'

'Oh. Quite handsome, I think. Yes.'

'Her hair?'

'Dark, with heavy braids, as though she were a girl or a foreigner.'

'What were her parents like, her stock? That she became such a person. It's interesting, you know.'

'From out of town. Professional people. The first to be divorced in their county. How's that? Enough?' I asked.

'With you, it's all a joke,' he said. 'What about the boy's father? Why didn't you mention him? Who was he? Or was the boy born out of wedlock?'

'Yes,' I said. 'He was born out of wedlock.'

'For godsakes, doesn't anyone in your stories get married? Doesn't anyone have the time to run down to City Hall before they jump into bed?'

'No,' I said. 'In real life, yes. But in my stories, no.'

'Why do you answer me like that?'

'Oh, Pa, this is a simple story about a smart woman who came to N.Y.C. full of interest love trust excitement very up-to-date, and about her son, what a hard time she had in this world. Married or not, it's of small consequence.'

'It is of great consequence,' he said.

'O.K.,' I said.

'O.K. O.K. yourself,' he said, 'but listen. I believe you that she's good-looking, but I don't think she was so smart.'

'That's true,' I said. 'Actually that's the trouble with stories. People start out fantastic. You think they're extraordinary, but it turns out as the work goes along, they're just average with a good education. Sometimes the other way around, the person's a kind of dumb innocent, but he outwits you and you can't even think of an ending good enough.'

'What do you do then?' he asked. He had been a doctor for a couple of decades and then an artist for a couple of decades and he's still interested in details, craft, technique.

'Well, you just have to let the story lie around till some agreement can be reached between you and the stubborn hero.'

'Aren't you talking silly, now?' he asked. 'Start again,' he said. 'It so happens I'm not going out this evening. Tell the story again. See what you can do this time.'

'O.K.,' I said. 'But it's not a five-minute job.' Second attempt:

Once, across the street from us, there was a fine handsome woman, our neighbor. She had a son whom she loved because she'd known him since birth (in helpless chubby infancy, and in the wrestling, hugging ages, seven to ten, as well as earlier and later). This boy, when he fell into the fist of adolescence, became a junkie. He was not a hopeless one.

He was in fact hopeful, an ideologue and successful con-
verter. With his busy brilliance, he wrote persuasive articles
for his high-school newspaper. Seeking a wider audience,
using important connections, he drummed into Lower
Manhattan newsstand distribution a periodical called *Oh!
Golden Horse!*

In order to keep him from feeling guilty (because guilt is
the stony heart of nine-tenths of all clinically diagnosed
cancers in America today, she said), and because she had
always believed in giving bad habits room at home where
one could keep an eye on them, she too became a junkie.
Her kitchen was famous for a while – a center for intellec-
tual addicts who knew what they were doing. A few felt
artistic like Coleridge and others were scientific and revolutionary like Leary. Although she was often high herself,
certain good mothering reflexes remained, and she saw to it
that there was lots of orange juice around and honey and
milk and vitamin pills. However, she never cooked anything but chili, and that no more than once a week. She
explained, when we talked to her, seriously, with neigh-
borly concern, that it was her part in the youth culture and
she would rather be with the young, it was an honor, than
with her own generation.

One week, while nodding through an Antonioni film,
this boy was severely jabbed by the elbow of a stern and
proselytizing girl, sitting beside him. She offered immediate
apricots and nuts for his sugar level, spoke to him sharply,
and took him home.

She had heard of him and his work and she herself
published, edited, and wrote a competitive journal
called *Man Does Live by Bread Alone*. In the organic heat
of her continuous presence he could not help but
become interested once more in his muscles, his arteries
and nerve connections. In fact he began to love them,
treasure them, praise them with funny little songs in
Man Does Live . . .

the fingers of my flesh transcend
my transcendental soul
the tightness in my shoulders end
my teeth have made me whole

To the mouth of his head (that glory of will and determination) he brought hard apples, nuts, wheat germ, and soy-bean oil. He said to his old friends, From now on, I guess I'll keep my wits about me. I'm going on the natch. He said he was about to begin a spiritual deep-breathing journey. How about you too, Mom? he asked kindly.

His conversion was so radiant, splendid, that neighborhood kids his age began to say that he had never been a real addict at all, only a journalist along for the smell of the story. The mother tried several times to give up what had become without her son and his friends a lonely habit. This effort only brought it to supportable levels. The boy and his girl took their electronic mimeograph and moved to the bushy edge of another borough. They were very strict. They said they would not see her again until she had been off drugs for sixty days.

At home alone in the evening, weeping, the mother read and reread the seven issues of *Oh! Golden Horse!* They seemed to her as truthful as ever. We often crossed the street to visit and console. But if we mentioned any of our children who were at college or in the hospital or dropouts at home, she would cry out, My baby! My baby! and burst into terrible, face-scarring, time-consuming tears. The End.

First my father was silent, then he said, 'Number One: You have a nice sense of humor. Number Two: I see you can't tell a plain story. So don't waste time.' Then he said sadly, 'Number Three: I suppose that means she was alone, she was left like that, his mother. Alone. Probably sick?'

I said, 'Yes.'

'Poor woman. Poor girl, to be born in a time of fools, to live among fools. The end. The end. You were right to put that down. The end.'

I didn't want to argue, but I had to say, 'Well, it is not necessarily the end, Pa.'

'Yes,' he said, 'what a tragedy. The end of a person.'

'No, Pa,' I begged him. 'It doesn't have to be. She's only about forty. She could be a hundred different things in this world as time goes on. A teacher or a social worker. An ex-junkie! Sometimes it's better than having a master's in education.'

'Jokes,' he said. 'As a writer that's your main trouble. You don't want to recognize it. Tragedy! Plain tragedy! Historical tragedy! No hope. The end.'

'Oh, Pa,' I said. 'She could change.'

'In your own life, too, you have to look it in the face.' He took a couple of nitroglycerin. 'Turn to five,' he said, pointing to the dial on the oxygen tank. He inserted the tubes into his nostrils and breathed deep. He closed his eyes and said, 'No.'

I had promised the family to always let him have the last word when arguing, but in this case I had a different responsibility. That woman lives across the street. She's my knowledge and my invention. I'm sorry for her. I'm not going to leave her there in that house crying. (Actually neither would Life, which unlike me has no pity.)

Therefore: She did change. Of course her son never came home again. But right now, she's the receptionist in a storefront community clinic in the East Village. Most of the customers are young people, some old friends. The head doctor has said to her, 'If we only had three people in this clinic with your experiences . . .'

'The doctor said that?' My father took the oxygen tubes out of his nostrils and said, 'Jokes. Jokes again.'

'No, Pa, it could really happen that way, it's a funny world nowadays.'

'No,' he said. 'Truth first. She will slide back. A person must have character. She does not.'

'No, Pa,' I said. 'That's it. She's got a job. Forget it. She's in that storefront working.'

'How long will it be?' he asked. 'Tragedy! You too. When will you look it in the face?'

The Immigrant Story

Jack asked me, Isn't it a terrible thing to grow up in the shadow of another person's sorrow?

I suppose so, I answered. As you know, I grew up in the summer sunlight of upward mobility. This leached out a lot of that dark ancestral grief.

He went on with his life. It's not your fault if that's the case. Your bad disposition is not your fault. Yet you're always angry. No way out but continuous rage or the nuthouse.

What if this sorrow is all due to history? I asked.

The cruel history of Europe, he said. In this way he showed ironic respect to one of my known themes.

The whole world ought to be opposed to Europe for its cruel history, Jack, and yet in favor of it because after about a thousand years it may have learned some sense.

Nonsense, he said objectively, a thousand years of outgoing persistent imperial cruelty tends to make enemies and if all you have to deal with these enemies is good sense, what then?

My dear, no one knows the power of good sense. It hasn't been built up or experimented with sufficiently.

I'm trying to tell you something, he said. Listen. One day I woke up and my father was asleep in the crib.

I wonder why, I said.

My mother made him sleep in the crib.

All the time?

That time anyway. That time I saw him.

I wonder why, I said.

Because she didn't want him to fuck her, he said.

No, I don't believe that. Who told you that?

I know it! He pointed his finger at me.

I don't believe it, I said. Unless she's had five babies all in a row or they have to get up at 6 a.m. or they both hate each other, most people like their husbands to do that.

Bullshit! She was trying to make him feel guilty. Where were his balls?

I will never respond to that question. Asked in a worried way again and again, it may become responsible for the destruction of the entire world. I gave it two minutes of silence.

He said, Misery misery misery. Grayness. I see it all very very gray. My mother approaches the crib. Shmul, she says, get up. Run down to the corner and get me half a pound of pot cheese. Then run over the drugstore and get a few ounces codliver oil. My father, scrunched like an old gray fetus, looks up and smiles smiles smiles at the bitch.

How do *you* know what was going on? I asked. You were five years old.

What do you think was going on?

I'll tell you. It's not so hard. Any dope who's had a normal life could tell you. Anyone whose head hasn't been fermenting with the compost of ten years of gluttonous analysis. Anyone could tell you.

Tell me what? he screamed.

The reason your father was sleeping in the crib was that you and your sister who usually slept in the crib had scarlet fever and needed the decent beds and more room to sweat, come to a fever crisis, and either get well or die.

Who told you that? He lunged at me as though I was an enemy.

You fucking enemy, he said. You always see things in a rosy light. You have a rotten rosy temperament. You were like that in

sixth grade. One day you brought three American flags to
school.

That was true. I made an announcement to the sixth-grade
assembly thirty years ago. I said: I thank God every day that I'm
not in Europe. I thank God I'm American-born and live on East
172nd Street where there is a grocery store, a candy store, and a
drugstore on one corner and on the same block a shul and two
doctors' offices.

One Hundred and Seventy-second Street was a pile of shit, he
said. Everyone was on relief except you. Thirty people had t.b.
Citizens and noncitizens alike starving until the war. Thank God
capitalism has a war it can pull out of the old feed bag every now
and then or we'd all be dead. Ha ha.

I'm glad that you're not totally brainwashed by stocks, bonds,
and cash. I'm glad to hear you still mention capitalism from time
to time.

Because of poverty, brilliance, and the early appearance of lots
of soft hair on face and crotch, my friend Jack was a noticeable
Marxist and Freudian by the morning of his twelfth birthday.

In fact, his mind thickened with ideas. I continued to put out
more flags. There were twenty-eight flags aflutter in different
rooms and windows. I had one tattooed onto my arm. It has
gotten dimmer but a lot wider because of middle age.

I am probably more radical than you are nowadays, I said.
Since I was not wiped out of my profession during the McCarthy
inquisitions, I therefore did not have to go into business for
myself and make a fortune.

You damn fool. Plenty are wiped out to this day. I mean brilliant guys – engineers, teachers, just broken – broken.

I believe I see the world as clearly as you do, I said. Rosiness is
not a worse windowpane than gloomy gray when viewing the
world.

Yes yes yes yes yes yes yes, he said. Do you mind? Just listen:

My mother and father came from a small town in Poland. They
had three sons. My father decided to go to America, to (1) stay out

of the army, (2) stay out of jail, (3) save his children from everyday wars and ordinary pogroms. He was helped by the savings of parents, uncles, grandmothers and set off like hundreds of thousands of others in that year. In America, New York City, he lived a hard but hopeful life. Sometimes he walked on Delancey Street. Sometimes like a bachelor he went to the theater on Second Avenue. Mostly he put his money away for the day he could bring his wife and sons to this place. Meanwhile, in Poland famine struck. Not hunger, which all Americans suffer six, seven times a day, but Famine, which tells the body to consume itself. First the fat, then the meat, the muscle, then the blood. Famine ate up the bodies of the little boys pretty quickly. My father met my mother at the boat. He looked at her face, her hands. There was no baby in her arms, no children dragging at her skirt. She was not wearing her hair in two long black braids. There was a kerchief over a dark wiry wig. She had shaved her head, like a backward Orthodox bride, though they had been serious advanced socialists like most of the youth of their town. He took her by the hand and brought her home. They never went anywhere alone, except to work or the grocer's. They held each other's hand when they sat down at the table, even at breakfast. Sometimes he patted her hand, sometimes she patted his. He read the paper to her every night.

They are sitting at the edge of their chairs. He's leaning forward reading to her in that old bulb light. Sometimes she smiles just a little. Then he puts the paper down and takes both her hands in his as though they needed warmth. He continues to read. Just beyond the table and their heads, there is the darkness of the kitchen, the bedroom, the dining room, the shadowy darkness where as a child I ate my supper, did my homework, and went to bed.

The Long-Distance Runner

One day, before or after forty-two, I became a long-distance runner. Though I was stout and in many ways inadequate to this desire, I wanted to go far and fast, not as fast as bicycles and trains, not as far as Taipei, Hingwen, places like that, islands of the slant-eyed cunt, as sailors in bus stations say when speaking of travel, but round and round the county from the seaside to the bridges, along the old neighborhood streets a couple of times, before old age and urban renewal ended them and me.

I tried the country first, Connecticut, which being wooded is always full of buds in spring. All creation is secret, isn't that true? So I trained in the wide-zoned suburban hills where I wasn't known. I ran all spring in and out of dogwood bloom, then laurel.

People sometimes stopped and asked me why I ran, a lady in silk shorts halfway down over her fat thighs. In training, I replied and rested only to answer if closely questioned. I wore a white sleeveless undershirt as well, with excellent support, not to attract the attention of old men and prudish children.

Then summer came, my legs seemed strong. I kissed the kids goodbye. They were quite old by then. It was near the time for parting anyway. I told Mrs. Raftery to look in now and then and give them some of that rotten Celtic supper she makes.

I told them they could take off any time they wanted to. Go lead your private life, I said. Only leave me out of it.

A word to the wise . . . said Richard.

You're depressed Faith, Mrs. Raftery said. Your boyfriend Jack, the one you think's so hotsy-totsy, hasn't called and you're as gloomy as a tick on Sunday.

Cut the folkshit with me, Raftery, I muttered. Her eyes filled with tears because that's who she is: folkshit from bunion to top-knot. That's how she got liked by me, loved, invented, and endured.

When I walked out the door they were all reclining before the television set, Richard, Tonto, and Mrs. Raftery, gazing at the news. Which proved with moving pictures that there had been a voyage to the moon and Africa and South America hid in a furious whorl of clouds.

I said, Goodbye. They said, Yeah, O.K., sure.

If that's how it is, forget it, I hollered and took the Independent subway to Brighton Beach.

At Brighton Beach I stopped at the Salty Breezes Locker Room to change my clothes. Twenty-five years ago my father invested $500 in its future. In fact he still clears about $3.50 a year, which goes directly (by law) to the Children of Judea to cover their deficit.

No one paid too much attention when I started to run, easy and light on my feet. I ran on the boardwalk first, past my mother's leafleting station – between a soft-ice-cream stand and a degenerated dune. There she had been assigned by her comrades to halt the tides of cruel American enterprise with simple socialist sense.

I wanted to stop and admire the long beach. I wanted to stop in order to think admiringly about New York. There aren't many rotting cities so tan and sandy and speckled with citizens at their salty edges. But I had already spent a lot of life lying down or standing and staring. I had decided to run.

*

After about a mile and a half I left the boardwalk and began to trot into the old neighborhood. I was running well. My breath was long and deep. I was thinking pridefully about my form.

Suddenly I was surrounded by about three hundred blacks.

Who you?

Who that?

Look at her! Just look! When you seen a fatter ass?

Poor thing. She ain't right. Leave her, you boys, you bad boys.

I used to live here, I said.

Oh yes, they said, in the white old days. That time too bad to last.

But we loved it here. We never went to Flatbush Avenue or Times Square. We loved our block.

Tough black titty.

I like your speech, I said. Metaphor and all.

Right on. We get that from talking.

Yes my people also had a way of speech. And don't forget the Irish. The gift of gab.

Who they? said a small boy.

Cops.

Nowadays, I suggested, there's more than Irish on the police force.

You right, said two ladies. More more, much much more. They's French Chinamen Russkies Congoleans. Oh missee, you too right.

I lived in that house, I said. That apartment house. All my life. Till I got married.

Now that *is* nice. Live in one place. My mother live that way in South Carolina. One place. Her daddy farmed. She said. They ate. No matter winter war bad times. Roosevelt. Something! Ain't that wonderful! And it weren't cold! Big trees!

That apartment. I looked up and pointed. There. The third floor.

They all looked up. So what! You blubrous devil! said a dark young man. He wore horn-rimmed glasses and had that intelligent look that City College boys used to have when I was eighteen and first looked at them.

He seemed to lead them in contempt and anger, even the littlest ones who moved toward me with dramatic stealth singing, Devil, Oh Devil. I don't think the little kids had bad feeling because they poked a finger into me, then laughed.

Still I thought it might be wise to keep my head. So I jumped right in with some facts. I said, How many flowers' names do you know? Wildflowers, I mean. My people only knew two. That's what they say now anyway. Rich or poor, they only had two flowers' names. Rose and violet.

Daisy, said one boy immediately.

Weed, said another. That *is* a flower, I thought. But everyone else got the joke.

Saxifrage, lupine, said a lady. Viper's bugloss, said a small Girl Scout in medium green with a dark green sash. She held up a *Handbook of Wildflowers.*

How many you know, fat mama? a boy asked warmly. He wasn't against my being a mother or fat. I turned all my attention to him.

Oh sonny, I said, I'm way ahead of my people. I know in yellows alone: common cinquefoil, trout lily, yellow adder'stongue, swamp buttercup and common buttercup, golden sorrel, yellow or hop clover, devil's-paintbrush, evening primrose, blackeyed Susan, golden aster, also the yellow pickerelweed growing down by the water if not in the water, and dandelions of course. I've seen all these myself. Seen them.

You could see China from the boardwalk, a boy said. When it's nice.

I know more flowers than countries. Mostly young people these days have traveled in many countries.

Not me. I ain't been nowhere.

Not me either, said about seventeen boys.

I'm not allowed, said a little girl. There's drunken junkies.

But *I! I!* cried out a tall black youth, very handsome and well dressed. I am an African. My father came from the high stolen plains. *I* have been everywhere. I was in Moscow six months, learning machinery. I was in France, learning French. I was in Italy, observing the peculiar Renaissance and the people's sweetness. I was in England, where I studied the common law and the urban blight. I was at the Conference of Dark Youth in Cuba to understand our passion. I am now here. Here am I to become an engineer and return to my people, around the Cape of Good Hope in a Norwegian sailing vessel. In this way I will learn the fine old art of sailing in case the engines of the new society of my old inland country should fail.

We had an extraordinary amount of silence after that. Then one old lady in a black dress and high white lace collar said to another old lady dressed exactly the same way, Glad tidings when someone got brains in the head not fish juice. Amen, said a few.

Whyn't you go up to Mrs. Luddy living in your house, you lady, huh? The Girl Scout asked this.

Why she just groove to see you, said some sarcastic snickerer.

She got palpitations. Her man, he give it to her.

That ain't all, he a natural gift-giver.

I'll take you, said the Girl Scout. My name is Cynthia. I'm in Troop 355, Brooklyn.

I'm not dressed, I said, looking at my lumpy knees.

You shouldn't wear no undershirt like that without no runnin number or no team writ on it. It look like a undershirt.

Cynthia! Don't take her up there, said an important boy. Her head strange. Don't you take her. Hear?

Lawrence, she said softly, you tell me once more what to do I'll wrap you round that lamppost.

Git! she said, powerfully addressing *me*.

In this way I was led into the hallway of the whole house of my childhood.

The first door I saw was still marked in flaky gold, 1A. That's where the janitor lived, I said. He was a Negro.

How come like that? Cynthia made an astonished face. How

come the janitor was a black man?

Oh Cynthia, I said. Then I turned to the opposite door, first floor front, 1B. I remembered. Now, here, this was Mrs. Goreditsky, very very fat lady. All her children died at birth. Born, then one, two, three. Dead. Five children, then Mr. Goreditsky said, I'm bad luck on you Tessie and he went away. He sent $15 a week for seven years. Then no one heard.

I know her, poor thing, said Cynthia. The city come for her summer before last. The way they knew, it smelled. They wropped her up in a canvas. They couldn't get through the front door. It scraped off a piece of her. My Uncle Ronald had to help them, but he got disgusted.

Only two years ago. She was still here! Wasn't she scared?

So we all, said Cynthia. White ain't everything.

Who lived up here, she asked, 2B? Right now, my best friend Nancy Rosalind lives here. She got two brothers, and her sister married and got a baby. She very light-skinned. Not her mother. We got all colors amongst us.

Your best friend? That's funny. Because it was *my* best friend. Right in that apartment. Joanna Rosen.

What become of her? Cynthia asked. She got a running shirt too?

Come on Cynthia, if you really want to know, I'll tell you. She married this man, Marvin Steirs.

Who's he?

I recollected his achievements. Well, he's the president of a big corporation, JoMar Plastics. This corporation owns a steel company, a radio station, a new Xerox-type machine that lets you do twenty-five different pages at once. This corporation has a foundation, The JoMar Fund for Research in Conservation. Capitalism is like that, I added, in order to be politically useful.

How come you know? You go over their house a lot?

No. I happened to read all about them on the financial page, just last week. It made me think: a different life. That's all.

Different spokes for different folks, said Cynthia.

I sat down on the cool marble steps and remembered Joanna's cousin Ziggie. He was older than we were. He wrote a poem which told us we were lovely flowers and our legs were petals, which nature would force open no matter how many times we said no.

Then I had several other interior thoughts that I couldn't share with a child, the kind that give your face a blank or melancholy look.

Now you're not interested, said Cynthia. Now you're not gonna say a thing. Who lived here, 2A? Who? Two men lives here now. Women coming and women going. My mother says, Danger sign: Stay away, my darling, stay away.

I don't remember, Cynthia. I really don't.

You got to. What'd you come for, anyways?

Then I tried. 2A. 2A. Was it the twins? I felt a strong obligation as though remembering was in charge of the existence of the past. This is not so.

Cynthia, I said, I don't want to go any further. I don't even want to remember.

Come on, she said, tugging at my shorts, don't you want to see Mrs. Luddy, the one lives in your old house? That be fun, no?

No. No, I don't want to see Mrs. Luddy.

Now you shouldn't pay no attention to those boys downstairs. She will like you. I mean, she is kind. She don't like most white people, but she might like you.

No Cynthia, it's not that, but I don't want to see my father and mother's house now.

I didn't know what to say. I said, Because my mother's dead. This was a lie, because my mother lives in her own room with my father in the Children of Judea. With her hand over her social-ist heart, she reads the paper every morning after breakfast. Then she says sadly to my father, Every day the same. Dying . . . dying, dying from killing.

My mother's dead Cynthia. I can't go in there.

Oh . . . oh, the poor thing, she said, looking into my eyes. Oh, if my mother died, I don't know what I'd do. Even if I was old as

you. I could kill myself. Tears filled her eyes and started down
her cheeks. If my mother died, what would I do? She is my pro-
tector, she won't let the pushers get me. She hold me tight. She
gonna hide me in the cedar box if my Uncle Rudford comes try to
get me back. She *can't* die, my mother.

Cynthia – honey – she won't die. She's young. I put my arm
out to comfort her. You could come live with me, I said. I got
two boys, they're nearly grown up. I missed it, not having a
girl.

What? What you mean now, live with you and boys. She
pulled away and ran for the stairs. Stay away from me, honky
lady. I know them white boys. They just gonna try and jostle my
black womanhood. My mother told me about that, keep you
white honky devil boys to your devil self, you just leave me be
you old bitch you. Somebody help me, she started to scream,
you hear. Somebody help. She gonna take me away.

She flattened herself to the wall, trembling. I was too frightened by her fear of me to say, Honey, I wouldn't hurt you, it's me.
I heard her helpers, the voices of large boys crying, We coming,
we coming, hold your head up, we coming. I ran past her fear to
the stairs and up them two at a time. I came to my old own door.
I knocked like the landlord, loud and terrible.

Mama not home, a child's voice said. No, no, I said. It's me! a
lady! Someone's chasing me, let me in. Mama not home, I ain't
allowed to open up for nobody.

It's me! I cried out in terror. Mama! Mama! let me in!

The door opened. A slim woman whose age I couldn't invent
looked at me. She said, Get in and shut that door tight. She took
a hard pinching hold on my upper arm. Then she bolted the door
herself. Them hustlers after you. They make me pink. Hide this
white lady now, Donald. Stick her under your bed, you got a
high bed.

Oh that's O.K. I'm fine now, I said. I felt safe and at home.

You in my house, she said. You do as I say. For two cents, I
throw you out.

I squatted under a small kid's pissy mattress. Then I heard the knock. It was tentative and respectful. My mama don't allow me to open. Donald! someone called. Donald!

Oh no, he said. Can't do it. She gonna wear me out. You know her. She already tore up my ass this morning once. Ain't *gonna* open up.

I lived there for about three weeks with Mrs. Luddy and Donald and three little baby girls nearly the same age. I told her a joke about Irish twins. Ain't Irish, she said.

Nearly every morning the babies woke us at about 6:45. We gave them all a bottle and went back to sleep till 8:00. I made coffee and she changed diapers. Then it really stank for a while. At this time I usually said, Well listen, thanks really, but I've got to go I guess. I guess I'm going. She'd usually say. Well. guess again. *I* guess you ain't. Or if she was feeling disgusted she'd say. Go on now! Get! You wanna go. I guess by now I have snorted enough white lady stink to choke a horse. Go on!

I'd get to the door and then I'd hear voices. I'm ashamed to say I'd become fearful. Despite my wide geographical love of mankind. I would be attacked by local fears.

There was a sentimental truth that lay beside all that going and not going. It *was* my house where I'd lived long ago my family life. There was a tile on the bathroom floor that I myself had broken. dropping a hammer on the toe of my brother Charles as he stood dreamily shaving, his prick halfway up his undershorts. Astonishment and knowledge first seized me right there. The kitchen was the same. The table was the enameled table common to our class, easy to clean, with wooden undercorners for indigent and old cockroaches that couldn't make it to the kitchen sink. (However, it was not the same table, because I have inherited that one, chips and all.)

The living room was something like ours, only we had less plastic. There may have been less plastic in the world at that time. Also, my mother had set beautiful cushions everywhere, on beds and chairs. It was the way she expressed herself, artistically, to embroider at night or take strips of flowered cotton and sew them across ordinary white or blue muslin in the most delicate designs, the way women have always used materials that live and die in hunks and tatters to say: This is my place.

Mrs. Luddy said, Uh huh!

Of course, I said, men don't have that outlet. That's how come they run around so much.

Till they drunk enough to lay down, she said.

Yes, I said, on a large scale you can see it in the world. First they make something, then they murder it. Then they write a book about how interesting it is.

You got something there, she said. Sometimes she said, Girl, you don't know *nothing*.

We often sat at the window looking out and down. Little tufts of breeze grew on that windowsill. The blazing afternoon was around the corner and up the block.

You say men, she said. Is that men? she asked. What you call — a Man?

Four flights below us, leaning on the stoop, were about a dozen people and around them devastation. Just a minute, I said. I had seen devastation on my way, running, gotten some of the pebbles of it in my running shoe and the dust of it in my eyes. I had thought with the indignant courtesy of a citizen, This is a disgrace to the City of New York, which I love and am running through.

But now, from the commanding heights of home, I saw it clearly. The tenement in which Jack my old and present friend had come to gloomy manhood had been destroyed, first by fire, then by demolition (which is a swinging ball of steel that cracks bedrooms and kitchens). Because of this work, we could see several blocks wide and a block and a half long. That weird guy Eddy — his house still stood, famous 1510 gutted, with black window frames, no glass, open laths. The stubbornness of the supporting beams! Some persons or families still lived on the lowest floors. In the lots between, a couple of old sofas lay on their fat faces, their springs sticking up into the air. Just as in wartime a half dozen ailanthus trees had already found their first quarter inch of earth and begun a living attack on the dead yards. At night, I knew animals roamed the place, squalling and howling, furious New York dogs and street cats and mighty rats. You would think you were in Bear Mountain Park, the terror of venturing forth.

Someone ought to clean that up. I said.

Mrs. Luddy said, Who you got in mind? Mrs. Kennedy? –

Donald made a stern face. He said. That just what I gonna do when I get big. Gonna get the Sanitary Man in and show it to him. You see that, you big guinea you, you clean it up right now! Then he stamped his feet and fierced his eyes.

Mrs. Luddy said. Come here, you little nigger. She kissed the top of his head and gave him a whack on the backside all at one time.

Well. said Donald, encouraged, look out there now you all! Go on I say, look! Though we had already seen, to please him we looked. On the stoop men and boys lounged, leaned, hopped about, stood on one leg, then another, took their socks off, and scratched their toes, talked, sat on their haunches, heads down, dozing.

Donald said, Look at them. They ain't got self-respect. They got Afros *on* their heads, but they don't know they black *in* their heads.

I thought he ought to learn to be more sympathetic. I said, There are reasons that people are that way.

Yes, ma'am, said Donald.

Anyway, how come you never go down and play with the other kids, how come you're up here so much?

My mama don't like me do that. Some of them is bad. Bad. I might become a dope addict. I got to stay clear.

You just a dope, that's a fact, said Mrs. Luddy.

He ought to be with kids his age more, I think.

He see them in school, miss. Don't trouble your head about it if you don't mind.

Actually, Mrs. Luddy didn't go down into the street either.

Donald did all the shopping. She let the welfare investigator in, the meterman came into the kitchen to read the meter. I saw him from the back room, where I hid. She did pick up her check. She cashed it. She returned to wash the babies, change their diapers, wash clothes, iron, feed people, and then in free half hours she sat by that window. She was waiting.

I believed she was watching and waiting for a particular man. I wanted to discuss this with her, talk lovingly like sisters. But before I could freely say, Forget about that son of a bitch, he's a pig, I did have to offer a few solid facts about myself, my kids, about fathers, husbands, passersby, evening companions, and the life of my father and mother in this room by this exact afternoon window.

I told her, for instance, that in my worst times I had given myself one extremely simple physical pleasure. This was cream cheese for breakfast. In fact, I insisted on it. sometimes depriving the children of very important articles and food.

Girl, you don't know nothing, she said.

Then for a little while she talked gently as one does to a person who is innocent and insane and incorruptible because of stupidity. She had had two such special pleasures for hard times, she said. The first, men, but they turned rotten, white women had ruined the best, give them the idea their dicks made of solid gold. The second pleasure she had tried was wine. She said, I do like wine. You *has* to have something just for yourself by yourself. Then she said, But you can't raise a decent boy when you liquor-dazed every night.

White or black, I said, returning to men, they did think they were bringing a rare gift, whereas it was just sex, which is common like bread, though essential.

Oh, you can do without, she said. There's folks does without.

I told her Donald deserved the best. I loved him. If he had flaws, I hardly noticed them. It's one of my beliefs that children do not have flaws, even the worst do not.

Donald was brilliant – like my boys except that he had an easier disposition. For this reason I decided, almost the second moment of my residence in that household, to bring him up to reading level at once. I told him we would work with books and newspapers. He went immediately to his neighborhood library and brought some hard books to amuse me. *Black Folktales* by Julius Lester and *The Pushcart War*, which is about another neighborhood but relevant.

Donald always agreed with me when we talked about reading and writing. In fact, when I mentioned poetry, he told me he knew all about it, that David Henderson, a known black poet, had visited his second-grade class. So Donald was, as it turned out, well ahead of my nosy tongue. He was usually very busy shopping. He also had to spend a lot of time making faces to force the little serious baby girls into laughter. But if the subject came up, he could take *the* poem right out of the air into which language and event had just gone.

An example: That morning, his mother had said, Whew, I just got too much piss and diapers and wash. I wanna just sit down by that window and rest myself. He wrote a poem:

Just got too much pissy diapers
and wash and wash
just wanna sit down by that window
and look out
  ain't nothing there.

Donald, I said, you are plain brilliant. I'm never going to forget you. For godsakes don't you forget me.

You fool with him too much, said Mrs. Luddy. He already don't even remember his grandma, you never gonna meet someone like her, a curse never come past her lips.

I do remember, Mama, I remember. She lying in bed, right there. A man standing in the door. She say, Esdras, I put a curse on you head. You worsen tomorrow. How come she said like that?

Gomorrah, I believe Gomorrah, she said. She know the Bible inside out.

Did she live with you?

No. No, she visiting. She come up to see us all, her children, how we doing. She come up to see sights. Then she lay down and died. She was old.

I remained quiet because of the death of mothers. Mrs. Luddy looked at me thoughtfully, then she said:

My mama had stories to tell, she raised me on. *Her* mama was a little thing, no sense. Stand in the door of the cabin all day, sucking her thumb. It was slave times. One day a young field boy come storming along. He knock on the door of the first cabin hollering, Sister, come out, it's freedom. She come out. She say, Yeah? When? He say, Now! It's freedom now! Then he knock at the next door and say, Sister! It's freedom! Now! From one cabin he run to the next cabin, crying out, Sister, it's freedom now!

Oh I remember that story, said Donald. Freedom now! Freedom now! He jumped up and down.

You don't remember nothing boy. Go on, get Eloise, she want to get into the good times.

Eloise was two but undersized. We got her like that, said Donald. Mrs. Luddy let me buy her ice cream and green vegetables. She was waiting for kale and chard, but it was too early. The kale liked cold. You not about to be here November, she said. No, no. I turned away, lonesomeness touching me, and sang our Eloise song:

Eloise loves the bees
the bees they buzz
like Eloise does.

Then Eloise crawled all over the splintery floor, buzzing wildly.

Oh you crazy baby, said Donald, buzz buzz buzz.

Mrs. Luddy sat down by the window.

You all make a lot of noise, she said sadly. You just right on noisy.

The next morning Mrs. Luddy woke me up.

Time to go, she said.

What?

Home.

What? I said.

Well, don't you think your little spoiled boys crying for you? Where's Mama? They standing in the window. Time to go lady. This ain't Free Vacation Farm. Time we was by ourself a little.

Oh Ma, said Donald, she ain't a lot of trouble. Go on, get Eloise, she hollering. And button up your lip.

She didn't offer me coffee. She looked at me strictly all the time. I tried to look strictly back, but I failed because I loved the sight of her.

Donald was teary, but I didn't dare turn my face to him, until the parting minute at the door. Even then, I kissed the top of his head a little too forcefully and said, Well. I'll see you.

On the front stoop there were about half a dozen mid-morning family people and kids arguing about who had dumped garbage out of which window. They were very disgusted with one another.

Two young men in handsome dashikis stood in counsel and agreement at the street corner. They divided a comment. How come white womens got rotten teeth? And look so old? A young woman waiting at the light said, Hush . . .

I walked past them and didn't begin my run till the road opened up somewhere along Ocean Parkway. I was a little stiff because my way of life had used only small movements, an occasional stretch to put a knife or teapot out of reach of the babies. I ran about ten, fifteen blocks. Then my second wind came, which is classical, famous among runners, it's the beginning of flying.

In the three weeks I'd been off the street, jogging had become popular. It seemed that I was only one person doing her thing, which happened like most American eccentric acts to be the most 'in' thing I could have done. In fact, two young men ran alongside of me for nearly a mile. They ran silently beside me and turned off at Avenue H. A gentleman with a mustache, running poorly in the opposite direction, waved. He called out, Hi, señora.

Near home I ran through our park, where I had aired my children on weekends and late-summer afternoons. I stopped at the northeast playground, where I met a dozen young mothers intelligently handling their little ones. In order to prepare them, meaning no harm, I said, In fifteen years, you girls will be like me, wrong in everything.

At home it was Saturday morning. Jack had returned looking as grim as ever, but he'd brought cash and a vacuum cleaner. While the coffee perked, he showed Richard how to use it. They were playing ticktacktoe on the dusty wall.

Richard said, Well! Look who's here! Hi!

Any news? I asked.

Letter from Daddy, he said. From the lake and water country in Chile. He says it's like Minnesota.

He's never been to Minnesota, I said. Where's Anthony?

Here I am, said Tonto, appearing. But I'm leaving.

Oh yes. I said. Of course. Every Saturday he hurries through breakfast or misses it. He goes to visit his friends in institutions. These are well-known places like Bellevue. Hillside, Rockland State, Central Islip, Manhattan. These visits take him all day and sometimes half the night.

I found some chocolate-chip cookies in the pantry. Take them, Tonto, I said. I remember nearly all his friends as little boys and girls always hopping, skipping, jumping, and cookie-eating. He was annoyed. He said, No! Chocolate cookies is what the commissaries are full of. How about money?

Jack dropped the vacuum cleaner. He said, No! They have parents for that.

I said, Here, five dollars for cigarettes, one dollar each.

Cigarettes! said Jack. Goddamnit! Black lungs and death! Cancer! Emphysema! He stomped out of the kitchen, breathing. He took the bike from the back room and started for Central Park, which has been closed to cars but opened to bicycle riders. When he'd been gone about ten minutes, Anthony said, It's really open only on Sundays.

Why didn't you say so? Why can't you be decent to him? I asked. It's important to me.

Oh Faith, he said, patting me on the head because he'd grown so tall, all that air. It's good for his lungs. And his muscles! He'll be back soon.

You should ride too, I said. You don't want to get mushy in your legs. You should go swimming once a week.

I'm too busy, he said. I have to see my friends.

Then Richard, who had been vacuuming under his bed, came into the kitchen. You still here, Tonto?

Going going gone, said Anthony, don't bat your eye.

Now listen, Richard said, here's a note. It's for Judy, if you get as far as Rockland. Don't forget it. Don t open it. Don't read it. I know he'll read it.

Anthony smiled and slammed the door.

Did I lose weight? I asked. Yes, said Richard. You look O.K. You never look too bad. But where were you? I got sick of Raftery's boiled potatoes. Where were you, Faith?

Well! I said. Well! I stayed a few weeks in my old apartment, where Grandpa and Grandma and me and Hope and Charlie lived, when we were little. I took you there long ago. Not so far from the ocean where Grandma made us very healthy with sun and air.

What are you talking about? said Richard. Cut the baby talk.

Anthony came home earlier than expected that evening because some people were in shock therapy and someone else had run away. He listened to me for a while. Then he said, I don't know what she's talking about either.

Neither did Jack, despite the understanding often produced by love after absence. He said, Tell me again. He was in a good mood. He said, You can even tell it to me twice.

I repeated the story. They all said, What?

Because it isn't usually so simple. Have you known it to

happen much nowadays? A woman inside the steamy energy of middle age runs and runs. She finds the houses and streets where her childhood happened. She lives in them. She learns as though she was still a child what in the world is coming next.

LATER
THE SAME
DAY
(1985)

Love

First I wrote this poem:

Walking up the slate path of the college park
under the nearly full moon   the brown oak leaves
  are red as maples
and I have been looking at the young people
they speak and embrace one another
because of them I thought I would descend
into remembering love   so   I let myself down
  hand over hand
until my feet touched the earth of the gardens
of Vesey Street

I told my husband, I've just written a poem about love.
What a good idea, he said.
Then he told me about Sally Johnson on Lake Winnipesaukee,
who was twelve and a half when he was fourteen. Then he told
me about Rosemarie Johanson on Lake Sunapee. Then he told
me about Jane Marston in Concord High, and then he told me about
Mary Smythe of Radcliffe when he was a poet at Harvard. Then
he told me about two famous poets, one fair and one dark, both
now dead, when he was a secret poet working at an acceptable

trade in an office without windows. When at last he came to my time – that is, the past fifteen years or so – he told me about Dotty Wasserman.

Hold on, I said. What do you mean, Dotty Wasserman? She's a character in a book. She's not even a person.

O.K., he said. Then why Vesey Street? What's that?

Well, it's nothing special. I used to be in love with a guy who was a shrub buyer. Vesey Street was the downtown garden center of the city when the city still had wonderful centers of commerce. I used to walk the kids there when they were little carriage babies half asleep, maybe take the ferry to Hoboken. Years later I'd bike down there Sundays, ride round and round. I even saw him about three times.

No kidding, said my husband. How come I don't know the guy?

Ugh, the stupidity of the beloved. It's you, I said. Anyway, what's this baloney about you and Dotty Wasserman?

Nothing much. She was this crazy kid who hung around the bars. But she didn't drink. Really it was for the men, you know. Neither did I – drink too much, I mean. I was just hoping to get laid once in a while or maybe meet someone and fall madly in love.

He is that romantic. Sometimes I wonder if loving me in this homey life in middle age with two sets of bedroom slippers, one a skin of sandal for summer and the other pair lined with cozy sheepskin – it must be a disappointing experience for him.

He made a polite bridge over my conjectures. He said, She was also this funny mother in the park, years later, when we were all doing that municipal politics and I was married to Josephine. Dotty and I were both delegates to that famous Kansas City National Meeting of Town Meetings. NMTM. Remember? Some woman.

No, I said, that's not true. She was made up, just plain invented in the late fifties.

Oh, he said, then it was after that. I must have met her afterward.

He is stubborn, so I dropped the subject and went to get the groceries. Our shrinking family requires more coffee, more eggs, more cheese, less butter, less meat, less orange juice, more grapefruit.

Walking along the street, encountering no neighbor, I hummed a little up-and-down tune and continued jostling time with the help of my nice reconnoitering brain. Here I was, experiencing the old earth of Vesey Street, breathing in and out with more attention to the process than is usual in the late morning – all because of love, probably. How interesting the way it glides to solid invented figures from true remembered wraiths. By God, I thought, the lover is real. The heart of the lover continues; it has been propagandized from birth.

I passed our local bookstore, which was doing well, with *The Joy of All Sex* underpinning its prosperity. The owner gave me, a dependable customer of poorly advertised books, an affectionate smile. He was a great success. (He didn't know that three years later his rent would be tripled, he would become a sad failure, and the landlord, feeling himself brilliant, an outwitting entrepreneur, a star in the microeconomic heavens, would be the famous success.)

From half a block away I could see the kale in the grocer's bin, crumbles of ice shining the dark leaves. In interior counterview I imagined my husband's north-country fields, the late autumn frost in the curly green. I began to mumble a new poem:

> *In the grocer's bin, the green kale shines*
> *in the north country it stands*
> > *sweet with frost*
> *dark and curly in a garden of tan hay*
> *and light white snow . . .*

Light white . . . I said that a couple of questioning times. Suddenly my outside eyes saw a fine-looking woman named Margaret, who hadn't spoken to me in two years. We'd had many years of political agreement before some matters relating to the

Soviet Union separated us. In the angry months during which we were both right in many ways, she took away with her to her political position and daily friendship my own best friend, Louise – my lifelong park, P.T.A., and antiwar-movement sister, Louise.

In a hazy litter of love and leafy green vegetables I saw Margaret's good face, and before I remembered our serious difference, I smiled. At the same moment, she knew me and smiled. So foolish is the true lover when responded to that I took her hand as we passed, bent to it, pressed it to my cheek, and touched it with my lips.

I described all this to my husband at suppertime. Well of course, he said. Don't you know? The smile was for Margaret but really you do miss Louise a lot and the kiss was for Louise. We both said, Ah! Then we talked over the way the SALT treaty looked more like a floor than a ceiling, read a poem written by one of his daughters, looked at a TV show telling the destruction of the European textile industry, and then made love.

In the morning he said, You're some lover, you know. He said, You really are. You remind me a lot of Dotty Wasserman.

Dreamer in a Dead Language

The old are modest, said Philip. They tend not to outlive one another.

That's witty, said Faith, but the more you think about it, the less it means.

Philip went to another table where he repeated it at once. Faith thought a certain amount of intransigence was nice in almost any lover. She said, Oh well, O.K. . . .

Now, why at that lively time of life, which is so full of standing up and lying down, *why* were they thinking and speaking sentences about the old.

Because Faith's father, one of the resident poets of the Children of Judea, Home for the Golden Ages, Coney Island Branch, had written still another song. This amazed nearly everyone in the Green Coq, that self-mocking tavern full of artists, entrepreneurs, and working women. In those years, much like these, amazing poems and grizzly tales were coming from the third grade, from the first grade in fact, where the children of many of the drinkers and talkers were learning creativity. But the old! This is very interesting, said some. This is too much. said others. The entrepreneurs said, Not at all – watch it – it's a trend.

Jack, Faith's oldest friend, never far but usually distant, said, I know what Philip means. He means the old are modest. They tend not to outlive each other by too much. Right, Phil?

Well, said Philip, you're right, but the mystery's gone.

In Faith's kitchen, later that night, Philip read the poem aloud. His voice had a timbre which reminded her of evening, maybe nighttime. She had often thought of the way wide air lives and moves in a man's chest. Then it's strummed into shape by the short-stringed voice box to become a wonderful secondary sexual characteristic.

Your voice reminds me of evening too! said Philip.

This is the poem he read:

There is no rest for me since love departed
no sleep since I reached the bottom of the sea
and the end of this woman, my wife.
My lungs are full of water. I cannot breathe.
Still I long to go sailing in spring among realities.
There is a young girl who waits in a special time and
*   place*
to love me, to be my friend and lie beside me all
*   through the night.*

Who's the girl? Philip asked.

Why, my mother of course.

You're sweet. Faith.

Of course it's my mother, Phil. My mother, young.

I think it's a different girl entirely.

No, said Faith. It has to be my mother.

But Faith, it doesn't matter who it is. What an old man writes poems about doesn't really matter.

Well, goodbye, said Faith. I've known you one day too long already.

O.K. Change of subject, smile, he said. I really am *crazy* about old people. Always have been. When Anita and I broke up, it was those great Sundays playing chess with her dad that I missed most. They don t talk to me, you know. People take everything personally. I don't, he said. Listen, I d love to meet your daddy *and* your mom. Maybe I'll go with you tomorrow.

We don't say mom, we don't say daddy. We say mama and papa, when in a hurry we say pa and ma.

I do too, said Philip. I just forgot myself. How about I go with you tomorrow. Damn it, I don't sleep. I'll be up all night. I can't stop cooking. My head. It's like a percolator. Pop! pop! Maybe it's my age, prime of life, you know. Didn't I hear that the father of your children, if you don't mind my mentioning it, is doing a middleman dance around your papa?

How about a nice cup of Sleepytime tea?

Come on Faith, I asked you something.

Yes.

Well, I could do better than he ever dreams of doing. I know — on good terms — more people. Who's that jerk know? Four old maids in advertising, three Seventh Avenue models, two fairies in TV, one literary dyke . . .

Philip . . .

I'm telling you something. My best friend is Ezra Kalmback. He made a fortune in the great American Craft and Hobby business — he can teach a four-year-old kid how to make an ancient Greek artifact. He's got a system and the equipment. That's how he supports his other side, the ethnic, you know. They publish these poor old dreamers in one dead language — or another. Hey! How's that! A title for your papa. 'Dreamer in a Dead Language.' Give me a pen. I got to write it down. O.K. Faith, I give you that title free of charge, even if you decide to leave me out.

Leave you out of what? she asked. Stop walking up and down. This room is too small. You'll wake the kids up. Phil, why does your voice get so squeaky when you talk business? It goes higher and higher. Right now you're above high C.

He had been thinking printing costs and percentage. He couldn't drop his answer more than half an octave. That's because I was once a pure-thinking English major — but alas, I was forced by bad management, the thoughtless begetting of children, and the vengeance of alimony into low practicality.

Faith bowed her head. She hated the idea of giving up the longed-for night in which sleep, sex, and affection would take their happy turns. What will I do, she thought. How can you talk like that to me Philip? Vengeance . . . you really stink Phil. Me. Anita's old friend. Are you dumb? She didn't want to hit him. Instead her eyes filled with tears.

What'd I do now? he asked. Oh, I know what I did. I know exactly.

What poet did you think was so great when you were pure?

Milton, he said. He was surprised. He hadn't known till asked that he was lonesome for all that Latin moralizing. You know, Faith, Milton was of the party of the devil, he said. I don't think I am. Maybe it's because I have to make a living.

I like two poems, said Faith, and except for my father's stuff, that's all I like. This was not necessarily true, but she was still thinking with her strict offended face. I like *Hail to thee blithe spirit bird thou never wert*, and I like *Oh what can ail thee knight at arms alone and palely loitering*. And that's all.

Now listen Philip, if you ever see my folks, if I ever bring you out there, don't mention Anita Franklin – my parents were crazy about her, they thought she'd be a Ph.D. medical doctor. Don't let on you were the guy who dumped her. In fact, she said sadly, don't even tell me about it again.

Faith's father had been waiting at the gate for about half an hour. He wasn't bored. He had been discussing the slogan 'Black Is Beautiful' with Chuck Johnson, the gatekeeper. Who thought it up, Chuck?

I couldn't tell you, Mr. Darwin. It just settled on the street one day, there it was.

It's brilliant, said Mr. Darwin. If we could've thought that one up, it would've saved a lot of noses, believe me. You know what I'm talking about?

Then he smiled. Faithy! Richard! Anthony! You said you'd come and you came. Oh oh, I'm not sarcastic – it's only a fact. I'm happy. Chuck, you remember my youngest girl? Faithy, this is

Chuck in charge of coming and going. Richard! Anthony! say hello to Chuck. Faithy, look at me, he said.

What a place! said Richard.

A castle! said Tonto.

You are nice to see your grandpa, said Chuck. I bet he been nice to you in his day.

Don't mention day. By me it's morning. Right Faith? I'm first starting out.

Starting out where? asked Faith. She was sorry so much would have to happen before the true and friendly visit.

To tell you the truth, I was talking to Ricardo the other day.

That's what I thought, what kind of junk did he fill you up with?

Faith, in the first place don't talk about their father in front of the boys. Do me the favor. It's a rotten game. Second, probably you and Ricardo got the wrong chemistry.

Chemistry? The famous scientist. Is that his idea? How's his chemistry with you? Huh?

Well, he talks.

Is Daddy here? asked Richard.

Who cares? said Tonto, looking at his mother's face. We don't care much, do we Faith?

No no, said Faith. Daddy isn't here. He just spoke to Grandpa, remember I told you about Grandpa writing that poetry. Well, Daddy likes it.

That's a little better, Mr. Darwin said.

I wish you luck Pa, but you ought to talk to a few other people. I could ask someone else – Ricardo is a smart operator, I know. What's he planning for you?

Well Faithy, two possibilities. The first a little volume, put out in beautiful vellum, maybe something like vellum, you know, *Poems from the Golden Age* . . . You like that?

Ugh! said Faith.

Is this a hospital? asked Richard.

The other thing is like this. Faithy, I got dozens of songs, you want to call them songs. You could call them songs or poems, whatever, I don't know. Well, he had a good idea, to put out a book also with some other people here – a series – if not a book. Keller for instance is no slouch when it comes to poetry, but he's more like an epic poet, you know . . . When Israel was a youth, then I loved . . . it's a first line, it goes on a hundred pages at least. Madame Nazdarova, our editor from *A Bessere Zeit* – did you meet her? – she listens like a disease. She's a natural editor. It goes in her ear one day. In a week you see it without complications, no mistakes, on paper.

You're some guy, Pa, said Faith. Worry and tenderness brought her brows together.

Don't wrinkle up so much, he said.

Oh shit! said Faith.

Is this a hospital? asked Richard.

They were walking toward a wall of wheelchairs that rested in the autumn sun. Off to the right under a great-leaf linden a gathering of furious arguers were leaning – every one of them – on aluminum walkers.

Like a design, said Mr. Darwin. A beautiful sight.

Well, *is* this a hospital? Richard asked.

It looks like a hospital, I bet, sonny. Is that it?

A little bit, Grandpa.

A lot, be honest. Honesty, my grandson, is *one* of the best policies.

Richard laughed. Only one, huh Grandpa.

See, Faithy, he gets the joke. Oh, you darling kid. What a sense of humor! Mr. Darwin whistled for the joy of a grandson with a sense of humor. Listen to him laugh, he said to a lady volunteer who had come to read very loud to the deaf.

I have a sense of humor too Grandpa, said Tonto.

Sure sonny, why not. Your mother was a constant entertainment to us. She could take jokes right out of the air for your grandma and me and your aunt and uncle. She had us in stitches, your mother.

She mostly laughs for company now, said Tonto, like if Philip comes.

Oh, he's so melodramatic, said Faith, pulling Tonto's ear. What a lie . . .

We got to fix that up, Anthony. Your mama's a beautiful girl. She should be happy. Let's think up a good joke to tell her. He thought for about twelve seconds. Well, O.K. I got it. Listen:

There's an old Jew. He's in Germany. It's maybe '39, '40. He comes around to the tourist office. He looks at the globe. They got a globe there. He says, Listen, I got to get out of here. Where you suggest, Herr Agent, I should go? The agency man also looks at the globe. The Jewish man says, Hey, how about here? He points to America. Oh, says the agency man, sorry, no, they got finished up with their quota. Ts, says the Jewish man, so how about here? He points to France. Last train left already for there, too bad, too bad. Nu, then to Russia? Sorry, absolutely nobody they let in there at the present time. A few more places . . . the answer is always, port is closed. They got already too many, we got no boats . . . So finally the poor Jew, he's thinking he can't go any-where on the globe, also he also can't stay where he is, he says oi, he says ach! he pushes the globe away, disgusted. But he got hope. He says, So this one is used up, Herr Agent. Listen – you got another one?

Oh, said Faith, what a terrible thing. What's funny about that? I hate that joke.

I get it, I get it, said Richard. Another globe. There is no other globe. Only one globe, Mommy? He had no place to go. On account of that old Hitler. Grandpa, tell it to me again. So I can tell my class.

I don't think it's so funny either, said Tonto.

Pa, is Hegel-Shtein with Mama? I don't know if I can take her today. She's too much.

Faith, who knows? You're not the only one. Who can stand her? One person, your mama, the saint, that's who. I'll tell you what – let the boys come with me. I'll give them a quick rundown on the place. You go upstairs. I'll show them wonderful sights.

Well, O.K. . . . will you go with Grandpa, boys?

Sure, said Tonto. Where'll you be?

With Grandma.

If I need to see you about anything, said Richard, could I?

Sure, sonny boys, said Mr. Darwin. Any time you need your mama say the word, one, two, three, you got her. O.K.? Faith, the elevator is over there by that entrance.

Christ, I know where the elevator is.

Once, not paying attention, rising in the gloom of her troubles, the elevator door had opened and she'd seen it – the sixth-floor ward.

Sure – the incurables, her father had said. Then to comfort her: Would you believe it, Faithy? Just like the world, the injustice. Even here, some of us start on the top. The rest of us got to work our way up.

Ha ha, said Faith.

It's only true, he said.

He explained that incurable did not mean near death necessarily, it meant, in most cases, just too far from living. There were, in fact, thirty-year-old people in the ward, with healthy hearts and satisfactory lungs. But they lay flat or curved by pain, or they were tied with shawls into wheelchairs. Here and there an old or middle-aged parent came every day to change the sheets or sing nursery rhymes to her broken child.

The third floor, however, had some of the characteristics of a hotel – that is, there were corridors, rugs, and doors, and Faith's mother's door was, as always, wide open. Near the window, using up light and the curly shadow of hanging plants, Mrs. Hegel-Shtein was wide awake, all smiles and speedy looks, knitting needles and elbows jabbing the air. Faith kissed her cheek for the awful sake of her mother's kindness. Then she sat beside her mother to talk and be friends.

Naturally, the very first thing her mother said was: The boys? She looked as though she'd cry.

No no, Ma, I brought them, they're with Pa a little.

I was afraid for a minute . . . This gives us a chance . . . So, Faithy, tell me the truth. How is it? A little better? The job helps?

The job . . . ugh. I'm buying a new typewriter, Ma. I want to work at home. It's a big investment, you know, like going into business.

Faith! Her mother turned to her. Why should you go into business? You could be a social worker for the city. You're very good-hearted, you always worried about the next fellow. You should be a teacher, you could be off in the summer. You could get a counselor job, the children would go to camp.

Oh, Ma . . . oh, damn it! . . . said Faith. She looked at Mrs. Hegel-Shtein, who, for a solid minute, had not been listening because she was counting stitches.

What could I do, Faithy? You said eleven o'clock. Now it's one. Am I right?

I guess so, said Faith. There was no way to talk. She bent her head down to her mother's shoulder. She was much taller and it was hard to do. Though awkward, it was necessary. Her mother took her hand – pressed it to her cheek. Then she said, Ach! what I know about this hand . . . the way it used to eat apple-sauce, it didn't think a spoon was necessary. A very backward hand.

Oh boy, cute, said Mrs. Hegel-Shtein.

Mrs. Darwin turned the hand over, patted it, then dropped it. My goodness! Faithy. Faithy, how come you have a boil on the wrist. Don't you wash?

Ma, of course I wash. I don't know. Maybe it's from worry, anyway it's not a boil.

Please don't tell me worry. You went to college. Keep your hands clean. You took biology. I remember. So wash.

Ma. For godsakes. I know when to wash.

Mrs. Hegel-Shtein dropped her knitting. Mrs. Darwin, I don't like to interfere, only it so happens your little kiddie is right. Boils on the wrist is the least from worry. It's a scientific fact. Worries what start long ago don't come to a end. You didn't realize. Only go in and out, in and out the heart a couple hundred times something like gas. I can see you don't believe me. Stubborn Celia Darwin. Sickness comes from trouble. Cysts, I got all over inside me since the Depression. Where the doctor could put a hand, Cyst! he hollered. Gallbladder I have since Archie married a fool. Slow blood, I got that when Mr. Shtein died. Varicose veins, with *hemorrhoids* and a crooked neck, I got when Mr. Shtein got social security and retired. For him that time nervousness from the future come to an end. For me it first began. You know what is responsibility? To keep a sick old man alive. Everything like the last supper before they put the man in the electric chair. Turkey. Pot roast. Stuffed kishkas, kugels all kinds, soups without an end. Oi. Faithy, from this I got arthritis and rheumatism from top to bottom. Boils on the wrist is only the beginning.

What you mean is, Faith said, what you mean is – life has made you sick.

If that's what I mean, that's what I mean.

Now, said Mr. Darwin, who was on his way to the roof garden with the boys. He had passed the room, stopped to listen; he had a comment to make. He repeated: Now! then continued, That's what I got against modern times. It so happens you're in the swim, Mrs. H. Psychosomatic is everything nowadays. You don't have a cold that you say, I caught it on the job from Mr. Hirsh. No siree, you got your cold nowadays from your wife, whose health is perfect, she just doesn't think you're so handsome. It might turn out that to her you were always a mutt. Usually then you get hay fever for life. Every August is the anniversary of don't remind me.

All right, said Mrs. Darwin, the whole conversation is too much. My own health doesn't take every lopsided idea you got in your head, Sid. Meanwhile, wash up a little bit extra anyway, Faith, all right? A favor.

O.K. Ma, O.K., said Faith.

What about me? said Mr. Darwin, when will I talk to my girl? Faithy, come take a little walk.

I hardly sat down with Mama yet.

Go with him, her mother said. He can't sit. Mr. Pins and Needles. Tell her, Sid, she has to be more sensible. She's a mother. She doesn't have the choice.

Please don't tell me what to tell her, Celia. Faithy, come. Boys, stay here, talk to your grandma. Talk to her friend.

Why not, boys. Mrs. Hegel-Shtein smiled and invited them. Look it in the face: old age! Here it comes, ready or not. The boys looked, then moved close together, their elbows touching.

Faith tried to turn back to the children, but her father held her hand hard. Faithy, pay no attention. Let Mama take care. She'll make it a joke. She has presents for them. Come! We'll find a nice tree next to a bench. One thing this place got is trees and benches. Also, every bench is not just a bench – it's a dedicated bench. It has a name.

From the side garden door he showed her. That bench there, my favorite, is named Jerome (Jerry) Katzoff, six years old. It's a terrible thing to die young. Still, it saves a lot of time. Get it? That wonderful circular bench there all around that elm tree (it should live to be old) is a famous bench named Sidney Hillman. So you see we got benches. What we do *not* have here, what I am suffering from daily, is not enough first-class books. Plenty of best sellers, but first-class literature? . . . I bet you're surprised. I wrote the manager a letter. 'Dear Goldstein,' I said. 'Dear Goldstein, Are we or are we not the People of the Book? I admit by law we're a little nonsectarian, but by and large we are here living mostly People of the Book. Book means mostly to you Bible, Talmud, etc., probably. To me, and to my generation, idealists all, book means BOOKS. Get me? Goldstein, how about putting a little from Jewish Philanthropies into keeping up the reputation for another fifty years. You could do it single-handed, adding very little to the budget. Wake up, brother, while I still got my wits.'

That reminds me, another thing, Faithy. I have to tell you a fact. People's brains, I notice, are disappearing all around me. Every day.

Sit down a minute. It's pressing on me. Last one to go is Eliezer Heligman. One day I'm pointing out to him how the seeds, the regular germinating seeds of Stalinist anti-Semitism, existed not only in clockwork, Russian pogrom mentality, but also in the everyday attitude of even Mensheviks to Zionism. He gives me a big fight, very serious, profound, fundamental. If I weren't so sure I was right, I would have thought I was wrong. A couple of days later I pass him, under this tree resting on this exact bench. I sit down also. He's with Mrs. Grund, a lady well known to be in her second, maybe third, childhood at least.

She's crying. Crying. I don't interfere. Heligman is saying, Madame Grund, you're crying. Why?

My mother died, she says.

Ts, he says.

Died. Died. I was four years old and my mother died.

Ts, he says.

Then my father got me a stepmother.

Oi, says Heligman. It's hard to live with a stepmother. It's terrible. Four years old to lose a mother.

I can't stand it, she says. All day. No one to talk to. She don't care for me, that stepmother. She got her own girl. A girl like me needs a mother.

Oi, says Heligman, a mother, a mother. A girl surely needs a mother.

But not me, I ain't got one. A stepmother I got, no mother.

Oi, says Heligman.

Where will I get a mother from? Never.

Ach, says Heligman. Don't worry, Madame Grund darling, don't worry. Time passes. You'll be healthy, you'll grow up, you'll see. Soon you'll get married, you'll have children, you'll be happy.

Heligman, oi, Heligman, I say, what the hell are you talking about?

Oh, how do you do, he says to me, a passing total stranger. Madame Grund here, he says, is alone in the world, a girl four years old, she lost her mother. (Tears are in his disappearing face.) But I told her she wouldn't cry forever, she'll get married, she'll have children, her time will come, her time will come.

How do you do yourself, Heligman, I say. In fact, goodbye, my dear friend, my best enemy, Heligman, forever goodbye.

Oh Pa! Pa! Faith jumped up. I can't stand your being here.

Really? Who says *I* can stand it?

Then silence.

He picked up a leaf. Here you got it. Gate to Heaven. Ailanthus. They walked in a wide circle in the little garden. They came to another bench: Dedicated to Theodor Herzl Who Saw the Light If Not the Land/In Memory of Mr. and Mrs. Johannes Mayer 1958. They sat close to one another.

Faith put her hand on her father's knee. Papa darling, she said.

Mr. Darwin felt the freedom of committed love. I have to tell the truth. Faith, it's like this. It wasn't on the phone. Ricardo came to visit us. I didn't want to talk in front of the boys. Me and your mother. She was in a state of shock from looking at him. She sent us out for coffee. I never realized he was such an interesting young man.

He's not so young, said Faith. She moved away from her father – but not more than half an inch.

To me he is, said Mr. Darwin. Young. Young is just not old. What's to argue. What you know, *you* know. What I know, *I* know.

Huh! said Faith. Listen, did you know he hasn't come to see the kids. Also, he owes me a chunk of dough.

Aha, money! Maybe he's ashamed. He doesn't have money. He's a man. He's probably ashamed. Ach, Faith, I'm sorry I told you anything. On the subject of Ricardo, you're demented.

Demented? Boy oh boy, I'm demented. That's nice. You have a kind word from Ricardo and I'm demented.

Calm down, Faithy, please. Can't you lead a more peaceful life? Maybe you call some of this business down on yourself. That's a terrible neighborhood. I wish you'd move.

Move? Where? With what? What are you talking about?

Let's not start that again. I have more to say. Serious things, my dear girl, compared to which Ricardo is a triviality. I have made a certain decision. Your mother isn't in agreement with me. The fact is, I don't want to be in this place anymore. I made up my mind. Your mother likes it. She thinks she's in a nice quiet kibbutz, only luckily Jordan is not on one side and Egypt is not on the other. She sits. She knits. She reads to the blind. She gives a course in what you call needlepoint. She organized the women. They have a history club, Don't Forget the Past. That's the real name, if you can believe it.

Pa, what are you leading up to?

Leading. I'm leading up to the facts of the case. What you said is right. This: I don't want to be here, I told you already. If I don't want to be here, I have to go away. If I go away, I leave Mama. If I leave Mama, well, that's terrible. But, Faith, I can't live here anymore. Impossible. It's not my life. I don't feel old. I never did. I was only sorry for your mother – we were close companions. She wasn't so well, to bother with the housework like she used to. Her operation changed her . . . well, you weren't in on that trouble. You were already leading your private life . . . well, to her it's like the Grand Hotel here, only full of *landsmen*. She doesn't see Hegel-Shtein, a bitter, sour lady. She sees a colorful matriarch, full of life. She doesn't see the Bissel twins, eighty-four years old, tragic, childish, stinking from urine. She sees wonderful! A whole lifetime together, brothers! She doesn't see, ach! Faithy, she plain doesn't see!

So?

So Ricardo himself remarked the other day, You certainly haven't the appearance of an old man, in and out, up and down the hill, full of ideas.

It's true. . . . Trotsky pointed out, the biggest surprise that comes to a man is old age. O.K. That's what I mean, I don't feel it. Surprise. Isn't that interesting that he had so much to say on every subject. Years ago I didn't have the right appreciation of him. Thrown out the front door of history, sneaks in the window to sit in the living room, excuse me, I mean I do not feel old. Do NOT. In any respect. You understand me, Faith?

Faith hoped he didn't really mean what she understood him to mean.

Oh yeah, she said. I guess. You feel active and healthy. That's what you mean?

Much more, much more. He sighed. How can I explain it to you, my dear girl. Well, this way. I have certainly got to get away from here. This is the end. This is the last station. Right?

Well, right . . .

The last. If it were possible, the way I feel suddenly toward life, I would divorce your mother.

Pa! . . . Faith said. Pa, now you're teasing me.

You, the last person to tease, a person who suffered so much from changes. No. I would divorce your mother. That would be honest.

Oh, Pa, you wouldn't really, though. I mean you wouldn't.

I wouldn't leave her in the lurch, of course, but the main reason — I won't, he said. Faith, you know why I won't. You must've forgot. Because we were never married.

Never married?

Never married. I think if you live together so many years it's almost equally legal as if the rabbi himself lassoed you together with June roses. Still, the problem is thorny like the rose itself. If you never got married, how can you get divorced?

Pa, I've got to get this straight. You are planning to leave Mama.

No, no, no. I plan to go away from here. If she comes, good, although life will be different. If she doesn't, then it must be goodbye.

Never married, Faith repeated to herself. Oh . . . well, how come?

Don't forget, Faithy, we were a different cut from you. We were idealists.

Oh, you were idealists . . . Faith said. She stood up, walking around the bench that honored Theodor Herzl. Mr. Darwin watched her. Then she sat down again and filled his innocent ear with the real and ordinary world.

Well, Pa, you know I have three lovers right this minute. I don't know which one I'll choose to finally marry.

What? Faith . . .

Well, Pa, I'm just like you, an idealist. The whole world is getting more idealistic all the time. It's so idealistic. People want only the best, only perfection.

You're making fun.

Fun? What fun? Why did Ricardo get out? It's clear: an idealist. For him somewhere, something perfect existed. So I say, That's right. Me too. Me too. Somewhere for me perfection is flowering. Which of my three lovers do you think I ought to settle for, a high-class idealist like me. *I* don't know.

Faith. Three men, you sleep with three men. I don't believe this.

Sure. In only one week. How about that?

Faithy. Faith. How could you do a thing like that? My God, how? Don't tell your mother. I will never tell her. Never.

Why, what's so terrible, Pa? Just what?

Tell me. He spoke quietly. What for? Why you do such things for them? You have no money, this is it. Yes, he said to himself, the girl has no money.

What are you talking about?

. . . Money.

Oh sure, they pay me all right. How'd you guess? They pay me with a couple of hours of their valuable time. They tell me their troubles and why they're divorced and separated, and they let me make dinner once in a while. They play ball with the boys in Central Park on Sundays. Oh sure, Pa, I'm paid up to here.

It's not that I have no money, he insisted. You have only to ask me. Faith, every year you are more mixed up than before. What did your mother and me do? We only tried our best.

It sure looks like your best was lousy, said Faith. I want to get the boys. I want to get out of here. I want to get away now.

Distracted, and feeling pains in her jaws, in her right side, in the small infection on her wrist, she ran through the Admitting Parlor, past the library, which was dark, and the busy arts-and-crafts studio. Without a glance, she rushed by magnificent, purple-haired, black-lace-shawled Madame Elena Nazdarova, who sat at the door of the Periodical Department editing the prizewinning institutional journal *A Bessere Zeit*. Madame

Nazdarova saw Mr. Darwin, breathless, chasing Faith, and called, Ai, Darwin . . . no love poems this month? How can I go to press?

Don't joke me, don't joke me, Mr. Darwin said, hurrying to catch Faith. Faith, he cried, you go too fast.

So. Oh boy! Faith said, stopping short on the first-floor landing to face him. You're a young man, I thought. You and Ricardo ought to get a nice East Side pad with a separate entrance so you can entertain separate girls.

Don't judge the world by yourself. Ricardo had his trouble with you. I'm beginning to see the light. Once before I suggested psychiatric help. Charlie is someone with important contacts in the medical profession.

Don't mention Charlie to me. Just don't. I want to get the boys. I want to go now. I want to get out of here.

Don't tell your mother is why I run after you like a fool on the stairs. She had a sister who was also a bum. She'll look at you and she'll know. She'll know.

Don't follow me, Faith yelled.

Lower your voice, Mr. Darwin said between his teeth. Have pride, do you hear me?

Go away, Faith whispered, obedient and frantic.

Don't tell your mother.

Shut up! Faith whispered.

The boys are down playing Ping-Pong with Mrs. Reis. She kindly invited them. Faith, what is it? you look black, her mother said.

Breathless, Mr. Darwin gasped, Crazy, crazy like Sylvia, your crazy sister.

Oh her. Mrs. Darwin laughed, but took Faith's hand and pressed it to her cheek. What's the trouble, Faith? Oh yes, you are something like Sylvie. A temper. Oh, she had life to her. My poor Syl, she had zest. She died in front of the television set. She didn't miss a trick.

Oh, Ma, who cares what happened to Sylvie?

What exactly is the matter with you?

A cheerful man's face appeared high in the doorway. Is this the Darwin residence?

Oh, Phil, Faith said. What a time!

What's this? Which one is this? Mr. Darwin shouted.

Philip leaned into the small room. His face was shy and determined, which made him look as though he might leave at any moment. I'm a friend of Faith's, he said. My name is Mazzano. I really came to talk to Mr. Darwin about his work. There are lots of possibilities.

You heard something about me? Mr. Darwin asked. From who?

Faithy, get out the nice china, her mother said.

What? asked Faith.

What do you mean what? What, she repeated, the girl says what.

I'm getting out of here, Faith said. I'm going to get the boys and I'm getting out.

Let her go, Mr. Darwin said.

Philip suddenly noticed her. What shall I do? he asked. What do you want me to do?

Talk to him. I don't care. That's what you want to do. Talk. Right? She thought, This is probably a comedy, this crummy afternoon. Why?

Philip said, Mr. Darwin, your songs are beautiful.

Goodbye, said Faith.

Hey, wait a minute, Faith. Please.

No, she said.

On the beach. the old Brighton Beach of her childhood, she showed the boys the secret hideout under the boardwalk, where she had saved the scavenged soda-pop bottles. Were they three cents or a nickel? I can't remember, she said. This was my territory. I had to fight for it. But a boy named Eddie helped me.

Mommy, why do they live there? Do they have to? Can't they get a real apartment? How come?

I think it's a nice place, said Tonto.

Oh shut up, you jerk, said Richard.

Hey boys, look at the ocean. You know you had a great-grand-father who lived way up north on the Baltic Sea, and you know what, he used to skate, for miles and miles and miles along the shore, with a frozen herring in his pocket.

Tonto couldn't believe such a fact. He fell over backwards into the sand. A frozen herring! He must've been a crazy nut.

Really Ma? said Richard. Did you know him? he asked.

No, Richie, I didn't. They say he tried to come. There was no boat. It was too late. That's why I never laugh at that story Grandpa tells.

Why does Grandpa laugh?

Oh Richie, stop for godsakes.

Tonto, having hit the sand hard, couldn't bear to get up. He had begun to build a castle. Faith sat beside him on the cool sand. Richard walked down to the foamy edge of the water to look past the small harbor waves, far far out, as far as the sky. Then he came back. His little mouth was tight and his eyes wor-ried. Mom, you have to get them out of there. It's your mother and father. It's your responsibility.

Come on, Richard, they like it. Why is everything my respon-sibility, every goddamn thing?

It just is, said Richard. Faith looked up and down the beach. She wanted to scream, Help!

Had she been born ten, fifteen years later, she might have done so, screamed and screamed.

Instead, tears made their usual protective lenses for the safe observation of misery.

So bury me, she said, lying flat as a corpse under the October sun.

Tonto immediately began piling sand around her ankles. Stop that! Richard screamed. Just stop that, you stupid jerk. Mom, I was only joking.

Faith sat up. Goddamn it, Richard, what's the matter with you? Everything's such a big deal. I was only joking too. I mean, bury me only up to here, like this, under my arms, you know, so I can give you a good whack every now and then when you're too fresh.

Oh, Ma . . . said Richard, his heart eased in one long sigh. He dropped to his knees beside Tonto, and giving her lots of room for wiggling and whacking, the two boys began to cover most of her with sand.

In the Garden

An elderly lady, wasted and stiff, sat in a garden beside a beautiful young woman whose two children, aged eight and nine, had been kidnapped eight months earlier.

The women were neighbors. They met every afternoon to speak about the children. Their sentences began: When Rosa and Loiza have come home . . . Their sentences often continued: I can't wait to show them the ice-cream freezer Claudina bought us . . . They will probably be afraid to go to school alone. At first Pepe will have to take them in the car . . . They will be thin. No, perhaps they will be too fat, having been forced to eat nothing but rice and beans and pampered with candy and toys to keep them quiet.

The elderly lady thought: When they come home, when they come home . . .

The beautiful young woman, their mother, said, This pillow cover for Loiza, I don't know if I'll finish it in time. I make so many mistakes, I have to rip. I want it to be perfect.

There were yellow *canario* flowers among green leaves on the pillow slip. There was a hummingbird in each corner.

The two husbands, accompanied by a stranger, came into the garden and waited under the bougainvillea while the father shouted, Coffee! Black! Black! Black! He always shouted these days. His wife retired to the kitchen to make a fourth pot of strong coffee. The father turned to the stranger, speaking as if the visitor were deaf. Now this is a garden, my friend. *This* is beautiful. The life here is good. You can see that. The criminal element is under control at last. The police patrol the area frequently. I can see you're a decent person and I'm glad to have you on this street. We do not rent to Communists or to what you call hippies. Right now in one of my houses the head of the Chicago Medical Center is sleeping. That house across the street there, with the enormous veranda. He sleeps late. It's his vacation from family troubles and business worries. You understand that. We, my colleagues and I, have been responsible for building nearly all the houses you see, the one you've rented. They are well constructed. We want people to come with children and grandchildren. We will not rent to just anyone.

The elderly woman cannot bear his shouting voice. She asks her husband to help her toward home. They slowly move across the lawn.

The stranger sits among the amazing flowers and birds for a few minutes. He is a well-dressed man, middle-aged, who happens to be a Communist. He is also a father of two children who are only a little older than the kidnapped daughters of this household. He is a tenderhearted but relentless person.

In the course of the next few days, as he shops and walks, he speaks to his neighbors, who are friendly. A woman in the corner house often stands at the wrought-iron gate, the *reja*, she calls it, of her veranda. When he asks, Did you know them? she bursts into tears. She says, They never cry anymore, I know. The little one, Loi, played with my granddaughter. When they were tiny, they sat with their dolls right there in the hammock in the back, rocking rocking, little mammies. I thought they would grow up and be friends in life.

He spoke to another neighbor whom he met in a shop. Returning together along the street of palms, the neighbor asked, Did he insult you in any way? No, said the stranger. Well, he often does, you know, some people think he's been driven mad.

I would be driven mad. I would sell and leave. But he has too much invested here. He hates every one of us.

Why? asked the stranger.

Why not? he replied. Wouldn't you? We are the witnesses of the entire event. Our children are skating up and down the street.

Yes, I see, said the stranger.

A third neighbor was washing his car. (This was another day.) He courteously turned down his car radio, which was singing evangelical songs of salvation. He said, Ah yes, it is terrible. Everyone knows, by the way, everyone knows it was his friends who did it. Perhaps he knows too. At least one was deeply involved. We have all been harassed by the police, but I for one am glad to be so pestered. It makes me believe they're doing their work, at least. But one, Carlo – the main one, I think, I'm not afraid to say his name – killed himself under investigation. Just last month. A Cuban. Always laughing.

Was it political? asked the stranger.

No, no, my friend, no politics. Money. Greed. Of course, I'm sure the kidnappers thought: The money will come. What is $100,000 to that person. The children blindfolded a day or so will be returned. No one the wiser. No problem. No one the wiser. They dreamed. A new car – two new cars. An expensive woman in the city. Restaurants. High life. But aha! something went wrong. I'm not afraid to tell you this. *Everyone* knows it. Clearly. The money did not go out quickly enough. Why? Let me tell you why. Because our friend is vain and foolish and believed himself too powerful and lucky to suffer tragic loss. Too quickly (because he is an important man), the police, all, the locals, the federals, moved in. Fear struck the kidnappers, you can see that. You may ask, Where are the children? Perhaps in another country, per- haps kindly treated by a frightened wife. Perhaps they will forget, go to school. they will think – oh! that childhood was a dream. Perhaps they are thrown into the sea. Garbage. Not good, not good.

He turned the radio up. Goodbye, sir, he said.

The very next house belonged to the elderly woman. She sat

on the front veranda, a shawl over her knees. Her husband sat beside her. She rolled little metal balls in her hands, an exercise designed to slow the degeneration of her finger muscles.

The stranger stepped up to the *reja* to say goodbye. His vacation was over. He would leave the island in the morning.

Look at this, just look at this, her husband said, waving a newspaper at him. The stranger looked at the article that had been encircled. The reporter had written: 'In an interview this afternoon in his summer home in the mountains, Sr. L –, father of the little girls kidnapped almost one year ago, said, Of course they will be returned. If I had less publicity they would have been returned long ago. We expect them home. Their room is ready for them. We believe, my wife and I believe, we are certain they will be returned.'

The elderly woman's husband said, What is in his mind? He thinks because he was once a poor boy in a poor country and he became very rich with a beautiful wife, he thinks he can bend steel with his teeth.

The woman spoke slowly. You see, sir, what the world is like. Her face was imperturbable. The wasting disease that deprived her limbs of movement had taken from her the delicate muscular gift of facial expression.

She had been told that this paralysis would soon become much worse. In order to understand that future and practice the little life it would have, she followed the stranger as he departed – without moving her head – with her eyes alone. She watched, from left to right, his gait, his clothes, his hair, his swinging arms. Sadly she had to admit that the eyes' movement even if minutely savored was not such an adventurous journey.

But she had become interested in her own courage.

Somewhere Else

Twenty-two Americans were touring China. I was among them. We took many photographs. We had learned how to say hello, goodbye, may I take your photograph? Frequently the people did not wish to be photographed.

Now, why *is* that? we asked. We take pictures in order to remember the Chinese people better, to be able to tell our friends about them after supper and give slide shows in churches and schools later on. Truthfully, we do it with politics in mind, if not in total command.

Mr. Wong, the political guidance counselor in the Travel Service, said it was because of Antonioni's film on China and his denigrating attraction to archaic charm. His middle-power chauvinism looked on China as the soufflé of Europe, to rise and fall according to the nourishment beaten into it by American capital investment and avant-garde art.

He said the high vigilance of the people would not allow us to imitate this filmmaker's disdain for technologies that visibly assert themselves in urban steel and all along the terraces of rice and soy and wheat.

One day, in the hotel meeting room. he said, You do not love the Chinese people.

Now, he shouldn't have said that. It made us stop listening –

especially Ruth Larsen, Ann Reyer, and me. We were to a tourist in love with the Chinese revolution, Mao Tse-tung, and the Chinese people. Those who were affectionate did once in a while hug a guide or interpreter. Others hoped that before the tour ended, they'd be able to walk along a street in Shanghai or Canton holding hands with a Chinese person of their own sex, just as the Chinese did – chatting politics, exchanging ideological news. Surreptitiously we looked into family courtyards every now and then to see real life, from which, though in love, we'd been excluded.

When we began to listen to Mr. Wong again, he was accusing one of us of taking pictures without permission. Where? When? Where? Who? we asked. We hoped we were not about to suffer socialist injustice, because we loved socialism.

Right here in Tientsin, in front of the hotel, Mr. Wong said.

Ah, we thought, it's possible. There were terrible temptations for photograph-taking right across the street from the hotel, in the beautiful small park. There the young played Ping-Pong, the old slowly at 1/25th did Tai Chi. Also, the middle-aged textile work-ers had left their sewing machines for a few days in order to participate in designing the cloth they fabricated. They stood around the rose garden drawing leaves and roses. One of us could have done that – just snapped a picture, too excited to say, May I please take your photograph?

Mr. Wong continued. The accused, he said, had photographed a lower-middle peasant lugging a two-wheel cart full of country produce into the city. A boy had been sleeping on top.

Ah, what a picture! China! The heavy cart, the toiling man, the narrow street – once England's street (huge buildings lined with first-class plumbing for the English empire's waste), like the downtown Free West anywhere. In the foreground the pho-tographed man labored – probably bringing early spring vegetables to some distant neighborhood in order to carry back to his commune honey buckets of the city's stinking gold.

This act, this photographing, had been reported by one vigilant Chinese worker incensed by Antonioni's betrayal. Mr. Wong pointed his political finger at our brilliant comrade Frederick J. Lorenz. You! he said. Especially *you* are not a friend.

A general gasp and three nervous snickers. Immediately Ruth Larsen touched Fred's shoulder to show loyalty. Freddy! Not Freddy! Joe Larsen jumped up. He walked to the door. He put his hand on the knob.

We had all assumed that Mr. Wong's guilty man would be Martin, a jolly friend to all revolutions, an old-time union organizer, history lover, passionate photographer. (Before our tour ended, he had taken 4,387 pictures, although his camera had been broken for two days. It was not exactly broken; it had simply closed its eye, exhausted.)

Ruth, Ann, and I had discussed Freddy. Ruth thought he should have been spoken to long ago, but not for his photography. In this China, where all the grownups dressed in modest gray, blue, and green, Freddy wore very short white California shorts with a mustard-colored California B.V.D. shirt and, above his bronze, blue-eyed face, golden tan California curly hair. She didn't think that was nice.

Who are you, Ruth? The commissar of underwear? Ann had asked.

At breakfast Ruth had started to address him: Freddy! Then she'd thought, Oh boy! There you go again – the typical analysis by the old, which is: Rough politics is O.K. if it leans on the arm of bourgeois appropriateness. So she'd said, You sure keep your suntan a long time, Freddy.

Fred closed his eyes in order to think in solitude. We suffered a tour-wide two-minute fear. We waited for Fred's decision. He opened his eyes, then rose in high courtroom style to rebut.

Mr. Wong made a little smile. He looked around at us all. His finger pointed once more: You, Mr. Lorenz, have been accused by still another worker of invading a noodle factory.

Cries of No! No! Christ! Come on! He's kidding! Three young people, who liked to see us older folks caught in political contradiction or treasonous bewilderment, simply laughed.

One of us, Duane Smith, had put his life savings into this trip.

He'd studied Chinese for six years in night school in order to come one day to this place and be understood by the Chinese people in Tienanmen Square. He didn't laugh. He whispered, This is serious. What if they throw us out?

Ruth said, Never!

Invading what? said Fred. Joe! he called out. He said, Oh, God! and sat down. What was China talking about?

Joe Larsen chewed sugarless gum very hard. He walked around and around in a little circle of annoyance near the door. Then he moved directly across the room to look at Mr. Wong. He believed in doing that. His politics was based on staring truthfully into the cruel eye of power.

Mr. Wong, he said, you know, in Peking I visited a street noodle factory too. One not far from the hotel.

Joe said he wanted to be absolutely clear. It was his fault that he and Fred had stopped at the noodle shop in the city of Tientsin. He was, when not in China, writing a novel, a utopia, a speculative fiction in which the self-reliant small necessary technology of noodle-making was one short chapter. He had considered it a good omen to have passed this street factory and to have been invited to observe all the soft hanging noodles and, in the bins, the stiff dried noodles. He admired the manageable machine that shaped, cut, and extruded them.

Why is he admitting all that? Duane Smith said. He'll get us thrown out.

Never, said Ruth.

The others had hoped for more interesting admissions. Joe often took long walks when the rest of us were visiting points of cultural interest. At supper he would tell us how he drank tea with old men, a condition he liked to consider himself a member of. He had taken a ferry ride with noisy Chinese families to the other side of a river. There, in an outlying district, two old people – guardians of the street – had shown him how to dispose of a banana peel.

Some of our people with poor character structures were jealous of his adventures. They'd been a little ashamed of their timidity when he spoke, but now that he was being spoken to, they were proud of their group discipline.

Mr. Wong, Joe said, Fred accompanied *me*. He was not alone. It was my idea. I'm crazy about your street noodle factories. Lane factories, I believe you call them?

Mr. Wong looked at Joe. Then he pretended Joe wasn't there and never had been. Mr. Wong did not like to be interfered with right in the middle of a political correction. Also, he did not seem to want to accuse two people at once. Why? Perhaps accusing one person was sharper, required only one finger and one harsh cry. At any rate, he ignored Joe and the interesting socialist question of decentralized neighborhood industry. Instead he said, Mr. Lorenz, why did you choose to photograph that peasant?

What? Me? Me? Me?

Fred said Me? so many times because he was (and is) one of our foremost movement lawyers. He's accustomed to approbation from his peers and shyness from petitioners. He can be depended upon to take the most hopeless case and to construct, out of his legal education and political experience, hope! – along with a furious protesting constituency.

So once more he cried, Me? Oh, take my film. Take it. Take the camera. You'll see. There's nothing . . .Take it. I don't even *like* to take pictures. I hate the lousy thing.

He tried to jerk the camera off his neck. He failed.

That's true, Mr. Wong, said Martin, trying out a reasonable tone (as one comrade *should* speak to another). My camera was broken last week and he gave me his. It didn't bother him at all.

We are not interested, said Mr. Wong. You will be here twelve more days. We wanted you to know that the Chinese people are vigilant. He made the tiniest bow, turned, and left.

Some of us gathered around Fred. Others gathered as far from Fred as possible.

Later that evening we were invited to share our folk heritage with the Tientsin Women's Federation. We sang 'I've Been Working on the Railroad.'

The next afternoon Ruth talked to Ho, one of our guides. We

all liked him, because he rolled his pants up to the knee when it was hot. She said, You know, Fred's one of our great poor-people's lawyers.

But you guys aren't into law so much, are you? said Ann. She has always been a little sarcastic.

You deserve this, I said to Ho. Who asked you to invite Antonioni, the star of the declining West? I bet lots of less-known people were dying to make the film.

Let's get off his back, said Martin, composing us nicely in his lens, snapping a group photograph. Duane Smith said, Please! Leave him alone.

Ho had become accustomed to our harassment. He folded his trouser legs one more lap above the knee. But it's right, is it not? he said. You must ask the people first, do they wish to be photographed.

Yes, I said, but that's not the point and you know it, Ho.

And tomorrow, when you visit the countryside and the fisheries, you will inquire before you take a picture of the poor or lower-middle peasant?

Sure, said Ann.

You will say, even if it is only a child, may I take your photograph?

O.K., O.K., we said. Relax! We heard you the first five hundred times.

About three months later, Martin invited us to a China reunion at his house, full of food, slides, insights, and commentary. Twelve people came. Ann had flown to Portugal that very morning. Duane Smith had written from California to say naturally he couldn't make it but would Martin lend his fishery slides for a couple of weeks and airmail them at once special delivery, certified. Fred was sure he'd see us; he was due in New York for a week of conferences.

The three young people were present, looking lovely. They were friendly. Two were still solemn with hard new politics, but one who had mocked us with sneers and gloom asked would we please begin the evening by holding hands and singing 'Listen, listen, listen to my heart's song, I'll never forget you, I'll never forsake you.'

I said, Why not? Let's see what happens.

Ruth said, My God' What's come over you? Anyway, where's Joe?

Someone said we should start either eating or looking. Joe was clearly impossible. He had been undisciplined in two countries. The younger people with the ache of youth were eating all the cheese.

Joe arrived forty minutes late, starved, sweaty. I have to tell you what happened, he said.

You know that nice park in the South Bronx, the one I like, where I've been working on and off this summer? Well, I finished up just a couple of hours ago. The boys I work with had already gone home – we had a great party – and I stuffed the camera and Juan's films of the fiesta into a musette bag.

I knew I was going to see all of you, so I sort of sauntered my way back to the subway, imagining our conversations and, well, excited – you know I get excited.

Those lousy streets. I've been in the neighborhood all these weeks with the summer work kids – not just the park but the lots – building some playgrounds and the kind of giant climber I showed you, Marty. Remember? And filming, getting the kids to see – not that anyone sees. Maybe just to keep a record. Sometimes we're raising a couple of beams and suddenly a building across the street begins to smolder – smoke, big white smoke, then flames out of every window. The Bronx kids usually keep going, but the other boys – they're Puerto Rican too, they come with me from the Lower East Side and one boy from Brooklyn – they're amazed. They can't believe – a block tougher than their own. After the fire engines, after the fire, when everything cools off, they like to see the junkies toss brass pipes, real old brass, out of the windows. Some of those houses were nice tenements once.

I know, said Ruth. I lived in one. Me too, said Martin.

That's right. We have some film if you ever want to see – the block is burning down on one side of the street, and the kids are trying to build something on the other.

Anyway, it's such a great day, I just walked along kind of dreaming. I passed a factory. There was a sign, EMPLEADOS NECESI- TADOS. Took a couple of shots. Women came out of the factory. It was about five-thirty, I guess. They waved, I took some pictures, they waved some more.

Now, you have to understand that on any street there, among a couple dozen abandoned buildings, there's always one or two that look nearly intact. Usually men and boys sit around the front of a building like that. That's what I saw, just a block or two after the factory. I hadn't planned on filming, but we did need a couple of good long background shots – the kids either do that wild back-and-forth panning or they shoot for the eye- ball. So I began this slow pan across the top floor – black windows and charred roofs – and as the camera slowly took it all in, I could see out of the corner of my eye a group of guys on one of the stoops. They were a distance away – playing a guitar, leaning on a wall, a mattress, the steps – with a couple of tran- sistors.

I had an awful uncomfortable feeling about including them in the long pan. In fact, I can't remember – did I, or did I stop short? I may have wanted to include them – because I hate those typical exposes, you know. It could have been right – correct – to show that energy those guys sometimes have in the early evening, not just the nodding-out residents of the famous South Bronx.

Still, I know that any non-Hispanic white man with a camera looks like a narc. So I put the camera away. Well, what did I do then? I guess I continued my walk toward the subway – a little quickly, maybe. I knew I'd better move.

About ten seconds after I began to feel safe, I heard a running thud. A human form flew past me, ripping the musette bag off my shoulder. He kept going, swerved, cut across an empty lot to the next street. He was so fast and so violent, but he'd just thrust his arm through the shoulder strap, moving it from my shoulder to his – hadn't hurt me at all, a craftsman – but I was shook up. I stood still. My heart was jumping. I watched him. I turned. Those guys down the block were all laughing. We were the only people on that long burned-out block.

What could I do? I started to resume my lifelong trip to the subway, but I'll tell you I couldn't stand for it to end that way. For some reason I wanted them to know who I was. Also, I didn't want to become scared of walking around that neighborhood. I work there, damn it. I don't know if those are the real reasons. Whatever – I had to talk to them. So I walked back and went up to them. They laughed. I said, Listen, I know it probably wasn't so great to have shot that film over your heads like that, but I don't think I included you.

I told them they probably knew me – I was working a couple of blocks away, and at least a couple of them must have been over there. I said the film I'd shot was not so important, but the other stuff had been taken by the Youth Corps kids and they'd feel bad.

The fellow on the top step said, That's one sad story, old man. I looked up. On the fire escape above us, the guy who'd snatched the musette bag was unraveling the film right out of the camera. Hopping around, dancing, laughing.

That's O.K., I said, like some kind of jerk. I don't really care, but I would like the other film. Can't do it, the guy says. I kept pushing: It isn't mine – it's the kids' on 141st. Then I just stood there looking at them. I didn't move. Couldn't. I must have looked so dumb, or maybe they recognized me. Anyway, they had a small speedy Spanish conference, and the leader, top-step man, hollered up, Paco, bring it down. No, no, Paco says. He was draping the exposed film in and out of the fireescape bars. Bring it down, top-step said. Paco looked absolutely miserable, but he handed the bag over. He was disgusted.

I told them thanks. They said, That's O.K., man. Then I did something strange. Why, I don't know. I said, It's true I need the film, but here, you take the camera.

No, no, said the leader.

Take it, I said.

No, no – you crazy, man?

Listen, take it, use it. We'll come over and help you out. You can make a movie.

Don't want it – you deaf? *No*. No.

I said, You've got to take it. I'll be on the 143rd Street lot.

I shoved the camera into their hands. I walked away fast. And here I am – that's all there is. What do you think?

What in the world! said Ruth.

Forget the world, said Joe. I'm sorry I told you the story. I don't know why I did. I must be nuts.

Martin said, I know why you told the story. You wanted to show that just because a person owns a camera they do not own the whole world and you understand it.

That's what you think, said Joe. I think I told it to you because it just happened. Don't make a big Marxist deal about it.

O.K., don't get upset, said Martin. He began to fuss with the projector. Now, let's be calm, he said. Get your chairs, everybody. Ruthie, put the lights out. Wait'll you see the color, folks. Number one. Here it comes, that old man, he's holding that grandchild in a pink and orange sweater – where was that?

Oh, Christ, said Joe, can't you remember anything? It was in a courtyard in a village near Nanking.

Lavinia: An Old Story

Lavinia was born laughing. That's how come her disposition so appealing, Robert, how come you in love with her, not Elsie Rose nor Rosemary. Pretty they be, they all come out of me with a grievance. *And* the boys, J. C. Charles and Edward William, from the first second it seem, louder than their sisters. UNcontrollable.

It come from nature, that fact. My opinion: What men got to do on earth don't take more time than sneezing. Now a woman walk away from a man, she just know she loaded down in her body nine months. She got that responsibility on her soul forever.

A man restless all the time owing it to nature to scramble for opportunity. His time took up with nonsense, you know his conversation got to suffer. A man can't talk. That little minute in his mind most the time. Once a while busywork, machinery cars, guns. Opposite of facts, you got to give in, Robert.

You listen now, boy, Lavinia born in good cheer. Nothing but a crumple sock, a newborn baby, she got a grin acrost her face .

Now, you say you love her. You got three rooms, front, sunny, you want her up there with you. I'm gonna ask you a question. How your job? You a happy worker? Or you dissatisfied, complaining to the boss, upsetting your mother with your dissatisfaction. Ask you another: You ever had welfare? You lie to the relief? I can't see a liar and am against a poor-dispositioned person.

Well, me and Mr. Grimble pull together. He didn't have a dollar, I made do. We live. When he pass away, it be all on me, them devilish boys and them mopey girls.

School, I said to them, you have had it. This here time is Depression. Mr. Roosevelt says so. The greengrocer hisself sitting amids barrels of plenty is skin and bones. Out, I said. You want to learn, learn by night. You spect to eat, work by day.

The big ones took it all right, little ones whine not to have their mama always about. Not Lavinia. Now, Robert, I got to tell you, she so cheerful with foolish stories to tickle the babies. She just rumple up the eldsters. A child, that's all. But I work for folks then, said: Bring that child, she just fine to talk to Granny while you ironing. We don't mind you bring *that* child.

So you see, Robert, when old John Stuart married our Rosemary last week, I said: Take her John Stuart. You and me play Spin the Bottle years and years ago and it some offense you prefer a hankering disarranged girl to a sensible widow that's got some feeling. It's a fact, though, that child does *need* protection. She lack caution. So I gives her to you my old friend, hoping you a better husband to her than you been to poor Mrs. Lucy Stuart gone only seven months.

In fact, who take Elsie is welcome to her. No matter she just sixteen, she never put her mind to nothing large and ain't going to soon.

Tell the truth Robert, it don't seem so far away in my mind, it don't seem distant from this front porch that Grimble first set his eye on me. I was a grade scholar then, aiming high. All in every way I look was on their back providing for men or on their knees cleaning up after them.

I said: Mama, I see you just defile by leaning on every will and whim of Pa's. Now I aim high. To be a teacher and purchase my own grits and not depend on any man.

That was my thought when Mr. Grimble turn to me. He was a

smart man, incline to understanding, but his heart been darken by moodiness. Oh my, he liked me.

Now, he was a smart man Robert, but no education. He turn it all to strength till he got shorn by pride. He could heave a meaty hog and that's no lie. In the WPA he was sought for.

I said: Grimble, I just determined not to set myself drifting in this animal way. I just as well live out a spinster's peevish time as be consumed by boiling wash water.

Grimble said: There is ways and means. If you wish not to have little ones, or just one or two for comfort, I say yes. I do not want you to pass your ma's pitiful days. I wish you well.

But you knows men as good as me. When they warm, they got to cool off. No ways out of that. Robert, you recollect your own ma, the children that grown ain't but half. Some discourage in me before they born, some scotch in my own flesh. And one little baby, crawling off, drown in springtime in that hole there by the creek.

Grimble tell me, Put that sorrow out of your mind. It can't be lived with. We got Elsie Rose and Rosemary and that glad Lavinia. J. C. Charles and Edward William look so hearty. Preserve yourself. The Lord says: Endure.

Well, he was sorry to see I never gain my strong desire to teach. But he provides no help nor no friendship neither, for lean days begun to gnaw into the fat ones.

Time pass and I sees him clear, but that time I was rancorous.

I near forgot my reading but that J. C. Charles was so slow and needed help and that was pleasure to do. In summer when the light was long, me and the boy studied. I come close to loving him best, but he was too slow for my affection.

Then one bad day a man from the quarry come running. Now listen to me, he say. What Grimble did. The foreman holler, Now you two hoist that rock from where it moored. Git it yonder. Well, listen, we went forward. Then Grimble brag, You scrawny hod carrier, if'n I can't hoist that pitiful rock myself, I'm made to swing a broom. No, then the pusher says, no. No, Grimble, that sandstone's got bottom. But him stubborn, gits to it, levers it up, hike his shoulder to it, heaves, and has it sure enough. Then down on his knees using what he got, a goddamn blockhead, and set it just so. Then – now listen – he stand up and turn to look at us. But his face got no appearance. And that Samson sets down and decline to fall but sets like an idiot. Mrs. Grimble, your man's blood vessel is busted.

I only giving you a true idea of life, Robert, for some folk *will* paint it prettier than it truly be.

What I mean about Lavinia – look here at me. Ain't nothing I own but this here apron and that Sunday hat Grimble give me twenty years ago. Now see Lavinia going about improving the foolish, singing in the choir, mending the lame. Now see her, Robert, that gal apt to be a lady preacher, a nurse, something great and have a name. Don't know what you see Robert, but I got in mind to be astonished.

That just what I said to Robert one year just past Christmas. Days still lean and mean. Old Grimble gone, save from misery. Then Robert said to me: How come you set on making me so fearful? You got to know I care for Lavinia. I don't mean no harm to her. Ain't she got her high school? I ain't a bad man. I don't lie. I like her hopeful nature. I like her smart way. Just what you got in mind, Ma?

That was all out of him. Call me Ma and slam the door.

Then a long time pass and all growed and gone, but Edward William, a boy concern with nastiness. Then this day come:

Just visiting Lavinia, I see her near scalded, deep in the wash-tub. Robert Grimble Fenner, Junior, my grandboy, is setting on a stool and squeaking out his schoolday story. Our Lavinia can't stop appreciating him a minute to heed my presence. By my side is Edward William, just wiggling to get away off someplace and start admiring hisself. He is fifteen and my patience is done. So I spurn him to look at that girl. Her little baby, Vynetta, is demanding her and Robert Junior follow her off to the cradle squeaking minus a letup.

I watch that gal. I just stare out my sad-old-sighted eyes at her. What I see: she is busy and broad.

Then I let out a curse, Lord never heard me do in this long life. I cry out loud as my throat was made to do, Damn you, Lavinia – for my heart is busted in a minute – damn you, Lavinia, ain't nothing gonna come of you neither.

Friends

To put us at our ease, to quiet our hearts as she lay dying, our dear friend Selena said, Life, after all, has not been an unrelieved horror – you know, I *did* have many wonderful years with her.

She pointed to a child who leaned out of a portrait on the wall – long brown hair, white pinafore, head and shoulders forward.

Eagerness, said Susan. Ann closed her eyes.

On the same wall three little girls were photographed in a schoolyard. They were in furious discussion; they were holding hands. Right in the middle of the coffee table, framed, in autumn colors, a handsome young woman of eighteen sat on an enormous horse – aloof, disinterested, a rider. One night this young woman, Selena's child, was found in a rooming house in a distant city, dead. The police called. They said, Do you have a daughter named Abby?

And with *him*, too, our friend Selena said. We had good times, Max and I. You know that.

There were no photographs of *him*. He was married to another woman and had a new, stalwart girl of about six, to whom no harm would ever come, her mother believed.

Our dear Selena had gotten out of bed. Heavily but with a

comic dance, she soft-shoed to the bathroom, singing, 'Those were the days, my friend . . .'

Later that evening, Ann, Susan, and I were enduring our five-hour train ride to home. After one hour of silence and one hour of coffee and the sandwiches Selena had given us (she actually stood, leaned her big soft excavated body against the kitchen table to make those sandwiches), Ann said. Well, we'll never see *her* again.

Who says? Anyway, listen, said Susan. Think of it. Abby isn't the only kid who died. What about that great guy, remember Bill Dalrymple – he was a non-cooperator or a deserter? And Bob Simon. They were killed in automobile accidents. Matthew, Jeannie, Mike. Remember Al Lurie – he was murdered on Sixth Street – and that little kid Brenda, who O.D.'d on your roof, Ann? The tendency, I suppose, is to forget. You people don't remember them.

What do you mean, 'you people'? Ann asked. You're talking to *us*.

I began to apologize for not knowing them all. Most of them were older than my kids, I said.

Of course, the child Abby was exactly in my time of knowing and in all my places of paying attention – the park, the school, our street. But oh! It's true! Selena's Abby was not the only one of that beloved generation of our children murdered by cars, lost to war, to drugs, to madness.

Selena's main problem, Ann said – you know, she didn't tell the truth.

What?

A few hot human truthful words are powerful enough, Ann thinks, to steam all God's chemical mistakes and society's slimy lies out of her life. We all believe in that power, my friends and I, but sometimes . . . the heat.

Anyway, I always thought Selena had told us a lot. For instance, we knew she was an orphan. There were six, seven other children. She was the youngest. She was forty-two years old before someone informed her that her mother had *not* died in

childbirthing her. It was some terrible sickness. And she had
lived close to her mother's body – at her breast, in fact – until she
was eight months old. Whew! said Selena. What a relief! I'd
always felt I was the one who'd killed her.

Your family stinks, we told her. They really held you up for
grief.

Oh, people, she said. Forget it. They did a lot of nice things for
me too. Me and Abby. Forget it. Who has the time?

That's what I mean, said Ann. Selena should have gone after
them with an ax.

More information: Selena's two sisters brought her to a Home.
They were ashamed that at sixteen and nineteen they could not
take care of her. They kept hugging her. They were sure she'd cry.
They took her to her room – not a room, a dormitory with about
eight beds. This is your bed, Lena. This is your table for your
things. This little drawer is for your toothbrush. All for me? she
asked. No one else can use it? Only me. That's all? Artie can't
come? Franky can't come? Right?

Believe me, Selena said, those were happy days at Home.

Facts, said Ann, just facts. Not necessarily the *truth*.

I don't think it's right to complain about the character of the
dying or start hustling all their motives into the spotlight like
that. Isn't it amazing enough, the bravery of that private inclusive
intentional community?

It wouldn't help not to be brave, said Selena. You'll see.

She wanted to get back to bed. Susan moved to help her.

Thanks, our Selena said, leaning on another person for the
first time in her entire life. The trouble is, when I stand, it hurts
me here all down my back. Nothing they can do about it. All the
chemotherapy. No more chemistry left in me to therapeut. Ha!
Did you know before I came to New York and met you I used to
work in that hospital? I was supervisor in gynecology. Nursing.
They were my friends, the doctors. They weren't so snotty then.
David Clark, big surgeon. He couldn't look at me last week. He
kept saying, Lena . . . Lena . . . Like that. We were in North Africa
the same year – '44, I think. I told him, Davy, I've been around a

long enough time. I haven't missed too much. He knows it. But I didn't want to make him look at me. Ugh, my damn feet are a pain in the neck.

Recent research, said Susan, tells us that it's the neck that's a pain in the feet.

Always something new, said Selena, our dear friend.

On the way back to the bed, she stopped at her desk. There were about twenty snapshots scattered across it – the baby, the child, the young woman. Here, she said to me, take this one. It's a shot of Abby and your Richard in front of the school – third grade? What a day! The show those kids put on! What a bunch of kids! What's Richard doing now?

Oh, who knows? Horsing around someplace. Spain. These days, it's Spain. Who knows where he is? They're all the same.

Why did I say that? I knew exactly where he was. He writes. In fact, he found a broken phone and was able to call every day for a week – mostly to give orders to his brother but also to say, Are you O.K., Ma? How's your new boyfriend, did he smile yet?

The kids, they're all the same, I said.

It was only politeness, I think, not to pour my boy's light, noisy face into that dark afternoon. Richard used to say in his early mean teens, You'd sell us down the river to keep Selena happy and innocent. It's true. Whenever Selena would say, I don't know, Abby has some peculiar friends, I'd answer for stupid comfort, You should see Richard's.

Still, he's in Spain, Selena said. At least you know that. It's probably interesting. He'll learn a lot. Richard is a wonderful boy, Faith. He acts like a wise guy but he's not. You know the night Abby died, when the police called me and told me? That was my first night's sleep in two years. I *knew* where she was.

Selena said this very matter-of-factly – just offering a few informative sentences.

But Ann, listening, said, Oh! – she called out to us all, Oh! – and began to sob. Her straightforwardness had become an arrow and gone right into her own heart.

Then a deep tear-drying breath: I want a picture too, she said.

Yes. Yes, wait, I have one here someplace. Abby and Judy and that Spanish kid Victor. Where is it? Ah. Here!

Three nine-year-old children sat high on that long-armed sycamore in the park, dangling their legs on someone's patient head – smooth dark hair, parted in the middle. Was that head Kitty's?

Our dear friend laughed. Another great day, she said. Wasn't it? I remember you two sizing up the men. I *had* one at the time – I thought. Some joke. Here, take it. I have two copies. But you ought to get it enlarged. When this you see, remember me. Ha-ha. Well, girls – excuse me, I mean ladies – it's time for me to rest.

She took Susan's arm and continued that awful walk to her bed.

We didn't move. We had a long journey ahead of us and had expected a little more comforting before we set off.

No, she said. You'll only miss the express. I'm not in much pain. I've got lots of painkiller. See?

The tabletop was full of little bottles.

I just want to lie down and think of Abby.

It was true, the local could cost us an extra two hours at least. I looked at Ann. It had been hard for her to come at all. Still, we couldn't move. We stood there before Selena in a row. Three old friends. Selena pressed her lips together, ordered her eyes into cold distance.

I know that face. Once, years ago, when the children were children, it had been placed modestly in front of J. Hoffner, the principal of the elementary school.

He'd said, No! Without training you cannot tutor these kids. There are real problems. You have to know *how to teach*.

Our P.T.A. had decided to offer some one-to-one tutorial help for the Spanish kids, who were stuck in crowded classrooms with exhausted teachers among little middle-class achievers. He had said, in a written communication to show seriousness and then in personal confrontation to *prove* seriousness, that he could not allow it. And the Board of Ed. itself had said no. (All this no-ness was to lead to some terrible events in the schools and neighborhoods of our poor yes-requiring city.) But most of the women in our P.T.A. were independent – by necessity and disposition. We were, in fact. the soft-speaking tough souls of anarchy.

I had Fridays off that year. At about 11 a.m. I'd bypass the principal's office and run up to the fourth floor. I'd take Robert Figueroa to the end of the hall, and we'd work away at story-telling for about twenty minutes. Then we would write the beautiful letters of the alphabet invented by smart foreigners long ago to fool time and distance.

That day, Selena and her stubborn face remained in the office for at least two hours. Finally, Mr. Hoffner, besieged, said that because she was a nurse, she would be allowed to help out by taking the littlest children to the modern difficult toilet. Some of them, he said, had just come from the barbarous hills beyond Maricao. Selena said O.K., she'd do that. In the toilet she taught the little girls which way to wipe, as she had taught her own little girl a couple of years earlier. At three o'clock she brought them home for cookies and milk. The children of that year ate cookies in her kitchen until the end of the sixth grade.

Now, what did we learn in that year of my Friday afternoons off? The following: Though the world cannot be changed by talk-ing to one child at a time, it may at least be known.

Anyway, Selena placed into our eyes for long remembrance that useful stubborn face. She said, No. Listen to me, you people. Please. I don't have lots of time. What I want . . . I want to lie down and think about Abby. Nothing special. Just think about her, you know.

In the train Susan fell asleep immediately. She woke up from time to time, because the speed of the new wheels and the resis-tance of the old track gave us some terrible jolts. Once, she opened her eyes wide and said, You know, Ann's right. You don't get sick like that for nothing. I mean, she didn't even mention him.

Why should she? She hasn't even seen him, I said. Susan, you still have him-itis, the dread disease of females.

Yeah? And you don't? Anyway, he *was* around quite a bit. He was there every day, nearly, when the kid died.

Abby. I didn't like to hear 'the kid.' I wanted to say 'Abby' the way I've said 'Selena' – so those names can take thickness and strength and fall back into the world with their weight.

Abby, you know, was a wonderful child. She was in Richard's classes every class till high school. Good-hearted little girl from the beginning, noticeably kind – for a kid, I mean. Smart.

That's true, said Ann, very kind. She'd give away Selena's last shirt. Oh yes, they were all wonderful little girls and wonderful little boys.

Chrissy *is* wonderful, Susan said.

She *is*, I said.

Middle kids aren't supposed to be, but she is. She put herself through college – I didn't have a cent – and now she has this fellowship. And, you know, she never did take any crap from boys. She's something.

Ann went swaying up the aisle to the bathroom. First she said, Oh, all of them – just wohunderful.

I loved Selena, Susan said, but she never talked to me enough. Maybe she talked to you women more, about things. Men.

Then Susan fell asleep.

Ann sat down opposite me. She looked straight into my eyes with a narrow squint. It often connotes accusation.

Be careful – you're wrecking your laugh lines, I said.

Screw you, she said. You're kidding around. Do you realize I don't know where Mickey is? You know, you've been lucky. You always have been. Since you were a little kid. Papa and Mama's darling.

As is usual in conversations, I said a couple of things out loud and kept a few structured remarks for interior mulling and right-eousness. I thought: She's never even met my folks. I thought: What a rotten thing to say. Luck – isn't it something like an insult?

I said, Annie, I'm only forty-eight. There's lots of time for me to be totally wrecked – if I live, I mean.

Then I tried to knock wood, but we were sitting in plush and leaning on plastic. Wood! I shouted. Please, some wood! Anybody here have a matchstick?

Oh, shut up, she said. Anyway, death doesn't count.

I tried to think of a couple of sorrows as irreversible as death. But truthfully nothing in my life can compare to hers: a son, a boy of fifteen, who disappears before your very eyes into a darkness or a light behind his own, from which neither hugging nor hitting can bring him. If you shout, Come back, come back, he won't come. Mickey, Mickey, Mickey, we once screamed, as though he were twenty miles away instead of right in front of us in a kitchen chair; but he refused to return. And when he did, twelve hours later, he left immediately for California.

Well, some bad things have happened in my life, I said.

What? You were born a woman? Is that it?

She was, of course, mocking me this time, referring to an old discussion about feminism and Judaism. Actually, on the prism of isms, both of those do have to be looked at together once in a while.

Well, I said, my mother died a couple of years ago and I still feel it. I think *Ma* sometimes and I lose my breath. I miss her. You understand that. Your mother's seventy-six. You have to admit it's nice still having her.

She's very sick, Ann said. Half the time she's out of it.

I decided not to describe my mother's death. I could have done so and made Ann even more miserable. But I thought I'd save that for her next attack on me. These constrictions of her spirit were coming closer and closer together. Probably a great enmity was about to be born.

Susan's eyes opened. The death or dying of someone near or dear often makes people irritable, she stated. (She's been taking a course in relationships *and* interrelationships.) The real name of my seminar is Skills: Personal Friendship and Community. It's a very good course despite your snide remarks.

While we talked, a number of cities passed us, going in the opposite direction. I had tried to look at New London through the dusk of the windows. Now I was missing New Haven. The conductor explained, smiling: Lady, if the windows were clean, half of you'd be dead. The tracks are lined with sharpshooters.

Do you believe that? I hate people to talk that way.

He may be exaggerating, Susan said, but don't wash the window.

A man leaned across the aisle. Ladies, he said, I do believe it. According to what I hear of this part of the country, it don't seem unplausible.

Susan turned to see if he was worth engaging in political dialogue.

You've forgotten Selena already, Ann said. All of us have. Then you'll make this nice memorial service for her and everyone will stand up and say a few words and then we'll forget her again – for good. What'll you say at the memorial, Faith?

It's not right to talk like that. She's not dead yet, Annie.

Yes, she is, said Ann.

We discovered the next day that give or take an hour or two, Ann had been correct. It was a combination – David Clark, surgeon, said – of being sick unto real death and having a tabletop full of little bottles.

Now, why are you taking all those hormones? Susan had asked Selena a couple of years earlier. They were visiting New Orleans. It was Mardi Gras.

Oh, they're mostly vitamins, Selena said. Besides, I want to be young and beautiful. She made a joking pirouette.

Susan said, That's absolutely ridiculous.

But Susan's seven or eight years younger than Selena. What did she know? Because: People *do* want to be young and beautiful. When they meet in the street, male or female, if they're getting older they look at each other's face a little ashamed. It's clear they want to say, Excuse me, I didn't mean to draw attention to mortality and gravity all at once. I didn't want to remind you, my dear friend, of our coming eviction, first from liveliness, then from life. To which, most of the time, the friend's eyes will courteously reply, My dear, it's nothing at all. I hardly noticed.

Luckily, I learned recently how to get out of that deep well of melancholy. Anyone can do it. You grab at roots of the littlest future, sometimes just stubs of conversation. Though some believe you miss a great deal of depth by not sinking down down down.

Susan, I asked, you still seeing Ed Flores?

Went back to his wife.

Lucky she didn't kill you, said Ann. I'd never fool around with a Spanish guy. They all have tough ladies back in the barrio.

No, said Susan, she's unusual. I met her at a meeting. We had an amazing talk. Luisa is a very fine woman. She's one of the office-worker organizers I told you about. She only needs him two more years, she says. Because the kids – they're girls – need to be watched a little in their neighborhood. The neighborhood is definitely not good. He's a good father but not such a great husband.

I'd call that a word to the wise.

Well, you know me – I don't want a husband. I like a male person around. I hate to do without. Anyway, listen to this. She, Luisa, whispers in my ear the other day, she whispers, Suzie, in two years you still want him, I promise you, you got him. Really, I may still want him then. He's only about forty-five now. Still got a lot of spunk. I'll have my degree in two years. Chrissy will be out of the house.

Two years! In two years we'll all be dead, said Ann.

I know she didn't mean all of us. She meant Mickey. That boy of hers would surely be killed in one of the drugstores or whore-houses of Chicago, New Orleans, San Francisco. I'm in a big beautiful city, he said when he called last month. Makes New York look like a garbage tank.

Mickey! Where?

Ha-ha, he said, and hung up.

Soon he'd be picked up for vagrancy, dealing, small thievery, or simply screaming dirty words at night under a citizen's window. Then Ann would fly to the town or not fly to the town to disentangle him, depending on a confluence of financial reality and psychiatric advice.

How *is* Mickey? Selena had said. In fact, that was her first sentence when we came, solemn and embarrassed, into her sunny front room that was full of the light and shadow of windy courtyard trees. We said, each in her own way, How are you feeling, Selena? She said, O.K., first things first. Let's talk about important things. How's Richard? How's Tonto? How's John? How's Chrissy? How's Judy? How's Mickey?

I don't want to talk about Mickey, said Ann.

Oh, let's talk about him, talk about him, Selena said, taking Ann's hand. Let's all think before it's too late. How did it start? Oh, for godsakes talk about him.

Susan and I were smart enough to keep our mouths shut.

Nobody knows, nobody knows anything. Why? Where? Everybody has an idea, theories, and writes articles. Nobody knows.

Ann said this sternly. She didn't whine. She wouldn't lean too far into Selena's softness, but listening to Selena speak Mickey's name, she could sit in her chair more easily. I watched. It was interesting. Ann breathed deeply in and out the way we've learned in our Thursday-night yoga class. She was able to rest her body a little bit.

We were riding the rails of the trough called Park-Avenue-in-the-Bronx. Susan had turned from us to talk to the man across the aisle. She was explaining that the war in Vietnam was not yet over and would not be, as far as she was concerned, until we repaired the dikes we'd bombed and paid for some of the hopeless ecological damage. He didn't see it that way. Fifty thousand American lives, our own boys – we'd paid, he said. He asked us if we agreed with Susan. Every word, we said.

You don't look like hippies. He laughed. Then his face changed. As the resident face-reader, I decided he was thinking: Adventure. He may have hit a mother lode of late counterculture in three opinionated left-wing ladies. That was the nice part of his face. The other part was the sly out-of-town-husband-in-New-York look.

I'd like to see you again, he said to Susan.

Oh? Well, come to dinner day after tomorrow. Only two of my kids will be home. You ought to have at least one decent meal in New York.

Kids? His face thought it over. Thanks. Sure, he said. I'll come.

Ann muttered, She's impossible. She did it again.

Oh, Susan's O.K., I said. She's just right in there. Isn't that good?

This is a long ride, said Ann.

Then we were in the darkness that precedes Grand Central.

We're irritable, Susan explained to her new pal. We're angry with our friend Selena for dying. The reason is, we want her to be present when we're dying. We all require a mother or mother-surrogate to fix our pillows on that final occasion, and we were counting on her to be that person.

I know just what you mean, he said. You'd like to have someone around. A little fuss, maybe.

Something like that. Right, Faith?

It always takes me a minute to slide under the style of her public-address system. I agreed. Yes.

The train stopped hard, in a grinding agony of opposing technologies.

Right. Wrong. Who cares? Ann said. She didn't have to die. She really wrecked everything.

Oh, Annie, I said.

Shut up, will you? Both of you, said Ann, nearly breaking our knees as she jammed past us and out of the train.

Then Susan, like a New York hostess, began to tell that man all our private troubles – the mistake of the World Trade Center, Westway, the decay of the South Bronx, the rage in Williamsburg. She rose with him on the escalator, gabbing into evening friendship and, hopefully, a happy night.

At home Anthony, my youngest son, said, Hello, you just missed Richard. He's in Paris now. He had to call collect.

Collect? From Paris?

He saw my sad face and made one of the herb teas used by his peer group to calm their overwrought natures. He does want to improve my pretty good health and spirits. His friends have a book that says a person should, if properly nutritioned, live forever. He wants me to give it a try. He also believes that the human race, its brains and good looks, will end in his time.

At about 11:30 he went out to live the pleasures of his eighteen-year-old nighttime life.

At 3 a.m. he found me washing the floors and making little apartment repairs.

More tea, Mom? he asked. He sat down to keep me company. O.K., Faith. I know you feel terrible. But how come Selena never realized about Abby?

Anthony, what the hell do I realize about you?

Come on, you had to be blind. I was just a little kid, and *I* saw. Honest to God, Ma.

Listen, Tonto. Basically Abby was O.K. She was. You don't know yet what their times can do to a person.

Here she goes with her goody-goodies – everything is so groovy wonderful far-out terrific. Next thing, you'll say people are darling and the world is so nice and round that Union Carbide will never blow it up.

I have never said anything as hopeful as that. And why to all our knowledge of that sad day did Tonto at 3 a.m. have to add the fact of the world?

The next night Max called from North Carolina. How's Selena? I'm flying up, he said. I have one early-morning appointment. Then I'm canceling everything.

At 7 a.m. Annie called. I had barely brushed my morning teeth. It was hard, she said. The whole damn thing. I don't mean Selena. All of us. In the train. None of you seemed real to me.

Real? Reality, huh? Listen, how about coming over for breakfast? – I don't have to get going until after nine. I have this neat sourdough rye?

No, she said. Oh Christ, no. No!

I remember Ann's eyes and the hat she wore the day we first

looked at each other. Our babies had just stepped howling out of the sandbox on their new walking legs. We picked them up. Over their sandy heads we smiled. I think a bond was sealed then, at least as useful as the vow we'd all sworn with husbands to whom we're no longer married. Hindsight, usually looked down upon, is probably as valuable as foresight, since it does include a few facts.

Meanwhile, Anthony's world – poor, dense, defenseless thing – rolls round and round. Living and dying are fastened to its surface and stuffed into its softer parts.

He was right to call my attention to its suffering and danger. He was right to harass my responsible nature. But I was right to invent for my friends and our children a report on these private deaths and the condition of our lifelong attachments.

At That Time,
or The History of a Joke

At that time most people were willing to donate organs. Abuses were expected. In fact there was a young woman whose uterus was hysterically ripped from her by a passing gynecologist. He was distracted, he said, by the suffering of a childless couple in Fresh Meadows. The young woman said, 'It wasn't the pain or the embarrassment, but I think any court would certainly award me the earliest uterine transplant that Dr. Heiliger can obtain.'

We are not a heartless people and this was done at the lowest judicial level, no need to appeal to state or federal power.

According to the *Times*, one of the young woman's ovaries rejected the new uterus. The other was perfectly satisfied and did not.

'I feel fine,' she said, but almost immediately began to swell, for in the soft red warm interior of her womb, there was already a darling rolled-up fetus. It was unfurled in due time, and lo! it was as black as the night which rests our day-worn eyes.

Then: 'Sing!' said Heiliger, the scientist, 'for see how the myth of man advances on the back of technological achievement, and behold, without conceiving, a virgin has borne a son.' This astonishing and holy news was carried to the eye of field, forest, and industrial park, wherever the media had thrust its wireless thumb. The people celebrated and were relatively joyful and the birth was reenacted on giant screens in theaters and on small screens at home.

Only, on the underside of several cities, certain Jews who had observed and suffered the consequence of other virgin births cried out (weeping) (as usual): 'It is not He! It is not He!'

No one knew how to deal with them; they were stubborn and maintained a humorless determination. The authorities took away their shortwave and antennae, their stereo screen TV and their temple videotapes. (People were not incarcerated at that time for such social intransigence. Therefore, neither were they rehabilitated.)

Soon this foolish remnant had nothing left. They had to visit one another or wander from town to town in order to say the most ordinary thing to a friend or relative. They had only their shawls and phylacteries, which were used by women too, for women (by that time) had made their great natural advances and were ministers, seers, rabbis, yogis, priests, etc., in well-known as well as esoteric religions.

In their gossipy communications, they whispered the hidden or omitted fact (which some folks had already noticed): The Child WAS A Girl, and since word of mouth is sound made in the echo of God (in the beginning there was the Word and it was without form but wide), ear to mouth and mouth to ear it soon became the people's knowledge, outwitting the computerized devices to which most sensible people had not said a private word for decades anyway.

Then: 'O.K.!' said Dr. Heiliger. 'It's perfectly true, but I didn't want to make waves in any water as viscous as the seas of mythology. Yes, it is a girl. A virgin born of a virgin.'

Throughout the world, people smiled. By that time, sexism and racism had no public life, though they were still sometimes practiced by adults at home. They were as gladdened by one birth as another. And plans were made to symbolically sew the generations of the daughters one to another by using the holy infant's umbilicus. This was luckily flesh *and* symbol. Therefore beside the cross to which people were accustomed there hung the circle of the navel and the wiggly line of the umbilical cord.

But those particular discontented Jews said again, 'Wonderful! So? Another tendency heard from! So it's a girl! Praise to the most Highess! But the fact is, we need another virgin birth like our blessed dead want cupping by ancient holistic practitioners.'

And so they continued as female and male, descending and undescending, workers in the muddy basement of history, to which, this very day, the poor return when requiring a cheap but stunning garment for a wedding, birth, or funeral.

Anxiety

The young fathers are waiting outside the school. What curly heads! Such graceful brown mustaches. They're sitting on their haunches eating pizza and exchanging information. They're waiting for the 3 p.m. bell. It's springtime, the season of first looking out the window. I have a window box of greenhouse marigolds. The young fathers can be seen through the ferny leaves.

The bell rings. The children fall out of school, tumbling through the open door. One of the fathers sees his child. A small girl. Is she Chinese? A little. Up u-u-p, he says, and hoists her to his shoulders. U-u-p, says the second father, and hoists his little boy. The little boy sits on top of his father's head for a couple of seconds before sliding to his shoulders. Very funny, says the father.

They start off down the street, right under and past my window. The two children are still laughing. They try to whisper a secret. The fathers haven't finished their conversation. The frailer father is uncomfortable; his little girl wiggles too much.

Stop it this minute, he says.

Oink oink, says the little girl.

What'd you say?

Oink oink, she says.

The young father says What! three times. Then he seizes the child, raises her high above his head, and sets her hard on her feet.

What'd I do so bad, she says, rubbing her ankle.

Just hold my hand, screams the frail and angry father.

I lean far out the window. Stop! Stop! I cry.

The young father turns, shading his eyes, but sees. What? he says. His friend says, Hey? Who's that? He probably thinks I'm a family friend, a teacher maybe.

Who're you? he says.

I move the pots of marigold aside. Then I'm able to lean on my elbow way out into unshadowed visibility. Once, not too long ago, the tenements were speckled with women like me in every third window up to the fifth story, calling the children from play to receive orders and instruction. This memory enables me to say strictly, Young man, I am an older person who feels free because of that to ask questions and give advice.

Oh? he says, laughs with a little embarrassment, says to his friend, Shoot if you will that old gray head. But he's joking, I know, because he has established himself, legs apart, hands behind his back, his neck arched to see and hear me out.

How old are you? I call. About thirty or so?

Thirty-three.

First I want to say you're about a generation ahead of your father in your attitude and behavior toward your child.

Really? Well? Anything else, ma'am.

Son, I said, leaning another two, three dangerous inches toward him. Son, I must tell you that madmen intend to destroy this beautifully made planet. That the murder of our children by these men has got to become a terror and a sorrow to you, and starting now, it had better interfere with any daily pleasure.

Speech speech, he called.

I waited a minute, but he continued to look up. So, I said, I can tell by your general appearance and loping walk that you agree with me.

I do, he said, winking at his friend; but turning a serious face to mine, he said again, Yes, yes, I do.

Well then, why did you become so angry at that little girl whose future is like a film which suddenly cuts to white. Why did you nearly slam this little doomed person to the ground in your uncontrollable anger.

Let's not go too far, said the young father. She *was* jumping around on my poor back and hollering oink oink.

When were you angriest – when she wiggled and jumped or when she said oink?

He scratched his wonderful head of dark well-cut hair. I guess when she said oink.

Have you ever said oink oink? Think carefully. Years ago, perhaps?

No. Well maybe. Maybe.

Whom did you refer to in this way?

He laughed. He called to his friend, Hey Ken, this old person's got something. The cops. In a demonstration. Oink oink, he said, remembering, laughing.

The little girl smiled and said, Oink oink.

Shut up, he said.

What do you deduce from this?

That I was angry at Rosie because she was dealing with me as though I was a figure of authority, and it's not my thing, never has been, never will be.

I could see his happiness, his nice grin, as he remembered this.

So, I continued, since those children are such lovely examples of what may well be the last generation of humankind, why don't you start all over again, right from the school door, as though none of this had ever happened.

Thank you, said the young father. Thank you. It would be nice to be a horse, he said, grabbing little Rosie's hand. Come on Rosie, let's go. I don't have all day.

U-up, says the first father. U-up, says the second.

Giddap, shout the children, and the fathers yell neigh neigh, as horses do. The children kick their fathers' horsechests, screaming giddap giddap, and they gallop wildly westward.

I lean way out to cry once more, Be careful! Stop! But they've gone too far. Oh, anyone would love to be a fierce fast horse carrying a beloved beautiful rider, but they are galloping toward one of the most dangerous street corners in the world. And they may live beyond that trisection across other dangerous avenues.

So I must shut the window after patting the April-cooled marigolds with their rusty smell of summer. Then I sit in the nice light and wonder how to make sure that they gallop safely home through the airy scary dreams of scientists and the bulky dreams of automakers. I wish I could see just how they sit down at their kitchen tables for a healthy snack (orange juice or milk and cookies) before going out into the new spring afternoon to play.

In This Country, But in Another Language, My Aunt Refuses to Marry the Men Everyone Wants Her To

My grandmother sat in her chair. She said, When I lie down at night I can't rest, my bones push each other. When I wake up in the morning I say to myself, What? Did I sleep? My God, I'm still here. I'll be in this world forever.

My aunt was making the bed. Look, your grandmother, she doesn't sweat. Nothing has to be washed — her stockings, her underwear, the sheets. From this you wouldn't believe what a life she had. It wasn't life. It was torture.

Doesn't she love us? I asked.

Love you? my aunt said. What else is worth it? You children. Your cousin in Connecticut.

So. Doesn't that make her happy?

My aunt said, Ach, what she saw!

What? I asked. What did she see?

Someday I'll tell you. One thing I'll tell you right now. Don't carry the main flag. When you're bigger, you'll be in a demonstration or a strike or something. It doesn't have to be you, let someone else.

Because Russya carried the flag, that's why? I asked.

Because he was a wonderful boy, only seventeen. All by

herself, your grandmother picked him up from the street – he was dead – she took him home in the wagon.

What else? I asked.

My father walked into the room. He said, At least *she* lived.

Didn't you live too? I asked my aunt.

Then my grandmother took her hand. Sonia. One reason I don't close my eyes at night is I think about you. You know it. What will be? You have no life.

Grandmother, I asked, what about us?

My aunt sighed. Little girl. Darling, let's take a nice walk.

At the supper table nobody spoke. So I asked her once more: Sonia, tell me no or yes. Do you have a life?

Ha! she said. If you really want to know, read Dostoevsky. Then they all laughed and laughed.

My mother brought tea and preserves.

My grandmother said to all our faces, Why do you laugh?

But my aunt said, Laugh!

Mother

One day I was listening to the AM radio. I heard a song: 'Oh, I Long to See My Mother in the Doorway.' By God! I said, I understand that song. I have often longed to see my mother in the doorway. As a matter of fact, she did stand frequently in various doorways looking at me. She stood one day, just so, at the front door, the darkness of the hallway behind her. It was New Year's Day. She said sadly, If you come home at 4 a.m. when you're seventeen, what time will you come home when you're twenty? She asked this question without humor or meanness. She had begun her worried preparations for death. She would not be present, she thought, when I was twenty. So she wondered.

Another time she stood in the doorway of my room. I had just issued a political manifesto attacking the family's position on the Soviet Union. She said, Go to sleep for godsakes, you damn fool, you and your Communist ideas. We saw them already, Papa and me, in 1905. We guessed it all.

At the door of the kitchen she said, You never finish your lunch. You run around senselessly. What will become of you?

Then she died.

Naturally for the rest of my life I longed to see her, not only in doorways, in a great number of places – in the dining room with my aunts, at the window looking up and down the block, in the country garden among zinnias and marigolds, in the living room with my father.

They sat in comfortable leather chairs. They were listening to Mozart. They looked at one another amazed. It seemed to them that they'd just come over on the boat. They'd just learned the first English words. It seemed to them that he had just proudly handed in a 100 percent correct exam to the American anatomy professor. It seemed as though she'd just quit the shop for the kitchen.

I wish I could see her in the doorway of the living room.

She stood there a minute. Then she sat beside him. They owned an expensive record player. They were listening to Bach. She said to him, Talk to me a little. We don't talk so much anymore.

I'm tired, he said. Can't you see? I saw maybe thirty people today. All sick, all talk talk talk talk. Listen to the music, he said. I believe you once had perfect pitch. I'm tired, he said.

Then she died.

Ruthy and Edie

One day in the Bronx two small girls named Edie and Ruthy were sitting on the stoop steps. They were talking about the real world of boys. Because of this, they kept their skirts pulled tight around their knees. A gang of boys who lived across the street spent at least one hour of every Saturday afternoon pulling up girls' dresses. They needed to see the color of a girl's underpants in order to scream outside the candy store, Edie wears pink panties.

Ruthy said, anyway, she liked to play with those boys. They did more things. Edie said she hated to play with them. They hit and picked up her skirt. Ruthy agreed. It *was* wrong of them to do this. But, she said, they ran around the block a lot, had races, and played war on the corner. Edie said it wasn't *that* good.

Ruthy said, Another thing, Edie, you could be a soldier if you're a boy.

So? What's so good about that?

Well, you could fight for your country.

Edie said, I don't want to.

What? Edie! Ruthy was a big reader and most interesting reading was about bravery – for instance Roland's Horn at Roncevaux. Her father had been brave and there was often a lot of discussion about this at suppertime. In fact, he sometimes modestly said,

Yes, I suppose I was brave in those days. And so was your mother, he added. Then Ruthy's mother put his boiled egg in front of him where he could see it. Reading about Roland, Ruthy learned that if a country wanted to last, it would require a great deal of bravery. She nearly cried with pity when she thought of Edie and the United States of America.

You don't want to? she asked.

No.

Why, Edie, why?

I don't feel like.

Why, Edie? How come?

You always start hollering if I don't do what you tell me. I don't always have to say what you tell me. I can say whatever I like.

Yeah, but if you love your country you have to go fight for it. How come you don't want to? Even if you get killed, it's worth it.

Edie said, I don't want to leave my mother.

Your mother? You must be a baby. Your mother?

Edie pulled her skirt very tight over her knees. I don't like when I don't see her a long time. Like when she went to Springfield to my uncle. I don't like it.

Oh boy! said Ruthy. Oh boy! What a baby! She stood up. She wanted to go away. She just wanted to jump from the top step, run down to the corner, and wrestle with someone. She said, You know, Edie, this is *my* stoop.

Edie didn't budge. She leaned her chin on her knees and felt sad. She was a big reader too, but she liked *The Bobbsey Twins* or *Honey Bunch at the Seashore*. She loved that nice family life. She tried to live it in the three rooms on the fourth floor. Sometimes she called her father Dad, or even Father, which surprised him. Who? he asked.

I have to go home now, she said. My cousin Alfred's coming. She looked to see if Ruthy was still mad. Suddenly she saw a dog. Ruthy, she said, getting to her feet. There's a dog coming. Ruthy turned. There *was* a dog about three-quarters of the way down the block between the candy store and the grocer's. It was an ordinary middle-sized dog. But it *was* coming. It didn't stop to sniff at curbs or pee on the house fronts. It just trotted steadily along the middle of the sidewalk.

Ruthy watched him. Her heart began to thump and take up too much space inside her ribs. She thought speedily, Oh, a dog has teeth! It's large, hairy, strange. Nobody can say what a dog is thinking. A dog is an animal. You could talk to a dog, but a dog couldn't talk to you. If you said to a dog, STOP! a dog would just keep going. If it's angry and bites you, you might get rabies. It will take you about six weeks to die and you will die screaming in agony. Your stomach will turn into a rock and you will have lockjaw. When they find you, your mouth will be paralyzed wide open in your dying scream.

Ruthy said, I'm going right now. She turned as though she'd been directed by some far-off switch. She pushed the hall door open and got safely inside. With one hand she pressed the apartment bell. With the other she held the door shut. She leaned against the glass door as Edie started to bang on it. Let me in, Ruthy, let me in, please. Oh, Ruthy!

I can't. Please, Edie, I just can't.

Edie's eyes rolled fearfully toward the walking dog. It's coming. Oh, Ruthy, please, please.

No! No! said Ruthy.

The dog stopped right in front of the stoop to hear the screaming and banging. Edie's heart stopped too. But in a minute he decided to go on. He passed. He continued his easy steady pace.

When Ruthy's big sister came down to call them for lunch, the two girls were crying. They were hugging each other and their hair was a mess. You two are nuts, she said. If I was Mama, I wouldn't let you play together so much every single day. I mean it.

Many years later in Manhattan it was Ruthy's fiftieth birthday. She had invited three friends. They waited for her at the round kitchen table. She had been constructing several pies so that this birthday could be celebrated in her kitchen during the day by any gathered group without too much trouble. Now and then one of the friends would say, Will you sit down, for godsakes! She would sit immediately. But in the middle of someone's sentence or even one of her own, she'd jump up with a look of worry beyond household affairs to wash a cooking utensil or wipe crumbs of flour off the Formica counter.

Edie was one of the women at the table. She was sewing, by neat hand, a new zipper into an old dress. She said, Ruthy, it wasn't like that. We both ran in and out a lot.

No, said Ruth. You would never have locked me out. You were an awful sissy, sweetie but you would never, never have locked me out. Just look at yourself. Look at your life!

Edie glanced, as people will, when told to do that. She saw a chubby dark-haired woman who looked like a nice short teacher, someone who stood at the front of the schoolroom and said, History is a wonderful subject. It's all stories. It's where we come from, who we are. For instance, where do you come from, Juan? Where do your parents and grandparents come from?

You know that, Mizz Seiden. Porto Rico. You know that a long-o time-o, Juan said, probably in order to mock both languages. Edie thought, Oh, to whom would he speak?

For Christsakes, this is a party, isn't it? said Ann. She was patting a couple of small cases and a projector on the floor next to her chair. Was she about to offer a slide show? No, she had already been prevented from doing this by Faith, who'd looked at the clock two or three times and said, I don't have the time, Jack is coming tonight. Ruth had looked at the clock too. Next week, Ann? Ann said O.K. O.K. But Ruthy. I want to say you have to quit knocking yourself. I've seen you do a million good things. If you were such a dud, why'd I write it down in my will that if anything happened to me, you and Joe were the ones who'd raise my kids.

You were just plain wrong. I couldn't even raise my own right.

Ruthy, really, they're pretty much raised. Anyway, how can you say an awful thing like that? Edie asked. They're wonderful beautiful brilliant girls. Edie knew this because she had held them in her arms the third or fourth day of life. Naturally, she became the friend called aunt.

That's true. I don't have to worry about Sara anymore, I guess.

Why? Because she's a married mommy? Faith asked. What an insult to Edie!

No, that's O.K., said Edie.

Well, I do worry about Rachel. I just can't help myself. I never know where she is. She was supposed to be here last night. She does usually call. Where the hell is she?

Oh, probably in jail for some stupid little sit-in or something, Ann said. She'll get out in five minutes. Why she thinks that kind of thing works is a mystery to me. You brought her up like that and now you're surprised. Besides which, I don't want to talk about the goddamn kids, said Ann. Here I've gone around half of most of the nearly socialist world and nobody asks me a single question. I have been a witness of events! she shouted.

I do want to hear everything, said Ruth. Then she changed her mind. Well, I don't mean everything. Just say one good thing and one bad thing about every place you've been. We only have a couple of hours. (It was four o'clock. At six, Sara and Tomas with Letty, the first grandchild, standing between them would be at the door. Letty would probably think it was her own birthday party. Someone would say, What curly hair! They would all love her new shoes and her newest sentence, which was Remember dat? Because for such a long time there had been only the present full of milk and looking. Then one day, trying to dream into an afternoon nap, she sat up and said, Gramma, I boke your cup. Remember dat? In this simple way the lifelong past is invented, which, as we know, thickens the present and gives all kinds of advice to the future.) So, Ann, I mean just a couple of things about each country.

That's not much of a discussion, for Christsake.

It's a party, Ann, you said it yourself.

Well, change your face, then.

Oh. Ruth touched her mouth, the corners of her eyes. You're right. Birthday! she said.

Well, let's go, then, said Ann. She stated two good things and one bad thing about Chile (an earlier visit), Rhodesia, the Soviet Union, and Portugal.

You forgot about China. Why don't you tell them about our trip to China?

I don't think I will, Ruthy; you'd only contradict every word I say.

Edie, the oldest friend, stripped a nice freckled banana she'd been watching during Ann's talk. The thing is, Ruth, you never simply say yes. I've told you so many times, *I* would have slammed the door on you, admit it, but it was your house, and that slowed me down.

Property, Ann said. Even among poor people, it begins early.

Poor? asked Edie. It was the Depression.

Two questions – Faith believed she'd listened patiently long enough. I love that story, but I've heard it before. Whenever you're down in the dumps, Ruthy. Right?

I haven't, Ann said. How come, Ruthy? Also, will you please sit with us.

The second question: What about this city? I mean, I'm kind of sick of these big international reports. Look at this place, looks like a toxic waste dump. A war. Nine million people.

Oh, that's true, Edie said, but Faith, the whole thing is hopeless. Top to bottom, the streets, those kids, dumped, plain dumped. That's the correct word, 'dumped.' She began to cry.

Cut it out, Ann shouted. No tears, Edie! No! Stop this minute! I swear, Faith said, you'd better stop that! (They were all, even Edie, ideologically, spiritually, and on puritanical principle against despair.)

Faith was sorry to have mentioned the city in Edie's presence. If you said the word 'city' to Edie, or even the cool adjective 'municipal,' specific children usually sitting at the back of the room appeared before her eyes and refused to answer when she called on them. So Faith said, O.K. New subject: What do you women think of the grand juries they're calling up all over the place?

All over what place? Edie asked. Oh, Faith, forget it, they're going through something. You know you three lead such adversarial lives. I hate it. What good does it do? Any way, those juries will pass.

Edie, sometimes I think you're half asleep. You know that woman in New Haven who was called? I know her personally. She wouldn't say a word. She's in jail. They're not kidding.

I'd never open my mouth either, said Ann. Never. She clamped her mouth shut then and there.

I believe you, Ann. But sometimes, Ruth said, I think, Suppose I was in Argentina and they had my kid. God, if they had our Sara's Letty, I'd maybe say anything.

Oh, Ruth, you've held up pretty well, once or twice, Faith said.

Yes, Ann said, in fact we were all pretty good that day, we were sitting right up against the horses' knees at the draft board – were you there, Edie? And then the goddamn horses started to rear and the cops were knocking people on their backs and heads – remember? And, Ruthy, I was watching you. You just suddenly plowed in and out of those monsters. You should have been trampled to death. And you grabbed the captain by his gold buttons and you hollered, You bastard! Get your goddamn cavalry out of here. You shook him and shook him.

He ordered them, Ruth said. She set one of her birthday cakes, which was an apple plum pie, on the table. I saw him. He was the responsible person. I saw the whole damn operation. I'd begun to run – the horses – but I turned because I was the one supposed to be in front and I saw him give the order. I've never honestly been so angry.

Ann smiled. Anger, she said. That's really good.

You think so? Ruth asked. You sure?

Buzz off, said Ann.

Ruth lit the candles. Come on, Ann, we've got to blow this out together. And make a wish. I don't have the wind I used to have.

But you're still full of hot air, Edie said. And kissed her hard. What did you wish, Ruthy? she asked.

Well, a wish, some wish, Ruth said. Well, I wished that this world wouldn't end. This world, this world, Ruth said softly.

Me too, I wished exactly the same. Taking action, Ann hoisted herself up onto a kitchen chair, saying, ugh my back, ouch my knee. Then: Let us go forth with fear and courage and rage to save the world.

Bravo, Edie said softly.

Wait a minute, said Faith . . .

Ann said, Oh, you . . . you . . .

But it was six o'clock and the doorbell rang. Sara and Tomas stood on either side of Letty, who was hopping or wiggling with excitement, hiding behind her mother's long skirt or grabbing her father's thigh. The door had barely opened when Letty jumped forward to hug Ruth's knees. I'm gonna sleep in your house, Gramma.

I know, darling, I know.

Gramma, I slept in your bed with you. Remember dat?

Oh sure, darling, I remember. We woke up around five and it was still dark and I looked at you and you looked at me and you had a great big Letty smile and we just burst out laughing and you laughed and I laughed.

I remember dat, Gramma. Letty looked at her parents with shyness and pride. She was still happy to have found the word 'remember,' which could name so many pictures in her head.

And then we went right back to sleep, Ruth said, kneeling now to Letty's height to kiss her little face.

Where's my Aunt Rachel? Letty asked, hunting among the crowd of unfamiliar legs in the hallway.

I don't know.

She's supposed to be here, Letty said. Mommy, you promised. She's really supposed.

Yes, said Ruth, picking Letty up to hug her and then hug her again. Letty, she said as lightly as she could, She *is* supposed to be here. But where can she be? She certainly is supposed.

Letty began to squirm out of Ruth's arms. Mommy, she called, Gramma is squeezing. But it seemed to Ruth that she'd better hold her even closer, because, though no one else seemed to notice – Letty, rosy and soft-cheeked as ever, was falling, already falling, falling out of her brand-new hammock of world-inventing words onto the hard floor of man-made time.

A Man Told Me
the Story of His Life

Vicente said: I wanted to be a doctor. I wanted to be a doctor with my whole heart.

I learned every bone, every organ in the body. What is it for? Why does it work?

The school said to me: Vicente, be an engineer. That would be good. You understand mathematics.

I said to the school: I want to be a doctor. I already know how the organs connect. When something goes wrong, I'll understand how to make repairs.

The school said: Vicente, you will really be an excellent engineer. You show on all the tests what a good engineer you will be. It doesn't show whether you'll be a good doctor.

I said: Oh, I long to be a doctor. I nearly cried. I was seventeen. I said: But perhaps you're right. You're the teacher. You're the principal. I know I'm young.

The school said: And besides, you're going into the army.

And then I was made a cook. I prepared food for two thousand men.

Now you see me. I have a good job. I have three children. This is my wife, Consuela. Did you know I saved her life?

Look, she suffered pain. The doctor said: What is this? Are you tired? Have you had too much company? How many children? Rest overnight, then tomorrow we'll make tests.

The next morning I called the doctor. I said: She must be operated immediately. I have looked in the book. I see where her pain is. I understand what the pressure is, where it comes from. I see clearly the organ that is making trouble.

The doctor made a test. He said: She must be operated at once. He said to me: Vicente, how did you know?

The Story Hearer

I am trying to curb my cultivated individualism, which seemed for years so sweet. It was my own song in my own world and, of course, it may not be useful in the hard time to come. So, when Jack said at dinner, What did you do today with your year off? I decided to make an immediate public accounting of the day, not to water my brains with time spent in order to grow smart private thoughts.

I said, Shall we begin at the beginning?

Yes, he said, I've always loved beginnings.

Men do, I replied. No one knows if they will ever get over this. Hundreds of thousands of words have been written, some freelance and some commissioned. Still no one knows.

Look here, he said, I like middles too.

Oh yes, I know. I questioned him. Is this due to age or the recent proliferation of newspaper articles?

I don't know, he said. I often wonder, but it seems to me that my father, who was a decent man – your typical nine-to-five – it seems to me he settled into a great appreciation of the middle just about the time my mother said, Well, Willy, it's enough. Goodbye. Keep the children warm and let him (me) finish high school at least. Then she kissed him, kissed us kids. She said. I'll call you next week, but never did speak to any of us again. Where can she be?

Now, I've heard that story maybe thirty times and I still can't bear it. In fact. whenever I've made some strong adversary point in public, Jack tells it to grieve me. Sometimes I begin to cry. Sometimes I just make soup immediately. Once I thought, Oh, I'll iron his underwear. I've heard of that being done, but I couldn't find the cord. I haven't needed to iron in years because of famous American science, which gives us wash-and-wear in one test tube and nerve gas in the other. Its right test tube doesn't know what its left test tube is doing.

Oh yes, it does, says Jack.

Therefore I want to go on with the story. Or perhaps begin it again. Jack said, What did you do today with your year off? I said, My dear, in the late morning I left our apartment. The *Times* was folded on the doormat of 1-A. I could see that it was black with earthquake, war, and private murder. Clearly death had been successful everywhere but not – I saw when I stepped out the front door – on our own block. Here it was springtime, partly because of the time of the year and partly because we have a self-involved block-centered street association which has lined us with sycamores and enhanced us with a mountain ash, two ginkgoes, and here and there (because we are part of the whole) ailanthus, city saver.

I said to myself, What a day! I think I'll run down to the store and pick up some comestibles. I actually thought that. Had I simply gone to the store without thinking, the word 'comestible' would never have occurred to me. I would have imagined – hungry supper nighttime Jack greens cheese store walk street.

But I do like this language – wheat and chaff – with its widening pool of foreign genes, and since I never have had any occasion to say 'comestible,' it was pleasurable to think it.

At the grocer's I met an old friend who had continued his life as it had begun – in the avant-garde, but not selfishly. He had also organized guerrilla theater demonstrations and had never spoken ill of the people. Most artists do because they have very small audiences and are angry at those audiences for not enlarging themselves.

How can they do that? I've often asked. They have word of mouth, don't they? most artists peevishly will reply.

Well, first my friend and I talked of the lettuce boycott. It was an old boycott. I told my friend (whose name was Jim) all about the silk-stocking boycott which coincided with the Japanese devastation of Manchuria and the disappearance of the Sixth Avenue El into Japanese factory furnaces to be returned a few years later – sometimes to the very same neighborhood – as shrapnel stuck in the bodies of some young New Yorkers of my generation.

Did that lead to Pearl Harbor? he asked respectfully. He was aware that I had witnessing information of events that had occurred when he was in grade school. That respect gave me all the advantage I needed to be aggressive and critical. I said, Jim, I have been wanting to tell you that I do not believe in the effectiveness of the way that you had the Vietnamese screaming at our last demonstration. I don't think the meaning of our struggle has anything to do with all that racket.

You don't understand Artaud, he said. I believe that the theater is the handmaiden of the revolution.

The valet, you mean.

He deferred to my correction by nodding his head. He accepts criticism gracefully, since he can always meet it with a smiling bumper of iron opinion.

You ought to know more about Artaud, he said.

You're right. I should. But I've been awfully busy. Also, I may have once known a great deal about him. In the last few years, all the characters of literature run together in my head. Sometimes King Ubu appears right next to Mr. Sparsit – or Mrs. . . .

At this point the butcher said, What'll you have, young lady? I refused to tell him.

Jack, to whom, if you remember, I was telling this daylong story, muttered, Oh God, no! You didn't do that again.

I did, I said. It's an insult. You do not say to a woman of my age who looks my age, What'll you have, young lady? I did not answer him. If you say that to someone like me, it really means, What do you want, you pathetic old hag?

Are you getting like that now too? he asked.

Look, Jack, I said, face facts. Let's say the butcher meant no harm. Eddie, he's not so bad. He spends two hours coming to New York from Jersey. Then he spends two hours going back. I'm sorry for his long journey. But I still mean it. He mustn't say it anymore.

Eddie, I said, don't talk like that or I won't tell you what I want.

Whatever you say, honey, but what'll you have?

Well, could you cut me up a couple of fryers?

Sure I will, he said.

I'll have a pork butt, said Jim. By the way, you know we're doing a show at City College this summer. Not in the auditorium – in the biology lab. It's a new idea. We had to fight for it. It's the most political thing we've done since *Scavenging*.

Did I hear you say City College? asked Eddie as he cut the little chicken's leg out of its socket. Well, when I was a boy, a kid – what we called City College – you know it was C.C.N.Y. then, well, we called it Circumcised Citizens of New York.

Really, said Jim. He looked at me. Did I object? Was I offended?

The fact of male circumcision doesn't insult me, I said. However, I understand that the clipping of clitorises of young girls continues in Morocco to this day.

Jim has a shy side. He took his pork butt and said goodbye.

I had begun to examine the chicken livers. Sometimes they are tanner than red, but I understand this is not too bad.

Suddenly Treadwell Thomas appeared at my side and embraced me. He's a famous fussy gourmet, and I was glad that the butcher saw our affectionate hug. Thought up any good euphemisms lately? I asked.

Ha ha, he said. He still feels bad about his life in the Language Division of the Defense Department. A year or two ago Jack interviewed him for a magazine called *The Social Ordure*, which ran five quarterly issues before the first editor was hired away by the *Times*. It's still a fine periodical.

Here's part of the interview:

Mr. Thomas, what is the purpose of the Language Division?

Well, Jack, it was organized to discontinue the English language as a useful way to communicate exact facts. Of course, it's not the first (or last) organization to have attempted this, but it's had some success.

Mr. Thomas, is this an ironic statement made in the afterglow of your new idealism and the broad range of classified information it has made available to us?

Not at all, Jack. It wasn't I who invented the expression 'protective reaction.' And it was Eisenhower, not I, who thought up (while thousands of hydrogen bombs were being tucked into silos and submarines) – it was not I who invented 'Atoms for Peace' and its code name, 'Operation Wheaties.'

Could you give us at least one expression you invented to stultify or mitigate? (Jack, I screamed, 'stultify' or 'mitigate,' you caught the disease. Shut up, said Jack, and returned to the interview.)

Well? he asked.

Well, said Treadwell Thomas, I was asked to develop a word or series of words that could describe, denote any of the Latin American countries in a condition of change – something that would by its mere utterance neutralize or mock their revolutionary situation. After consultation, brainpicking, and the daydreaming that is appropriate to any act of creation, I came up with 'revostate.' The word was slipped into conversations in Washington; one or two journalists were glad to use it. It was just lingo for a long time. But you have no doubt seen the monograph *The Revostationary Peasant in Brazil Today*. Even you pinkos use it. Not to mention Wasserman's poetic article, 'Rain Forest, Still Water, and the Culture of the Revostate,' which was actually featured in this journal.

Right on, Treadwell – as our black brothers joyfully said for a couple of years before handing that utterance on for our stultification or mitigation.

Still, it's true Thomas could have gone as far as far happens to be in our time and generation, hundreds of ambitious jobless college students at the foot of his tongue on Senior Defense Department Recruiting Day, but apart from cooking a lot of fish he has chosen to guffaw quite often. Some people around here think that guffawing, the energetic cleansing of the nasal passage, is the basic wisdom of the East. Other people think that's not true.

Which reminded me as we waited for the packaging of the meat, how's Gussie?

Gus? Oh yeah, she's into hydroponics. She's got all this stuff standing around in tubs. We may never have to go shopping again.

Well, I laughed and laughed. I repeated the story to several others before the day was over. I mocked Gussie to Jack. I spoke of her mockingly to one or two strangers. And the fact is, she was already the wave of the future. I was ignorant. It wasn't my ocean she was a wave in.

In fact, I am stuck here among my own ripples and tides. Don't you wish you could rise powerfully above your time and name? I'm sure we all try, but here we are, always slipping and falling down into them, speaking their narrow language, though the subject, which is how to save the world – and quickly – is immense.

Goodbye, Treadwell, I said sadly. I've got to get some greens.

The owner of our grocery was hosing down the vegetables. He made the lettuce look fresher than it was. Little drops of water stood on the broccoli heads among the green beady buds and were just the same size.

Orlando, I said, Jack was walking the dog last week at 2 a.m. and I was out at 7 a.m. and you were here both times.

That's true, he said. I was.

Orlando, how can you do that, how can you get to work, how can you live? How can you see your kids and your wife?

I can't, he said. Maybe once a week.

Are you all right?

Yes. He put down his hose and took my hand in his. You see, he said, this is wonderful work. This is food. I love all work that has to do with food. I'm lucky. He dropped my hand and patted a red cabbage. Look at me, I'm a small businessman. I got an A&P on one side, a Bohack on another, and a fancy International full of cheese and herring down the block. If I don't put in sixteen hours a day I'm dead. But Mrs. A., just look at that rack, the beans, that corner with all the parsley and the arugula and the dill, it's beautiful, right?

Oh yes, I said, I guess it is, but what *I* really love are the little bunches of watercress – the way you've lined the carrot bin with them.

Yeah, Mrs. A., you're O.K. You got the idea. The beauty! he said, and went off to take three inferior strawberries out of a perfect box. A couple of years later – in the present, which I have not quite mentioned (but will) – we fought over Chilean plums. We parted. I was forced to shop in the reasonable supermarket among disinterested people with no credit asked and none offered. But at that particular moment we were at peace. That is, I owed him $275 and he allowed it.

O.K., said Jack, if you and Orlando are such pals, why aren't all these strawberries ripe? He picked up a rather green eroded one. I invented an anthropological reply. Well, Orlando's father is an old man. One of the jobs Orlando's culture has provided for his father's old age is the sorting of strawberries into pint and quart boxes. Just to be fair, he has to hide one or two greenish ones in each box.

I think I'll go to bed, said Jack.

I was only extrapolating from his article in the third issue of *The Social Ordure* – 'Food Merchandising, or Who Invented the Greedy Consumer.' I reminded him of this.

He said politely, Ah . . .

The day had been too long and I hadn't said one word about the New Young Fathers or my meeting with Zagrowsky the Pharmacist. I thought we might discuss them at breakfast.

So we slept, his arms around me as sweetly as after the long day he had probably slept beside his former wife (and I as well beside my etc. etc. etc.). I was so comfortable; our good mattress and our nice feelings were such a cozy combination that I remembered a song my friend Ruthy had made up about ten years earlier to tease the time, the place, us:

oh, the marriage bed, the marriage bed
can you think of anything nicer
for days and nights of years and years
you lie beside your darling
your arms are hugging one another
your legs are twined together
until the dark and certain day
your lover comes to take you
   away   away   away

At about 3 a.m. Jack cried out in terror. That's O.K., kid, I said, you're not the only one. Everybody's mortal. I leaned all my softening strength against his skinny back. Then I dreamed the following in a kind of diorama of Technicolor abstraction – that the children had grown all the way up. One had moved to another neighborhood, the other to a distant country. *That* one was never to be seen again, the dream explained, because he had blown up a very bad bank, and in the dream I was the one who'd told him to do it. The dream continued; no – it circled itself, widening into my very old age. Then his disappearance made one of those typical spiraling descents influenced by film technique. Unreachable at the bottom, their childhood played war and made jokes.

I woke. Where's the glass of water, I screamed. I want to tell you something, Jack.

What? What? What? He saw my wide-awake eyes. He sat up. What?

Jack, I want to have a baby.

Ha ha, he said. You can't. Too late. A couple of years too late, he said, and fell asleep. Then he spoke. Besides, suppose it worked; I mean, suppose a miracle. The kid might be very smart, get a scholarship to M.I.T., and get caught up in problem solving and godalmighty it could invent something worse than anything us old dodos ever imagined. Then he fell asleep and snored.

I pulled the Old Testament out from under the bed where I keep most of my bedtime literature. I jammed an extra pillow under my neck and sat up almost straight in order to read the story of Abraham and Sarah with interlinear intelligence. There was a lot in what Jack said – he often makes a sensible or thought-provoking remark. Because you know how that old story ends – well! With those three monotheistic horsemen of perpetual bossdom and war: Christianity, Judaism, and Islam.

Just the same, I said to softly snoring Jack, before all that popular badness wedged its way into the world, there *was first* the little baby Isaac. You know what I mean: looking at Sarah just like all our own old babies – remember the way they practiced their five little senses. Oh, Jack, that Isaac, Sarah's boy – before he was old enough to be taken out by his father to get his throat cut, he must have just lain around smiling and making up diphthongs and listening, and the women sang songs to him and wrapped him up in such pretty rugs. Right?

In his sleep, which is as contentious as his waking, Jack said yes – but he should not have been allowed to throw all that sand at his brother.

You're right, you're right. I'm with you there, I said. Now all you have to do is be with me.

This Is a Story about My Friend George, the Toy Inventor

He is a man of foreign parentage who suffers waves of love, salty tears that crest in his eyes. The shores attacked by those waves are often his children. This isn't a story about his children.

One day, George failed. He had had many successes, so the failure was not a life failure. It was the failure of a half year's work and included, as failure often does, an important loss of income.

He had invented a pinball machine. When we saw it, we said, George! This is not a pinball machine alone. This is the poem of a pinball machine, the essence made delicately concrete, and so forth.

This is what it looked like: Instead of hard metal balls which are propelled into a box with decorated flashing lights and illuminated athletes and planets, balls of blue water are shot into the box. The blue water breaks and scatters in tiny blue droplets of varying volume. The action is swift, the sky-blue droplets skitter and collect again on the magnetic white ground. There are resting places with numbers for scoring.

It is certainly beautiful and stands so far ahead of its time that we were not surprised to learn it had been rejected. After the rejection, George rented a couple of ordinary pinball machines (because he's a serious person, an inventor, an artist) in order to try to understand his failure. He installed them in the boys' attic room. The family played and investigated them for several weeks. Then, to his sorrow, he added understanding and amazement.

How could he have believed he was the one to improve on the pinball machine, that old invention of cumulative complication. He had offered only a small innovation.

Beauty! we said. Bringing all our political theory to bear on the matter, we suggested that there was money to be extracted – even from that – inside the opportunistic life of coopting capitalism.

No, George said, you don't understand. The pinball machine – any pinball machine you play in any penny arcade – is so remarkable, so fine, so shrewdly threaded. It is already beautiful in necessity and sufficiency of wire, connection, possibility.

No, no, George said. The company was right. They gave me six months to make a better pinball machine. They were fair. What gall I had to think I could. No, they were fair. It's as though I had expected to invent the violin.

Zagrowsky Tells

I was standing in the park under that tree. They call it the Hanging Elm. Once upon a time it made a big improvement on all kinds of hooligans. Nowadays if, once in a while . . . No. So this woman comes up to me, a woman minus a smile. I said to my grandson, Uh oh, Emanuel. Here comes a lady, she was once a beautiful customer of mine in the pharmacy I showed you.

Emanuel says, Grandpa, who?

She looks O.K. now, but not so hot. Well, what can you do, time takes a terrible toll off the ladies.

This is her idea of a hello: Iz? what are you doing with that black child? Then she says, Who is he? Why are you holding on to him like that? She gives me a look like God in judgment. You could see it in famous paintings. Then she says, Why are you yelling at that poor kid?

What yelling? A history lesson about the park. This is a tree in guidebooks. How are you by the way, Miss . . . Miss . . . I was embarrassed. I forgot her name absolutely.

Well, who is he? You got him pretty scared.

Me? Don't be ridiculous. It's my grandson. Say hello Emanuel, don't put on an act.

Emanuel shoves his hand in my pocket to be a little more

glued to me. Are you going to open your mouth sonny yes or no?

She says, Your grandson? Really, Iz, your grandson? What do you mean? your grandson?

Emanuel closes his eyes tight. Did you ever notice children get all mixed up? They don't want to hear about something, they squinch up their eyes. Many children do this.

Now listen Emanuel, I want you to tell this lady who is the smartest boy in kindergarten.

Not a word.

Goddamnit, open your eyes. It's something new with him. Tell her who is the smartest boy — he was just five, he can already read a whole book by himself.

He stands still. He's thinking. I know his little cute mind. Then he jumps up and down yelling, Me me me. He makes a little dance. His grandma calls it his smartness dance. My other ones (three children grown up for some time already) were also very smart, but they don't hold a candle to this character. Soon as I get a chance, I'm gonna bring him to the city to Hunter for gifted children; he should get a test.

But this Miss . . . Miss . . . she's not finished with us yet. She's worried. Whose kid is he? You adopt him?

Adopt? At my age? It's Cissy's kid. You know my Cissy? I see she knows something. Why not? I had a public business. No surprise.

Of course I remember Cissy. She says this, her face is a little more ironed out.

So my Cissy, if you remember, she was a nervous girl.

I'll *bet* she was.

Is that a nice way to answer? Cissy *was* nervous . . . The nervousness, to be truthful, ran in Mrs. Z.'s family. Ran? Galloped . . . tarum tarum tarum.

When we were young I used to go over there to visit, and while me and her brother and uncles played pinochle, in the kitchen the three aunts would sit drinking tea. Everything was Oi! Oi! Oi! What for? Nothin to oi about. They got husbands . . . Perfectly fine gentlemen. One in business, two of them real professionals.

They just got in the habit somehow. So I said to Mrs. Z., one oi out of you and it's divorce.

I remember your wife very well, this lady says. *Very* well. She puts on the same face like before; her mouth gets small. Your wife *is* a beautiful woman.

So . . . would I marry a mutt?

But she was right. My Nettie when she was young, she was very fair, like some Polish Jews you see once in a while. Like for instance maybe some big blond peasant made a pogrom on her great-grandma.

So I answered her, Oh yes, very nice-looking; even now she's not so bad, but a little bit on the grouchy side.

O.K., she makes a big sigh like I'm a hopeless case. What did happen to Cissy?

Emanuel, go over there and play with those kids. No? No.

Well, I'll tell you, it's the genes. The genes are the most important. Environment is O.K. But the genes . . . that's where the whole story is written down. I think the school had something to do with it also. She's more an artist like your husband. Am I thinking of the right guy? When she was a kid you should of seen her. She's a nice-looking girl now, even when she has an attack. But then she was something. The family used to go to the mountains in the summer. We went dancing, her and me. What a dancer. People were surprised Sometimes we danced until 2 a.m.

I don't think that was good, she says. I wouldn't dance with my son all night . . .

Naturally, you're a mother. But 'good,' who knows what's good? Maybe a doctor. I could have been a doctor, by the way. Her brother-in-law in business would of backed me. But then what? You don't have the time. People call you day and night. I cured more people in a day than a doctor in a week. Many an M.D. called me, said, Zagrowsky, does it work . . . that Parke-Davis medication they put out last month, or it's a fake? I got immediate experience and I'm not too stuck up to tell.

Oh, Iz, you are, she said. She says this like she means it but it makes her sad. How do I know this? Years in a store. You observe.

You watch. The customer is always right, but plenty of times you know he's wrong and also a goddamn fool.

All of a sudden I put her in a certain place. Then I said to myself, Iz, why are you standing here with this woman? I looked her straight in the face and I said, Faith? Right? Listen to me. Now you listen, because I got a question. Is it true, no matter what time you called, even if I was closing up, I came to your house with the penicillin or the tetracycline later? You lived on the fourth-floor walk-up. Your friend what's-her-name, Susan, with the three girls next door? I can see it very clear. Your face is all smeared up with crying, your kid got 105°, maybe more, burning up, you didn't want to leave him in the crib screaming, you're standing in the hall, it's dark. You were living alone, am I right? So young. Also your husband, he comes to my mind, very jumpy fellow, in and out, walking around all night. He drank? I betcha. Irish? Imagine you didn't get along so you got a divorce. Very simple. You kids knew how to live.

She doesn't even answer me. She says . . . you want to know what she says? She says, Oh shit! Then she says, Of course I remember. God, my Richie was sick! Thanks, she says, thanks, godalmighty thanks.

I was already thinking something else: The mind makes its own business. When she first came up to me, I couldn't remember. I knew her well, but where? Then out of no place, a word, her bossy face maybe, exceptionally round, which is not usual, her dark apartment, the four flights, the other girls – all once lively, young . . . you could see them walking around on a sunny day, dragging a couple kids, a carriage, a bike, beautiful girls, but tired from all day, mostly divorced, going home alone? Boyfriends? Who knows how that type lives? I had a big appreciation for them. Sometimes, five o'clock I stood in the door to see them. They were mostly the way models *should* be. I mean not skinny – round, like they were made of little cushions and bigger cushions, depending where you looked; young mothers. I hollered a few words to them, they hollered back. Especially I remember her friend Ruthy – she had two little girls with long black braids, down to here. I told her, In a couple of years, Ruthy, you'll have some beauties on your hands. You better keep an eye on them. In those days the women always answered you in a pleasant way, not afraid to smile. Like this: They said, You really think so? Thanks, Iz.

But this is all used-to-be and in that place there is not only good but bad and the main fact in regard to *this* particular lady: I did her good but to me she didn't always do so much good.

So we stood around a little. Emanuel says, Grandpa, let's go to the swings. Go yourself – it's not so far, there's kids, I see them. No, he says, and stuffs his hand in my pocket again. So don't go – Ach, what a day, I said. Buds and everything. She says, That's a catalpa tree over there. No kidding! I say. What do you call that one, doesn't have a single leaf? Locust, she says. Two locusts, I say.

Then I take a deep breath: O.K. – you still listening? Let me ask you, if I did you so much good including I saved your baby's life, how come you did *that*? You know what I'm talking about. A perfectly nice day. I look out the window of the pharmacy and I see four customers, that I seen at least two in their bathrobes crying to me in the middle of the night, Help help! They're out there with signs. ZAGROWSKY IS A RACIST. YEARS AFTER ROSA PARKS, ZAGROWSKY REFUSES TO SERVE BLACKS. It's like an etching right *here*. I point out to her my heart. I know exactly where it is.

She's naturally very uncomfortable when I tell her. Listen, she says, we were right.

I grab on to Emanuel. You?

Yes, we wrote a letter first, did you answer it? We said, Zagrowsky, come to your senses. Ruthy wrote it. We said we would like to talk to you. We tested you. At least four times, you kept Mrs. Green and Josie, our friend Josie, who was kind of Spanish black . . . she lived on the first floor in our house . . . you kept them waiting a long time till everyone ahead of them was taken care of. Then you were very rude, I mean nasty, you can be extremely nasty, Iz. And then Josie left the store, she called you some pretty bad names. You remember?

No, I happen not to remember. There was plenty of yelling in the store. People *really* suffering; come in yelling for codeine or what to do their mother was dying. That's what I remember, not some crazy Spanish lady hollering.

But listen, she says – like all this is not in front of my eyes, like the past is only a piece of paper in the yard – you didn't finish with Cissy.

Finish? *You* almost finished my business and don't think that Cissy didn't hold it up to me. Later when she was so sick.

Then I thought, Why should I talk to this woman. I see myself: how I was standing that day how many years ago? – like an idiot behind the counter waiting for customers. Everybody is peeking in past the picket line. It's the kind of neighborhood, if they see a picket line, half don't come in. The cops say they have a right. To destroy a person's business. I was disgusted but I went into the street. After all, I knew the ladies. I tried to explain, Faith, Ruthy, Mrs. Kratt – a stranger comes into the store, naturally you have to serve the old customers first. Anyone would do the same. Also, they sent in black people, brown people, all colors, and to tell the truth I didn't like the idea my pharmacy should get the reputa-tion of being a cut-rate place for them. They move into a neighborhood . . . I did what everyone did. Not to insult people too much, but to discourage them a little, they shouldn't feel so welcome. They could just move in because it's a nice area.

All right. A person looks at my Emanuel and says, Hey! he's not altogether from the white race, what's going on? I'll tell you what: life is going on. You have an opinion. I have an opinion. Life don't have no opinion.

I moved away from this Faith lady. I didn't like to be near her. I sat down on the bench. I'm no spring chicken. Cock-a-doodle-do, I only holler once in a while. I'm tired, I'm mostly the one in charge of our Emanuel. Mrs. Z. stays home, her legs swell up. It's a shame.

In the subway once she couldn't get off at the right stop. The door opens, she can't get up. She tried (she's a little overweight). She says to a big guy with a notebook, a big colored fellow, Please help me get up. He says to her, You kept me down three hundred years, you can stay down another ten minutes. I asked her, Nettie, didn't you tell him we're raising a little boy brown like a coffee bean. But he's right, says Nettie, we done that. We kept them down.

We? We? My two sisters and my father were being fried up for Hitler's supper in 1944 and you say we?

Nettie sits down. Please bring me some tea. Yes, Iz, I say: *We.*

I can't even put up the water I'm so mad. You know, my Mrs., you are crazy like your three aunts, crazy like our Cissy. Your whole family put in the genes to make it for sure that she wouldn't have a chance. Nettie looks at me. She says, Ai ai. She doesn't say oi anymore. She got herself assimilated into ai . . . That's how come she also says 'we' done it. Don't think this will make you an American, I said to her, that you included yourself in with Robert E. Lee. Naturally it was a joke, only what is there to laugh?

I'm tired right now. This Faith could even see I'm a little shaky. What should she do, she's thinking. But she decides the discussion ain't over so she sits down sideways. The bench is damp. It's only April.

What about Cissy? Is she all right?

It ain't your business how she is.

O.K. She starts to go.

Wait wait! Since I seen you in your nightgown a couple of times when you were a handsome young woman . . . She really gets up this time. I think she must be a woman's libber, they don't like remarks about nightgowns. Bathrobes, she didn't mind. Let her go! The hell with her . . . but she comes back. She says, Once and for all, cut it out, Iz. I really *want* to know. Is Cissy all right?

You want. She's fine. She lives with me and Nettie. She's in charge of the plants. It's an all-day job.

But why should I leave her off the hook. Oh boy, Faith, I got to say it, what you people put on me! And you want to know how Cissy is. *You!* Why? Sure. You remember you finished with the picket lines after a week or two. I don't know why. Tired? Summer maybe, you got to go away, make trouble at the beach. But I'm stuck there. Did I have air conditioning yet? All of a sudden I see Cissy outside. She has a sign also. She must've got the idea from you women. A big sandwich board, she walks up and down. If someone talks to her, she presses her mouth together.

I don't remember that, Faith says.

Of course, you were already on Long Island or Cape Cod or someplace – the Jersey shore.

No, she says, I was not. I was not. (I see this is a big insult to her that she should go away for the summer.)

Then I thought, Calm down, Zagrowsky. Because for a fact I didn't want her to leave, because, since I already began to tell, I have to tell the whole story. I'm not a person who keeps things in. Tell! That opens up the congestion a little – the lungs are for breathing, no secrets. My wife never tells, she coughs, coughs. All night. Wakes up. Ai, Iz, open up the window, there's no air. You poor woman, if you want to breathe, you got to tell.

So I said to this Faith, I'll tell you how Cissy is but you got to hear the whole story how we suffered. I thought, O.K. Who cares! Let her get on the phone later with the other girls. They should know what they started.

How we took our own Cissy from here to there to the biggest doctor – I had good contacts from the pharmacy. Dr. Francis O'Connel, the heavy Irishman over at the hospital, sat with me and Mrs. Z. for two hours, a busy man. He explained that it was one of the most great mysteries. They were ignoramuses, the most brilliant doctors were dummies in this field. But still, in my place, I heard of this cure and that one. So we got her massaged fifty times from head to toe, whatever someone suggested. We stuffed her with vitamins and minerals – there was a real doctor in charge of this idea.

If she would take the vitamins – sometimes she shut her mouth. To her mother she said dirty words. We weren't used to it. Meanwhile, in front of my place every morning, she walks up and down. She could of got minimum wage, she was so regular.

Her afternoon job is to follow my wife from corner to corner to tell what my wife done wrong to her when she was a kid. Then after a couple months, all of a sudden she starts to sing. She has a beautiful voice. She took lessons from a well-known person. On Christmas week, in front of the pharmacy she sings half the *Messiah* by Handel. You know it? So that's nice, you think. Oh, that's beautiful. But where were you you didn't notice that she don't have on a coat. You didn't see she walks up and down, her socks are falling off ? Her face and hands are like she's the super in the cellar. She sings! she sings! Two songs she sings the most: one is about the Gentiles will see the light and the other is, Look! a virgin will conceive a son. My wife says, Sure, naturally, she wishes she was a married woman just like anyone. Baloney. She could of. She had plenty of dates. Plenty. She sings, the idiots applaud, some skunk yells, Go, Cissy, go. What? Go where? Some days she just hollers.

Hollers what?

Oh, I forgot about you. Hollers anything. Hollers, Racist! Hollers, He sells poison chemicals! Hollers, He's a terrible dancer, he got three left legs! (Which isn't true, just to insult me publicly, plain silly.) The people laugh. What'd she say? Some didn't hear so well; hollers, You go to whores. Also not true. She met me once with a woman actually a distant relative from Israel. Everything is in her head. It's a garbage pail.

One day her mother says to her, Cissile, comb your hair, for godsakes, darling. For this remark, she gives her mother a sock in the face. I come home I see a woman not at all young with two black eyes and a bloody nose. The doctor said, Before it's better with your girl, it's got to be worse. That much he knew. He sent us to a beautiful place, a hospital right at the city line – I'm not sure if it's Westchester or the Bronx, but thank God, you could use the subway. That's how I found out what I was saving up my money for. I thought for retiring in Florida to walk around under the palm trees in the middle of the week. Wrong. It was for my beautiful Cissy, she should have a nice home with other crazy people.

So little by little, she calms down. We can visit her. She shows us the candy store, we give her a couple of dollars; soon our life is this way. Three times a week my wife goes, gets on the subway with delicious foods (no sugar, they're against sugar); she brings something nice, a blouse or a kerchief – a present, you understand, to show love; and once a week I go, but she don't want to look at me. So close we were, like sweethearts – you can imagine how I feel. Well, you have children so you know, little children little troubles, big children big troubles – it's a saying in Yiddish. Maybe the Chinese said it too.

Oh, Iz. How could it happen like that? All of a sudden. No signs?

What's with this Faith? Her eyes are full of tears. Sensitive I suppose. I see what she's thinking. Her kids are teenagers. So far they look O.K. but what will happen? People think of themselves. Human nature. At least she doesn't tell me it's my wife's fault or mine. I did something terrible! I loved my child. I know what's on people's minds. I know psychology *very* well. Since this happened to us, I read up on the whole business.

Oh, Iz . . .

She puts her hand on my knee. I look at her. Maybe she's just a nut. Maybe she thinks I'm plain old (I almost am). Well, I said it before. Thank God for the head. Inside the head is the only place you got to be young when the usual place gets used up. For some reason she gives me a kiss on the cheek. A peculiar person.

Faith, I still can't figure it out why you girls were so rotten to me.

But we were right.

Then this lady Queen of Right makes a small lecture. She don't remember my Cissy walking up and down screaming bad language but she remembers: After Mrs. Kendrick's big fat snotty maid walked out with Kendrick's allergy order, I made a face and said, Ho ho! the great lady! That's terrible? She says whenever I saw a couple walk past on the block, a black-and-white couple, I said, Ugh – disgusting! It shouldn't be allowed! She heard this remark from me a few times. So? It's a matter of taste.

Then she tells me about this Josie, probably Puerto Rican, once more – the one I didn't serve in time. Then she says, Yeah, and really, Iz, what about Emanuel?

Don't you look at Emanuel, I said. Don't you dare. He has nothing to do with it.

She rolls her eyes around and around a couple of times. She got more to say. She also doesn't like how I talk to women. She says I called Mrs. Z. a grizzly bear a few times. It's my wife, no? That I was winking and blinking at the girls, a few pinches. A lie . . . maybe I patted, but I never pinched. Besides, I know for a fact a couple of them loved it. She says, No. None of them liked it. Not one. They only put up with it because it wasn't time yet in history to holler. (An American-born girl has some nerve to mention history.)

But, she says, Iz, forget all that. I'm sorry you have so much trouble now. She really is sorry. But in a second she changes her mind. She's not so sorry. She takes her hand back. Her mouth makes a little O.

Emanuel climbs up on my lap. He pats my face. Don't be sad, Grandpa, he says. He can't stand if he sees a tear on a person's face. Even a stranger. If his mama gets a black look, he's smart, he doesn't go to her anymore. He comes to my wife. Grandma, he says, my poor mama is very sad. My wife jumps up and runs in. Worried. Scared. Did Cissy take her pills? What's going on? Once, he went to Cissy and said, Mama, why are you crying? So this is her answer to a little boy: she stands up straight and starts to bang her head on the wall. Hard.

My mama! he screams. Lucky I was home. Since then he goes straight to his grandma for his troubles. What will happen? We're not so young. My oldest son is doing extremely well – only he lives in a very exclusive neighborhood in Rockland County. Our other boy – well, he's in his own life, he's from that generation. He went away.

She looks at me, this Faith. She can't say a word. She sits there. She opens her mouth almost. I know what she wants to know. How did Emanuel come into the story. When?

Then she says to me exactly those words. Well, where does Emanuel fit in?

He fits, he fits. Like a golden present from Nasser.

Nasser?

O.K., Egypt, not Nasser – he's from Isaac's other son, get it? A close relation. I was sitting one day thinking, Why? why? The answer: To remind us. That's the purpose of most things.

It was Abraham, she interrupts me. He had two sons, Isaac and Ishmael. God promised him he would be the father of generations; he was. But you know, she says, he wasn't such a good father to those two little boys. Not so unusual, she has to add on.

You see! That's what they make of the Bible, those women; because they got it in for men. Of *course* I meant Abraham. Abraham. Did I say Isaac? Once in a while I got to admit it, she says something true. You remember one son he sent out of the house altogether, the other he was ready to chop up if he only heard a noise in his head saying, Go! Chop!

But the question is, Where did Emanuel fit. I didn't mind telling. I wanted to tell. I explained that already.

So it begins. One day my wife goes to the administration of Cissy's hospital and she says, What kind of a place you're running here. I have just looked at my daughter. A blind person could almost see it. My daughter is pregnant. What goes on here at night? Who's the supervisor? Where is she this minute?

Pregnant? they say like they never heard of it. And they run around and the regular doctor comes and says, Yes, pregnant. Sure. You got more news? my wife says. And then: meetings with the weekly psychiatrist, the day-by-day psychologist, the nerve doctor, the social worker, the supervising nurse, the nurse's aide. My wife says, Cissy knows. She's not an idiot, only mixed up and depressed. She *knows* she has a child in her womb inside of her like a normal woman. She likes it, my wife said. She even said to her, Mama, I'm having a baby, and she gave my wife a kiss. The first kiss in a couple of years. How do you like that?

Meanwhile, they investigated thoroughly. It turns out the man is a colored fellow. One of the gardeners. But he left a couple months ago for the Coast. I could imagine what happened. Cissy always loved flowers. When she was a little girl she was planting seeds every minute and sitting all day in front of the flower pot to see the little flower cracking up the seed. So she must of watched him and watched him. He dug up the earth. He put in the seeds. She watches.

The office apologized. Apologized? An accident. The supervisor was on vacation that week. I could sue them for a million dollars. Don't think I didn't talk to a lawyer. That time, then, when I heard, I called a detective agency to find him. My plan was to kill him. I would tear him limb from limb. What to do next. They called them all in again. The psychiatrist, the psychologist, they only left out the nurse's aide.

The only hope she could live a half-normal life – not in the institutions: she must have this baby, she could carry it full term. No, I said, I can't stand it. I refuse. Out of my Cissy, who looked like a piece of gold, would come a black child. Then the psychologist says, Don't be so bigoted. What nerve! Little by little my wife figured out a good idea. O.K., well, we'll put it out for adoption. Cissy doesn't even have to see it in person.

You are laboring under a misapprehension, says the boss of the place. They talk like that. What he meant, he meant we got to take that child home with us and if we really loved Cissy . . . Then he gave us a big lecture on this baby: it's Cissy's connection to life; also, it happens she was crazy about this gardener, this son of a bitch, a black man with a green thumb.

You see I can crack a little joke because look at this pleasure. I got a little best friend here. Where I go, he goes, even when I go down to the Italian side of the park to play a little bocce with the old goats over there. They invite me if they see me in the supermarket: Hey, Iz! Tony's sick. You come on an' play, O.K.? My wife says, Take Emanuel, he should see how men play games. I take him, those old guys they also seen plenty in their day. They think I'm some kind of a do-gooder. Also, a lot of those people are ignorant. They think the Jews are a little bit colored anyways, so they don't look at him too long. He goes to the swings and they make believe they never even seen him.

I didn't mean to get off the subject. What is the subject? The subject is how we took the baby. My wife, Mrs. Z., Nettie, she plain forced me. She said, We got to take this child on us. I will move out of here into the project with Cissy and be on welfare. Iz, you better make up your mind. Her brother, a top social worker, he encouraged her, I think he's a Communist also, the way he talks the last twenty, thirty years . . .

He says: You'll live, Iz. It's a baby, after all. It's got your blood in it. Unless of course you want Cissy to rot away in that place till you're so poor they don't keep her anymore. Then they'll stuff her into Bellevue or Central Islip or something. First she's a zombie, then she's a vegetable. That's what you want, Iz?

After this conversation I get sick. I can't go to work. Meanwhile, every night Nettie cries. She don't get dressed in the morning. She walks around with a broom. Doesn't sweep up. Starts to sweep, bursts into tears. Puts a pot of soup on the stove, runs into the bedroom, lies down. Soon I think I'll have to put her away too.

I give in.

My listener says to me, Right, Iz, you did the right thing. What else could you do?

I feel like smacking her. I'm not a violent person, just very excitable, but who asked her? – Right, Iz. She sits there looking at me, nodding her head from rightness. Emanuel is finally in the playground. I see him swinging and swinging. He could swing for two hours. He likes that. He's a regular swinger.

Well, the bad part of the story is over. Now is the good part. Naming the baby. What should we name him? Little brown baby. An intermediate color. A perfect stranger.

In the maternity ward, you know where the mothers lie, with the new babies, Nettie is saying, Cissy, Cissile darling, my sweetest heart (this is how my wife talked to her, like she was made of gold – or eggshells), my darling girl, what should we name this little child?

Cissy is nursing. On her white flesh is this little black curly head. Cissy says right away: Emanuel. Immediately. When I hear this, I say, Ridiculous. Ridiculous, such a long Jewish name on a little baby. I got old uncles with such names. Then they all get called Manny. Uncle Manny. Again she says – Emanuel!

David is nice, I suggest in a kind voice. It's your grandpa's, he should rest in peace. Michael is nice too, my wife says. Joshua is beautiful. Many children have these beautiful names nowadays. They're nice modern names. People like to say them.

No, she says, Emanuel. Then she starts screaming, Emanuel Emanuel. We almost had to give her extra pills. But we were careful on account of the milk. The milk could get affected.

O.K., everyone hollered. O.K. Calm yourself, Cissy. O.K. Emanuel. Bring the birth certificate. Write it down. Put it down. Let her see it. Emanuel . . . In a few days, the rabbi came. He raised up his eyebrows a couple times. Then he did his job, which is to make the bris. In other words, a circumcision. This is done so the child will be a man in Israel. That's the expression they use. He isn't the first colored child. They tell me long ago we were mostly dark. Also, now I think of it, I wouldn't mind going over there to Israel. They say there are plenty black Jews. It's not unusual over there at all. They ought to put out more publicity on it. Because I have to think where he should live. Maybe it won't be so good for him here. Because my son, his fancy ideas . . . ach, forget it.

What about the building, your neighborhood, I mean where you live now? Are there other black people in the community?

Oh yeah, but they're very snobbish. Don't ask what they got to be so snobbish.

Because, she says, he should have friends his own color, he shouldn't have the burden of being the only one in school.

Listen, it's New York, it's not Oshkosh, Wisconsin. But she gets going, you can't stop her.

After all, she says, he should eventually know his own people. It's their life he'll have to share. I know it's a problem to you, Iz, I know, but that's the way it is. A friend of mine with the same situation moved to a more integrated neighborhood.

Is that a fact? I say, Where's that?

Oh, there are . . .

I start to tell her, Wait a minute, we live thirty-five years in this apartment. But I can't talk. I sit very quietly for a while, I think and think. I say to myself, Be like a Hindu, Iz, calm like a cucumber. But it's too much. Listen, Miss, Miss Faith – do me a favor, don't teach me.

I'm not teaching you, Iz, it's just . . .

Don't answer me every time I say something. Talking talking. It's true. What for? To whom? Why? Nettie's right. It's our business. She's telling me Emanuel's life.

You don't know nothing about it, I yell at her. Go make a picket line. Don't teach me.

She gets up and looks at me kind of scared. Take it easy,

Emanuel is coming. He hears me. He got his little worried face. She sticks out a hand to pat him, his grandpa is hollering so loud.

But I can't put up with it. Hands off, I yell. It ain't your kid. Don't lay a hand on him. And I grab his shoulder and push him through the park, past the playground and the big famous arch. She runs after me a minute. Then she sees a couple friends. Now she has what to talk about. Three, four women. They make a little bunch. They talk. They turn around, they look. One waves. Hiya, Iz.

This park is full of noise. Everybody got something to say to the next guy. Playing this music, standing on their heads, juggling – someone even brought a piano, can you believe it, some job.

I sold the store four years ago. I couldn't put in the work no more. But I wanted to show Emanuel my pharmacy, what a beautiful place it was, how it sent three children to college, saved a couple lives – imagine: one store!

I tried to be quiet for the boy. You want ice cream, Emanuel? Here's a dollar, sonny. Buy yourself a Good Humor. The man's over there. Don't forget to ask for the change. I bend down to give him a kiss. I don't like that he heard me yell at a woman and my hand is still shaking. He runs a few steps, he looks back to make sure I didn't move an inch.

I got my eye on him too. He waves a chocolate popsicle. It's a little darker than him. Out of that crazy mob a young fellow comes up to me. He has a baby strapped on his back. That's the style now. He asks like it's an ordinary friendly question, points to Emanuel. Gosh what a cute kid. Whose is he? I don't answer. He says it again, Really some cute kid.

I just look in his face. What does he want? I should tell him the story of my life? I don't need to tell. I already told and told. So I said very loud – no one else should bother me – how come it's your business, mister? Who do you think he is? By the way, whose kid you got on your back? It don't look like you.

He says, Hey there buddy, be cool be cool. I didn't mean anything. (You met anyone lately who meant something when he opened his mouth?) While I'm hollering at him, he starts to back away. The women are gabbing in a little clutch by the statue. It's a considerable distance, lucky they got radar. They turn around sharp like birds and fly over to the man. They talk very soft. Why are you bothering this old man, he got enough trouble? Why don't you leave him alone?

The fellow says, I wasn't bothering him. I just asked him something.

Well, he thinks you're bothering him, Faith says.

Then her friend, a woman maybe forty, very angry, starts to holler, How come you don't take care of your own kid? She's crying. Are you deaf? Naturally the third woman makes a remark, doesn't want to be left out. She taps him on his jacket: I seen you around here before, buster, you better watch out. He walks away from them backwards. They start in shaking hands.

Then this Faith comes back to me with a big smile. She says, Honestly, some people are a pain, aren't they, Iz? We sure let him have it, didn't we? And she gives me one of her kisses. Say hello to Cissy – O.K.? She puts her arms around her pals. They say a few words back and forth, like cranking up a motor. Then they bust out laughing. They wave goodbye to Emanuel. Laughing. Laughing. So long, Iz . . . see you . . .

So I say, What is going on, Emanuel, could you explain to me what just happened? Did you notice anywhere a joke? This is the first time he doesn't answer me. He's writing his name on the sidewalk. EMANUEL. Emanuel in big capital letters.

And the women walk away from us. Talking. Talking.

The Expensive Moment

Faith did not tell Jack.

At about two in the afternoon she went to visit Nick Hegstraw, the famous sinologist. He was not famous in the whole world. He was famous in their neighborhood and in the adjoining neighborhoods, north, south, and east. He was studying China, he said, in order to free us all of distance and mystery. But because of foolish remarks that were immediately published, he had been excluded from wonderful visits to China's new green parlor. He sometimes felt insufficiently informed. Hundreds of people who knew nothing about Han and Datong visited, returned, wrote articles; one friend with about seventy-five Chinese words had made a three-hour documentary. Well, sometimes he did believe in socialism and sometimes only in the Late T'ang. It's hard to stand behind a people and culture in revolutionary transition when you are constantly worried about their irreplaceable and breakable artifacts.

He was noticeably handsome, the way men are every now and then, with a face full of good architectural planning. (Good use of face space, Jack said.) In the hardware store or in line at the local movie, women and men would look at him. They might turn away saying, Not my type, or, Where have I seen him before? TV? Actually they had seen him at the vegetable market. As an unmarried vegetarian sinologist he bought bagfuls of broccoli and waited with other eaters for snow peas from California at $4.79 a pound.

Are you lovers? Ruth asked.

Oh God, no. I'm pretty monogamous when I'm monogamous. Why are you laughing?

You're lying. Really, Faith, why did you describe him at such length? You don't usually do that.

But the fun of talking, Ruthy. What about that? It's as good as fucking lots of times. Isn't it?

Oh boy, Ruth said, if it's that good, then it's got to be that bad.

At lunch Jack said, Ruth is not a Chinese cook. She doesn't mince words. She doesn't sauté a lot of imperial verbs and docile predicates like some women.

Faith left the room. Someday, she said, I'm never coming back.

But I love the way Jack talks, said Ruth. He's a true gossip like us. And another thing, he's the only one who ever asks me anymore about Rachel.

Don't trust him, said Faith.

After Faith slammed the door, Jack decided to buy a pipe so he could smoke thoughtfully in the evening. He wished he had a new dog or a new child or a new wife. He had none of these things because he only thought about them once in ten days and then only for about five minutes. The interest in sustained shopping or courtship had left him. He was a busy man selling discount furniture in a rough neighborhood during the day, and reading reading reading, thinking writing grieving all night the bad world-ending politics which were using up the last years of his life. Oh, come back, come back, he cried. Faith! At least for supper.

On this particular afternoon, Nick (the sinologist) said, How are your children? Fine, she said. Tonto is in love and Richard has officially joined the League for Revolutionary Youth.

Ah, said Nick. L.R.Y. I spoke at one of their meetings last month. They threw half a pizza pie at me.

Why? What'd you say? Did you say something terrible? Maybe it's an anti-agist coalition of New Left pie throwers and Old Left tomato throwers.

It's not a joke, he said. And it's not funny. And besides, that's not what I want to talk about. He then expressed opposition to the Great Leap Forward and the Cultural Revolution. He did this by walking back and forth muttering, Wrong. Wrong. Wrong.

Faith, who had just read *Fanshen* at his suggestion, accepted both. But he worried about great art and literature, its way of rising out of the already risen. Faith, sit down, he said. Where were the already risen nowadays? Driven away from their type-writers and calligraphy pens by the Young Guards – like all the young, wild with a dream of wildness.

Faith said, Maybe it's the right now rising. Maybe the already risen don't need anything more. They just sit there in their lawn chairs and appreciate the culture of the just rising. They may even like to do that. The work of creation is probably too hard when you are required because of having already risen to be always distinguishing good from bad, great from good . . .

Nick would not even laugh at serious jokes. He decided to show Faith with mocking examples how wrong she was. None of the examples convinced her. In fact, they seemed to support an opposing position. Faith wondered if his acquisitive mind was not sometimes betrayed by a poor filing system.

Here they are anyway:

Working hard in the fields of Shanxi is John Keats, brilliant and tubercular. The sun beats on his pale flesh. The water in which he is ankle-deep is colder than he likes. The little green shoots are no comfort to him despite their light-green beauty. He is thinking about last night – this lunar beauty, etc. When he gets back to the commune he learns that they have been requested by the province to write poems. Keats is discouraged. He's thinking, This lunar beauty, this lunar beauty . . . The head communard, a bourgeois leftover, says, Oh, what can ail thee, pale individualist?

He laughs, then says, Relax, comrade. Just let politics take command. Keats does this, and soon, smiling his sad intelligent smile, he says, Ah . . .

This lunar beauty
   touches Shanxi province
in the year of the bumper crops
   the peasants free of the landlords
stand in the fields
   they talk of this and that
   and admire
the harvest moon.

Meanwhile, all around him peasants are dampening the dry lead pencil points with their tongues.

Faith interrupted. She hoped someone would tell them how dangerous lead was. And industrial pollution.

For godsakes, said Nick, and continued. One peasant writes:

This morning the paddy
   looked like the sea
At high tide we will
   harvest the rice
This is because of Mao Zedong
   whose love for the peasants
has fed the urban proletariat.

That's enough. Do you get it? Yes, Faith said. Something like this? And sang.

On the highway to Communism
the little children put plum blossoms
In their hair and dance
on the new-harvested wheat

She was about to remember another poem from her newly

invented memory, but Nick said, Faith, it's already 3:30, so – full
of the play of poems they unfolded his narrow daybed to a comfortable three-quarter width. Their lovemaking was ordinary but
satisfactory. Its difference lay only in difference. Of course, if
one is living a whole life in passionate affection with another,
this differentness on occasional afternoons is often enough.

And besides that, almost at once on rising to tea or coffee, Faith
asked, Nick, why do they have such a rotten foreign policy? The
question had settled in her mind earlier, resting just under the
light inflammation of desire.

It was not the first time she had asked this question, nor was
Nick the last person who answered.

Nick: For godsakes, don't you understand anything about politics?

Richard: Yeah, and why does Israel trade probably every day
with South Africa?

Ruth (*although her remarks actually came a couple of years
later*): Cuba carries on commercial negotiations with Argentina.
No?

The boys at supper: Tonto (*softly, with narrowed eyes*): Why
did China recognize Pinochet just about ten minutes after the
coup in Chile?

Richard (*tolerantly explaining*): Asshole, because Allende
didn't know how to run a revolution, that's why.

Jack reminded them that the U.S.S.R. may have had to over-
come intense ideological repugnance in order to satisfy her old
longing for South African industrial diamonds.

Faith thought, But if you think like that forever you can be sad
forever. You can be cynical, you can go around saying no hope,
you can say import-export, you can mumble all day, World Bank.
So she tried thinking: The beauty of trade, the caravans crossing
Africa and Asia, the roads to Peru through the terrible forests of
Guatemala, and then especially the village markets of underde-

veloped countries, plazas behind churches under awnings and tents, not to mention the Orlando Market around the corner; also the Free Market, which costs so much in the world, and what about the discount house of Jack, Son of Jake.

Oh sure, Richard said, the beauty of trade. I'm surprised at you, Ma, the beauty of trade — those Indians going through Guatemala with leather thongs cutting into their foreheads holding about a ton of beauty on their backs. Beauty, he said.

He rested for about an hour. Then he continued. I'm surprised at you Faith, really surprised. He blinked his eyes a couple of times. Mother, he said, have you ever read any political theory? No. All those dumb peace meetings you go to. Don't they ever talk about anything but melting up a couple of really great swords?

He'd become so pale.

Richard, she said. You're absolutely white. You seem to have quit drinking orange juice.

This simple remark made him leave home for three days.

But first he looked at her with either contempt or despair.

Then, because the brain at work pays no attention to time and speedily connects and chooses, she thought: Oh, long ago I looked at my father. What kind of face is that? he had asked. She was leaning against their bedroom wall. She was about fourteen. Fifteen? A lot you care, she said. A giant war is coming out of Germany and all you say is Russia. Bad old Russia. I'm the one that's gonna get killed. You? he answered. Ha ha! A little girl sitting in safe America is going to be killed. Ha ha!

And what about the looks those other boys half a generation ago had made her accept. Ruth had called them put-up-or-shut-up looks. She and her friends had walked round and round the draft boards with signs that said I COUNSEL DRAFT REFUSAL. Some of those young fellows were calm and holy, and some were fierce and grouchy. But not one of them was trivial, and neither was Richard.

Still, Faith thought, what if history should seize him as it had actually taken Ruth's daughter Rachel when her face was still as round as an apple; a moment in history, the expensive moment when everyone his age is called but just a few are chosen by conscience or passion or even only love of one's own agemates, and they are the ones who smash an important nosecone (as has been recently done) or blow up some building full of oppressive money or murderous military plans; but, oh, what if a human creature (maybe rotten to the core but a living person still) is in it? What if they disappear then to live in exile or in the deepest underground and you don't see them for ten years or have to travel to Cuba or Canada or farther to look at their changed faces? Then you think sadly, I could have worked harder at raising that child, the one that was once mine. I could have raised him to become a brilliant economist or finish graduate school and be a lawyer or a doctor maybe. He could have done a lot of good, just as much *that* way, healing or defending the underdog.

But Richard had slipped a note under the door before he left. In his neat handwriting it said: 'Trade. Shit. It's production that's beautiful. That's what's beautiful. And the producers. They're beautiful.'

What's the use, said Ruth when she and Faith sat eating barley soup in the Art Foods Deli. You're always wrong. She looked into the light beyond the plate-glass window. It was unusual for her to allow sadness. Faith took her hand and kissed it. She said, Ruthy darling. Ruth leaned across the table to hug her. The soup spoon fell to the floor, mixing barley and sawdust.

But look, Ruth said, Joe got this news clipping at the office from some place in Minnesota. 'Red and green acrylic circles were painted around telephone poles and trees ringing the Dakota State Prison last night. It was assumed that the Red and the Green were planning some destructive act. These circles were last seen in Arizona. Two convicts escaped from that prison within a week. Red and green circles were stenciled on the walls of their cells. The cost for removing these signatures will probably go as high as $4,300.'

What for? said Faith.

For? asked Ruth. They were political prisoners. Someone has to not forget them. The green is for ecology.

Nobody leaves that out nowadays.

Well, they shouldn't, said Ruth.

This Rachel of Ruth and Joe's had grown from girl to woman in far absence, making little personal waves from time to time in the newspapers or in rumor which would finally reach her parents on the shores of their always waiting – that is, the office mailbox or the eleven o'clock news.

One day Ruth and Joe were invited to a cultural event. This was because Joe was a cultural worker. He had in fact edited *The Social Ordure*, a periodical which published everything Jack wrote. He and Ruth had also visited China and connected themselves in print to some indulgent views of the Gang of Four, from which it had been hard to disengage. Ruth was still certain that the bad politics and free life of Jiang Qing would be used for at least a generation to punish ALL Chinese women.

But isn't that true everywhere, said Faith. If you say a simple thing like, 'There are only eight women in Congress,' or if you say the word 'patriarchy,' someone always says, Yeah? look at Margaret Thatcher, or look at Golda Meir.

I love Golda Meir.

You do? Oh! said Faith.

But the evening belonged to the Chinese artists and writers who had been rehabilitated while still alive. All sorts of American cultural workers were invited. Some laughed to hear themselves described in this way. They were accustomed to being called 'dreamer poet realist postmodernist.' They might have liked being called 'cultural dreamer,' but no one had thought of that yet.

Many of these Chinese artists (mostly men and some women) flew back and forth from American coast to coast so often (sometimes stopping in Iowa City) that they were no longer interested in window seats but slept on the aisle or across the fat center where the armrests can be adjusted . . . while the great deep dipping Rockies, the Indian Black Hills, the Badlands, the good and endless plains moved slowly west under the gently trembling jet. They never bother anymore to dash to the windows at the circling of New York as the pattern holds and the lights of our city engage and eliminate the sky.

Ruth said she would personally bring Nick to the party since China was still too annoyed to have invited him. It wasn't fair for a superficial visitor like herself to be present when a person like Nick, with whole verses of his obsession falling out of his pockets, was excluded.

That's O.K., Ruth. You don't have to ask him, Faith said. Don't bother on my account. I don't even see him much anymore.

How come?

I don't know. Whenever I got to like one of his opinions he'd change it, and he never liked any of mine. Also, I couldn't talk to you about it, so it never got thick enough. I mean woofed and warped. Anyway, it hadn't been Nick, she realized. He was all right, but it was travel she longed for – somewhere else – the sexiness of the unknown parts of far imaginable places.

Sex? Ruth said. She bit her lips. Wouldn't it be interesting if way out there Rachel was having a baby?

God, yes, of course! Wonderful! Oh, Ruthy, Faith said, remembering babies, those round, staring, day-in day-out companions of her youth.

Well, Faith asked, what was he like, Nick – the poet Ai Qing? What'd he say?

He has a very large head, Nick said. The great poet raised from exile.

Was Ding Ling there? The amazing woman, the storyteller, Ding Ling?

They're not up to her yet, Nick said. Maybe next year.

Well, what did Bien Tselin say? Faith asked. Nick, tell me.

Well, he's very tiny. He looks like my father did when he was old.

Yes, but what did they say?

Do you have any other questions? he asked. I'm thinking about something right now. He was writing in his little book – thoughts, comments, maybe even new songs for Chinese modernization – which he planned to publish as soon as possible. He thought Faith could read them then.

Finally he said, They showed me their muscles. There were other poets there. They told some jokes but not against us. They laughed and nudged each other. They talked Chinese, you know. I don't know why they were so jolly. They kept saying, Do not think that we have ceased to be Communists. We are Communists. They weren't bitter. They acted interested and happy.

Ruthy, Faith said, please tell me what they said.

Well, one of the women, Faith, about our age, she said the same thing. She also said the peasants were good to her. But the soldiers were bad. She said the peasants in the countryside helped her. They knew she felt lonely and frightened. She said she loved the Chinese peasant. That's exactly the way she said it, like a little speech: I'll never forget and I will always love the Chinese peasant. It's the one thing Mao was right about – of course he was also a good poet. But she said, well, you can imagine – she said, the children . . . When the entire working office was sent down to the countryside to dig up stones, she left her daughters with her mother. Her mother was old-fashioned, especially about girls. It's not so hard to be strong about oneself.

Some months later, at a meeting of women's governmental organizations sponsored by the UN, Faith met the very same Chinese woman who'd talked to Ruth. She remembered Ruth well. Yes, the lady who hasn't seen her daughter in eight years. Oh, what a sadness. Who would forget that woman. I have known a few. My name is Xie Feng, she said. Now you say it.

The two women said each other's strange name and laughed. The Chinese woman said, Faith in what? Then she gathered whatever strength and aggression she'd needed to reach this country; she added the courtesy of shyness, breathed deep, and said, Now I would like to see how you live. I have been to meetings, one after another and day after day. But what is a person's home like? How do you live?

Faith said, Me? My house? You want to see my house? In the mirror that evening brushing her teeth, she smiled at her smiling face. She had been invited to be hospitable to a woman from half the world away who'd lived a life beyond foreignness and had experienced extreme history.

The next day they drank tea in Faith's kitchen out of Chinese cups that Ruth had brought from her travels. Misty terraced hills were painted on these cups and a little oil derrick inserted among them.

Faith showed her the boys' bedroom. The Chinese woman took a little camera out of her pocket. You don't mind? she asked. This is the front room, said Faith. It's called the living room. This is our bedroom. That's a picture of Jack giving a paper at the Other Historian meeting and that picture is Jack with two guys who've worked in his store since they were all young. The skinny one just led a strike against Jack and won. Jack says they were right.

I see – both principled men, said the Chinese woman.

They walked around the block a couple of times to get the feel of a neighborhood. They stopped for strudel at the Art Foods. It was half past two and just in time to see the children fly out of the school around the corner. The littlest ones banged against the legs of teachers and mothers. Here and there a father rested his length against somebody's illegally parked car. They stopped to buy a couple of apples. This is my Chinese friend from China, Faith said to Eddie the butcher, who was smoking a cigar, spitting and smiling at the sunlight of an afternoon break. So many peaches, so many oranges, the woman said admiringly to Eddie.

They walked west to the Hudson River. It's called the North River but it's really our Lordly Hudson. This is a good river, but very quiet, said the Chinese woman as they stepped onto the beautiful, green, rusting, slightly crumpled, totally unused pier and looked at New Jersey. They returned along a street of small houses and Faith pointed up to the second-floor apartment where she and Jack had first made love. Ah, the woman said, do you notice that in time you love the children more and the man less? Faith said, Yes! but as soon as she said it, she wanted to run home and find Jack and kiss his pink ears and his 243 last hairs, to call out, Old friend, don't worry, you are loved. But before she could speak of this, Tonto flew by on his financially rewarding messenger's bike, screaming, Hi, Mom, *nee hau*, *nee hau*. He has a Chinese girlfriend this week. He says that means hello. My other son is at a meeting. She didn't say it was the L.R.Y.'s regular beep-the-horn-if-you-support-Mao meeting. She showed her the church basement where she and Ruth and Ann and Louise and their group of mostly women and some men had made leaflets, offered sanctuary to draft resisters. They would probably do so soon again. Some young people looked up from a light board, saw a representative of the Third World, and smiled peacefully. They walked east and south to neighborhoods where our city, in fields of garbage and broken brick, stands desolate, her windows burnt and blind. Here, Faith said, the people suffer and struggle, their children turn round and round in one place, growing first in beauty, then in rage.

Now we are home again. And I will tell you about my life, the Chinese woman said. Oh yes, please, said Faith, very embarrassed. Of course the desire to share the facts and places of her life had come from generosity, but it had come from selfcenteredness too.

Yes, the Chinese woman said. Things are a little better now. They get good at home, they get a little bad, then improve. And the men, you know, they were very bad. But now they are a little better, not all, but some, a few. May I ask you, do you worry that your older boy is in a political group that isn't liked? What will be his trade? Will he go to university? My eldest is without skills to this day. Her school years happened in the time of great confusion and running about. My youngest studies well. Ah, she said, rising. Hello. Good afternoon.

Ruth stood in the doorway. Faith's friend, the listener and the answerer, listening.

We were speaking, the Chinese woman said. About the children, how to raise them. My youngest sister is permitted to have a child this year, so we often talk thoughtfully. This is what we think: Shall we teach them to be straightforward, honorable, kind, brave, maybe shrewd, self-serving a little? What is the best way to help them in the real world? We don't know the best way. You don't want them to be cruel, but you want them to take care of themselves wisely. Now my own children are nearly grown. Perhaps it's too late. Was I foolish? I didn't know in those years how to do it. Yes, yes, said Faith. I know what you mean. Ruthy? Ruth remained quiet. Faith waited a couple of seconds. Then she turned to the Chinese woman. Oh, Xie Feng, she said. Neither did I.

Listening

I had just come up from the church basement with an armful of leaflets. Once, maybe only twenty-five, thirty years ago, young women and men bowled in that basement, played PingPong there, drank hot chocolate, and wondered how in God's separating world they could ever get to know each other. Nowadays we mimeograph and collate our political pamphlets among the bowling alleys. I think I'm right when I remember that the leaflets in my arms cried out, *U.S. Honor the Geneva Agreements.* (Jack did not believe the U.S. would ever honor the Geneva Agreements. Well, then, sadness, Southeast Asian sadness, U.S. sadness, all-nation sadness.)

Then I thought: Coffee. Do you remember the Art Foods Deli? The Sudarskys owned it, cooked for us, served us, argued Europe Israel Russia Islam, played chess in the late evening on the table nearest the kitchen, and in order to persuade us all to compassion and righteousness exhumed the terrible town of his youth – Dachau.

With my coffee, I ordered a sandwich named after a neighbor who lives a few blocks away. (All sandwiches are so honored.) I do like the one I asked for – Mary Anne Brewer – but I must say I really prefer Selena and Max Retelof, though it's more expensive. The shrimp is not chopped quite so fine, egg is added, a

little sweet red pepper. Selena and Max were just divorced, but
their sandwich will probably go on for another few years.

At the table next to mine, a young man leaned forward. He was
speaking to an older man. The young man was in uniform, a soldier. I thought, When he leaves or if I leave first, I'll give him a
leaflet. I don't want to but I will. Then I thought, Poor young
fellow, God knows what his experience has been; his heart, if it
knew, would certainly honor the Geneva Agreements, but it
would probably hurt his feelings to hear one more word about
how the U.S.A. is wrong again and how he is an innocent instrument of evil. He would take it personally, although we who are
mothers and have been sweethearts – all of us know that 'soldier'
is what a million boys have been forced to be in every single one
of a hundred generations.

Uncle Stan, the soldier boy was saying, I got to tell you, we
had to have a big wedding then, Mamasan Papasan, everybody
was there. Then I got rotated. I wrote to her, don't think I didn't.
She has a nice little baby girl now. If I go back I'll surely see her.
But, Stan, basically I want to settle down. I already reenlisted
once. It would be good if I got to be a construction worker. If you
know someone, one of Tommy's friends. If you got a contact.
Airfields or harbors – something like that. I could go over for a
year or two now and then. She wouldn't want to come back here.
Here's the picture, see? She has her old grandma, everybody's
smiling, right? I'm not putting her down, but I would like to find
a good-looking American girl, someone nice, I mean, and fall in
love and settle down, because, you know, I'm twenty-four
already.

Uncle Stan said, Twenty-four, huh? Then he asked for the
check. Two coffees, two Helen someone or others. While the
waitress scribbled, I, bravely, but against my better judgment,
passed one of the leaflets to the young man. He stood up. He
looked at it. He looked at me. He looked at the wall, sighing. Oh
shit. He crumpled the leaflet in one hand. He looked at me again.
He said, Oh, I'm sorry. He put the leaflet on the table. He
smoothed it out.

Let's go, said Uncle Stan.

I'd finished my lunch, but Art Foods believes that any eating time is the body's own occasion and must not be hurried. In the booth behind me two men were speaking.

The first man said: I already have one child. I cannot commit suicide until he is at least twenty or twenty-two. That's why when Rosemarie says, Oh, Dave, a child? I have to say, Rosemarie, you deserve one. You do, you're a young woman, but no. My son (by Lucy) is now twelve years old. Therefore if things do not work out, if life does not show some meaning, MEANING by God, if I cannot give up drinking, if I become a terrible drunk and know I have to give it up but cannot and then need to commit suicide, I think I'd be able to hold out eight or nine years, but if I had another child I would then have to last twenty years. I cannot. I will not put myself in that position.

The other man said: I too want the opportunity, the freedom to commit suicide when I want to. I too assume that I will want to in ten, twenty years. However, I have responsibilities to the store, the men that work there. I also have my real work to finish. The one serious thing that would make me commit suicide would be my health, which I assume will deteriorate – cancer, heart disease, whatever. I refuse to be bedridden and dependent and therefore I am sustained in the right to leave this earth when I want to do so and on time.

The men congratulated each other on their unsentimentality, their levelheadedness. They said almost at the same time, You're right, you're right. I turned to look at them. A little smile just tickled the corners of their lips. I passed one of my leaflets over the back of the booth. Without looking up, they began to read.

Jack and I were at early-morning breakfast when I told him the two little stories. And Jack, I said, one of those men was you.

Well, he said, I know it was me. You don't have to remind me. I saw you looking at us. I saw you listening. You don't have to tell stories to me in which I'm a character, you know. Besides which, all those stories are about men, he said. You know I'm more interested in women. Why don't you tell me stories told by women about women?

Those are too private.

Why don t you tell them to me? he asked sadly.

Well, Jack. you have your own woman stories. You know, your falling-in-love stories, your French-woman-during-the-Korean-War stories, your magnificent-woman stories, your beautiful-new-young-wife stories, your political-comrade-though-extremely-beautiful stories . . .

Silence – the space that follows unkindness in which little truths growl.

Then Jack asked, Faith, have you decided not to have a baby?

No, I've just decided to think about it, but I haven't given it up.

So, with the sweetness of old forgiving friendship, he took my hand. My dear, he said, perhaps you only wish that you were young again. So do I. At the store when young people come in waving youth's unfurled banner HOPE, meaning their pockets are full of someone's credit cards, I think: New toasters! Brand-new curtains! Sofa convertibles! Danish glass!

I hadn't thought of furniture from the discount store called Jack, Son of Jake as a song of beginnings. But I guess that's what it is – straw for the springtime nest.

Now listen to me, he said. And we began to address each other slowly and formally as people often do when seriousness impedes ease some stately dance is required. Listen. Listen, he said. Our old children are just about grown. Why do you want a new child? Haven't we agreed often, haven't we said that it had become noticeable that life is short and sorrowful? Haven't we said the words 'gone' and 'where'? Haven't we sometimes in the last few years used the word 'terrible' and we mean to include in it the word 'terror'? Everyone knows this about life. Though of course some fools never stop singing its praises.

But they're right, I said in my turn. Yes, and this is in order to encourage the young whom we have, after all, brought into the world – they must not be abandoned. We must, I said, continue pointing out simple and worthwhile sights such as – in the

countryside – hills folding into one another in light-green spring
or white winter, the sky which is always astonishing either in its
customary blueness or in the configuration of clouds – the way
they're pushed in their softest parts by the air's breath and change
shape and direction and density. Not to mention our own beloved
city crowded with day and night workers, shoppers, walkers, the
subway trains which many people fear but they're so handsomely
lined with pink to dark dark brown faces, golden tans and yellows scattered amongst them. It's very important to emphasize
what is good or beautiful so as not to have a gloomy face when
you meet some youngster who has begun to guess.

Well, Jack said.

Then he said, You know, I like your paragraphs better than
your sentences. That comment wasn't made (I knew) in order to
set the two forms in hostile opposition. It was still part of the
dance, a couple of awkward, critical steps from theory to practice.

Perhaps, he continued, if we start making love in the morning,
your body will be so impressed and enlivened by the changes in
me that it will begin again all its old hormonal work of secreting,
womb cleaning, and egg making.

I doubt it, I said. Besides, I'm busy, you know. I have an awful
lot to do.

By this, I meant that our early mornings are usually so full of
reading last night's paper, dissenting and arguing appropriate
actions, waking the boys, who should really be old enough to
understand an alarm clock when it speaks to them – without
their mother's translation. Also, we had once had the moral or
utilitarian idea that brainy labor must happen early; it must pre-
cede the work of love or be damaged by the residual weight of all
that damp reality.

But Jack said, Oh, come on. He unbuttoned his shirt. My face
is very fond of the gray-brown hairs of his chest. Thanks, I said,
but it won't work, you know. Miracles don't happen, and if they
do they're absolutely explainable. He began to get a very rosy
look about him, which is a nice thing to happen to a man's face.

It's not called blushing. Blushing is an expression of shyness and female excitement at the same time. In men it's observed as an energetic act the blood takes on its determined own.

Think think, talk talk, that's you, stop it! Come on, kid, he said, touching my knee, my thigh, breast, all the outsides of love. So we lay down beside one another to make a child, with the modesty of later-in-life, which has so much history and erotic knowledge but doesn't always use it.

How else is one to extract a new person from all-refusing Zeus and jealous Hera? My God, said Jack, you've never mentioned Greek gods in bed before. No occasion, I said.

Later on he called the store to tell the salesmen not to sell too many kitchen sets without him, he couldn't afford to give away all that commission. Wouldn't you think that would annoy the men? Jack says I don't understand the way men talk to one another.

I had just started the coffee when Richard, my very large and handsome son, appeared. He is known far and wide for his nosy ear. Why are you still in your pajamas? I asked. He answered, What is this crap, Mother, this life is short and terrible. What is this metaphysical shit, what is this disease you intelligentsia are always talking about.

First we said: Intelligentsia! Us? Oh, the way words lie down under decades, then the Union of Restless Diggers out of sheer insomnia pulls them up: daggers for the young but to us they look like flowers of nostalgia that grew in our mother's foreign garden. What *did* my mother say? Darling, you should have come to Town Hall last night, the whole intelligentsia was there. My uncle, strictly: The intelligentsia will never permit it!

So I laughed. But Jack said, Don't you dare talk to your mother like that, Richard! Don't you dare! Ma, Richard said, get his brains out of the pickle jar, it's no insult. Everyone knows, the intelligentsia strikes the spark, so that they'll be relevant for a long time, striking sparks here and there.

Of course, he explained, the fire of revolution would only be advanced, contained, and put to productive use by the working class. Let me tell you, Jack, the intelligentsia better realize this. And another thing, where'd you get that don't-dare-talk-to-my-mother stuff . . . I know her a lot longer than you do. I've been talking to her for maybe almost eighteen years and you've been sitting around our house maybe three years tops.

Sorry, Richard. I heard a character on a TV show last night say exactly that. 'Don't you dare talk to your mother like that.' I had gone over to see Anna about something. She turned on the TV the minute I came in.

Wow! Really? Listen, the same thing happened to me too. I went to see Caitlin, you know Caitlin, around the corner, the doctor's daughter. The one whose kid brother tried to set fire to the nun a couple of years ago? Well, you know, she did that too the minute I came in, she turned on the TV.

Huh! They were surprised that the girl and the woman unknown to one another had done exactly the same thing to each of them. Richard offered Jack a cigarette and sat down at the kitchen table. Coffee, Ma, he said.

Then Jack asked, Richard, tell me, do you forgive your father for having run out on you kids years ago?

I don't forgive him and I don't not forgive him. I can't spend my life on personal animosities. The way imperialism's leaning so hard on the Third World the way it does . . .

Jack said, Ah . . . He blinked his eyes a couple of times, which a person who can't cry too well often does. Richard, did you know my father was a junk peddler. He had a pushcart. He yelled (in Yiddish), Buy old clothes, buy old clothes. I had to go with him, walk up to the fifth floor, pick up stuff; I guess we crawled up and down every street in the Bronx . . . Buy old clothes . . . old clothes.

Richard said, Oh!

What do you think, Jack asked. Rich, do you think my daughter, I mean Kimmy, will she ever call me up and say, It's O.K., Dad?

Well, said Richard, nodding his head, shrugging his shoulders.

I have to go to work now, I said. I don't happen to own my own business. Also, I have a late meeting tonight. O.K.?

The two men nodded. They sat quietly together expanding their lungs to the tiniest thread of tissue with smoke. Breathing deeply, dangerously, in and out.

Then, as often happens in stories, it was several years later. Jack had gone off to Arizona for a year to clear his lungs and sinuses and also to have, hopefully, one last love affair, the kind that's full of terrific longing, ineluctable attraction, and so forth. I don't mean to mock it, but it's only natural to have some kind of reaction. Lots of luck, Jack, I said, but don't come home grouchy. The boys were in different boroughs trying to find the right tune for their lives. They had been men to a couple of women and therefore came for supper only now and then. They were worried for my solitariness and suggested different ways I could wear my hair.

Of course, because of this planet, which is dropping away from us in poisonous disgust, I'm hardly ever home. The other day, driving down the West Side – Broadway – after a long meeting, I was stopped at a red light. A man in the absolute prime of life crossed the street. For reasons of accumulating loneliness I was stirred by his walk, his barest look at a couple of flirty teenage girls; his nice unimportant clothes seemed to be merely a shelter for the naked male person.

I thought, Oh, man, in the very center of your life, still fitting your skin so nicely, with your arms probably in a soft cotton shirt and the shirt in an old tweed jacket and your cock lying along your thigh in either your right or left pants leg, it's hard to tell which, why have you slipped out of my sentimental and carnal grasp?

He's nice, isn't he? I said to my friend Cassie.

I suppose so, she said, but Faith, what is he, just a bourgeois on his way home.

To everyday life, I said, sighing with a mild homesickness.

To whose everyday life, she said, goddamnit, whose?

She turned to me, which is hard to do when you're strapped and stuffed into a bucket seat. Listen, Faith, why don't you tell my story? You've told everybody's story but mine. I don't even mean my whole story, that's my job. You probably can't. But I mean you've just omitted me from the other stories and I was there. In the restaurant and the train, right there. Where is Cassie? Where is *my* life? It's been women and men, women and men, fucking, fucking. Goddamnit, where the hell is my woman and woman, woman-loving life in all this? And it's not even sensible, because we *are* friends, we work together, you even care about me at least as much as you do Ruthy and Louise and Ann. You let them in all the time; it's really strange, why have you left me out of everybody's life?

I took a deep breath and turned the car to the curb. I couldn't drive. We sat there for about twenty minutes. Every now and then I'd say, My God! or, Christ Almighty! neither of whom I usually call on, but she was stern and wouldn't speak. Cassie, I finally said, I don't understand it either; it's true, though, I know what you mean. It must feel for you like a great absence of yourself. How could I allow it. But it's not me alone, it's them too. I waited for her to say something. Oh, but it *is* my fault. Oh, but why did you wait so long? How can you forgive me?

Forgive you? She laughed. But she reached across the clutch. With her hand she turned my face to her so my eyes would look into her eyes. You are my friend, I know that, Faith, but I promise you, I won't forgive you, she said. From now on, I'll watch you like a hawk. I do not forgive you.